Award-winning author  been an avid reader her chapters she's managed marry her doctor hero a̲s̲o̲n̲s̲.̲ Now she writes chapters of her own in the medical romance, contemporary romance and women's fiction genres. Louisa's books have variously been nominated for the coveted RITA® Award and the New Zealand Koru Award, and have been translated into twelve languages. She lives in Auckland, New Zealand.

Sue MacKay lives with her husband in New Zealand's beautiful Marlborough Sounds, with the water on her doorstep and the birds and the trees at her back door. It is the perfect setting to indulge her passions of entertaining friends by cooking them sumptuous meals, drinking fabulous wine, going for hill walks or kayaking around the bay—and, of course, writing stories.

REUNITED BY THE NURSE'S SECRET

LOUISA GEORGE

RESISTING THE PREGNANT PAEDIATRICIAN

SUE MacKAY

MILLS & BOON

First published in Great Britain 2023
by Mills & Boon, an imprint of HarperCollins*Publishers* Ltd,
1 London Bridge Street, London, SE1 9GF

www.harpercollins.co.uk

HarperCollins*Publishers* Macken House, 39/40 Mayor Street Upper, Dublin 1, D01 C9W8, Ireland

ISBN: 978-0-263-30625-5

11/23

REUNITED BY THE NURSE'S SECRET

LOUISA GEORGE

MILLS & BOON

PROLOGUE

AS LEAVING DOS WENT, this one was a disaster. Not because no one had come, but because *everyone* was here, from his direct boss and shift colleagues to the admin staff, the call receivers and the boss's boss's boss.

Either they were all sad to see him go or it was just a good excuse for a booze-up. Either way, the bar was heaving, the chatter and laughter closing in on him. It always happened: that sense of disconnection, of being an observer rather than part of it all. As if he were floating out of his body and looking down on himself, sitting at a table on the first floor of a crowded bar, overlooking Auckland's Viaduct basin out onto a marina full of very expensive yachts, hemmed in by people he'd likely never see again.

He'd clearly had too much of the delicious craft beer they sold here. Time to make a discreet exit.

He went to stand but Lewis, his boss—senior Intensive Care paramedic—and good friend, clapped him on the back. He was swaying and his eyes looked unfocused—another victim of the craft-beer allure. 'Brin, my mate. Are you sure we can't convince you to stay?'

Brin laughed. 'Ah. If you could have a word with Immigration and get them to magic me a new visa, that would be amazing. I love New Zealand.'

'Not enough to commit to a permanent job, though? They won't issue a visa on a temporary contract.'

But that was all Brin was prepared to sign up for. He shrugged; he had his reasons to keep on moving. 'I might come back—you never know. I just need to see a bit more of this side of the world first.'

'Australia's lucky to have you. But there's always a job for you here.'

'Cheers, mate. Thanks.' Brin squeezed out of his seat and indicated he was heading to the loo. But, once out of eyeshot of the crowd, he swerved left, took the escalator to the ground floor and walked out into the pedestrianised area filled with bars, restaurants and hotels, where he took a deep breath and slowly let it out.

He wasn't big on goodbyes. Had anyone noticed? He glanced up to the first floor, where laughter floated a decibel above a regular bass beat. No. He stuck his hands in his pockets, still looking up at the bar, double-checking for anyone noticing his departure, and strode towards his fancy hotel—a treat for his last night in the country.

The first thwack hit his gut.

The second took out his right hip.

What the hell?

Fists clenched, he whirled round one-eighty degrees, but there was no apparent assailant. He hauled in a breath.

God, that hurt his belly.

Then he heard a groan. A woman was sprawled on the ground in front of him. She must have tripped and grabbed him as she slid to the ground. She was wearing a sparkly silver dress and some seriously sexy stilettos.

And noticing them was entirely inappropriate. He squatted down to make eye contact. 'Hey. Are you okay? God, I'm sorry. I wasn't looking—'

'Sorry, I wasn't looking.'

They both spoke at the same time.

'Well, that'll teach us.' He quickly assessed her. She didn't seem injured, just a little stunned. Clearly, she hadn't had the wind knocked out of her, as he had. 'Yell out if anything hurts.'

'Only my ego.' She looked up at him, all big brown eyes and amazing mouth, silky with red lipstick. Then she shifted position to sit on the ground and check her legs. 'But if I was wearing tights they'd be ruined.'

Which drew his eyes to her legs: good legs, a great body and pretty face. She had the kind of tan that came from being outdoors, not a bottle, a cloud of blonde curls and soft, large brown eyes.

Then she glanced behind her, the way he'd done a moment ago, as if checking she wasn't being followed.

His sore gut squeezed. 'Hey, are you in some kind of danger?'

'Of being caught leaving a thirtieth birthday party at the crucial tequila-shots-and-dancing-on-the-tables-stage…?' She laughed and something about the sweet sound was a balm to his heart. She put up her hands. 'Guilty as charged.'

'Aw, that's the best bit. *Dancing Queen* on repeat.'

'Over there.' She pointed to a nearby bar displaying a *Private Party* sign outside. 'Feel free. I doubt anyone would mind.'

'No thanks. To be honest, I'm escaping too.'

'Oh? Tell me everything.' She undid her sandal straps and slid them off her feet, then stuck out her hand, which he took as a sign to help her stand. Which he did. As he levered her up, he noted a few things: she was light as air; her scent, with a hint of jasmine and sea salt, wrapped around him and made him think of warm summer nights; she was entirely happy to walk barefoot—a real New Zealand thing, he'd learnt; and she wasn't wearing a wedding ring.

She walked to the marina railing, leant against it, took a deep breath and let it out very slowly, as if she was trying to calm herself. All thoughts of telling her why he was run-

ning away from…well, life…disappeared. 'You sure you're
not hurt?'

'Sure.' She nodded. 'Where's your accent from?'

'Ireland.'

'Ah. I couldn't decide if you were Scottish or Irish.'

'Like me and the Kiwi and Australian accents. I always get
them mixed up. And probably cause offence in the process.'

'Too right.' She gaped at him. 'We sound nothing alike.'

'You sound exactly alike. But I'm heading to Australia tomorrow, so maybe I'll notice the difference when I'm there.'

Her head tilted to one side as she looked at him. 'You're
leaving? Tomorrow?'

'Aye. Australia for a four-month contract. Then…who
knows? Maybe Asia or South America.'

Her eyes narrowed. 'What are you running from, Mr Irish?'

Ah, yes. That. 'Brin. Sure, you don't want to know.'

Her smile was all kinds of seductive. 'Oh, I really do, Brin.'

'Seriously, the less you know about me, the better. What's
your name?'

She turned to look out at the boats. 'Mi…chelle.'

He wasn't sure if she'd hesitated or hiccupped. And he also
wasn't sure if she was telling him the truth. Or maybe that was
just the way they pronounced 'Michelle' around here. 'Well,
Mi…chelle, nice to meet you.'

She took his hand and looked up at him. 'You too, Brin the
Irish man.' The way she said his name made his chest heat
and his skin fizz.

'Will you be okay getting home or can I help you…?'

Her face brightened. 'I'm not going home.'

'No? A real runaway, then.'

'I'm staying there.' She pointed towards *his* hotel. 'My
friend treated me to a night of luxury. I don't get the chance
to come to the city very often.'

Was it a coincidence that they were staying at the same

hotel? He wasn't sure he believed in coincidences, or fate. Was she staying there alone? Was she single? 'Because of your family?'

That seemed a good way of finding out the answers to his questions.

She whirled round, eyes suddenly guarded. 'What?'

Oh, he'd touched a nerve there. He backtracked a little, not wanting to upset her more. Up to now, and discounting the bruised gut, this had been a fine encounter and he was having fun. 'You don't visit the city often…because you have a brood of kids and a husband you adore, somewhere rural?'

To be fair, she looked far too young to have a brood. Maybe one or two.

A family? As if he knew what that was. If he'd touched anyone's nerve, it was his own.

'Somewhere rural? Kind of.' She nodded. 'No kids. No husband. No…' She suddenly looked bone-tired and very, very sad. She pressed her lips together and stared back out to sea. He wondered why she was so sad and if there was anything he could do to help her.

Then he wondered why he was even thinking that. He'd just met her. She was a stranger—a beautiful stranger. And he was leaving in the morning. So, he had nothing to lose, right?

'Hey. Sorry if I said something wrong.' He reached out and touched her shoulder. Was that too much? Could he touch her? Was that okay? Probably not; he took his hand away.

She looked at him, eyes swimming with unshed tears, and his heart kind of folded in on itself. She looked lost as she said, 'No. No, nothing at all. I'm just…ah…you know. Probably drank too much wine. I shouldn't. It makes me depressed.'

'I get that. Best not to have too much. That's why I was running away too. People kept buying me farewell drinks, and it's rude not to take them, but then I get drunk and I think about things I shouldn't…' Images of what he'd left back in Ireland swam in his head. He forced them away.

'Two runaways.' She touched his arm and brought him back to the present, which was a hell of a lot prettier than his past. So now he'd touched her, and she'd touched him, and he felt a whole lot better about everything. Her eyes were still misted but there was something else there—a glimmer of mischief— and he liked that. A lot.

She smiled. 'We could probably get into a whole lot of trouble.'

'If we're lucky,' he quipped.

Her eyes widened in response. 'I don't believe in luck. But I do believe in getting into the right kind of trouble.'

Oh, God.

She was seriously something. In another life he might have made a move on her. But he was getting on that plane tomorrow and she looked like the kind of woman who'd want more. Who *deserved* more. More than he could give for sure.

But, just in case, so as to not misread her context, he asked, 'What kind of trouble, exactly?'

She leaned closer. 'I'm not sure yet. But I guess if we're both here in the city for one night and we literally bump into each other and we're both on the run…' She smiled, slow and tantalising. 'There must be a reason. Something's brought us together. I mean, I never come to town, and this is your last night here. So why did we meet tonight? Why you? Why me? Why here? Why now?'

'I've no idea.' He shrugged. 'Coincidence? Fate?'

'Fate?' She giggled. 'You believe in all that?'

'That a higher force has brought us to this spot, this moment?' Nah, he didn't believe that. And yet, she did have a point.

She shrugged and giggled. 'It would be a shame not to

honour the Fates if they do exist, though. Or we might incur their wrath.'

He chuckled. As come-on lines went, this was right up there. 'Yeah, best not annoy the Fates. What do you think they have in mind for us, Mi...chelle?'

'I don't know.' She drummed her fingers against her bottom lip. 'I'm just trying to decide...'

'Anything I can do to help crystallise your ideas, let me know.'

She edged closer, close enough for him to see the smattering of freckles over her nose, the layer of mascara on long, thick eyelashes and the quick dart of her tongue across her lips before she said, 'Talk with me, Brin.'

Talk? That was out of left field.

'Sure. About what?'

'I don't care. I just like listening to your accent. It takes me away from...' She shivered, clearing her throat, as if trying to clear her head too. 'It's lyrical and soft and so different to what I'm used to. I like the way you sound.'

Oh, hell.

His body prickled as his libido sprang fully into life. 'To be honest, I like the way you...everything.'

He had to admit feeling intrigued as to what exactly the sound of his voice was taking her away from.

'That makes two of us.' She put her hand on his chest and stepped closer. 'So, tell me something—anything. Just keep talking...and we'll see where we end up.'

CHAPTER ONE

Three years later...

THE ROAR OF helicopter blades as they flew across the tempestuous Hauraki Gulf just about smothered the raging clatter of Mia's heart and the rush of panic whistling through her head.

It had all happened so fast. One minute she'd been celebrating the sale of her late parents' property—an outdoors education camp—which had made her, if not exactly rich, then financially comfortable. She'd been raising a glass and planning a night of partying in Auckland city before waving her best friend off on an exciting adventure. The next minute, they'd received news so terrifying her legs had almost buckled beneath her.

Her beloved home, Rāwhiti Island, twenty-two kilometres off the Auckland coast, was suffering an ugly storm and a passenger ferry had capsized in one of the bays—a ferry no doubt carrying people she knew and loved who could be in danger. The storms could be cruel here, Mia knew to her cost. Roofs got blown off, trees felled and power cut.

People died.

Her daughter, Harper, was on the island too. The beautiful little girl who had, if not saved Mia's life, then given her something to live for. So, she wouldn't be able to breathe properly until she had Harper safely in her arms. She'd decided to return immediately. Mia wasn't about to lose anyone else.

But there was more…so much more she could barely believe.

As she climbed into the rescue chopper to go back and help her island *whanau*—her family, not by blood but by choice—she found the space occupied by two guys in green paramedic uniforms. Their faces were half-obscured by baseball caps and the chopper headsets. One of them, though, was unmistakable: tall with short, black hair…and startling navy-blue eyes.

Her past caught up with her as her heart stuttered and her gut clenched.

Why now? Why today of all days? Why this helicopter, at this exact moment, on this day?

The guy sitting opposite her was an Irishman called Brin. Clearly a paramedic, although he hadn't told her that when they'd met three years ago. And, judging by the way he was looking at her, he was just as blindsided seeing her again as she was seeing him. His shocked gaze caught hers as the chopper juddered roughly through grey clouds. A crosswind dumped them a few metres down towards the sea. Mia yelped as the skipper wrestled with the controls. Would they even survive this flight?

Next to her, her best friend and sister-in-law, Carly, squeezed her hand.

Mia tore her eyes away from Brin, still trying to reconcile the fact he was here and wondering where to start, what to say. How to explain…?

'Hey, it's going to be okay,' Carly mouthed over the din.

'I don't think so.' She shrugged at her friend. She was not okay at all. She wasn't ready for this, neither her head nor her heart. Not amongst the turmoil of a rescue and God knew what else they'd be facing on Rāwhiti.

'Prepare for a bumpy landing,' the skipper's voice crackled through her headset.

She gripped Carly's hand, then they were descending fast through lumps and bumps that buffeted them like a washing machine spin-cycle. Carly's face was pale. Brin was steadfastly looking out the front window into the darkness.

'Welcome to Rāwhiti.' The skipper chuckled. 'Good luck out there.'

Then the door hatch opened. Mia took off her headset, unclipped her safety buckle and was bundled out into a wind that hit her in the chest and whipped most of her breath away. The skipper shoved their suitcases into their arms...so excitedly packed and sadly unused...and they ran out of chopper-blade range to be met by one of the locals, Nikau.

He took her bag and shouted, 'Carly, Mia, thank God you're here. Everyone's evacuated to the camp and the injured are being taken there too.'

Carly nodded and raced ahead. Having been the island's first responder, she no doubt wanted to get into the thick of the rescue efforts. Mia supposed she should tell the paramedics where they were headed but they just followed Carly. Mia trailed behind, descending the steep path towards the back of the outdoor education camp—the place she had just sold.

Chaos...in her head, in her body, here at the camp. Rain lashed the windows and wind rattled the window frames as people bustled around the huge kitchen-dining room, trying to dry off or attend to the injured. Added to the battering wind and rain were the raised voices of people in pain, people who were frightened, people at risk.

She ran from group to group, trying to find Harper, then stumbled outside into the downpour, only to have a woman with a nasty gash on her forehead thrust at her.

There was no time to think, so Mia helped the woman to

the makeshift minor-injury assessment area in a cordoned-off area of the room.

She'd left Harper in the care of Owen, the island doctor, and his four-year-old son, Mason. Owen would not have let anything happen to them. They wouldn't have been on the ferry. They were safe; she was sure.

But, hell, how many times had she told herself that that terrible night when her parents and brother hadn't come home?

They are safe. How many times had she repeated those words for the next week until reality had crashed in? How many hours had she and Carly sat together, hoping, wishing, praying for their family to return? And then no one had. Mia had been left without her parents and brother, Rafferty. Carly had been made a widow. All they'd had left was each other, and Harper had cemented the bond: mother, auntie, baby.

Mia pulled herself together. She was sure her baby was okay…but where was she?

'Have you got any painkillers?' The woman in front of her moaned and Mia forced herself to focus on her job. She was the island nurse-practitioner. Everyone depended on her to stay focused and calm. She grabbed a first-aid kit, explained to her patient what she was going to do and made sure the woman had no other injuries she needed to deal with.

And, always, she was aware of the feeling she was being watched. She turned her head and saw Brin kneeling on the floor, attending to a boy who looked around nine years old. Not a local kid. As if he felt her eyes on him, Brin turned and looked at her. His expression was one of confusion, his eyes narrowed as if he was trying to get a better look at her.

She looked away and focused on cleaning the head wound. *Not here. Not now.*

When? How? Why? What the hell was she going to say?

Because, now he was here in front of her, she had to tell him. He said something to the boy's mum then stood.

Was he coming over? What was he going to say?

She didn't want to hear him speak. That cute Irish accent had been the undoing of her three years ago. He'd seduced her with his words. Hell, she'd been putty in his hands. But the ramifications of where that voice had taken her, what they'd done that night, were still rippling and would do so for the rest of Mia's life.

Her heart thumped in time with each of his steps as he strode towards her.

'Mia! You're here! Thank God.' Anahera, Mia's friend and receptionist at Mia's workplace, Rāwhiti Medical Clinic, slid in front of Brin and wrapped her in a hug. Over her friend's shoulder, she watched Brin pause and frown.

Mia. Hell—he'd heard. No matter; she had more immediate things to worry about. She grasped Anahera's shoulders. 'Where's Harper?'

Anahera stroked Mia's arm. 'Breathe, Mia. Breathe. Don't worry, hon. She's fast asleep in one of the bunk rooms upstairs. Nicole's in there, and her babies too. I just left them to come down here to help out. I'm so glad you came home. Is Carly...? Did she go?'

Having lost her husband, and too afraid to let herself fall in love with Owen, Carly had booked a one-way ticket around the world, planning to leave the country tomorrow. But, as she and Mia had celebrated the camp sale and contemplated their futures, Carly had realised she loved Owen and had come back to see if he felt the same about her. 'She's come home too, but I don't know where she is now. We jumped off the helicopter and she disappeared in a huge rush.'

'Probably gone to find Owen. He's co-ordinating the rescue in North Bay.'

'Right. Yes. Good. They'll need all the help they can to rescue the boat passengers.'

'Poor guy's first emergency on his own. Well… I guess he has Carly now too.' Anahera smiled.

'Oh, I think he has.' Mia forced a smile of her own. At least one good thing was coming out of this fated night. Carly and Owen's relationship had stalled when she'd decided to head overseas but now Mia could only hope they'd get back on track. But this night, the storm and these injuries, would bring back fearful memories for Carly too.

Anahera nodded. 'That's something, then. Little Mason's in the bunk room upstairs too.'

All her loved ones were accounted for. Mia did what Anahera had asked and finally breathed out. *Good. Right, focus, Mia.*

'I've set up a major injury space in the accessible room down the corridor and the walking wounded are over there.' Anahera pointed towards Brin. 'I don't know what we'll do when this place changes hands. Nowhere on the island has this kind of space.'

Mia grimaced. She and Carly had signed the sale and purchase agreement only hours ago, although it felt like a lifetime. This place was no longer hers and she had no idea what it might turn into. The last rumour had been about a fancy upmarket resort.

Guilt worried down her spine as she looked around the familiar room used by generations of school children to learn bush skills and sailing. Memories came of her parents teaching those skills: the love they'd had for their jobs; her brother joining the teaching team as he'd grown older. Then Carly marrying him and coming to live here five years ago.

So many memories were imprinted on these walls. Her whole life until eighteen had been lived here…then three years away at nursing college and subsequent years in a little cottage in a different part of the island. But the camp had always been her home. Until a perfect storm of issues—Carly leaving and not being able to find a replacement; much-needed renovation they'd been unable to afford; and Mia's own little cottage requiring some serious TLC—had collided and they'd decided to sell Camp Rāwhiti.

But had she made a mistake by selling? Had she betrayed her family's memory? No. She couldn't think about that right now.

'Mia!' Nikau was standing in the doorway, his arm wrapped around the waist of a man who was hopping on one foot.

Mia glanced at Brin. He stared back at her, then turned away.

I can explain...

Mia's heart jerked as she watched him stride to the door, his back rigid as he nodded at Nikau, then head towards the high-need assessment area.

A peal of thunder roared above them, shaking the windows. The sky lit up with a flash of bright white. Someone screamed. A baby started to cry. Noise filled her ears, her chest.

And suddenly she did want to hear Brin's voice, to have his soothing words whispered against her neck.

'It's okay. It's okay. You are beautiful. You are amazing. I want you. You feel... God, you feel so good. I'm so glad I found you. It's okay. It's okay. It's okay...' he'd said as she'd blubbed against his chest, overwhelmed by so much emotion from the singular act of love-making. As she'd lost herself in sensory overload with this smooth-talking man, his mind-melting kisses, his heat. Had sought pleasure, given pleasure, unburdened herself of six months' worth of grief in touch, feel and sensation.

Then he'd made her laugh with stupid jokes and they'd talked about...what? Books, movies, travel, likes, dislikes, other things... But not everything. She hadn't told him her real name, where she lived and what she did because it hadn't seemed important. They'd only had one night, after all. But she had talked about her hopes and her dreams. It had been liberating to be effervescent, carefree Michelle instead of tragic Mia.

Right now, she ached to feel as unburdened and free as she had that night. To have him hold her again. To feel less alone. To explore *him* again. To relive every delicious second…and maybe even tell him the truth, at least about her name.

But she had so much truth to tell him she didn't know how to begin.

Mia?

Brin walked away from the woman he'd thought was Michelle. Was it her? He was sure of it. She had the same halo of blonde curls; the dark, soulful eyes. But his Michelle…*his*? What the hell? He gave a rueful laugh, then corrected himself. The woman he'd spent the night with would have shown some sort of recognition other than aversion and avoidance, surely? It had been one of the most memorable nights of his life. The connection had been instant, the attraction off the scale. But had it been more than just great sex?

Yeah, he'd thought so. Hell, he'd almost considered staying in Auckland just to spend more time with her, but with his visa expiring the next day he hadn't been able to take the risk. They'd agreed not to swap contact details. The mystery had amped up the sex appeal and he'd preferred to keep his heart intact by not investing too deeply or too much.

Besides, he'd left his tattered roots in Ireland. He wasn't about to start putting any down in this tiny country at the end of the world.

He trawled through possible scenarios. Maybe she had an identical twin, and this was indeed that twin called Mia. Maybe Michelle had had a reason to lie to him—perhaps she had had a husband and a brood of kids. Perhaps she was scared he might blurt out what they'd done in front of everyone here and put her in a difficult situation. Surely, she'd think better of him than that?

Truth was, he couldn't second-guess what any woman was thinking these days, if his failed marriage and the lies that were embroidered through it were anything to go by.

The major assessment space was empty, which he knew could only be a good thing. They'd been told to expect serious casualties, but the rescue team had clearly done a great job of getting the ferry passengers to safety without too much physical trauma. Although, the emotional trauma of being on a sinking boat in the dark and a raging storm would probably last longer.

But out here he could breathe for a moment, get his head round seeing this woman again before heading back in and working with her. When she'd stepped on to the helicopter and their eyes had met, he'd wanted to grin and wrap her in his arms. But the guarded way she'd looked at him had given him a very strong message of rebuttal, even denial.

A high-pitched wail had him turning round to find a woman holding a crying toddler. A girl, around two years old, maybe a little more. She was a mess of black curls, with pale skin and sleepy blue eyes. She rubbed the silky border of a well-worn blanket between her fingers. Cute kid…but obviously very upset. Then the blanket floated to the ground and the wailing intensified. Brin picked it up and handed it back to her.

'Hey, you don't want to lose your blankie. I know it's precious. I had one just like it when I was your age.'

Funny; he'd forgotten until this minute.

Fat tears dotted her cheeks and her chest juddered as she breathed in, telling him she'd been crying for a while. She held the blanket close to her chest and stared at him. But he laughed at her possessiveness. 'Don't worry, *mo stór*. I won't take it away from you.'

'Blankie.' She stared at him, and he wondered if she was warning him not to touch it or just repeating the word.

'Yes, blankie.' Suddenly desperate to see her smile, he flicked the bottom of the blanket over her head. 'Oh? Where's she gone? Where is she?'

A sniff.

'Where's she gone?' he tried again.

A gurgle.

Then she pulled the blanket down and giggled. Someone had taught her hide-and-seek.

He flicked it up again to cover her face. 'She's gone again. Where is she?'

The giggle became a full belly-laugh as she tugged the comforter away from her face. The tears were gone. And, oh, those huge dark-blue eyes and that messy hair, a tangle of black…kind of like his had been before he'd had it cut. The sullen pout that had transformed into the prettiest smile he'd ever seen was too cute.

There was something about her that made his chest feel warm.

Mo stór. My darling.

How many times had he said that? His heart suddenly ached for the little girl he'd left behind in Ireland. She was a few years older than this one, but he remembered the toddler stage all too well: the tantrums and the cuteness overload, the beginnings of a real personality. She'd been like him, he'd thought—a dreamer and a pleaser. Funny, too, just like him.

Yeah. Not so funny now.

He rubbed at his chest and the little girl started to cry again.

'It's okay, Harper. It's okay. Let's see if we can find your mammy in the dining room.' The woman flashed Brin a weary smile and bustled past him. He held the door open and let her through.

As he followed her into the noisy room, his eyes immediately and instinctively found Michelle again. She was crouched on her haunches, taking an elderly man's blood pressure. The old man was wrapped in a foil blanket and even from here Brin could see him shivering. But Michelle was tender and reassuring…he knew because he'd seen her in action earlier. She was assured in her medical skills, and compassionate. A nurse—he hadn't even known that.

The woman with the girl walked over to Michelle and handed her the crying toddler. Michelle's face creased into a grin, then crumpled into a grimace as she started to cry too. She wrapped the child in her arms, rocking her back and forth.

He remembered the way Michelle had cried in his arms that night, the breathless sobs she'd said were from making love with him. From being touched after a long time. From giving and taking pleasure, the overwhelm of their attraction. But he'd sensed there'd been more to it as she'd gripped him and her tears had soaked his chest.

And he'd been right.

Michelle had been on the chopper and had a small suitcase. How long had she been away?

And was she the little girl's mother?

Clearly this was her reason not to have told him the truth about her home life. She *did* have a family.

Hell. One thing he really hated was lying—lying where children were involved, in particular.

'Brin. Can you give me a hand?' Lewis, his old and new colleague, called over to him and gestured towards a woman with a badly misshapen leg. 'Going to need your silky skills for this one.'

'On it.' Brin shook away the emotion he thought he'd got a handle on and threw himself back into his work.

At least that was something he could rely on.

CHAPTER TWO

IT FELT AS if the stream of injuries was never going to end, but as the last of the passengers, the boat skipper, Carly, Owen and the rescue team all piled into the dining room, things started to calm down. Everyone had been safely rescued, but the boat was sinking.

At least the casualties were relatively minor, save for a couple of patients who needed fairly quick evacuation to Auckland General Hospital, which Lewis was trying to organise, but he kept getting rebutted because of the downturn in the weather.

Mia had managed to get Harper to go back upstairs with Nicole and she hadn't heard a peep from her since. And, yes, she knew Brin had seen her with her daughter. She hadn't dared look at him, so had no idea what he might be thinking.

This was all such a mess. Her thoughts and emotions were all over the place. She'd cried, holding Harper, in front of all those people. Her guard had dropped, she'd felt so protective, he was here and…oh, God. Her heart felt as if it were going to hammer out of her chest. Did he know? Had he guessed?

A steaming mug of hot chocolate was pushed into her hands. Carly smiled at her. 'You've done a great job with all these patients. Drink this. It'll keep your strength up.'

'Thanks.' Mia took the cup and noticed her hands were trembling.

It seemed as though Carly had noticed too. 'Can I say, you look terrible, Mia. Are you okay?'

'Thanks muchly. You don't look so great yourself,' Mia threw back, laughing. Carly was soaked to the skin, hair plastered to her face, and sporting a tinfoil blanket. But she was bright and cheery and had a very secretive smile every time she looked over at Owen.

'I'm going for a shower as soon as I get the chance,' Carly said. 'Do you want to go upstairs for a while to be with Harper?'

'I need to stay here in case we have any further medical problems.' Plus, she wanted to make sure Brin got on that chopper soon and headed off the island.

'There are enough of us to cope without you,' her friend said.

'No. I'm fine.' Mia realised she'd snapped. 'I'm sorry. I'm—'

'Hey, it's okay.' Carly smiled softly. 'This must be bringing up all kinds of emotions for you. I know it did for me. I just had a bit of a wobble out there on the boat with Owen.'

Her friend didn't know the half of it. Mia shrugged. 'I'll be okay. What about you? What kind of wobble?'

'I had a meltdown when I thought there might be some people left on the ferry and were going to drown. I screamed a bit and there were tears as the memories piled in. But Owen got me through. And no one died.' Carly wrapped her in a hug, avoiding spilling the hot chocolate. 'I'm okay. But tell me what you need, Mia. If you want to go hug your girl, then go. If you need a shower, go right ahead. Some quiet time? I can muster a room for you upstairs.'

'Gosh, where would I be without you?' Mia hugged her friend, trying not to cry. 'I'm so glad you decided to stay.'

'Me too. I was overwhelmed by the feelings I'd grown for Owen and I panicked and wanted to run away. But, as soon as I left this island, I knew I'd made a mistake.' Carly squeezed Mia tightly. 'After Rafferty died, I didn't want to fall in love and then risk losing it all again. And I didn't want you to think I'd ever forget him.'

'I know you won't ever forget my brother. But I also know you love Owen, and you need to celebrate it. Wallow in it.'

'Oh, I will.' Carly's eyes crinkled. 'So, what do you need, Mia?'

I want to rewind to that night in the hotel.

The thought almost brought her to her knees: comfort; peace; exhilaration; being held. Finding pleasure that had wiped away some of her grief, if only for a few hours. For that, she'd been eternally grateful. And there'd been that ethereal…*something* between them. Something she'd never forgotten and had never found with any other man since. Not that there'd been any who had got past the first-date stage.

It had been a bone-deep connection. *A knowing.* An understanding she couldn't even begin to describe. But then, it had been laced through with her lies, so maybe she was just looking back with rose-coloured glasses.

She extricated herself from Carly's hug and forced another smile. 'I'm good. Honestly. I've already had a big hug with Harper. She needs to sleep now, or it'll be Miss Grumpy Pants tomorrow, and I really don't have the energy to deal with that.'

'Okay, if you're sure.' Carly was looking at her with a puzzled expression which Mia was not going to solve for her any time soon. She'd spent the last three years avoiding any discussion about Harper's parentage and wasn't about to start talking now. Not here. Not ever, if possible.

But it wasn't going to be possible; she knew that now. He was back. 'I'm sure.'

Her friend sighed. 'Okay. Well, I've just heard that the weather's too bad for the paramedics to evacuate the tibial fracture and the collarbone injury in the short term. So, we need to make up a room for them to rest in. Owen was hoping that between you, him and the two paramedics you could do a roster, to take it in turns to get a break while the others monitor the patients.'

Which might mean she would spend more time with Brin. Mia shuddered. 'Sure.'

'Great. I'll sort out a room in the annexe with bedding, if you could take this tray of drinks over to the guys?' Carly pointed to a tray on the table next to her and then flitted towards the exit.

'The guys' meaning Brin and the senior paramedic, Lewis, who was a regular on the medical evacs. Taking the drinks meant she'd have to look Brin in the eye, which she'd so far managed to avoid, but there wasn't anything she could do about it now. So, she picked up the tray and walked towards the makeshift screen, her heart in her mouth, her stomach in knots.

As she entered the space, Brin looked up from attending a patient and caught her gaze. She tried to look away but couldn't. He was...well...just as gorgeous as he'd been that night, with searching eyes, strong jaw and a rugged, toned body—tanned now, even though he'd laughed that his Irish skin usually went bright red in the sun rather than brown.

She forced some calm into her body. 'Hey, here's some hot chocolate.' She turned to the two patients. 'I'll check with the doc to see if you're allowed anything to eat or drink. It depends on how soon we can get you medevaced out of here. They might want you nil-by-mouth if they think we can get you to the hospital soon.'

'Might not be until tomorrow, I'm afraid. It's too wild right now.' Lewis jumped up and took the tray. 'Thanks a lot, Mia. This is great.'

She shot a look at Brin at the mention of her name. His expression was like stone. She turned back to Lewis and put as much levity into her tone as she could. 'Carly's making beds up in a bunk room in the annexe. We can take it in turns to monitor this lovely pair and then alternate getting some rest.'

'Great idea. Hey…' Lewis's expression turned serious. 'I was thinking…'

'Yes?' Mia stared up at him. He was a nice guy. Around her age, maybe a little older. Single, good-looking, outdoorsy. Not her type or anything, but she got on well with him. Maybe if she hadn't kept Brin in her heart she might have thought other men might be her type, but he'd ruined her for anyone else.

'Are you okay? I mean, this must be giving you some bad flashbacks, right?'

She briefly closed her eyes and let memories wash through her. The boat that hadn't come back. Her whole family…gone.

Then she opened them but refused to look at Brin and let him see all the emotions she carried with her. Emotions she'd wrangled into submission but were mingling with her anxiety and making her blood pressure spiral. Bereaved Mia was not bright and bubbly Michelle, although he'd probably guessed that by now. 'Yeah. It's not the best night I've ever had.'

Understatement of the year.

'I'm so sorry, Mia.' Lewis touched her arm. 'Is there anything I can do?'

'I'm okay. But thank you.' She took a deep breath. 'The best thing is for all this to be over. I'd really like the wind to die down and the sun to come out in the morning.'

'Us too. We need to get our patients to the hospital asap.' Lewis grimaced, then looked at his colleague. 'Okay. Brin, you take the first rest. Mia, would you mind showing Brin where the bunk rooms are? It's a warren up there, and especially difficult in the dark.'

No. Please, no.

'Sure.'

But Brin shook his head warily. 'I'll find it, no worries. Don't bother yourself, Mia.'

His Irish accent had the faintest Aussie tinge in it. Had he been there all this time? He'd said he was going to travel through Asia, maybe head to South America—his 'great adventure', he'd called it.

She glanced at Lewis, who was frowning as he looked first at Brin then at Mia. Then his eyes widened. 'God, sorry. Stupid of me. You two don't know each other. Mia Edwards, this is Brin O'Connor. He's our newest team member, but he's been here before. A few years ago…two?'

'Three.' Brin nodded.

'But you never came out to Rāwhiti, no?' Lewis was babbling on, totally oblivious that Brin and Mia knew each other, intimately. 'Well, this is Mia. She's our very capable nurse-practitioner here on Rāwhiti. Which is usually a gorgeous place to visit, except when it's blowing a gale.'

'Pleased to meet you…Mia.' Brin's tone was flat but this time he did look at her and his expression was guarded, confused and possibly angry.

She didn't blame him. At least he'd been honest that night. She swallowed back her anxiety. *O'Connor*—Brin O'Connor. How much easier things could have been if she'd known that little piece of information three years ago. 'Hi, Brin. Welcome to Rāwhiti.'

'Better head upstairs, mate. Time's ticking. You have an hour and counting.' Lewis tapped his watch. 'Mia, do us a favour and show him the bunk room or he'll waste all his rest time trying to find it.'

She felt the weight of everyone looking at her, so she nodded quickly then headed out of the room. If they could do this in double-quick time, she might be able to avoid awkward conversations until she was ready to answer the many questions he'd no doubt have.

Don't ask. Don't ask. Don't ask.

Once outside, there was no opportunity to talk. The wind howled and the trees bent almost sideways. The roar of the sea filled the air and the lashing rain made it undesirable to stop even for a moment. But, once inside the annexe, silence fell, weighty and laden with their history and all those unasked questions.

She ran up the steps and opened the bunk-room door, irritated to find that Carly had finished making up the beds and had obviously long gone.

She pointed to the bunks. 'There you go. Bathroom's at the far end of the corridor. Bye.' Then she turned and headed away.

'Michelle.' His voice stopped her, the way it had that night. The voice that she still dreamt of almost as often as the way he'd kissed her, held her, made love to her... They were all regular stalkers through her dreams. 'Mia. Whoever you are...'

Her heart hammered against her chest like the storm waves crashing against the rocks. She slowly turned to face him. This was it—the reckoning. 'Mia. My name's Mia, not Michelle.'

He nodded, his expression unreadable. 'I assume you had your reasons for giving me a different name.'

'I did.' It hadn't been her intention. She'd grasped a chance to be someone else for a few hours. But she needed to be honest now. She walked back into the bunk room, preferring to have this conversation out of earshot of anyone else.

He followed her inside but didn't close the door. He even stepped to one side to allow her a direct escape route. The result of training in dealing with difficult situations? Or maybe he was just giving her space.

'Is he here?' he asked.

'Who?' Mia frowned.

He sat down on one of the beds. 'Your partner—husband?'

'I don't have one.'

'Oh. I thought...' He looked at the floor. 'Okay.'

'It's...complicated.'

'Isn't it always?' His tone was sharper as he looked at her again. 'But you had one, right? Someone significant enough that you lied to me about your name, and God knows what else.'

His words stung. 'No, Brin. I'm not the kind of person who has affairs. Honestly. That's not who I am. I've never been married, and I didn't have a partner when I met you. That one night we had together? I was single. I was free to be with you.'

'So why lie about who you were?'

'I…' How to explain everything? 'Does it matter? Really?'

He huffed out a breath, stood, stalked over to the window and put his hands on the ledge, staring out into the wild night. 'It shouldn't matter, right? We both knew the score. It was a bit of harmless fun. But, yet, somehow it does. That night felt… I don't know…significant. I thought we'd connected. I was honest wit' you.'

There was his accent again, stroking her nerve endings while the emotions swirling in her chest gave the raging gale outside some serious competition. 'Really? You told me everything about your life?'

'Not everything, no. We didn't have enough time for everything.' He turned round to look at her, leaned back against the window ledge and crossed his ankles. 'It was the first time I met you. I wasn't going to bore you with my life history.'

'Exactly. So, you held things back too.' God knew, she was trying for time, absolution or…what? She didn't know.

'It was our first night,' he reiterated.

'And the last.'

'Yeah.' He held her gaze with those lovely blue eyes…eyes she looked into every day when she gazed at her daughter. But they turned dark. 'We both knew it was a one-time thing.'

'We did.' And it had been amazing, magical, life-affirming. Life-giving—literally.

He shook his head and the anger seemed to steam out of him. 'I'm sorry. I'm getting all heavy over nothing. It's okay, I get it. I was thrown by the name thing. And, to be honest, blindsided by seeing you again after all these years. It's not my business why you told me your name was Michelle.' He hesitated then huffed out a breath. 'Look, I had a bad time of it a few years back with a woman who lied to me. It messed me up for a while—makes me wary. I don't like being lied to.'

'I don't blame you.' She didn't want to think he'd been hurt before and that she had added to it. This serious Brin was another layer to add to the funny, sexy, gentle one she remembered.

'And…' He gave her a rueful smile. 'Ah, look ya. I guess I'd built up this idea of what things could have been like if we'd stayed in touch, you know? Or what our reunion might have been like.'

She'd been there too, many times, going over and over what she might say. 'Yes, me too. Didn't think it'd be like this—in a bunk room in a storm.'

'I definitely had other ideas.' His eyes briefly lit up and she wondered if his ideas featured a rerun of that night. 'But there it is.'

They both knew this conversation about wishful thinking was going nowhere so she didn't say anything else. But for a moment she allowed herself to imagine a romantic reunion where the timing and the place had been perfect. Where they'd stayed in touch, or where he hadn't left. Where she'd told him her real name and he'd told her his surname. Where she'd found him on social media. Where he'd known where she lived, or the island, at least.

Things could have been very different.

Silence filled the conversation gap and she was about to leave and try to get her head around everything. Maybe delay the important conversation to another time. Maybe…never?

But then he said, 'What did Lewis mean by "flashbacks"?'

'I'm sorry?'

'I mean…you don't have to explain, but I'm sinking here.' He ran his palm across his cropped hair and gazed at her. It dawned on her that he wasn't angry, just confused. 'I know

I don't have a right to ask, Mia, but this is like a huge puzzle and I don't have a clue what's going on. Did your partner die in a storm or something? I mean…if that's what happened I don't blame you for not wanting to talk about it that night. Or…what?'

He looked lost. He thought the lie about her name was tied up in some sort of relationship tragedy. No, that was poor Carly's cross to bear. And just thinking about everything she'd lost brought Mia's barriers crashing down. 'Oh, Brin. No, I didn't lose my partner. I lost my whole family—my mum, dad and brother. In a boating accident…before I met you. About six months or so before.'

Those navy-blue eyes darkened and he looked genuinely upset for her. Almost as if he felt her grief. 'God, Mia, that's terrible. I'm so sorry. I didn't know.'

'Why would you? That night, you said something along the lines of, "the less you know about me, the better". And I thought…yeah. Actually, let's play. It's been a long time since I played. I'd spent six months battered by grief. Everywhere I went, people looked at me with such sadness, I felt the weight of their grief piled on mine. I was exhausted and lonely. Then one of my old nursing friends invited me to a party. I really wasn't going to go but Carly, my brother's widow, pushed me into it with the lure of a luxury hotel. And I eventually caved.'

'Then you met me.'

Oh, yes. A major turning point in her life. 'We were having a good time flirting…' She paused, caught his eye and hoped to find the…something again, but it wasn't there—just bewilderment. 'I didn't want to bring all my past into our fun conversation. I wanted to be someone else. To step out of my crappy life, leave all that grief and emotion behind just for one night. Can you blame me for wanting some respite from that? My family were dead. I didn't want to be that "sole survivor" person, the one everyone pities. I wanted mysterious, exciting, sexy. Man, I just wanted to be wanted.'

He closed his eyes and she wondered what he was thinking. When he opened them again he looked at her and smiled cautiously. 'You were certainly that, Mia. I almost didn't get on the plane.'

'Because of me?' He'd thought about stalling his plans for her?

'Yeah.' He laughed. 'Crazy, eh?'

'That would have been mad.' So much had happened since. 'Did you get to do all the travelling you'd planned?'

'Some. A few months working in Aussie to boost the financials, then I got to Asia as the world went into lockdown. Bad timing, eh? I hopped on one of the last flights out of Hanoi and hunkered down back in Perth. Went straight back to the job I'd just left. My visa got extended so I stayed a while longer. Then back here.'

'Why didn't you go back home?'

He frowned. 'Home?'

'Ireland.'

He straightened and spat out, 'There's nothing for me there. Nothing at all.'

'Or stay in Perth, then? Why come back here?' Was she fishing? Was she hoping his reasons for returning were to do with her? And why such a vociferous reaction to her question?

He held up his palms. 'Lewis called me out of the blue and offered me a promotion.'

'Lewis. Of course.' All this time her friend had kept in touch with Brin and she hadn't even known. And, she noted, Brin hadn't come back to look for her—he'd come for the job opportunity. She wasn't sure she could put a name to the feelings that news instilled in her but they weren't happy ones. Damn, even now she felt intensely moved by him.

He shrugged. 'To be fair, he sounded pretty desperate, and

there's a new scheme here that fast-tracks Irish paramedics. Makes getting a visa a lot easier. So why not? I like the place and the people.' He shot her a look that had her insides melting. 'It seemed like a good idea.'

'Well, you've certainly done a lot more than I have. I've just stayed here the whole time.'

'Ah, no. I wouldn't say that. In between you've had a baby. Harper, is it—your little girl? I saw you with her earlier—cute as a button.'

Oh, God.

Trepidation flooded through her, making her heart jitter and her gut tighten. She wished he'd leave, so she didn't have to tell him the truth, but that was the coward's way out. He needed to know…even if this cold, sparse room on a wild night wasn't the best time or place. The words would no doubt rock his world.

There was no easy way to say it. She felt blindsided, unprepared, even though she'd been rehearsing how and what she was going to say for almost three years. She took a breath and held his gaze.

'*Our* little girl, Brin.'

'I'm sorry?' He shook his head and took a step towards her, his eyes suddenly wild with an emotion she couldn't identify but was a lot like panic, with a flash of anger…distrust. He raised his hands, wanting answers. 'What the hell?'

'*Our* little girl.'

She swallowed. This was not the reaction she'd been hoping for. Confusion, yes—surprise, definitely—but anger, mistrust? Did he think she was lying? Trying to trap him?

But she'd gone this far, so she had to tell him the truth. 'That child is our baby, Brin. Harper is your daughter.'

CHAPTER THREE

THIS COULDN'T BE HAPPENING.

This could not freaking be happening.

Brin took a deep breath, let it out slowly and tried to control his reactions as he looked at Mia. He'd been in her presence what—three hours, four? And already his emotions were on a rollercoaster ride. She was still beautiful, guarded, soft, sexy. Oh, yes...he'd registered the physical tug towards her.

But this news?

He backed away. 'No, Mia. You've made a mistake. She's not my child.'

She blinked quickly, her tone fervent, her words coming out in a rush, as if she had so much to say and couldn't stop them. 'Yes, she is. There was no one else but you. No one. She was born thirty-seven weeks after our night.'

'But...whoa, Mia. Are you sure?'

'One hundred percent.' Her eyes widened. 'Look at her. She's got your eyes, Brin, not mine. Your fair skin. I don't know what your hair was like when you were younger, but she's certainly not inherited my blonde.'

The little girl with the blankie who'd cried then giggled and done something to his heart.

Mo stór.

That little tiny scrap of giggling prettiness was his child? He couldn't deny the hair was exactly like his at that age, the eyes blue like his, not brown like Mia's. But that was where the likeness ended, surely?

She'd been upset and he'd tried to soothe her. But why? Why not just pick up the blanket and give it to her then walk away? Why get involved?

Because there'd been something about her that had made him stop, that had called to him. Jeez, the way her mother had called to him too. Something that had made him want her to be happy, a marrow-deep, soul-deep need to protect her that had been visceral, undeniable.

If that wee girl was his child, he would love her until he died—he knew that without a doubt.

No.

No.

He wasn't going to believe her. He couldn't do that to himself again—allow himself to slide into loving a child only to have it cruelly snatched away. A pack of lies.

No.

Mia was staring at him, her lip trembling as if she was on the verge of tears. 'Say something, Brin.'

'Like what?' He didn't trust himself to stay calm. He needed to think. He couldn't do that with her here; there was too much of her: her scent, her pretty face, the soft lilt of her voice… the tenderness. God, he remembered that—the sweet sounds she'd made when he'd slid inside her. The way she'd tasted; the swell of her breasts. Too many memories that would make him soften.

And harden.

So he left her there, in that soulless room, and walked out into the night.

Raindrops pelted his body as he wandered…to where? He didn't know where he was, save for some outdoor camp on a tiny island in the middle of a big sea. He followed the path that took him past the major-injury room, the large kitchen-dining block with condensation-covered windows and the hum of chatter, past the drying room and lecture room and out onto a flat piece of grass about the size of half a football pitch. Fifty metres or so further on he could see the large, dark shape of a building, so he headed for it. Squinting through the water running down his face, he saw a sign: *Boat Shed*. He tried the door but it was locked.

Beyond that was a small bay. The crash of waves against the pebbles assaulted him, tumultuous and messy; the squawk of birds trying to settle in a storm; the roaring wind; the groaning and rustling of trees. A child was crying somewhere inside.

His child?

His heart jerked. 'Harper.'

He tried to see how it felt to say it out loud. He didn't dislike it, it was just unfamiliar. Not a name he'd have chosen but…

But what? He'd given his first daughter an Irish name. Would he have chosen something Irish for Harper?

A daughter. Another daughter. He closed his eyes and tried to breathe, but his chest hurt, as if there was a thick weight pressing on his rib cage. He'd had no name choice to make this time, no build-up, no excitement. No going for scans or buying the cot. No birth, no firsts, just a blanket statement of fact.

A cute kid with a blankie. If she was telling the truth.

'Brin?'

Mia's voice, behind him, was tentative. He turned to see her holding a blue-and-white-striped beach towel over her head to protect herself from the rain. And as she approached his heart did a funny leap. His whole body prickled with recognition.

I see you. I know you. I remember.

No. He was not going there, not after this bombshell.

She cleared her throat as she stared up at him. 'Um… Lewis asked me to wake you. Your break finished ten minutes ago. He thinks you're still asleep.'

Hell. Had he been out here that long? He nodded, his mind a whirl of thoughts. 'Okay.'

But he didn't move. How the hell was this going to play out? What did she expect him to do, to say?

She tilted her chin up and met his gaze. There was steel in there now. The possessiveness of a mother who was not going to let her child down. 'If I'd found out I had a daughter, I'd be… Well, I'd be thrilled.'

'You sure about that? Right out of the blue? One day someone randomly throws that at you—you had no inkling, no idea? No one had thought to let you know…what, three years ago?… that this was happening?' He almost laughed at his history repeating. You'd have thought he'd have learnt his lesson by now.

But she didn't know about his past—the lies he'd been told, the love he'd given. He did not want to go there and get his heart stomped on again.

Hell, to have one woman pretend her child was his had been heart-breaking. To have a second woman do the same thing… Did he have 'mug' written across his face? Was he some sort of easy target? But it wasn't just the women he fell for, was it? His brother had been complicit too.

His *brother*. His own kin, his blood.

Betrayal ran deep and he was not going to put himself in line for that again.

And yet… Harper. That hair. That smile. That tug.

It wasn't impossible, right? The dates worked. They'd made love more than once that night. Had they used protection? He tried to remember, but knew he always did. And also knew that no contraception was one hundred percent safe.

Harper. He refused to allow her into his heart.

She was cute as hell.

Mia lowered the towel and scrunched it into a ball. Rain dripped onto her top from her sodden hair. Mascara ran down her cheeks. She was impossibly pretty, even so. And pissed off at him now. She glowered. 'Well, yes, it would be a surprise, and I'm sorry there was no other way of telling you. But she's, well, she's the absolute best thing that ever happened to me.'

She didn't have to say the words; her love for her child shone from her. He'd seen the way she'd cried when she'd held Harper earlier, heard the gentle voice, seen the immediate and unstoppable smile through the tears.

'Good, Mia. I'm glad you found some happiness after what you've been through.' But that didn't mean he was going to be a pushover 'And you want what from me, exactly?'

'Nothing.' She stepped back and shook her head. 'I…don't know. I thought I should tell you.'

'Because, if I took one look at her and did the maths, I'd guess?' Because he couldn't deny there was a familial likeness. His brother had the same eyes and hair, and Niamh. His heart cleaved at the memory.

'Because you have a right to know and to see her. If you want to. And she has every right to know her father.'

He didn't reply.

She screwed the towel up tightly in her hands. Her eyes blazed and her voice raised a notch. Because she was getting angry with him or because of the howling wind? 'For God's sake, Brin, I tried to find you, but I didn't even know your surname. The hotel refused to give out any personal information, no matter how much I begged them to. I even called the bar you'd been in, but they said there hadn't been any bookings that night.'

'Ah, no, it was just an informal thing.'

She glared at him. 'You disappeared. I looked for you on social media but there was nothing.'

'I don't do any of that.' He didn't want reminders of Ireland. Of the broken relationships he'd left behind or of his brother's treachery, his ex's lies.

'Did you know that if you put *Brin from Ireland* into a

search engine you get nearly five million hits? I went through so many of them, night after night. But I found nothing about you, so I gave up looking. Resigned myself to bringing her up on my own. I didn't know you'd come back. I didn't think I'd ever see you again.' Her eyes were wet and he wasn't sure if it was all from the rain. 'This is a shock, Brin.'

'Too right.' Seeing her again on the helicopter had been a jolt to his heart. He'd fleetingly thought…maybe? He was here again; maybe they could reconnect? But then he'd seen her reaction. She'd been scared…or wary. Or…she'd had something fundamentally important to tell him and didn't know where to begin.

But how could he untangle Mia and Harper from his ex and from the girl he'd thought was his daughter back in Ireland? How could he separate out emotions? Learn to trust that Mia was telling the truth in the aftermath of lies she'd thought were inconsequential, but had mapped out the routes they'd both taken from that night onwards?

Mia wiped the back of her hand across her face. Her clothes clung to her body, outlining contours he didn't remember. She was softer in places, thinner in others but still stunning—more so. She gave him a tentative smile. She was anxious, nervous. 'Look, I know it's a lot to take in. But if you want to…I don't know…see her, we can arrange something. I don't know what…but we should probably talk some time when we're not surrounded by chaos.'

His heart was still raging, echoing the storm that blew around them. 'Right now, the only thing I want you to arrange is a paternity test.'

'What?' Her mouth fell open.

He nodded sharply. He was not going to soften towards either of them. He was not going backwards. 'Once we get the result, then we'll know exactly where we stand.'

Without looking at her he made his way back towards the

dining room. He wondered how the hell he could focus on work when his life…his whole damned life…had come crashing down.

Again.

Mia fought the hurt that swelled through her.

Not just for her but for Harper too. If there was going to be any contact between father and daughter, she'd have to be very careful Harper didn't get hurt. Brin was a traveller, a nomad, constantly moving. He didn't think of the place he grew up in as his home. Would he just as easily move on from here, from them?

Harper was his daughter. Mia had absolutely no doubt about that. He'd have to deal with it, the way she'd dealt with it the last three years.

But she'd expected him to be kinder about it. And, worse, despite everything she couldn't help feeling the pull towards him like a moth to a flame. The immediate and devastating attraction she'd felt that first night reverberated through her. Her body remembered him—his touch, his laugh, his kisses.

But she knew better now. The way he'd reacted to this news showed her he wasn't the compassionate man she remembered.

She followed him back up to the camp buildings, swatting rain from her face and tears from her eyes. She would not cry in front of him, not again. The Mia he'd known before had grown up. She was stronger now, independent, a mother. She was capable, efficient and honest.

The door flew open and Carly bounded out. 'Mia, there you are. Harper's awake and looking for…' She paused, looking at Brin then at Mia. 'Sorry, did I interrupt…?'

Mia ignored the question, her focus entirely on her daughter's well-being. 'Where is she?'

'Anahera's got her in the dining room. Don't look so worried, she's fine—just a bit tearful.'

That makes two of us.

'Thanks.'

She headed inside and straight for her daughter, but kept half an eye on Brin, who marched over to the cordoned-off area and disappeared behind the screen.

'Mumma!' Harper slipped off Anahera's knee and ran towards her, clutching her favourite and very faded yellow-and-white-checked blanket.

'Hey, cutie.' Mia whipped her daughter up into her arms and gave her neck a nuzzle. 'I missed you.'

Harper patted Mia's face. 'Ugh. Wet.'

'Yes, sweetie. It's pouring with rain out there.'

'Playground?'

Mia laughed. The camp had a little play area with a slide, a climbing frame and a little plastic blue seesaw in the shape of a whale—but who knew for how much longer, now it had been sold?

She'd never wanted to run the camp and finding people to help Carly run it had proved difficult, never mind the cost of upkeep and much-needed renovation. Plus, she was a nurse, trying to make a life for herself and her daughter on a nurse's salary. The money from the sale of her old home would give her some breathing space. Although, now Brin was back, she felt as if she couldn't get enough oxygen into her lungs.

How much easier might her life have been—*their* lives have been—if Harper's father had been around? Would she have needed to sell her parents' beloved home?

'Mumma! Playground.' Harper patted Mia's face, bringing her back to the current most pressing needs of her offspring. It was way too late to trawl through those kinds of thoughts.

She gently rubbed her daughter's head with her knuckles. 'No, darling. Not right now. It's windy and rainy and night-time. The slide will be wet and you might get blown away in the wind.'

'Please.'

'You'll get pneumonia if you go out there. No.'

'Playground.' Harper's mouth formed a pout and Mia sighed.

'Tomorrow, maybe. Once things have dried off. Not right now.'

'Playground.' Her daughter threw her blankie onto the floor.

Mia leant forward and picked it up. This was her daughter's most favourite thing in the whole world. 'Don't let it get dirty. I think it's back to bed for you, little miss. You obviously haven't had enough sleep.'

She hated saying no, but there it was—the parent's burden. Not that Brin would know. She'd been the one parenting single-handed for three years. She didn't condemn him: the poor guy hadn't known. But, now he did, would he challenge the way she'd brought up her daughter? Would he want to do things differently? Would he want joint custody? That was, if he even wanted anything to do with them when the DNA test provided the proof.

DNA test! She wanted to scream. So many questions, niggles and worries had reared their heads and pummelled this already difficult day.

Lewis appeared from behind the screen with a wheelchair. The man with the displaced collarbone sat in it upright, pale and tired. Then Brin appeared, pushing another wheelchair in which sat the woman with the broken leg. Voices crackled through their walkie-talkies and she heard something about a weather window. He was leaving.

He looked around the room and his gaze fell on Harper and her.

Mia's breath caught. This could be the last chance they had to talk, but what more was there to say? He knew where she lived now and her real name. If he wanted to get involved with his daughter, he just had to contact her. As for anything more…the one thing she'd craved ever since that wonderful night…well, that was definitely off the table. There was too much distrust now, too much space between them—three years, for a start.

But Harper wriggled off her lap and ran towards him, beaming and laughing. His gaze followed and there was a hint of reluctant amusement in his face.

Please smile.

'Blankie.' His daughter held her precious blanket out to him. Was she offering it to him?

What? Weird.

She'd never done anything like that before to anyone. In fact, she was extremely possessive when it came to her blankie; she couldn't get to sleep without it.

How was he going to react now he knew what he knew?

'Harper, stop.' Mia would not let her daughter be hurt by this man. She jumped up and started to walk towards them. 'Harper, don't bother Brin, he's busy.'

Startled, Harper turned round and the blankie dropped to the floor.

Brin looked over at Mia then at Harper.

'No bother.' He picked up the blanket, held it out and smiled. He smiled! And it transformed his face back to the way he'd looked that night. Carefree. Gorgeous. Sexy as hell. 'Here ya go…Harper.'

Their daughter beamed at the sound of her name in his soft, lilting voice. Then she did something very strange. She put the blanket over her face.

What the heck?

Brin momentarily looked stricken then he crouched down and said something Mia couldn't catch.

Harper tugged the blanket down and giggled, then put it over her face again.

Once again, a flicker of discomfort scudded across Brin's face, then he smiled. 'Where's she gone?'

Harper pulled the blanket down and laughed again.

He patted her head and grinned, then stood, rubbed his chest and drew his eyes away from his daughter. For a beat he looked haunted, then his gaze collided with Mia's.

She'd covered the distance and was now standing in front of him. Exhaustion nipped at his features and she felt a glimmer of sympathy. He'd stayed well beyond the time his shift was supposed to finish. He was also dealing with a shock revelation.

She gently rubbed her daughter's back. 'Harper, say goodbye to Brin.'

Not Daddy, or Dad or Papa—just Brin. If it bothered him, he didn't show it.

'Bye, Bwin.' Her little girl both broke and raised the tension. He gave her another sad smile. 'Bye, Harper.'

Then he turned to Mia. 'Could you give me your contact details? For the…' he had the good grace to lower his voice '…test.'

So he hadn't changed his mind. Her stomach was in knots, her heart deflating. In a flat tone, she gave him her details.

'Okay.' He nodded as he put them into his phone. The smile was gone.

Then, in another beat, so was he.

Again.

CHAPTER FOUR

THE LONG NIGHT turned into an even longer six days that Mia thought would never end. She helped clean up the camp, dropped Harper off at nursery, then returned home to find her little cottage under a couple of feet of water. She managed to save what she could, called the insurance company then walked to work to find a very soggy clinic. Sometimes, even the best of buildings couldn't stop a very determined storm.

She'd been cleaning up for six days. It felt like six years.

And every moment was dogged by thoughts of Brin. Flashbacks to that night and the sexy way he'd looked at her intersected with his expression when she'd told him about Harper. All the while her heart jumped and jittered. She was exhausted physically, mentally and emotionally.

Looking forward to clocking off for the weekend, she was putting the closed sign on the clinic door when Carly bounded in. 'Hey, Mia! How's things?'

Mia grinned, always pleased to see her friend. 'You look very energised! Clearly you haven't been elbow-deep in flood water and storm damage for the last few days.'

'We were lucky our cottage stayed reasonably dry. But, anyway, I barely noticed. I am fuelled by love.' Carly waved her hand in the air and giggled. 'And I can't believe I even said that.'

'Oh, God, please—you're making me nauseous.' But it was so lovely to see Carly find happiness again after so many years in the dark, grieving for her beloved Rafferty. Mia felt a tinge of envy.

'I'm making me nauseous.' Carly giggled again. 'Sorry. Do you need a hand?'

'No, I'm done. Ready for the weekend.' Mia walked back to the reception desk and powered down the computer.

Carly leaned against the door jamb. 'Hey, are you okay? I've been worried about you all week. You seem, I don't know, distracted. Upset.'

And for good reason. 'I'm fine, honestly.'

'And yet you don't look it. What's wrong, hun?' Carly walked across the room and frowned sadly over the desk at her. 'Did the storm bring back some bad memories?'

Oh, hell.

Mia didn't need sympathy. She'd never asked anyone for help or discussed her thoughts and feelings, at least not since her mum had died. God, she missed her. But Carly was her best friend; they'd shared so much grief and trauma together, and she'd kept secrets from her for too long. Plus, she was going to explode if she didn't talk this through with someone.

She looked up at her friend and grimaced. 'Good memories, actually.'

Carly's frown deepened. 'I'm sorry?'

Oops, her mouth was running away. If she started to talk, she didn't know if she would be able to stop. 'Nothing. Ignore me.'

'Mia Edwards, what are you not telling me?' Carly peered at her suspiciously. 'Come on, talk to me. Sometimes it helps to share stuff. What good times are we talking here, you dark horse?'

'Oh, God. I need to tell someone before I go completely mad.' Mia took a deep breath and blew it out slowly. 'You remember Brin...from the other night?'

'The gorgeous Irish paramedic?' Carly shrugged at Mia's frown. 'Can't blame a girl for noticing.'

'Yes. That Brin.'

'I saw you two outside, deep in conversation. What was that all about?' Carly's frown melted into a huge smile. 'Oh, my God. He asked you out?'

'It's a little more complicated than that.'

Carly walked round the desk and leaned against it, peering closely at Mia. 'Oh?'

Mia took another deep breath. 'Well…he's…he's Harper's father.'

Her friend's eyes almost popped out of her head. She opened her mouth, closed it and opened it again. 'What? I think I might need my ears syringed—I thought you said he's Harper's dad.'

'I did. He is.' Mia watched her friend's reaction, which appeared to go from shock to confusion to delight to worry. Kind of how Mia felt but nowhere near as intense.

Carly grimaced too. 'I think I'm going to have to sit down. Every time I've tried to bring up the subject, you've hedged or flat out refused to say anything. But Brin? He's… Wow… I don't believe it.'

You're not the only one.

Mia stood and started to pace across the floor. 'I didn't think telling you about him was relevant. It was a one-night thing, fun and exciting, never to be repeated.'

'I guessed that much already. When you came back from that party you were different, somehow. Can't quite explain it. But you had a definite smile on your face. You had a great time.'

'We did. It was meant to be just a bit of fun. I didn't even tell him my real name. We didn't talk jobs. It wasn't an interview. It was sex. Great sex.'

Carly's eyes widened. 'Good. Okay. Why not? No judgement here.'

'Then he went off travelling. There were a lot of things I didn't know about him…like his surname, for a start. When I found out I was pregnant, I couldn't just call him and tell him. I couldn't find him.'

'And now he's come back.' Her eyes narrowed. 'For you?'

Mia shook her head, ignoring the sting in her chest. 'No. He got a job here. He's just doing Lewis a favour, I think. Plus, it's a promotion. But he was in Perth—Perth in Australia, not Perth in Scotland. Oh, and I'm babbling. I'm just…thrown.'

Carly patted the chair next to her. 'This is so unlike you, Mia. Come and sit down. You never panic. Does he know about Harper?'

Mia preferred to pace. 'Yes. I told him as soon as I could. It seemed only fair.'

'And?' Carly bugged her eyes. 'And?'

'He demanded a DNA test. I received a call from a company in Auckland the morning after the storm, confirming my details, so he must have contacted them the minute he left here. They couriered over a test pack, I did Harper's mouth swab and sent it back the same day. The results will be emailed in the next few days.'

Carly exhaled on a smile. 'That's good news, right?'

Mia stopped pacing. 'Why?'

'It means he's considering things. He wants a quick answer.'

Mia hadn't considered that. 'Why won't he just believe me?'

'Why should he?'

Mia stared at her friend. Wasn't it obvious? 'Because I wouldn't lie about something like this. I mean, I know it's a shock, but it's very clear he doesn't trust me. In fact, he wasn't very nice about the whole thing. Nothing like the kind guy I remember. Showing his true colours, eh?'

Carly scowled. 'To be honest, Mia, you only had one night with him. That's not long enough to get to know or trust someone. He might think you want to sue him for back-dated child support, or God knows what. He's right to be wary.'

Oh, Carly had all the reasonable answers. 'I wouldn't do anything like that. And we clicked, Carly. The chemistry was real, off the scale. But maybe I was wrong about him. Maybe he's the kind of man who's going to run. Maybe Brin O'Connor is just a heartless, unreliable jerk I don't want my daughter to get involved with.'

Never mind about me.

A shiver in the atmosphere had her turning to look towards the door. Carly had left it open and a figure had walked in. He was tall, dark-haired and gorgeous, looking every bit as shocked at her words as he had been when she'd stepped on to the helicopter.

Despite everything, Mia's heart did a little dance at the sight of him, while her head told it to quieten the hell down. This man could be dangerous to her equilibrium and her heart, not to mention to her daughter's.

Brin was back.

Great.

He'd heard her not-so-glowing description of him. And she knew he'd heard. *Awkward.*

Both women were staring at him, mouths open. For a split second he felt like doing exactly what she thought he'd do— running. Not from Harper and her, but from the feelings swirling in his chest. From the panic and immediate desire at seeing her again. From the dismay that she didn't seem to like him much. That he was going to be just like his brother: a royal jerk.

Ex-brother. *Persona non grata.*

But the last ferry had pulled out of the harbour and he was stuck here, at least for the night. And, no matter how far he ran, he couldn't escape himself, could he?

Why the hell he'd come back, he wasn't sure. But, the minute he'd clocked off for two days, he'd rushed home, packed a bag and ran for the ferry. He hadn't been able to fight the need to be here.

He didn't know what he was expecting or looking for. But here he was. 'Hey, Mia. Hi, Carly.'

The two women glanced at each other. Carly gave Mia a hug and, loudly enough for him to hear and heed the hidden warning, she whispered in her Kiwi-English accent, 'Love you, Mia. Call me if you need me. I'll come straight over.'

Then she nodded at him and left.

He wanted to smile. It was good to know Mia had people who had her back. Who'd hopefully been there for her over the last few years, given she had no family now, except Harper.

His family...

He wasn't very nice. He was unreliable.

The words pierced his chest. He'd spent all thirty-four years of his life trying to be kind, fair and honest, the exact opposite of his father and brother. He'd been there for Niamh at every step, all the firsts.

'Hey, Mia.'

'Brin.' Her eyes were dark, her posture rigid, far from the carefree woman he remembered. But hell, she was so beautiful, just looking at her made his chest heat.

He inhaled. 'Look, I wanted to apologise for the way I behaved the other day...night. You know...' God, he was making a mess of this.

Her hands were on her hips. 'You could have just called or emailed. Actually, yes, an email would have been better. It would have saved you a trip.'

'I...wanted to see you face-to-face. Things are always better that way. I was shocked and I acted badly. I can be nice. I *am* nice.' Was the real truth that he'd wanted to see her face? He hadn't stopped thinking about her all week. Not just because of Harper, although she'd been in his head all week too, and what the future might hold. *If* she was his daughter.

But Mia had been at the forefront of his mind too much: the soft sway of her hips; the curve of her lips; her scent that he recognised even now, all these years later. It was something floral and intoxicating—a little musk.

He tried for a smile, which was not reflected by her face as she said, 'Has the test result come back? Only, it hadn't last time I checked my emails.'

'What? No. Not the last time I checked either.' He'd been refreshing his email account endlessly for the last few hours. His nerves were shredded, and hers too, judging by her curt attitude. Although, that could also likely be because of the way he'd responded to her news the other day.

Her eyebrows rose. 'So, you're here because…?'

'I thought we needed to talk some more.'

'No. Not until the DNA results come through.'

Wow, this was a turnaround. This was not a woman who wanted someone to fund her child's education and expenses. Not that he'd thought that about Mia, but it happened. It had happened to him.

She held up a palm and continued. 'In fact, I don't want you getting involved with my daughter until I know I can trust you, Brin O'Connor.'

He was not his father. He would not walk away from his responsibilities. He was not his brother. He would not betray his family.

But she knew nothing about him, really. They'd only shared one night, after all. 'Fair enough. I wouldn't trust me either. Maybe I am just a heartless…what was it?…jerk?'

Red bloomed in her cheeks. 'I—'

'Hey there!' Owen popped his head round the door. 'There you go, Harper. Here's your mummy. Oh hey, Brin, good to see you.'

The little girl ran into the room, beaming. 'Mumma! Mumma!'
And your daddy?

Brin tried to dampen down the flicker of hope in his chest.
He didn't want to be this little girl's father. He didn't want to
get involved with this family, not if it meant putting his heart
at risk.

He didn't know the DNA results yet but still his whole body
smiled at the toddler running across the room, her arms out-
stretched as she reached her mum.

'Hi there, sweetie. Did you have a good day at nursery?' Mia bent, picked Harper up, kissed her and whirled
her round, all rigidity and stuffiness gone. Harper put her
chubby hands on her mum's face and gave her a kiss. Mia's
eyes were brown and her hair blonde, in stark contrast to
her daughter's blue eyes and black curls. But the smile...
that was pure Mia.

Something tightened in his chest and he realised, with a
shock, that it was a kind of yearning...for these two? For that
feeling of warmth at the end of a hard week? For someone to
greet him with a smile? For *his people*?

Hell, one minute in their company and he was jelly. He
didn't have any people. He knew that well enough. And he
was just fine on his own.

Why had he come here?

What a mistake to think he might fix some of this mess
he'd found himself in. He should get on the first ferry out tomorrow morning.

Owen was looking at him. 'What's happened? Is there an
evac?' He looked at Mia. 'Why didn't you call me?'

She held her hand up and gave the doctor a wavering
smile.

'No.'

'No.'

They spoke at the same time, and he heard the panic in her

voice mirror the same feelings in his chest. 'Stand down, doc. There's no emergency. I'm just here for the weekend; thought I'd check the place out.'

'Well, you wouldn't believe a storm blew through last week, eh?' Owen glanced out at the dazzling sunshine outside. 'It's a stunning day and good forecast.'

A little cold in here, though.

'Weekend?' Mia blinked.

But before any of them could say anything more, Harper ran across to Brin and offered him her blanket. His heart folded. Oh God, this was their game now. She looked so eager to play, he couldn't resist.

He bent down and threw the blanket over Harper's face, waiting for the giggle. It quickly came and felt like sunshine in his chest.

Sunshine that scudded under a cloud as Mia asked flatly, 'Where are you staying?'

'B and B down the road. Next to the yacht club.'

Totally oblivious to the dynamic between Brin and Mia, Owen nodded. 'Ah, Wiremu's place. He'll look after you. But you should have called me. You are more than welcome to stay at ours for free. Any time.' His young boy was tugging at his hand. 'Daddy! Come on. Kayaking with Carly.'

'Duty calls.' Owen rolled his eyes and laughed. 'Hey, mate, what do you have planned while you're here?'

'Not much, really. A hike, maybe a kayak. Relaxing.' As if that was going to be possible, being so close to Mia. 'Not sure.'

'I don't suppose you could help out at the regatta tomorrow? It's just me and Mia and we could do with another pair of hands, especially as we'll have our kids with us.'

'Regatta?' Brin looked from Owen to Mia then back again. Mia's stony expression had returned and her eyes were blazing, as if she was trying to send him some sort of message. Probably along the lines of, *don't say yes*.

Owen nodded and pointed to a poster on the wall. 'Boat race. Leaving the yacht club at nine o'clock, but the festivities will go on all morning. There's a sausage sizzle and craft fair. We're running the medical tent—giving out sunscreen, raising awareness of being sun- and sea-smart. Plus, any injuries. It's usually just the odd splinter. Nothing you can't handle.'

He felt the weight of Mia's stare on his back, but he could hardly say no, could he? He didn't have any other plans, the island was small and he could probably explore it all in one afternoon. He had until Sunday evening here. 'It'll give me something to do. Sure.'

Owen nodded as he made his way to the door. 'Great. Cheers, mate. See you in the morning, then.'

Then there was just the three of them—Mia, Harper and him.

There wasn't any point staying around for more of this awkward exchange, so he followed in Owen's wake towards the door, his chest aching a little. God knew what he'd expected but it wasn't to feel so deflated. But yeah...he'd been delusional to think Mia would be as excited about his visit as he was.

He turned for a last look. 'I'll see you tomorrow.'

'Brin. Wait.' She looked as if she was having a struggle between her head and her heart. More like between being polite and unfriendly.

His chest warmed in anticipation. 'Yes?'

'Look, there aren't many places to eat on the island, and I don't imagine you've brought much food with you.'

'I was going to eat at the yacht club—apparently they do excellent food.'

'They do. And we always have a table there on a Friday, eh, Harper? Go to see Wiremu for some hot chips?'

As Harper did a happy wiggle and repeated, 'Hot chips, hot chips…' on a loop, Mia's expression became guarded.

'It's just a treat. We eat healthily the rest of the time. She has a very balanced diet for her growing needs.'

He laughed. 'You don't want to know what rubbish I eat most of the time. Whatever I can stuff in my mouth between call-outs, and ramen if I'm being fancy. I am not judging. A portion of hot chips is perfect for a day like today.'

The guardedness slipped a little into a sort-of smile. 'Which is what, exactly?'

Oh, so many things. Joy at little Harper's happy squeals when she'd played their game. Pride at the burgeoning friendship with Owen. All of it mixed with trepidation, panic and confusion about potentially being a father, and the question of Mia…whose smile, when it came, entranced him, reeled him in, speared his chest.

He settled on, 'Difficult?'

Her shoulders finally dropped, and she blew out a long sigh. 'Yes. Difficult indeed.'

'I probably should have prepared you for me turning up again out of the blue. I'm sorry. Next time I will most definitely call.'

Her eyes widened. 'Next time?'

'Yes. Next time.' If he was this girl's father, there would be many, many times. He just had to try and wrestle his attraction to Mia under control. Because he couldn't let anything derail his relationship with Harper. Nothing could happen between Mia and him—nothing at all. 'I don't want it to be difficult.'

'Me neither.'

He blew out a breath and couldn't help smiling. Maybe they'd reached a detente? 'So how about we have a chat? Nothing heavy. Just an end-of-the-week catch-up over hot chips.'

'Okay, yes. Sounds good.' She nodded and smiled a really wide grin. Boy, that blew his mind and had his skin, his whole body, prickling with heat.

Which was a warning sign he needed to listen to.

CHAPTER FIVE

OF COURSE, EVERYONE REMEMBERED Brin from the storm, and they were all pleased to see him, and not even a little taken aback that he was with Mia and Harper.

It seemed as if Mia was the only one taken aback by his sudden appearance. Harper was thrilled. Owen seemed happy to have found a new buddy, offering him a free place to stay and asking him to help out.

After placing their order, they sat outside at her usual table, overlooking the small marina. Brin's eyebrows rose as he scanned the myriad yachts, launches and dinghies in the bay. 'Wow, there are a lot of boats here.'

'It's not usually like this. They're here for the regatta.'

'It's got a great vibe.' He tapped his foot along to a four-piece band playing summer classics and she relaxed a little. Sure, her heart had stalled when he'd walked into the clinic, but now… Now she needed—wanted—to try and smooth things out for Harper's sake.

She was glad to be in the warmth of the late-afternoon sun, able to breathe a bit more freely, rather than being confined in a small room with him. He dominated every space and assaulted her senses with his intoxicating scent and gorgeous eyes.

Right now, he was sitting next to Harper and playing 'hide the teddy'. The way he looked at their child snagged her heart. He was the father: there was no doubt, never any doubt at all. But seeing the way they were together proved it beyond anything.

It was hard to think rationally around him but they had important things to discuss. She wasn't going to let him barrel over her parenting with his ideas or change the routine she'd developed with her little girl.

Might he take her away? Oh, God, no. He couldn't do that. Could he?

'Hey.' He dipped his head to look at her across the table, catching her gaze and giving her a smile. 'You zoned out for a minute. I was just saying, this is an idyllic place to grow up. Did you grow up here too? Or somewhere else?'

'Sorry, I was miles away.' She'd been too engrossed in panicked fantasies to be in the present. 'Here. At the camp, actually. My parents used to run the place.'

'Wow. I bet you ran wild with all that bush out the back.'

'Not at all. I wasn't allowed to go too far from the cottage, not until I got older. And I learnt to share all my things from a young age, my home and my very large garden, not just with my brother but with kids from all over the *motu* who had come to learn sailing and bush skills.'

'Motu?' He shook his head.

'It means "country". Sorry.'

'Don't be. I'm getting used to the way Kiwis slip *te reo Māori* into their sentences. It's cool. I wish I'd learnt Gaelic at school.'

'Do you miss Ireland?'

'It's a pretty place. A lot of weather. A bit like here.'

She frowned. 'That's not an answer. Do you have family there?'

Did Harper have family there? Cousins, aunties and uncles he might want her to meet?

His jaw tightened. 'Not any more.'

'No one?' He was like her, then, all alone in the world. She should have been relieved but there was something in the way he looked at her, as if he was trying to decide what to say, before he settled on, 'No one.'

She wasn't sure he was being completely honest here. But she imagined he had his reasons and decided not to push him—yet. 'That's too sad. I mean, growing up here wasn't all roses. My brother could be a royal pain sometimes. Boy, could we fight.'

Brin's jaw relaxed. 'Nothing like having a sibling to keep you grounded, right?'

They both looked at Harper and Mia's stomach felt like a stone. A sibling? Another baby?

He winced. 'I'm sorry, that was careless of me. You must miss your brother very much.'

'I do.' Not wanting to dwell on her own tragedy she asked, 'Your parents…?'

'Mum died a few years ago.' He shrugged but she could see the pain in his eyes.

'I'm sorry. And your dad…?' She let her words fade, hoping he hadn't had the same kind of tragedy she'd had.

'Left. Mammy said he was good at making babies but terrible at caring for them.' His blue eyes darkened. 'I have different things to say about him.'

'Like what?' Babies…plural. What had happened to his siblings?

He cautiously flicked his eyes towards Harper. 'I'm not going to ruin this evening. The best thing said about my da is nothing at all.' His tone was light again but there were dark edges to his eyes. There was more to this story but he clearly wasn't going to talk about it here or now.

Harper tugged at her sleeve. 'Mumma. Ice-cream, please?'

'Finish your dinner first, then we'll decide.' She looked up to see Brin watching the interaction and her mood took a nosedive. 'You probably think I'm too soft on her.'

'I'm not going to judge how you've brought her up.' He

winked at Harper, who instinctively knew they were talking about her, so gave them both a beaming smile. He chuckled. 'Butter wouldn't melt, eh? She's an angel. Great manners. Bright as a button. She's happy, that's the most important thing.'

He sounded almost as proud of their daughter as she felt. 'I'm glad you think so.'

He dipped a chip into some aioli then slipped it into his mouth. 'You were right, Mia. These are some great chips.'

'Tomorrow you should try the steak-and-cheese pies—award-winning. It's blue cheese too. The best.'

'Stop it, temptress.' He bugged his eyes at her but there was something more there: the glitter and tease she'd been so attracted to *before*.

Fantasies of a very different kind slipped into her head. Of her holding him, kissing him…and more. And, oh yes, she wanted to tempt him, to allow herself to fall into flirting with him, just like before.

But she couldn't. She wiped Harper's hands with a tissue. 'Right, missy. Time to get going.'

'Ice-cream?' her daughter asked hopefully but she looked exhausted.

Mia knew her daughter well enough to see that a tantrum was on the horizon. 'We'll have some at home. We've got hokey-pokey, your favourite.'

Brin was still looking at Mia, the light very much in his eyes as he watched her. 'Thanks for this, Mia.'

'It's no trouble.'

He walked with them down the steps and onto the path that ran between the buildings and the marina. 'I should make sure you get home safely.'

'You just did.' She laughed.

He frowned then followed her pointed finger to the house three doors down from where they were standing: her old villa, painted white wood with a row of sandbags along the ground at the front. It was small, cosy and needed a new coat of paint. But it had potential and an amazing view of the marina and across the bay. Mia loved it.

His eyebrows rose. 'Cute house. The sandbags are from the storm?'

'Yes.' She sighed. 'The house needed work before the storm, but it's worse now. The carpet in the front room got saturated and I had to lift everything I could to waist height. Some of Harper's toys started to float away but we rescued them.'

'Sounds bad.'

'Not as bad as some. In the end, the water didn't get as high as the electricity sockets, or we'd really be in a pickle.'

'You should have told me.'

'And you'd have done what? You were too busy choppering people to hospital.'

He grimaced. 'Given you support, at least.'

'It's okay. We weren't exactly talking, were we?'

A shadow slid across his face. 'I think we both needed a bit of space.'

'I know I did.' She was glad he understood her reluctance to dive right in. Glad, too, that he was serious about doing the right thing. 'We're okay and that's the main thing. I've spent the last few days drying everything out and getting air into the rooms. Coupled with that, everywhere needs a decent coat of paint. And I need a new kitchen, which I've ordered and am beyond excited about, which is a thing I never thought I'd say, or be. Excited about a kitchen? Where is that Mia who wanted to travel and get a tattoo and play the drums?'

'She's still there.' His grin was infectious. 'Drums? Wicked.'

She laughed. 'No. Terrible, actually.'

'Well, I see her—playing terrible drums and getting a tattoo.'

'And getting all hot over paint shades.' She was probably babbling and talking nonsense.

I see her.

His words almost whipped her breath away and made her head whirl a little. Did he see the real Mia, the way he had that night? Mia stripped bare and raw… Her body prickled at the memory. No…it was at having him here, so close. It was that smile; his touch. *God*, he'd felt so good. He'd kissed like a demon too.

Her insides started to melt. She was getting hot over a lot more than paint shades. 'You don't want to hear about all this.'

'I do, actually.' Probably because he wanted to make sure Harper was living in a sanitary, habitable house. 'I could… No.'

He shook his head and took a step back.

Her heart hammered. What had he been about to say? 'You could…?'

Come in?

Help renovate?

Kiss me?

That last thought slid to the front of her mind, obliterating all reasoning. To kiss him, taste him, hold him close… So tantalisingly tempting and so *not* a good idea.

'Mumma.' Harper put out her hands to be picked up and Mia hauled her onto her hip. Immediately, Harper laid her head on Mia's shoulder, stuck her thumb in her mouth and rubbed the satin edge of her blanket between her fingers.

Brin's eyes softened as he looked at his daughter. 'Looks like it's someone's bedtime.'

'Yes, I think we've had enough excitement for one day.' Mia looked up at him. Had she imagined the flicker of awareness in his eyes? The subtle slide of his gaze from her eyes to her mouth? The flare of…something?

Deep in her belly, she felt a responsive stirring of desire.

Heat hit her cheeks and she started to turn away before he saw it.

'Mia Edwards.' Her name sounded like poetry, with the way he'd said it, and she wanted him to say it over and over. She was bewitched by the gentle lilt of his accent. Again.

She turned back to get a glimpse of him. Again.

'Yes, Brin O'Connor?' The way she replied sounded wanton.

'Sleep well.' The smile he gave her was filled with generosity, with a good helping of seductiveness.

She wasn't sure she was going to sleep at all, with images of him running through her mind. 'Good night, Brin. See you in the morning.'

'Definitely.' He scuffed his fingertips through Harper's hair. 'Night-night, little one.'

The effect of his smile, his warmth and…everything…had her wishing things had been different. Had her wanting him to touch her.

She wanted his hands on her. Wanted his mouth on her… everywhere.

No. That couldn't happen. She'd lost everything she'd loved when her family had been drowned. Then she'd found solace and more than enough love in her daughter. It had been a hard road, getting to this state of tranquillity. She liked being calm, and prided herself on being efficient, friendly and kind, and a respected member of the island community. She didn't want or need a man to upset everything she'd worked so hard for.

She wasn't going to risk losing another love again or change her hard-won, happy life here. She had her sanity, her equilibrium. Her emotions had been wrangled under control. She did not want to be out of control. She was going to be resolutely single. For the rest of her life.

She nodded at him. 'See you.' And then she went into her house, hoping its cool interior would soothe the heat in her body.

Thirty minutes later she was putting a bathed and very sleepy Harper to bed when her phone pinged.

It was an incoming email from the DNA test lab.

Her heart rattled but she couldn't understand why. She knew the facts. But the thought of having Brin in her life made her anxious, excited and panicked. The attraction to him was growing stronger and she didn't know how to deal with it.

He could break her heart. Worse, he could break her daughter's by moving on.

She slid her phone into her jeans pocket, kissed her...*their*... now-sleeping daughter on the cheek and left the room.

Truth was on her side. But knowing that didn't settle the panic. Things were going to change, regardless of whether she wanted them to or not.

After clearing up the mess from this morning's rush to get out of the house to nursery and work, she needed some peace and fresh air, so opened the front door and set up her deck chair on the kerb side. The sky was cloudless with a thick slick of purple stars and the Milky Way.

Up the road at the yacht club, people were laughing. The lap of water against the jetty that usually lulled her did nothing to soothe her nerves.

Brin O'Connor was going to be in her daughter's life and, inevitably, in Mia's too. She needed to learn how to deal with it.

And not think about kissing him again.

CHAPTER SIX

So HE WAS a father. A real one this time. Although he'd feel as if Niamh was his daughter for the rest of his life, someone else was her daddy now.

Brin shoved his phone back into his pocket and tried to breathe. The bedroom was stuffy. He opened a window and stood at it, trying to shift the ache in his lungs. It wasn't working. He needed to be outside and feel the fresh night air against his skin.

He ran downstairs and out the front door into the cool evening, stuck his hands into his jeans pockets and headed along the road, trying to work out how to navigate this strange situation. Last time it had been easy, as he'd lived with Niamh's mother. But this time? He had no idea. And he'd already missed so much. He was suddenly greedy to know everything about Harper.

Sure, he already knew the basics. His daughter had pilfered a piece of his heart that he knew he'd never get back. Her smile was like sunshine. Her tears pierced his chest. He'd do everything in his power to protect her and love her. Anything else was icing on the cake.

And Mia? His pulse quickened at the thought of her. The glitter in her eyes when he'd jokingly called her a temptress... over a pie! The effect on him had been instant, a direct arrow to his groin. But also...and far more dangerously...to his heart.

Ah, Mia.

The pull to her was getting hard to ignore.

As if the Fates were looking down and playing games, she appeared outside her house, carrying a mug of steaming liquid. Her eyes widened as he approached.

He couldn't exactly turn round and walk away. 'Mia?'

She nodded and put her mug on the windowsill 'You got the email?'

An email that had changed his life. 'She's my daughter.'

'Yes. I told you. You are the only person I've had sex with in...well, you know.' Her cheeks reddened. 'A very long time.'

He didn't want to think of her having sex with anyone but him—ever. 'So, what do we do now?'

She rubbed her palms down her thighs. She'd changed out of her nurse's scrubs into a T-shirt that skimmed her curves, and shorts that highlighted her gorgeous legs. 'I have no idea.'

'Do you want me to be involved?'

'Oh, Brin, yes of course. You're her father, you have every right.' She exhaled. 'But...can I be honest with you?'

'Always. Please. I want to know what you're thinking.'

She worried at her bottom lip. 'She's been just mine for so long. I've never had to think about sharing her and now I'm worried.'

'You think I might...what?'

'I don't know. Take her away?' She looked haunted at the thought, bereft. 'To Ireland.'

Never. 'God, Mia. No way. This is her home.' He'd lived the nightmare of having his child cruelly taken away from him, and he wasn't about to inflict that poison on someone else.

Unless, of course, it was his brother. Who, while not being in a relationship with Niamh's mother, was still seeing Niamh on a regular basis.

Mo stór.

Mia pierced him with a dark look. She still didn't trust him. 'And where is your home?'

Good question.

'I haven't had one for a long time.'

'But it's not here, right? You've already left here once, looking for more excitement.' She raised her palm. 'It's not Australia. It's not Ireland. You're still looking. It could be somewhere far away. You're a city boy, right? Dublin and Perth, not a tiny community on an island in the middle of nowhere.'

'Whoa. I've known about her for less than a week. I've got no plans to take her anywhere. I'd like to get to know her. To spend time with her.' He leaned against the wall and looked at her. She was so defensive, protective…*good.* Their daughter needed a strong woman like Mia in her life. But she'd done it all on her own and he couldn't imagine how she'd managed. 'Tell me about it.'

She frowned. 'About what?'

'All of it. The birth. Her firsts.'

Her eyebrows rose. 'Oh, sure… Well, I've got child-bearing hips, so the pregnancy was fine.' She ran her hands over her hips, drawing his eyes down.

She had an amazing body with which she'd carried and given birth to his child. He could barely breathe at the thought, and at what he'd missed. 'No complications?'

'None.' She smiled. 'Quick and easy.'

'Where?'

'Here. At the camp.' Her gaze flitted across the bay. 'A home birth.'

'Wasn't that a bit risky?'

'Actually, a surprise. I wasn't due for another couple of weeks and I'd planned to go over to the city in good time. But Harper was in a hurry.' Her eyes had a faraway look about them. She smiled and rubbed her belly and he ached to press his fingers there. He wondered what it would have been like to feel the swell of his child inside her.

'Luckily Anahera's well used to helping deliver babies in extremis. And, double luck, I had a midwife friend staying on the island. And Carly, of course. My three musketeers. Everything was fine. Once we'd delivered her and I felt well enough, we went over to the mainland to get checked out with the doctor.'

'Wasn't Owen here?'

'No, he's new. We didn't have a doctor then.'

'Who helped you afterwards? Cooked meals, made sure you got some rest?'

'Mother hen.' She nudged him and laughed. 'I moved into Carly's cottage for the first few weeks after Harper was born and she looked after me. She's really good family.'

This was confusing. He was sure Carly was from England. 'She's your family? But she has an English accent. You're very Kiwi.'

Mia smiled. 'Oh, of course, I keep forgetting you don't know the history. She was married to my brother. We're not blood family. Sisters by marriage, best friends by choice.'

A far cry from his relationship with his brother. Blood wasn't always thicker. 'Sometimes that's better than the real thing.'

'Oh?' Her eyebrows rose in question and he realised she was too easy to talk to.

'Nah. No. Not going there.'

Her eyebrows slumped into a frown and he could see her emotionally retreat at his refusal to answer her question. But he wasn't going to taint this conversation with tales of his broken family. There was too much he was greedy to know about Harper, about them both. 'Tell me about my girl.'

Mia's eyes grew soft and he wasn't sure if he saw a sheen of tears there. But she looked away and cleared her throat. 'She was a big baby. Three-point-eight kilogrammes, and long. She's got your long legs, Brin.'

Her gaze drifted down his body then back to capture his gaze. He saw pride and love there as she talked about Harper.

She looked so beautiful, it made his heart hurt. He remembered the way she'd been so soft in his arms. The feel of her skin against his. The way she'd tasted.

'She's got your smile.' He wasn't sure what else to do or say. He knew what he *wanted* to do. But he was not going to kiss Mia Edwards.

'She's a good kid. My heart.' She put her hand on her chest. 'Please don't upset her.'

'Of course not. At least, I'll try not to. But you know how teenagers can be sometimes. I'm bound to be embarrassing at some point.'

'Teenagers?' She chuckled. 'She's barely turned two.'

'They start early these days. Grow up too fast.'

But she turned serious. 'I meant, please don't say you're going to do something and then not do it. Turn up on time. Be reliable.'

'Hey.' He touched her shoulder. 'I'm not a bad guy.'

'I know. I couldn't bear it if you hurt her.'

That thought pierced him too. 'I won't. At least, I'll try not to.'

She nodded. 'Good. And it's going to be confusing for her if you suddenly start being around all the time.'

'I know. Slowly does it. Will she understand if we tell her?'

'I...don't know. Let's see how it pans out.'

He wanted Harper to know who he was right now but needed to take Mia's lead on this. 'Okay. And I will want regular visits. I need to get to know her after everything I've missed.' In case she took that as a criticism, he added, 'It must have been hard, facing a future as a solo mum with no grandparents to help out.'

'Yes. But everyone here's family.'

'I get that feeling. It's a good place.'

'I was well looked after. We both were. Harper is Rāwhiti Island's baby.'

'So, I'd better be careful?' He laughed, but knew it was the truth. Also, that leaving here and living somewhere else was not on Mia's radar. This was her home.

Where was his? Currently Auckland, where his job was. It wasn't a thousand miles away but it was hardly next door. And she was right: he'd never planned it to be permanent.

'Don't say you haven't been warned.' She chuckled, picked up her mug and frowned. 'My tea's gone cold. You want one?'

'Are you sure?'

'I think we can manage to be civil, right?'

'More than civil.' He followed her into her house. Maybe she was starting to trust him after all.

The front door led straight into a lounge in disarray. A blue sofa and two cosy-looking blue-and-white-checked chairs had been pushed against the back wall. Piled on top of them were a box of toys and a basket of laundry. There was no carpet, just bare floorboards. A dehumidifier hummed in the corner. It was in disarray, but the overriding scent was lavender cleaning fluid, and it was spotlessly clean.

She watched him take it all in. 'I've had the insurance people over and there's a new carpet coming. Everything else is salvageable. It's safe. She's not living in squalor.'

'Jeez, Mia, I don't think that. You're amazing to have done all this on your own.' He wanted to scoop them up, take them back to his apartment on the mainland and look after them. But he got the impression Mia wouldn't let that happen in a million years.

'I made it into a game for Harper. She was a good little helper.'

'If you need anything, let me know.'

She shook her head. 'I've got this. I can manage just fine.' *On my own. Like the last three years.*

The unspoken words filled the room.

'Mia, I mean it. Let me help.' But he knew she was a resilient, independent woman. She would ask for help *if* she needed it, not because he thought she did. 'I know you've probably been saying "I've got this" for the last three years, but you don't have to do this on your own any more.'

She pressed her lips together and took a deep breath. 'Guess I'm not very good at sharing after all.'

'Baby steps, right?'

She looked grateful he hadn't pushed the issue. 'Yep. Baby steps.'

Despite the flooding there were still photographs of his daughter on every wall: as a tiny new-born, strapped to Carly in a sling; at her first birthday, with a paper hat on; in the garden. And so many with her mum, giddy with pride. He rubbed his fist against the ache in his chest as he stopped at one where Harper was in a pink party dress and Mia was bent over, holding her hands. They looked as if they were dancing at a party. He traced the outline of his daughter's face. 'She's beautiful.'

Mia came and stood next to him, close enough to touch. And, man, he wanted to. She sighed. 'My little ray of sunshine. That was at Anahera's youngest's wedding in the yacht club.'

He laughed. 'You weren't escaping *Dancing Queen* that time?'

'You remembered.' She looked up at him, her brown eyes alight, her mouth a crescent of joy. 'Your daughter loves to dance, Brin. *Dancing Queen* is her favourite song. After *Baby Shark*, of course.'

'She's got great taste.'

She frowned. 'Have you ever heard *Baby Shark*?'

'No, thank you.'

She looked at the photograph. 'I'm sorry you missed those years. We should have stayed in touch.' She moved slightly and her hand brushed against his. The air seemed to sizzle around them. He struggled to fill his lungs with the Mia-scented air.

'I wish we had.'

She turned to face him, so close her fingers pressed against his. Her smile was soft and sexy, her eyes searching his. And suddenly it was three years ago. Just him, her and the most amazing night ahead.

He reached for her hand, entwining his fingers with hers. She looked down at them, a little gasp escaping her lips. But she didn't pull away; instead, she looked back at him. A wary smile played on her lips, as if she was as confused by all of this as he was.

A beat passed, two...the atmosphere thickened with need. He wanted to...everything. He wanted her so damned much. Which was crazy and messed up because he knew that anything between them would be a risk to him, to him seeing his daughter and to his equilibrium. But she held his gaze and he couldn't, wouldn't, look away.

It was all too much too soon. It was crazy to feel like this. He ran his thumb over hers. 'God, Mia...'

'Yes?' Her breath stuttered in her chest, her mouth a fraction open.

He saw it then, in her eyes: a mirrored need. The chemistry was real and raw. It was like the first time, an incomprehensible attraction. She was the only thing he was aware of: her sensual mouth; her soft skin; her sultry eyes. Just...Mia.

Not wanting to let go of her, he slid the fingers of his free hand across her cheek, cupping her face. Her mouth was inches away. He could feel her hitched breath against his jaw. Maybe she didn't trust him, maybe she did. But she wanted this.

He should have walked away then, knowing that they were on a trajectory that could only end in disaster. But she grasped his wrist, held it in place then rose up on tiptoes and pressed her mouth against his.

'God. Mia.'

He let go of her hand and slid his fingers across her other

cheek to her hairline. His heart raced. His chest constricted. His skin felt too tight.

His head screamed at him to go. But he couldn't.

She tasted exactly as he remembered: intoxicating and fresh, and of the herbal tea she'd sipped. Of something pure Mia. Her body fitted against his and he felt the press of her breasts against his chest. It felt like an extension of that night, without three years in between. No re-learning, just pleasure and need.

A squeak of a cry came from another room.

Harper. His daughter. She was the most important person in all of this. He couldn't think this was going to end in happy families. It never did. In fact, he wasn't sure that such a thing existed.

He pulled away, his body shaking. 'Look, sorry. That shouldn't have happened. It'll only complicate things.'

Mia nodded quickly, looking turned on and yet torn as she straightened her clothes. 'Brin...yes. Sorry. I need to go to her.'

He watched her disappear into the back recess of the house. He already missed the feel of her in his arms—the soft lips, the hot kisses.

Mia. His heart rattled against his rib cage. Mia and Harper. This was how it could have been: both parents together, taking it in turns to soothe the little one. The other making tea or pouring wine. An evening shared. A bed shared.

But he'd done all that before and it had broken his god-damned heart.

So, he took a deep breath and reined in all his strength to put one foot in front of the other and walk away.

CHAPTER SEVEN

MIA WAS GLAD of the steady stream of customers at the little gazebo they'd erected outside the clinic, taking her mind off the fact Brin was standing so close to her. And she pushed back the memories of that kiss.

The island was alive with tourists and locals out to watch the boat race. Crowds filled the jetty and thronged the road and beach. There was a happy vibe, which she would normally sink into, but today she felt weird—short-changed, actually. The kiss had been amazing, but nowhere near long enough. Even though they shouldn't have done it in the first place, because it could only muddy things.

How could she be so attracted to this man? She'd never forgotten him, that much was true. She'd dreamt about him. Ached for him. But to have such an immediate and undeniable connection again scared her. There were so many reasons why they needed to keep this purely platonic.

What didn't help was the way Harper gravitated to him all morning, wanting him to play, showing him her shell collection, asking him to fasten her sandals. Watching him with their daughter—the gentle tone of his voice, the patience at the never-ending game of hide-and-seek—had her heart contracting.

The kiss had been such a shock, and so wanted in that moment, she'd been blinded by her need for his touch. But now, in the fresh light of day, and after having ruminated about it for most of the night, she knew that anything between them had to be purely and totally about what was good for Harper.

Kissing Brin was not good for Harper.

Mooning over Brin was not good for Harper.

Thinking about happy families, trying to create something like that, was *not* good. Mia had had one of those once and losing it had made her almost insane with grief. Harper had been a wonderful surprise, but reconciling having a child with her fear of losing her had been difficult. She'd carved out a protected space in her heart for her daughter and now that was all she had the capacity for.

She was not prepared to love anyone else. Because what if she lost them too? She wouldn't be able to cope a second time. So keeping a level head around him would definitely be good.

Owen came out of the clinic, carrying a tray. 'Lemonade for the workers. Is it okay if I finish up now?'

'Sure. There's only an hour until we close up anyway. And we're not exactly run off our feet.' Mia took a glass from the tray as Brin sauntered over after treating someone for a wasp sting. Keeping busy kept him at arm's length.

Owen put the tray on the fold-up table under the gazebo. 'Thanks. I'm meeting Carly and we're taking Mason for a quick swim over in our bay. Would you like us to take Harper too?'

No doubt Carly had already told Owen about the Mia-Harper-Brin saga and, even though he hadn't mentioned anything so far, was the doctor doing a bit of match-making here, or giving them space to talk in private? Did he genuinely want to take Harper to play with his son?

And why was she suddenly suspicious of her friends?

But she looked over at her daughter, who was putting sticking plasters on her doll's knee, and started to feel a bit wobbly about being left here on her own with Brin. There was safety in numbers... 'Oh, she's fine.'

But Harper tugged at Mia's sleeve. '*Please*, Mumma. Swim.'

'It's mighty hot, that's for sure.' Brin smiled at Harper, and Mia read that as a capitulation.

Rather than argue in front of everyone, Mia numbly nodded, ran back to her cottage, stuffed Harper's swim stuff into a bag then arrived back at the gazebo in about two minutes flat.

She watched the happy trio saunter off down the hill. Then, her body bristling with irritation, she turned to Brin, who was straightening a pile of 'Sun Smart' flyers. 'Brin, we put the leaflets here, not there.' She picked up the leaflets and put them on the opposite side of the table.

His nostrils flared but he nodded. 'Sorry. I thought I was helping.'

'I said she couldn't go swimming.' Her irritation had got the better of her, or maybe it was nerves.

He put his hands up in surrender. 'Hey, I didn't say she could.'

'No, but you said it was hot. Which kind of meant she should go cool off.' She didn't know why she was so irked about this.

'I didn't say she should get wet. I'm sorry if you think I overstretched.'

'I've spent the whole of her life making decisions with her and for her. I'm not used to someone else having an opinion. Or, at least, voicing one.'

'I'm sorry. I understand.' He came a little closer and put his hand on her arm. And why, oh why, did it make her heart jump for joy when it should have been hardening against him? 'Hey, this isn't about Harper, is it?' he crooned in his gorgeous accent. 'You've been tetchy all morning.'

She felt a little called out. 'I have not.'

But he didn't rise to her irritation. He laughed. He laughed! 'Mia, you have been Miss Grumpy all morning. At least, with me. "Brin, we put the leaflets here, not there",' he said in an almost perfect imitation of Mia's voice and words. And she had to admit she'd been...*picky* this morning. But she was confused. She didn't know how to act around him in front of Owen or her daughter. Not when all she wanted to do was sink into another kiss with him. Her voice was always high-pitched when she talked to him, her breath always thready. She wasn't her usual calm and composed self. He *got* to her.

Brin sighed and ran his palm down her arm, making her want to curl into his embrace instead of rebuild her emotional barriers. 'Look, I know we overstepped with the kiss and everything. And I apologise.'

She shrugged away from his touch in case she did something stupid, like snuggle against him. 'Do we have to talk about this?'

The smile hadn't left his mouth. 'We do. Yes. Otherwise it'll be buzzing around in my head. If I deal with it, it'll go.'

She couldn't help smiling at this admission. 'So, you too?'

'Yep. I can't stop thinking about it and how much I'd like to do it again. But I know it's not good for us. Or for Harper. She's the most important person in all of this.'

That was one thing they could agree on, at least. 'Exactly what I was thinking.'

'So, can we put it behind us?'

I'd like to do it again.

Me too.

She didn't know if she could put all these weird feelings behind her, but she nodded. 'Yes.'

'Good. Normal service is resumed.' He inhaled, then exhaled slowly.

'Can I have some sunscreen, please?' Lochie Taylor, from Harper's nursery, thrust out his hand. Mia squirted some into it, then made sure he was thoroughly covered. A hooter sounded and a roar came up from the crowds.

The race was on.

'Thanks!' Lochie tore away from her and ran towards his

mum on the crowded jetty, and Mia watched as he ran between the legs of an elderly lady, sending her flying onto the concrete road.

'Whoa!'

'Got it,' Brin called as he ran to help the woman, who wasn't moving. Lochie looked horrified, so Mia rushed over to find his mum in the throng. By the time she arrived back, Brin had the lady sitting up on the ground, saying, 'Hey, now, Marion love—don't you be moving yourself until we've looked at the damage.'

She had a lump and bruising over her right temple, but nothing else. He looked up, caught Mia watching him, smiled and gave her a thumbs-up.

Mia nodded, knowing Marion was in safe hands. She'd felt the security in those hands herself; the safety and solace he provided, along with a whole lot more.

He wasn't easily ruffled. Except, she recalled, when she'd stepped on to the helicopter, and during every moment alone with her since. He wasn't ruffled around Harper, he was a pushover. He wasn't ruffled around Owen, or anyone else. Mia shook her head. Maybe he was just ruffled around her. That made her belly tighten. Because she was definitely ruffled around him, whether she wanted to be or not. 'I'll grab some ice.'

'Great. And we'll walk slowly over to the chair, eh, Marion?'

They managed to get her into a chair, took her blood pressure and put some ice on her bump. They calmed her down and called her relatives, who were in another bay, waiting for the race to come through.

Brin popped inside to get Marion a glass of water and, as she drank it, Mia took him to one side. 'If you want to have a wander round or watch the race, feel free. I can manage on my own.'

He frowned. 'I'm fine here.'

'But it's your day off. I feel bad you're working when you came here for a rest.'

'I came to see you.' His gaze latched on to hers and she felt the enormity of what he was saying. He'd come to make amends. To do his best. To get to know his daughter. And Mia had kissed him and then snapped at him. But he smiled. 'It's hardly taxing work. I'll tell you what—when we're done here, you can show me around the place.'

'Okay. Deal.' She laughed. 'It won't take long—it's not exactly a huge place. Once Harper's done playing with Mason, we'll take you for a tiki tour.'

'Excellent.' He gave a sharp nod and started back towards their patient with a quick, 'It's a date.'

It's a date.

Her belly fluttered. She knew it was just a turn of phrase and, especially after what they'd agreed, she knew it didn't mean anything. But part of her was excited about the prospect of spending more time with him...for Harper's sake. A platonic relationship between parents who were friends was a good thing.

They were interrupted by someone with a blister, then a child with a grazed knee, someone with hay fever and another with a heat rash. All of this took up the next hour, which flew by very quickly, yet at the same time seemed to stretch and stretch—usually coinciding with Mia thinking about the 'date'.

As Marion's relatives finally led her away, with strict instructions from Brin to take her to her GP back on the mainland later this afternoon, Mia's phone rang: Carly. Even though Mia knew that there was bound to be nothing wrong, her heart still stuttered. Ever since the day she'd lost her family to the sea, she panicked at personal calls. 'Hi, Carly. What's up?'

Carly's voice was light. 'Hey! The kids are happily building sandcastles and I've said they can stay a while longer. Why don't you pick Harper up later?'

Mia glanced at Brin, who was starting to tidy away the things on the table. 'I'm fine to collect her as soon as we've finished packing up here.'

'It's all good, honestly. Mason will only complain that he's bored if she goes home. Take the afternoon off.'

Show Brin around on her own…? 'It's okay, I'll be over soon.'

'Well, I have her now. She's my niece and I'm not giving her back until later.' Carly chuckled and Mia knew there was definitely a little meddling going on here. 'When was your last child-free afternoon?'

Mia thought. 'When we went to Auckland to sign the sale of the camp.'

'Exactly. We didn't even get to spend the night there before flying back here, and you've worked non-stop ever since. It's only a few hours. Have fun.'

'Carly—'

'Love you. Bye.'

Carly had gone before Mia had a chance to answer. Damn it—she couldn't hide behind her daughter now. She was going to have to show him around the island on her own.

'It's a date.' *Eejit.*

They'd decided they weren't going to act any further on their undeniable attraction and then he'd said the 'D' word. What was it about Mia that made him reckless and impulsive?

She looked gorgeous today, in a pink-and-white gingham sundress. Her blonde hair was tied back into a ponytail, her skin was fresh and make-up-free and she looked impossibly pretty and younger than her thirty-two years.

'A boat?' He blinked as she walked him to the jetty. He followed her down a ramp and onto a white fibreglass motorboat.

He didn't know much about boats, but this looked well-loved, with its two padded seats, navy-blue canopy, bow rails, space for fishing rods and storage.

She grinned at him. 'How else do we get round an island?'

'By foot?'

'We are literally going *round* the island, Brin. Sit down and hold on.' She gunned the engine and the boat juddered as she steered it out of the marina towards open water. She was confident and obviously very experienced in handling the boat.

They turned right out of the harbour and then into a smaller bay, where the water was so clear he could see large stingrays slithering along the ocean bottom. There was a tiny sandy beach and a smattering of buildings dotted on a bush-lined hill. He didn't know the names of all the native New Zealand trees but could identify ferns and palm trees. Moored boats bobbed in the bay and seabirds dive-bombed the water to catch the myriad silver fish he saw darting beneath the surface.

Mia killed the engine and sighed. 'This is one of my favourite bays. It's so peaceful and there's shelter from the wind.'

'It's gorgeous.'

She pointed to a little cottage near the shore. 'That's Owen and Mason's place. Carly's too, now, I imagine.'

He frowned. 'They're together? Of course they're together—I saw them at the camp after the storm.'

'Carly was going to go overseas but she decided to stay here with Owen.' Mia peered at the beach then at the cottage. 'They must have finished playing and gone inside. Never mind, I'll pop back later.'

'Nice place, but it's a bit isolated.' There were few roads on the island, he'd learnt, but every house had beach access and a boat.

She looked at him and her eyes narrowed. 'It's only a few

minutes round to the yacht club from here. Their neighbours are just over the hill. But, yes, the island is a long way from anywhere.'

'Not sure I could live somewhere so far from a cinema and pubs and…life. You have to be very organised, right? Can't forget a pint of milk and pop back for one.'

'Really?' She shook her head. 'You couldn't imagine living here? It's beautiful.'

'Remotely beautiful.'

She frowned. 'It's a good life. The yacht club has a little store off to the side where they stock essentials, and the Mansion House has open-air movie nights in the summer. But the remoteness is why we're such a tight community here. We need each other's help. That's also why Owen and I take it in turns to be on call every other night. If someone needs something, we have to give them a hand, no matter what.'

If he'd been in any doubt, he now knew she was utterly committed to this place and its people. 'What do you do with Harper if you get called out?'

'To be fair, it's a rarity, but Anahera babysits. She's round in North Bay, so it's not too far.'

'You drive the boats at night?' He tried to hide his naïvety but clearly failed.

She laughed, her eyes shining in amusement. 'Of course. We have lights, Brin. It is the twenty-first century.'

'I've got a lot to learn.'

She'd kicked off her sandals and stood barefoot at the wheel, wind tugging wisps of her ponytail free. The breeze played with the hem of her dress, every now and then lifting the fabric to reveal a glimpse of her gorgeous legs.

The memory of that kiss slammed into his brain. His body prickled and he had to force himself to walk to the other end of the boat before he reached for her again.

Luckily, she restarted the engine and the cool breeze and

the hull skidding over the waves distracted him. Not enough, but some.

Next, they visited the outdoor camp with its huge red *SOLD* sticker across the Camp Rāwhiti sign. It looked a completely different place from what he remembered of a few days ago. His impression had been of panicked people, pain and shock. But now it looked pretty, with scarlet-flowered flax bushes and blue agapanthus lining the gravel paths. The boat shed was locked up, but he imagined school kids playing about on the water in little boats with white sails.

Back from the beach, the main camp building dominated the space. It was two-storey with the kitchen-diner at the front, where he'd spent the uncomfortable night trying to work out who Mia was. And there was the little annexe higher up the hill behind the main block, where he'd learnt that Harper was his daughter.

As they drew closer, he noticed Mia became quieter. Her shoulders slumped forward and she stared at the buildings with haunted eyes. Jeez, he had enough memories of this place to last him a few years, but she had a lifetime of them. Of growing up, losing her family and giving birth, all here in this little bay.

He wanted to slide his arm around her shoulder and give her comfort but thought better of it. They'd agreed not to kiss, so touching her was far too much temptation. 'So, you sold the camp?'

'We did. Carly and I.' She shrugged, then slowed the boat and steered towards the jetty.

'Do you mind me asking why?'

'Carly wanted to travel, and the camp needed renovating. I couldn't do it, not with my job and little Harper to look after.'

'It's a lot of work.' Her life would have been simpler if he'd been aware of Harper's existence. He could have helped, shouldered some of the burden.

'Now it's someone else's problem.' She looked towards the wooden buildings as she wrapped her arms tight round her chest, looking every bit as if it were still her problem.

'I was talking about working and looking after a child being hard.'

She blinked. 'I love my job and my daughter. I can do both.'

'I have no doubt. I'm not judging you. Just acknowledging how hard it's been for you. Is the new owner going to keep it as a camp?'

'Last thing we heard, there were plans to turn it into some kind of fancy resort.' This shrug was filled with sadness.

'How do you feel about that?'

'Weird. I know it's just bricks and mortar, and I thought I was okay with it. But I do feel guilty. Maybe I should have tried harder to keep it going in my parents' memory.' She rubbed her palms up and down her arms. 'It was their life's work. When I'd thought about selling the place, I'd been wooed by the prospect of a good future for me and Harper, but actually signing on the dotted line made me rethink. Too late now, of course. But sometimes I worry I've sold their memory down the river so I can have a new kitchen.'

If only she'd found him earlier, he might have been able to spare her this kind of worry. 'Harper is my daughter too. I'll help you out financially, obviously.'

She turned to look at him. 'I can't even think about that right now.'

No. This was all about her grief and some misplaced guilt. 'When my mam died, I felt the same. Like, how do I keep her memory alive?'

'What did you do? I have a bench with their names on, which we concreted into the ground by the playground. I've asked the new owner if I can have it and I've got permission to put it next to the marina. But do you think I should do something else?' The boat rocked under the swell of the waves, and she reached for a rail to steady herself. In the wispy dress, and with the haunted look in her eyes, she looked so vulnerable it made his chest hurt.

Without second-guessing himself, he put his hand on her shoulder. Felt her warmth under his fingertips. 'You'll keep your family alive in stories you tell Harper. You are testament to them. Your parents' legacy is inside you, Mia. In everything you do, how you treat people, who you are.'

'Not *everything* I do, I hope. I've made a few poor choices.' She smiled but still looked thoughtful.

'You mean me? That night?' He laughed. But he also knew there was a part of his father and brother inside him too. People didn't just inherit the good DNA.

She put her hand on his chest. 'Oh, Brin. It was a good night. Just with a complicated outcome.'

'A beautiful one.'

'Yes.' She smiled and it was as if she'd been dipped in sunshine, glowing in the soft light. His chest felt cracked open, just looking at her and thinking of everything she'd been through.

The moment lengthened as they looked at each other. The memory of last night's kiss seeped into his brain. She was so close...

He ran his fingers over her jaw.

Her eyes misted.

One kiss. How easy would it be to give in? To lean into the feeling, to take what they both wanted?

Her mouth opened slightly and her tongue dipped out and wetted her lower lip.

He ran his thumb there.

She gasped.

One kiss.

A bird squawked overhead, breaking the moment. He could not be lured in by the fact she'd asked his opinion about something so deeply personal. Or by the fact he'd never seen anyone or anything as beautiful as she was in this moment. He couldn't deepen this connection.

He stepped back and cleared his throat, hoping to clear the blurring in his head. 'Um, you don't mind being on boats after everything that happened?'

She stepped away too, as if realising this increased intimacy wasn't a great idea. 'I've got the ocean in my veins, Brin. I don't have the option of liking or not liking boats. This island is my home and boating is the quickest way to get from A to B. Besides, it's a beautiful day, and we're only going round the headland, so I reckon we're okay. Hold on.'

She turned and restarted the boat engine. The moment was gone.

But, no matter how much he tried, the need he felt for her still lingered.

CHAPTER EIGHT

MIA PULLED UP into the next bay and breathed out. Being this close to Brin was not good for her. The gentle way he spoke, the way he listened and answered her questions so honestly, made her feel seen and heard. Made her believe she was doing the right things, making the right decisions in her life. It was good to have that validation. Empowering.

Except the decision to kiss him last night—and again just now, when she'd almost given in—was not a wise decision at all. She had to stay strong. Maybe at the end of this weekend he'd leave and never come back and she'd be right back where she'd started: a solo mum with a lovely daughter and just a little bit lonely.

But that was okay. She'd been fine being that person. She didn't need upheaval. And, even if she craved them, she didn't *need* kisses from a gorgeous man with a sexy accent and good heart. She couldn't risk any more heartbreak in her life.

She moored up and climbed the steps to the jetty, aware he was following her and unsure if she could keep her cool around him much longer. So she adopted a tour-guide role and pointed to the magnificent white two-storey colonial building on the reserve. It had wide verandas and filigree ironwork on the railings. 'This is the Mansion House. Built in the eighteen-hundreds for one of the first governor generals in New Zealand.'

He looked impressed. 'Very fancy.'

'Indeed. There are peacocks around somewhere and there used to be olive groves out the back. And monkeys and zebras, apparently.'

'Wow. You wouldn't expect that in a place like this.'

'It's not the right environment for them. I think only the peacocks are left now. But...' she grinned, pointing towards the café '...the best thing about this place is the home-made ice-cream.'

'Now you're talking my language.' He laughed and ran towards the café, the way Harper might have. The way Mia might have, once upon a time, before the weight of everything had crushed her. Sometimes, she thought, she'd forgotten how to have fun.

They sat in the sunshine on the reserve eating their ice-creams and watched as a ferry docked and a small group of teenagers piled onto the jetty.

Brin turned to her. 'I've realised I have no idea about so much of your island life. What do the kids here do for school?'

'We have a small primary over the hill there.' She pointed towards Jackson's Point round the headland. 'The older kids can choose to board on the mainland, do correspondence school or home school.'

'What did you do?' He licked a drip of strawberry ice-cream from his fingers. She watched hungrily, remembering the amazing things he'd done with that tongue. With those fingers. Heat suffused her skin.

She swallowed. 'My parents home-schooled us. We were around other kids all the time anyway, so we didn't miss out on the social side. Plus, there are plenty of families here now. Anahera's kids were and still are some of my best friends.'

'What do you think we'll do for Harper?'

We.

Warmth spread through her at the way he'd embraced his new role. She'd never had to discuss these things with anyone so totally invested in Harper's life, because she'd always been the sole decision-maker where her daughter was concerned. Sure, Carly, Anahera and other friends gave opinions but, in the end, the decision was always hers to make.

She suddenly turned cold. Now she'd be sharing making these decisions with Brin. But, despite their amazing chemistry, she didn't know him well enough to trust him, did she? Not really. They'd known each other for a matter of hours. He didn't know Harper, her strengths, or what kind of schooling would suit her needs. 'The primary here is as good as any I know in Auckland. Once she gets to year eight, we'll discuss options. Where did you go to school?'

'Dublin.'

'Did you like it?'

He crunched the rest of his cone, swallowed then leaned back on his elbows. 'I loved school. Loved learning things. I was captain of the football team and the chess club. You?'

'I aced maths and English. Got a few medals for dancing.'

'So, she's got grace, music and intellect on her side.'

Mia smiled, relenting. She knew her daughter better than anyone else. She would discuss the future, but she would very much advocate what she thought was best and make sure that happened. 'She's very clever. Loves reading... I guess you'd call it *practising* reading. She can recite all the stories, and knows if you're missing bits out so you can hurry story time up—'

Any further thought was cut short by the sound of a high-pitched scream.

Brin scrambled upright and ran towards the commotion, Mia tight at his heels. The kids were pointing into the water.

'What's happened?' Brin asked.

One of the kids turned to him, pale. 'Logan's fallen off the jetty.'

They looked to where he was pointing and saw a boy wedged between the jetty and the ferry, his face just about out of the deep water, and moaning in pain.

Brin peered down. 'Hey, Logan. I'm a paramedic. My name's Brin. There's some steps over there—can you swim over and climb out?'

'No,' Logan moaned.

'Did you hit something when you fell in? What hurts?'

The boy grimaced, raising his chin above the water as it lapped close to his mouth. 'My foot…it's stuck in something.'

'Oi! Grab this rope and I'll pull you out,' the ferry skipper shouted as he threw a swim-float attached to rope towards him, then side-mouthed to Brin, 'Bloody kids, messing about.'

'Let's get him out first,' Brin huffed. 'Then you can read him the riot act.'

'Stuck…' Logan's voice was muffled as water lapped into his mouth. He'd grasped the slippery, seaweed-covered jetty post but was struggling to keep his head above the waterline. 'Help me.'

'Grab the float.' The skipper's annoyance was laced with panic. 'Can you wriggle free? Is it reeds? Rope? What?'

'I don't know…' Logan's breath came fast as he coughed. The float bobbed on the top of the waves then got caught in the swell and swept away to the right, out of Logan's reach.

The skipper hauled the float back in and threw it again. It got caught between the ferry's hull and the jetty and lodged there, unusable.

Logan began to shake, kicking his legs. 'Help me.'

'Hey, man. Try to stay calm.' Heart jumping, Brin peered into the murky water, trying to see what was pinning Logan down.

The boy pressed tight back against the side of the jetty as the ferry loomed close, undulating in the waves. There were only a few inches or so between boat and boy.

'Move the ferry,' Brin ordered the skipper. 'Or he's going to get crushed.'

'My—my foot…' Logan started to splutter as water filled his mouth. 'Caught. Stuck. Can't move.'

Or he's going to drown.

'Wait. If you start the engine, he could drown in the wash.' Mia was by Brin's side, her hand on his back. Her touch was a comfort.

The skipper knelt and looked at the water, his face red and blotchy. 'It's not high tide yet but the tide's coming in. We need to get his foot free before he drowns.'

'Well, I'm not waiting.' Brin whipped off his T-shirt and dived into the water just beyond the boat's stern. Visibility was poor, as the ferry had disturbed the silt and sand, and Logan's kicking had made the water turbulent. Above him he could see light and shapes but down here, nothing.

Need air.

When he surfaced, he saw Mia kneeling at the edge of the jetty trying to hold Logan's head above the rising water. She looked calm as she talked to the boy, but he knew how much this must be affecting her. She'd said the water was part of her blood, but it had cruelly taken her family too.

No more. Not on his watch.

He dived down again. Peering hard, he made out some old rope attached to the side of the jetty. Somehow Logan's foot had become tangled and the more he writhed the more stuck he became.

Damn.

Brin kicked to the surface, trying not show the worry he felt to Logan or Mia. 'His foot is caught on some rope, and we need to cut him free. We need space.' Brin touched Logan's shoulder. 'I need you to stop…stop kicking, mate. Please.'

Mia called to a deck hand. 'Knife! Get me a knife. Quickly.'

It felt like for ever until the deck hand returned and passed

the knife to Mia. She handed it down to Brin. 'Here you go.'
Her eyes were dark and her face pale. She was trembling and
stretching to hold Logan's face out of the water. But she nodded and gave him a small smile. 'You've got this, Brin. But
please, be careful. We… Harper needs you to be okay.'

His daughter's name galvanised him. Brin's heart hammered against his rib cage. He wasn't a great swimmer. He
didn't know what he was going to do if he couldn't cut the
rope. And he most certainly didn't know if he'd *got* anything,
let alone the capability to hold his breath long enough to get
this boy free. But he was damned well going to prove Mia's
belief in him. This boy was someone's child. He nodded to
her, hauled in more air then dived back down.

The rope was gnarly and old but thick. He grabbed Logan's
foot to stop him kicking, and so he wouldn't cut the lad. But
Logan was scared, the water was rising and he was kicking
for his life.

Brin scraped the knife against the rope. It barely made a
scratch. The knife wasn't sharp enough. The rope too thick.
It was going to take longer than he'd thought.

Do it, man. This is someone's child.

He'd want someone to do this for his kid if they were in
danger. He'd want someone to go above and beyond. With the
image of little Harper at the forefront of his mind, Brin cut, cut
and cut. But it wasn't working. With the water and the blunt
serrations, it wasn't working.

His lungs burned and his desperate need for air forced him
back up. He broke the surface, panting and coughing.

Mia's face screwed up in torment. 'Brin?'

'I can't… It's not…' He greedily gulped snatches of air as
his words taunted him.

I can't.

Not good enough.

Someone's child. Someone's son.

That was not how this was going to play out. He gulped more air into his lungs and dived back down into the murky water. He angled the knife and sawed and sawed, putting all his strength into each action. Some of the rope began to fray but not enough.

Come on! Come on!

Next to him Logan's kicking started to slow. Was he drowning? Was it too late?

No.

No!

Brin's chest was on fire.

Air. Need air.

He kicked up to the surface and saw the boy's mouth barely above the water. 'Logan, hold on, man. Hold on.'

Mia's face crumpled. 'Brin, please.'

Please...what? Stop? Try harder?

He couldn't let this boy die and then go back to his little girl and be the man he wanted to be, knowing he hadn't done everything, given everything.

He dived back down. Sawed and sawed and sawed and sawed.

Come on...come on!

Suddenly, the rope sprang apart. Logan's foot was free and disappearing up and out of the water.

Brin's lungs were screaming, his thoughts blurring. But he managed to grab hold of the jetty post and clawed his way up into beautiful fresh air. 'Is—is he okay?' he choked out.

'He's...he's coughing. But he's okay. He's safe up here.' Mia offered him her hand and pulled him up out of the water. Her eyes were glistening and her smile was sweet with relief. 'I thought... Oh, Brin. Thank you.'

She wrapped her arms round him and pressed her face against his chest, her whole body trembling. He held her the way he had that night and stroked her back. 'Hey, it's okay. It's okay.'

He imagined how she must have felt when she'd watched him dive down over and over again, wondering if he'd resurface. Her life and her losses were inextricably connected to the sea.

'Brin, please.'

Her voice had been laced with distress. For Logan or for him? Had she been reliving that tragedy all over again?

She eased back and shook her head, her eyes haunted. 'I'm so glad you're okay.'

'Yeah. Me too.' He wanted her back in his arms but knew the hug had probably been a friend-to-friend, relief kind of hug and nothing more. So instead he bent to look at the boy. His ankle was red from rope burns and he was pale, shaking and coughing. Someone had wrapped him in a towel and there was a huddle of concerned adults round him. 'You okay, Logan?'

'I'm…good.' The boy looked up at him and shook his head. 'Thanks. I thought… I thought I was going to drown.'

'Yeah, I was worried too.' Brin's chest was hurting and he couldn't quite catch his breath properly. 'But all we got was a bit wet, right? And a sore foot. But you'll live to fight another day.'

Logan gave him a weak smile. 'I'm going to watch where I walk in future.'

'Good lad.' Brin tousled the kid's hair. Then he turned and found Mia looking at him, holding his T-shirt tight to her chest and wearing a strange expression that he couldn't quite name.

Mia was still shaking by the time they got back to her boat. She grabbed a towel and threw it over Brin's shoulders. 'I thought… You were down there a long time.'

'The rope was so thick, it took a bit of effort to cut it.' He shook his head and started to rub his chest dry.

He said thick without the *'h'*: *'t'ick'*. It was desperately sexy and cute, and made her want him even more, but she was shaken by the strength of her panic when he'd dived into the water. Then, when he hadn't surfaced for such a long time, she'd prayed and hoped he'd be okay. It was like a rerun of her life: the worst bits, the waiting. Only this time it had been minutes, not days.

He'd been prepared to risk his life for someone he didn't know. But then, that was his job. He cared for people; he looked out for them, looked after them. He saved them. As did she. She might not fully trust him with her heart, but she understood him, saw his motivation to help and felt it resonate deep inside her. If he'd do that for someone else's child, what would he be prepared to do for his own? He wouldn't walk away, surely?

'Okay, big-shot hero, let's get you back to the B and B so you can get some dry clothes on.' She inhaled on a shiver, and he must have noticed, because he stopped rubbing and looked at her.

'You okay?'

'Not really.' She felt shaken, turned on and anxious all rolled into one. She *liked* him, so that made everything worse, and now she realised she cared about him. Cared for him. Just how much after such a short time, she wasn't prepared to explore.

She flicked the key, started the boat engine and steered slowly out of the bay, homeward bound. What could she do with all these feelings inside her? It was overwhelming. 'I was worried about you, Brin.'

'Really?' He sidled up next to her and grinned. 'Well, that's nice.'

'Nice? I thought you were going to drown or get crushed. *Nice?*'

'Fortunately, I'm very much uncrushed, although slightly damp.' But his grin was replaced with something more serious. 'Look, Mia, I know how you must have been feeling. I'm sorry if it brought back bad memories.'

'It did. But I'm okay, thanks. You rescued Logan and you're alive, and my concern is apparently *nice*.' She couldn't help laughing then, because it was such an underwhelming word to describe everything she was feeling.

He winked at her and spread his arms as if to say, *here I am*. 'If you don't like nice, would you prefer naughty?'

Giggling, she flicked her hand at him. 'Not with you, Brin O'Connor. Get away from me.'

But he'd made her laugh and the tension of the last few minutes ebbed away. How could she go from panicked to laughter so easily?

Brin—that was why. She sneaked a quick glance at him as he rubbed down his legs. The last few years had been good to him. It wasn't only his face that was tanned. His whole body was gorgeously sun-kissed. He worked out, that much was obvious, had strong, toned arms, a solid wall of abdominal muscle and a smattering of dark hair arrowing from his belly button…down.

She turned away…and looked back.

She turned away again. A movement in the water to her left had her peering closer. She stopped the engine.

Brin frowned. 'What's the matter?'

'I wanted to show you…' She pointed to a group of little blue-and-cream birds in the water, diving and swimming. 'Little blue penguins.'

His eyes lit up as he watched the tiny birds. 'They're incredible. Great little divers. I could get some tips from them.'

She smiled, glad of the distraction from him and all these feelings. 'They're so cute. The smallest penguins in the world. They nest over there in the bay, up the hill a little in burrows and tree roots.'

'They nest up the hill? Not on the beach?'

'Mostly up in the scrubby areas. They waddle up at night and then back down here for food and a swim in the morning.'

'Sounds like my kind of life—swimming and snacks.' He chuckled.

She laughed too. 'You don't waddle.'

'I could.' He dropped the towel and wiggled his backside with his arms straight by his sides, a poor but funny impression of a penguin.

She giggled. 'Well, I'll drop you off over in the bay and you can go waddle with your mates.'

'I think I've got wet enough for one day, *thanks*.' He rubbed the towel across his hair. Then he stopped and looked at her, his eyes softening. 'Mia, really, thank you.'

Her heart thrummed. 'For...?'

'This day. Showing me the island. The penguins, the Mansion House, your favourite bay... It's been more than I hoped for.'

She tried to wave him off with nonchalance. 'You need to know where your daughter lives.'

'And now I can picture her here when I'm back in the city in my apartment.'

He was really smitten. And, even though she knew he was only smitten with their daughter and not with her island, she felt a sliver of hurt spear her heart at his absolute intention to leave. 'Rāwhiti is a good place to live. She loves it here.'

'It's very different to what I'm used to, that's for sure.' His eyebrows rose. 'And thanks, Mia, for giving me a chance. Getting to know me.'

'It's important, you know, for Harper. I needed to make sure you're trustworthy and reliable.' She had to detach from her own feelings about him. He was going back to Auckland. He did not want to live here.

But, oh, it was more than that. She'd watched him dive into the water and prayed he'd come back up. He'd been down there so long, she'd thought… She couldn't lose another person to the ocean. When he'd surfaced, her heart had been so full, she'd wanted to wrap him in her arms and hold him. To be sufficiently freed up in her heart to be able to take what she wanted and not worry about losing him.

'And?' He smiled, waiting for her judgement of him. 'Am I? Trustworthy and reliable?'

She shook her head. 'The jury is still out.'

'Looks like I've got my work cut out to prove myself.'

'We've a long way to go yet, Brin.' She looked away, knowing her confusion and desire must be mirrored on her face.

But he touched her arm, bringing her to face him again. 'I get it. I do. And this…seeing you again after all this time… it's unreal, Mia.'

'Brin…' It was meant to be a warning, but it was more like a sigh. Or a prayer. *Brin.* How many times had she sobbed his name over the years, wondering where he was? Wishing he'd been here…when she'd seen the two blue lines on the pregnancy test. When she'd thrown up in those early months. When she'd held their baby for the first time she'd whispered his name into her daughter's perfect little ears, hoping that by some miracle she'd find him and show him what they'd made. When Harper had been sick and Mia had been at her wits' end. When she'd been exhausted from breastfeeding. When Harper had taken her first steps.

Brin.

He smiled. 'This is all… I didn't expect. Didn't think… I don't know. It's a lot.'

'It is.' It was too much—his closeness, his smile, the gentle look in his eyes as they talked about Harper. The hope— yes, the hope that things might be a little bit better, now he was back.

He was so close…and there was an expanse of broad chest

that looked so inviting she ached to put her head there and breathe him in.

She closed her eyes, trying to fight the need rushing through her.

'Mia?' His breath whispered over her cheek. 'What's wrong?'

'Nothing. Everything. I…' She opened her eyes, barely able to breathe, the desperation to touch him so overwhelming, it suffused her whole body. 'Is it weird that we only had one night together but I missed you for the next few weeks?'

'Months?' He spoke at the same time as her. He chuckled. 'If you're weird, then I am too.'

She looked into his eyes and saw that he meant it. He'd missed her the way she'd missed him.

But she'd lied. She'd missed him for the last three years.

'I never forgot you.' His gaze slid to her mouth. 'I couldn't get you out of my head. That night, Mia…'

Her heart drummed against her chest bone. 'We can't… shouldn't…'

He opened his arms, hands palm-up, and shrugged.

Your choice. Your move.

And, oh, she couldn't resist—just a hug, not a kiss. She stroked her fingertips down his bare chest, walked into his open arms, rested her head against his shoulder and held him.

It felt… Oh, *God*. It felt so good to be right there in his arms, skin on skin. Heat skittered through her, and she felt the fast beat of his heart against her chest. She ran her fingers up his arms, stroking his soft skin, running over the swell of his biceps. She felt him shudder in pleasure. He pressed his forehead to hers, closing his eyes and inhaling a shaky breath. His movements were slow…too slow…but the power and sensuality of his touch had her fizzing with desire.

He cupped the back of her neck, then traced forward over her shoulder, skimming her décolletage, and lower, until his fingers grazed her nipples over her dress. He ran his knuckles over them, then palmed her breast, watching her reaction. No doubt *feeling* her reaction as her nipples beaded.

'Brin.' She gasped and her eyes fluttered closed, savouring his touch.

'Mia... Mia...' He rubbed his forehead against hers, then pressed his mouth to her cheek. 'Mia.'

'Yes. Yes.' She turned her head and his mouth was there, his head tilted towards her, and there was no way she could stop this. She angled her head and he touched his lips to hers.

It was a whisper of a kiss, a feather's touch. But it set her aflame.

'Brin.' She moaned as she wound her arms round his neck and tugged him closer, pressing all of her against all of him. She slid her mouth over his. He tasted of the sea, salt and fresh air. Of something so intensely elemental and sensual, she couldn't get enough.

He pressed her against the seat, his hardness hot against her core as he opened his mouth to kiss her with the same hunger she felt. She raked her hands across his back, urging him closer, pulsing against his erection.

He slid his hands down her legs and grasped the hem of her dress, bunching it up her thighs, his caress rough and desperate. His fingers traced the inside of her thigh, a tease she couldn't bear. Because she wanted him inside her.

She angled her legs until his fingers flicked the hem of her panties, stroking her centre.

'God, Mia. I need to be—'

Honk!

From somewhere behind them, a horn sounded and, through eyes barely able to focus, she whirled round to see a flotilla of yachts sailing towards them.

Hot damn. The race!

She jumped away from him, wiping a trembling hand across

her mouth. Bad enough that they'd given in to temptation again, but a whole fleet of sailors and friends had caught them at it. 'Quick! We're in the path of the race.'

She flicked the engine on and steered them out of the direct line. 'The finish is round that headland.'

He grinned and held on to the back of her seat. 'Caught out like naughty school kids.'

'It isn't funny,' she threw at him.

His eyes roamed her face, scrutinising her reaction, and his smile melted away. 'No. You're right. It isn't funny at all. It's actually very serious.'

'This is where I live, Brin. This is my home. I don't need them all knowing my private business. We need to stop this. You can see Harper, of course. But all this…us spending time together…it's not going to work. It's too much. Too…everything.' And, with hands that would not stop shaking, she steered them home.

Who knew how far they might have gone if they hadn't been disturbed? Who knew how deep she'd have let herself fall when she needed to be vigilant around him? Twice today they'd been so intimate, it had made her thoughts blurry. She had to steel herself against him.

No kissing. No messing about in boats.

No falling for him.

Thank God the flotilla had arrived when it did.

CHAPTER NINE

'IS THERE ANYONE HERE? Please, help me.' A woman staggered through the clinic door, clutching her pregnant stomach. She had a nasty gash above her eye and was clearly shocked and breathless.

'Hey, sure.' Mia jumped up and helped the woman into her consulting room, where she plumped up the pillow and assisted her to climb onto the examination couch. 'My name's Mia. I'm the nurse-practitioner on the island. What's your name?'

'Ruth.' The woman looked down at palms which were grazed, gritty and bleeding.

'Looks like you've been through the wars. What's happened?'

'I tripped on the path and landed heavily on my side. Now I think I've started bleeding...down there. I don't know... I'm all wet, but I daren't look.' Tears shone in her eyes and worry nipped at her features. 'Is my baby okay?'

Mia knew how that worry felt. Carrying a baby had been the most precious, wonderful and scary thing she'd ever done. Suddenly she was responsible for another life that depended utterly on her for everything. She made sure her tone was gentle and reassuring, even though placental abruption was her first and worrying thought. 'Okay, let's take a look. How far along are you?'

'Thirty-two weeks.'

'Your first?'

'Yes.' Ruth ran her hand over her swollen belly then her face creased in anguish. 'Oh. Oh…it hurts.'

Mia put her palm on Ruth's belly and felt the ripple under her fingers. 'Looks like the fall might have brought on early labour.'

Ruth grabbed Mia's hand tightly. 'Is there…a doctor here?'

'Usually, yes. But he's away for the next couple of days.' Owen had gone to the mainland for an emergency-management course, leaving Mia in sole charge, which was always a challenge, but one she relished. She'd completed extra courses over the years to equip her to handle most things that came her way.

Before Owen had arrived, she'd had to manage emergencies on her own. But, as the island population had grown, and therefore the demand, the community had decided they needed more than one medically trained expert, so had petitioned the powers that be to help provide one.

Mia held the woman's hand until the contraction had passed, all the while assessing her patient. 'You're doing great. I need to do an examination. Is that okay?'

'Yes, yes, please. Make sure my baby's okay.'

'First, I'll check baby's heartbeat.' Mia squeezed her hand, aware that every mum wanted to be reassured that all was well.

She lifted the Doppler from the drawer, squeezed jelly onto Ruth's bump and ran the transducer over her skin. The welcome sound of a quick heartbeat filled the air. Mia breathed out in relief, then went on to do the vaginal examination. 'What were you hoping for, for your birth care and plan?'

'I was going to stay with my mum on the mainland from next week, then go to the hospital from there.'

Mia pulled off her blood-stained gloves and threw them in the bin. Ruth was spotting but not haemorrhaging. The baby's heartbeat was normal but she still needed to get her to hospital as soon as possible. 'Well, you might have to be flexible. Your cervix is definitely softening, which usually means early labour. It's best we get you to hospital quickly so you can have a full examination and ultrasound. The doctors can give you something to slow things down or hopefully stop the contractions altogether, and they'll want to monitor you. We like to keep baby cooking for as long as we can.'

'But what if he comes soon? Will he be okay? He's very little.'

'Thirty-two weeks is early, yes, and he might need a little help once he's born, so we need to get you both the right care. The sooner the helicopter gets here, the better.'

'Okay. Should I go pack a bag or something?'

'Do you live here? I thought I knew everyone on the island.' But she'd been distracted the last couple of weeks and not paying attention to the comings and goings on her little island home. It was all because of Brin, course—the restless nights and daydreams, making her heart sore yet hopeful. Making her excited about a future with him in it and scared about how to navigate it all in the midst of such an intense and unsustainable attraction. After the boat kiss, she'd cried off any further communication that day and hidden at home, pretending to have a headache, so she wouldn't have to face him again.

Yes, she was a coward.

He'd been gone four days now and she'd received one text a day enquiring about how she and Harper were. She'd answered them all with politeness, trying to not let her desire infiltrate her thoughts and messaging.

Ruth nodded. 'We moved here a couple of weeks ago. We're renovating over in Beth's Bay. But my husband's gone back to the city to tie up some loose ends and get some more supplies.'

'Okay. Well, I don't want you moving around too much. We need to keep you on bed rest until you've been properly assessed. I could ask our receptionist to go to your house and grab some of your things.'

'Please. There's a spare key in a plant pot to the left of the door.'

'No problem. And, while we're waiting, I'll clean up those grazes. And perhaps you'd like to call your husband, let him know what's happening? Or I could do that for you?'

'I'll call him. He'll be so worried.' Ruth's bottom lip wobbled. 'It's taken us so long to get pregnant—three rounds of IVF and a lot of anxiety.'

Mia's heart went out to the young woman. She gave her hand a squeeze. 'I understand completely. I'll go and call the helicopter, then I'll be right back.'

Mia left the room and took a deep breath. Luckily, when she'd gone into labour, she'd only been a couple of weeks early, with no risk to her baby and no one to else to worry about. She put the emergency evacuation request through and called Anahera, who was on her lunch break. Then she went back to stay with Ruth until the chopper arrived.

Of course, it was Brin who arrived twenty minutes later, along with another paramedic, Emma. Mia breathed a sigh of relief as he walked in, as if she didn't have to worry any more.

But that was weird. This was her job, and she did it every day. She could deal with the emotional fallout from the more intense or complicated situations. Only, things seemed easier when he was around. His ready smile and willingness to help were endearing and attractive.

But things became a lot more complicated when he was around too.

He breezed in, smiled at Mia then turned his attention to their patient. 'Hi there, I'm Brin, and this is Emma. We're here to transport you to Auckland Women's.'

'The…cavalry?' Ruth breathed through another contraction.

He grinned and jokily flexed his biceps. 'That's us. Right, what's been going on?'

Mia gave him the details and watched as he slid his hand

over Ruth's and squeezed it, saying, 'What an adventure you've been having. Don't worry, we'll get you to the hospital safe and sound. Just need to put in a drip to keep you hydrated, and I've some pain relief if you need it.'

Ruth grimaced. 'Only when the contractions hit.'

'Oh, I've something in my bag of tricks for that, don't you be worrying.'

Ruth's shoulders relaxed as she smiled up at him, as if he were some sort of superhero. 'Thank you.'

'No worries. Let's get you and your precious cargo into the wheelchair, then we'll scoot you up to the chopper.' They assisted Ruth into the chair and Emma took hold of the wheelchair handle. 'I'll get her up there if you can bring the bags.'

'Right behind you.'

Brin watched them leave then turned to Mia, his expression guarded. 'Hey, how are you doing?'

Despite the frostiness between them, her heart fluttered. But a fluttering heart wasn't going to keep him at arm's length. She stepped away. 'I'm fine.'

His eyes narrowed, as if he was assessing her response. 'And Harper?'

'Fine, too. She's at kindy.'

'Right.' He smiled but there was something brittle about it. 'Look, I know things got heavy the other day, but we're bigger than that, right?'

'Of course.'

'I was thinking...wondering...whether you wanted to come over to spend some time with me in Auckland? You and Harper?'

Stupid, fluttering heart.

'Actually, I was thinking of coming over to the city next weekend. Work's starting on my house on Monday and I need to order some new tiles, soft furnishings and furniture. I don't like to do that online. I like to see the colours in person. So perhaps we could meet up, yes.'

'Grand. You're welcome to stay at mine. I've a spare room.'

'For Harper?' she clarified.

'Of course. You can have my room and there's a couch in the lounge I can sleep on.' His nod was quick and sharp, as if there'd never been any doubt about where Mia would sleep.

Just looking at him, at those vibrant blue eyes and strong arms, her body tilted towards him. But her head stayed strong. 'I've booked a hotel.'

'Okay.' He didn't argue or try to push the issue. He'd clearly had second thoughts about the wisdom of kissing too. 'Well, you could come over for food or something. I'd like Harper to come visit my place.'

Mia's gut tightened into a knot. 'Because she needs to get used to being with you, at your house?' She heard the tremor in her voice.

He nodded. 'It's early days, and I wouldn't want you or her to feel pressured in any way, but yes—I'd like to see her regularly. Get some sort of routine going. I mean, it's not always easy with shift work, but I can put in requests for regular days off.'

She'd imagined this happening. She knew that Brin would be keen to see his daughter whenever he could, as he was that kind of man. But she hadn't expected her gut to hollow out at the thought of not seeing her daughter every other weekend.

For the rest of her life.

She swallowed back her feelings, not wanting to show them. It was better for Harper to get to know her father than for Mia to keep her here, preventing her from having a relationship with blood family just because she didn't want to share. It didn't mean it didn't hurt, though.

She nodded and dug for a smile. 'Okay. We'll come over on Saturday morning.'

'We could take her to the zoo or something, in between the heavy shopping itinerary? Or I could look after her while you do the sofa buying stuff.'

Did he want sole charge for the afternoon? She imagined the two of them playing their hide-behind-the-blanket game, or eating ice-creams together, and felt excluded before it had even happened. 'I don't know how I feel about you having sole care of her. You don't know her little foibles and habits. Things are moving a bit too fast.'

'But they do have to move, Mia. I'm experienced...' He hesitated and frowned, shaking his head. 'A fast learner. And I've got two and a bit years of catching up to do. You have to see that.'

She did. But, oh, she was conflicted. And he seemed so unaffected by the fact they'd made out—twice. His focus was all about Harper. It was what they'd agreed and what she wanted, but she couldn't get over how being in his presence made her thoughts blur and her limbs turn to jelly.

His radio crackled and he pressed the button to reply. 'On my way, Em. Sorry. Be there in five. Okay, Mia, I've got to go. See you next week.' He leaned in and kissed her cheek. A chaste little peck, nothing other than a friendly gesture. Nothing at all like what her body craved. She turned instinctively at his touch, wanting that mouth on hers.

But he'd stepped away.

She inhaled, getting a whiff of his delicious scent, and breathed out slowly as she watched him dart out of the door. She called out to him, 'I'll let you know the ferry times.'

'Grand,' he called back, his hand raised in a wave.

Which left her even more confused. How could she be this emotionally invested in what he did, thought and wanted after such a short time? How could she survive the next few years, having him flit in and out of her life like this and not have more of him to herself?

How could she spend a weekend with this man and get out sane?

CHAPTER TEN

BRIN'S CHEST HURT as he waited for the ferry to dock on Saturday morning. He felt a whole load of excitement mixed with a good dollop of anxiety. He'd never been nervous around kids before and had been a natural, good father to Niamh. But truth was he wanted to be the best father for Harper and to have Mia see that. He wanted her to trust him, because they were going to be in each other's lives for a long time, now they shared Harper.

And yet, at the same time, he had this gnawing worry that it was all going to be snatched away from him at any moment. He was going to lose all over again. He felt cleaved in two—wanting to run into this, giving his full heart, but at the same time wanting to run away from it and keep his heart safe.

Because the last time when he'd been happy he hadn't been ready when the truth had come out. It had blindsided him, shaken the foundations of what he'd thought it was to be family—to be a brother, to be loved and to love. So, he had to be ready for the next time. He was not going to go let himself be lulled by the promise of happy families.

Would he always feel like this—that he could never fully lean into happiness for fear he was going to lose it? His jaw clenched. His brother and his ex had a lot to answer for.

His brother... How could anyone do something so horrific to his own kin?

He peered at the line of people streaming off the ferry,

looking for Mia's pretty smile and his happy, chatty daughter. But as the stragglers at the back disembarked his heart folded in on itself.

They weren't here. They weren't coming. Mia had obviously changed her mind. She didn't trust him.

He pulled out his phone and checked his messages—none.

He took one last look. The deck hands were opening the gates for the next load of passengers to walk on board.

They weren't coming.

Déjà vu. A different daughter and a different woman, but the same gut-wrenching feelings. He swallowed back the hurt and turned to walk away. He'd been right not to get too invested; he'd have to work out parental access through more formal avenues. But she could at least have let him down gently.

'Brin!'

Whoa!

He turned to see Mia rushing towards him, dragging a holdall on wheels and carrying another bag over her shoulder while pushing a pushchair with Harper in it, kicking her legs and waving at him. Mia was wearing a white tank top, a pink silk skirt that fell just below her knees, white trainers and an anxious frown. His heart danced at the sight of them.

He was next to her before he could think and took the shoulder bag and holdall from her hands. He made sure not to kiss her cheek this time. Last time, he'd been too close to kissing her full on the lips. 'Hey, it's good to see you both.'

But Mia frowned. 'Were you leaving? Did you think we weren't coming?'

They'd been delayed, that was all. He should have had more faith in her. He'd misjudged her and jumped to conclusions instead of believing in her. 'Yes… No… I thought you might have changed your mind.'

'I'd have messaged you, silly. I don't *not* turn up. Missy

needed the loo just at docking time—potty training.' She rolled her eyes with a smile. 'Got to take advantage of the moment.'

'Fun times. Don't worry, I totally understand. You have to carry a potty around everywhere you go and it's often a little unpredictable at first.' He grinned with relief and felt as silly as she'd called him. But old traits died hard. How many times had he waited outside the house, or at the bus station, or in a café to see Niamh, only for her mother not to bother bringing her? How many times had his heart been dashed, from hope and excitement to disappointment?

But Mia wasn't Grainne, his ex; he needed to remember that.

Harper had her arms out to be hugged, so he put down the bags again, unclipped the pushchair straps and whipped her up into his arms, kissing her cheeks. 'Hey, cheeky chops. How are you?'

'Bwin!' Harper patted his cheeks and beamed at him. 'Cheek chops.'

'Did you do a wee in the toilet?' he asked, oddly pleased to hear all about it.

'No.' Mia shook her head. 'But we will next time, right, Harper?'

'Yes, Mumma.' Harper wriggled to be put down, so he helped her back into the buggy and picked up the bags.

'These things take time, but you'll get the hang of it.'

'You seem to know a lot about potty training. Are you the Wee Whisperer?' Mia laughed and Brin's gut jolted. He had never wanted to talk about what had happened between his ex and him, and the complication of his brother, and he wasn't about to start. It wasn't as if Niamh was a part of his life now, or his brother. And he knew that hurt would radiate from him if he so much as mentioned anything, so why darken the mood?

He smiled at his daughter. 'Ah, no. Been reading up on toddler taming.'

'Nothing like being prepared.' Mia laughed, but she was looking at him as if she wanted to ask him a question but didn't know what to say. 'Although, nothing can prepare you for the terrible twos.'

'Don't listen to her. She doesn't know what she's saying. You're not terrible, so you're not! You're gorgeous.' He winked at Harper and walked them to his car. Mia had messaged about car seats, so he'd bought one to make life easier for when Harper was visiting. It got the smile of approval and a corresponding punch of pride in his solar plexus at not only doing something right for Harper, but impressing Mia too.

The journey to his place involved a lot of chattering, Harper telling him what she'd been doing at kindergarten and wanting a drink, then needing a real wee this time and stopping at the public loos, everyone cheering at her success. It was good to have her there as a distraction because having Mia so close was muddling his brain. He'd thought a few days' respite from her would ease his attraction to her but…no. His car now smelt of her delicious scent, that was a constant seduction, and his body prickled and heated every time he looked at her.

'Nice place,' Mia said breezily as they finally got to his first-floor apartment in Ōrākei, and nodded as she looked round, clearly impressed. 'Renting, right?'

He'd tried to make it as homely as possible, but it was probably still very much a bachelor pad. 'Yes. But I'm hoping to buy somewhere at some point.'

'You're planning on staying, then?'

Was he?

'I've no plans to leave.'

'Which isn't the same thing.' She peered at him, waiting for a clearer answer. But he didn't know what to say. Before Harper, he'd planned to stay in New Zealand for a couple of years then move on. But now…? His plans had been utterly derailed.

But he'd had plans before—family plans; a future and a life that he'd thought was complete and settled—and they'd been derailed too. Making more concrete plans seemed foolish. Who knew what other shocks and surprises might be around the corner?

He shrugged, not wanting to illuminate her any further. 'I'm here for the foreseeable. None of us knows what the future holds, right? Until a couple of weeks ago I wouldn't have imagined my life changing so drastically. But here we are.'

'Here we are.' She looked up at him and smiled warily. But he could see the softness in her gaze and the way she tried to shrug it off by blinking. She was as confused by all of this as he was. 'Want to show us round?'

'Won't take long.' He laughed. 'It's not the biggest of places.'

But it had a decent-sized lounge, a spotlessly clean kitchen, a master bedroom with *en suite* bathroom and a spare room. Pale grey walls and sleek lines. A couple of minutes later, they were standing in his spare room, which with permission from the landlady he'd painted soft pink.

Mia sighed as she took it all in—the white wooden bed, white toy box waiting to be filled and white bookcase. 'Oh, you've bought a big girl's bed too. Look, Harper.'

Mum and daughter both went to test the mattress in a fit of giggles.

Watching them playing in the space he'd created gave him a shot of pride right in the middle of his chest. 'I thought Harper could pick out her own duvet cover, but I bought one just in case.'

Mia patted the duvet. 'I think *Frozen* will work fine.'

'An easy bet. Most girls her age are *Frozen*-obsessed.'

'You know a lot about children, Brin. What's popular, how to potty train…'

Damn. He'd given too much away again. 'It's my job to.

Got to find a way of distracting the little ones when they're in pain, right?'

'Oh, yes. Of course.' She tickled Harper's tummy until the toddler was rolling about and giggling. 'Is it still okay if we stay?'

'Sure. I got everything ready in case you wanted to. Or Harper fell asleep here or something.' His heart squeezed at the thought of getting involved in his daughter's bedtime routine, spending those precious moments together.

Mia smiled tentatively. 'Thanks. I…um…cancelled the hotel. Seemed silly to splash out on something so frivolous when we can bunk down here.'

'No bunking. You can have my room. I'll take the sofa.' He was thrilled to have the chance to read Harper a bedtime story for the first time in his life. But, hell, how was he going to cope with having Mia so close, in the next room?

All night…

She breathed out. 'Thanks. But I'm okay on the sofa, honestly.'

'My bed it is.' He tried not to look at her; he really did. But his gaze collided with hers and he couldn't miss the heat in her eyes, the flare of something. He imagined her in his bed, doing the things they'd done that one night together. Remembered the way she'd held him, gripped him, the way they'd fitted together so perfectly.

He swallowed back his reaction because they had to do this right. They couldn't keep falling into each other's arms. Couldn't allow their attraction to override sense. 'Right, we have things to do. Let's go shopping for…what was it…tiles? Sofas?'

Mia picked Harper up from the bed and followed him back into the lounge. 'Maybe tomorrow. Perhaps we can go to Kelly Tarlton's today?'

'The aquarium place down the road?'

She nodded and looked at Harper. 'I think that will be much more exciting for us all, hey, Harper? Go see the fishes and penguins?'

Being with Harper was exciting—learning about her, becoming a father. But being with Mia was different...more scintillating, more tempting. He needed ordinary—shopping, boring things. Things that wouldn't involve Mia laughing or cooing at penguins, making her more adorable and more appealing.

Sofa shopping...that was where it was at.

But Harper tugged on his hand and her large blue O'Connor eyes tugged at his heart. ''Quarium, Bwin. Fish.'

How could he resist?

'I guess I'm just one big pushover.' He took her chubby little hand in his. 'Okay, come on, princess.'

Mia's hand rested on his back as she chuckled, whispering, 'What is it with daddies and their girls?'

Yeah. His throat tightened. He'd been here before and it had been the best thing that had ever happened in his whole damned life. And this was a great second chance to have it all over again.

A chance and a threat. A huge, scary and dangerous threat.

Pushover—yeah. Been there, done that.

And it had hurt him badly in the end.

He didn't know if he could cope with all of this.

He was a natural, she had to admit.

He listened to Harper's endless chatter, as if she were a wise mentor giving him worldly advice. He laughed at her showing off. He played the blankie game until even Harper got bored of it. Read out all the information posters about each fish and sea creature, pulled faces at the sharks and held Harper when, randomly, she was scared of the penguins. He gave her food before she started to complain about being hungry. Anticipated her toilet needs and gave her space when she needed it, keeping her close in the crowd. His enthusiasm was endless, his patience even more so. It was as if he knew exactly what a good father was and had determined to be exactly that.

And with every smile, cuddle and adoration of Harper, with every side-smile towards her, with every brief accidental touch or brush of fingers…and some not so accidental…she wanted him more.

But something niggled at the back of her mind. Something that wasn't quite ready to take full form as an idea. Something that wasn't quite right. He was a great parent. Fantastic. He anticipated Harper's needs and knew how to soothe her when she cried. But how? Most people needed time to get used to a child they'd only just met. He wasn't just a 'wee whisperer', he was perfect.

No one was ever perfect.

But he hadn't believed they'd actually turn up today. Why not? Why did he hold some things back? What wasn't he telling her? What had happened to make him so untrusting? She couldn't put her finger on it, but she was going to be more alert to his words and reactions going forward.

By the time they'd got Harper back to the apartment, fed and bathed her, she was exhausted. Mia left Brin reading a bedtime story on the bed with his daughter, snuggled under one of his arms. Unable to hear the soft lilt of his voice without wanting to slide under his other arm and listen to him until she fell asleep too, or at the very least climb right into the bed with him, she wandered into the kitchen, poured herself a wine and sat in the lounge, staring out to sea.

Regardless of her niggling brain, today had gone well. Harper and Brin had a bond, she could see that. She had to make this work.

'She's finally gone to sleep.' His voice jolted her from her daydreams. 'I'm ready to do the same.'

'It was a big day.'

His eyebrows rose. 'For us all.'

'Not one I imagined ever having.'

He'd brought the bottle of wine and another glass through and hovered by the back door. 'Do you want to watch the TV? A film?'

The way he said the word sounded like 'fillum' and it made her chuckle. 'No. I'd like to sit for a while and chill.'

'I have chocolate.' He waved a bar of expensive dark chocolate under her nose.

'Yes please!'

He laughed. 'Come outside and chill, then. Eat chocolate. Watch the sunset. Well, you can't see the actual sunset from here, but the sky is a riot of colour.'

'Chocolate, wine and a beautiful sunset. You know how to treat a girl.'

'My girls.' His gaze latched on to hers and she saw that, regardless of what they'd agreed or how mistrusting he was, he *wanted* this. Wanted her. Which made her heart jitter and her belly squeeze.

There was more to this than a physical attraction. She wanted to know more about him, wanted to understand him. Wanted him with an intensity that took her by surprise.

And it felt so natural to sit next to him on the large wicker sofa, chocolate melting on her tongue, wine in her hand, and look at the beautiful evening sky, which was indeed streaked with vivid oranges and pinks. She gazed up at it and sighed. 'Red sky at night...'

'Shepherd's delight. In Ireland, that means it's going to be a nice day tomorrow. But it means nothing as straightforward here.' He chuckled, his nose crinkling and his eyes glittering. 'New Zealand weather is a mystery to me. One minute it's raining, then it's sunny. Sometimes it's sunny and rainy at the same time. And I've never been anywhere else in the world where you have rain when there's no clouds.'

She nudged him and laughed. 'You'll get used to it. Carry a sunhat and an umbrella wherever you go.'

'Right you are.' He smiled at her. 'I don't suppose you heard anything about Ruth Taylor—the pregnant woman I med-evaced last week? How did she get on?'

She didn't want to do small talk. She wanted to curl into his arms, lean her head on his shoulder and watch the colourful clouds scud by. 'Her husband called to let us know she was being kept in hospital to be monitored, but they'd managed to stop the contractions. Baby is happy and snug, Mum's just a bit bored.'

'As you would be for any length of time. It got me think-ing, though, about what you went through. I keep trying to imagine you and Harper. Who held her first?'

'Carly. She delivered her, with guidance. She has such love for her niece. That's a bond that will never be broken.'

He blinked, almost as if he was flinching, but recovered. 'Did she cry straight away?'

'Carly? She was sobbing through it all. Worse than me, to be honest.'

He bugged his eyes at her. 'I meant Harper.'

'I know.' She giggled, delighted he wanted to hear so much about it. 'Harper yelled her guts out. She was not entirely happy to be out in the world, despite the hurry.'

'That's my girl—making a big noise.' He winked. 'Stat-ing her place.'

'Oh, she can do that well enough. She doesn't lack confi-dence. That must come from you.'

He shrugged. 'I hope I'm not too full of myself.'

'Just enough.' Enough confidence, enough sense of humour, enough sex appeal. She looked at the shadows and light in his features. There was so much about him that she liked. But so much about him that she still didn't know. Such as why he'd reacted at the mention of Carly. Or had it been the niece bit?

She slipped her sandals off, twisted to lean against the sofa's arm, popped her feet onto the cushion next to him and looked at him. 'Have you seen many births?'

'More often than not we're getting them to hospital in the nick of time, but I've attended a few. Eleven all up.' He ran his hand over her bare toes, as if they'd spent many evenings like this, chatting about their jobs and lives. Her heart made more space for him. She wiggled her toes and he tickled them, then his palm slid up her calf.

It was difficult to have any kind of proper conversation with his hand on her like this but she persevered. 'Any drama?'

'Actually, no. Just…well, miracles. Special stuff. Magical stuff. It's amazing. All that work and all that worry and then there's this perfect little scrap of life in your hands. Holding your little one when they first breathe or blink… Being the first person they ever see in their whole lives, with those little button eyes… That primeval squawk… Ah.' He looked at her, his eyes bright and soft, and she could see the wonder of it all in his face. Could see the love right there. Then his face fell, and he stopped stroking her leg. 'God, I'm sorry, Mia. I wasn't getting at you.'

Love for who, exactly? Had he been there, feeling that? 'Not at all. I did everything I could to find you, Brin, and I wish you'd been there too. Because you've described exactly how I felt—such joy and worry, this tiny little dot of a thing depending on you, and you love it fiercely, so fiercely, even though it's the first time you've ever met. I get that. I know that, Brin. But there's something else, isn't there? That look in your eye.' She made her tone gentle and enquiring. He'd actually opened up more in that sentence than she'd ever heard before. 'As if you've been there, holding your baby for the first time.'

He shook his head and looked away. 'Ah, you know. Just what I've seen of other fathers.'

'But it isn't, is it? There's something you're not telling me.' She stroked his shoulder, desperate for him to tell her what had happened.

He blinked and she saw a flicker of panic in his features, which confirmed her suspicions. He blew out a long breath. 'Leave it, Mia. Don't go there. I don't.'

'So there *is* something.'

'Mia.' His tone was a warning. He lifted her feet from his thigh, got up, walked across to the rail and leaned against it, looking out at the sky. Then he turned, his features wrestled into something benign again. 'The problem with my job is that we don't get to hear about many outcomes, so it's nice to find out what's going on with Ruth.'

She held his gaze, waiting for him to rewind back to her questions. She wanted answers. He held her gaze then gave a minute shake of his head, enough to tell her not to intrude any more deeply into his personal life.

Well, something bad had happened, that much she could tell. Was that what had made him leave Ireland? Was that why he was running from job to job and country to country?

And why wouldn't he tell her?

And how would it impact his life going forward?

Because, when it came down to it, they really didn't know each other much at all. Sure, there was an amazing attraction, but heart to hearts, sharing truths and dreams...? Not since that one and only night together.

They were different people now. Getting to know and understand someone took time. Opening themselves up and trusting each other would take even longer. He wasn't going to tell her about his past. Not now, not today. Probably not tomorrow, or next month. Her heart stung at him keeping secrets from her. Their physical distance now felt like an emotional chasm.

But she tried to salvage something of the conversation and followed his lead to not pry. 'Whereas we're there for them before and after. I love the continuity from birth through to old age. No doubt I'll be seeing a lot more of Ruth and her baby when she comes home.'

'You clearly love your job.'

She pulled her feet up and wrapped her arms around her knees. 'I do.'

'And you intend to stay on Rāwhiti?'

'Yes. Why?'

'I wondered if you'd ever thought about moving away?'

Where was this going? 'I spent three years in the city doing my nursing degree then had various stints in hospitals and clinics across the country, getting more qualified, but no. I don't want to live anywhere else.'

'What about travelling? I remember you said you wanted to explore the world.'

She sighed. 'With a child? That would be difficult.'

'There are ways. You could go and I could look after her.'

'What?' She frowned. He was planning a life without her in it. And, even though she had no right to feel hurt by this, the sting of it rippled through her. 'You're encouraging me to go on holiday and leave her with you?'

'Sure, why not? When she's older, maybe.'

'I can't go away and leave my daughter behind.' A wedge of pain slid into her chest.

He frowned. '*Our* daughter. I'm talking years in the future, Mia. Not tomorrow.'

She'd sold her family home and the guilt and sadness of that rippled through her daily. She was dealing with a flood in her house and her workplace, managing solo parenting and reacquainting with this man who didn't trust her yet. It was a lot.

She was trying to make sense of it all but she felt as if her routine and future were suddenly slipping from under her feet and she was scrambling to stay upright. 'Things are moving too quickly here, Brin. Let's be honest, we need to get to know each other a lot better before we start to make those sorts of plans.' She jumped up and walked to the door.

He followed her. 'Where are you going?'

'To bed. Harper and I have got a lot to do tomorrow.'

'But…'

She put up her hand to silence him. 'It's for the best, I think.'

CHAPTER ELEVEN

A HIGH-PITCHED CRY startled Mia awake. She glanced at the clock: two forty-seven. Her heart raced as she listened again.

Footsteps passed her door.

Harper?

Heart pounding, she jumped out of bed, ran to Harper's room and found Brin about to go in there too. 'What's happening? Is she okay?' he whispered.

Mia put her finger to her lips, aware that she was dressed only in her summer sleepwear comprising a pale blue tank top and barely-there shorts. Aware that his eyes had appraised her as she'd walked towards him.

And that her eyes had appraised his bare chest and dark boxers, toned abdomen and muscled shoulders. Her body thrummed at the sight of his half-naked body. 'Let's take a look.'

They opened the door and peeked in. He was standing behind her and the warmth of his body so close to hers made her breath catch.

Harper was lying on her back, her blankie gripped firmly in one hand, a toy penguin that Brin had bought her from the aquarium in the other.

Mia's heart rippled with love as she edged back out of the room, nudging Brin behind her. 'She's fast asleep. She does that sometimes, just a little cry or a snore. Sleep talking—nothing major.'

'Worth checking, though.'

'Always.'

He started to make his way back down to the lounge but stopped at her…his…bedroom door. 'You okay? You dashed off earlier and you seemed upset.'

Was this really the time for that conversation? But, if not now, when? Over a busy breakfast with Harper? When they were shopping? She wanted Brin to open up with her so she had to talk the talk. 'Oh, you know. I'm confused, to be honest. I'm emotionally all over the place.'

'You too? I was lying there going over and over what we need to do, how to deal with it all. What I'd said that might have upset you. I was an *eejit* to suggest you go on holiday without your daughter. I'm sorry.' His smile almost melted her heart. 'I'm just eager to cram all those missed years into now.'

'Well, I could have dealt with it better. It's wrong of me to be scared you two will develop a bond and freeze me out.' She'd looked deep inside herself and found this ugly jealousy. But she'd had three years carrying and getting to know their daughter—he hadn't. 'I jumped when I should have stayed and talked it through with you. I do want you to spend time with her. Honestly, I do.'

'I wouldn't want someone coming into my life and taking over, taking my daughter away from me. I'm sorry if you thought I was going to do that. Jeez, I would *never* do that. *Ever.* I know what that would do to you.' He looked at her with such conviction that she wondered again: what had happened to him to make him so adamant about this? He breathed out. 'It's early days. We need to take this at your pace, and we've all got to get used to the new status quo. But promise you'll talk to me about how you're feeling. I don't want to break anything you have with Harper, but I do want to grow my own bond with her.'

'I know. I don't want things to change.'

'They will. It's inevitable. But I'll try make it a good change. For us all.'

'Thanks. I know I'll come round to it; just give me time.' He seemed so adamant that he wouldn't take Harper away, she had to believe him.

He clapped his hands. 'Right. I reckon this calls for emergency hot chocolate.'

He walked into the kitchen, switched a light on under one of the cupboards and flicked on the kettle. Mia lifted out cups and put them on the counter. 'That's exactly what my friend Carly would say. She reckons hot chocolate makes everything better.'

He spooned chocolate mix into the cups and turned to look at her. 'She's right about that.'

'And I'm sorry I pried. It's your life. You don't have to tell me everything about your past. But I do want to get to know you better.'

'For Harper or for you?' He stirred water into the cups then carried them through to the lounge and put them on the coffee table.

Good question. She sat next to him on the sofa, picked up her hot chocolate and sipped it. Awareness of his half-naked body fingertips' stretch away thrummed through her body. She wanted to get to know him better in so many ways. And she couldn't keep hiding behind her daughter.

In the dim light his face was shadows. He wouldn't see her reaction. And, if she wanted him to be honest, she had to start too. 'For me, Brin. I want to know you. I feel as if you're giving me only what you want me to see.'

'I'm giving you all I can. I'm sorry if that's not enough. You don't trust me, is that it?'

She stared into her mug. '*I* don't trust *me*.'

'In what way?'

She tried to find words to describe the commotion inside her but came up with nothing that made sense. 'Ignore me.

Sorry, it's late, and I'm not making sense. This was probably a mistake.'

'What was?' His fingers found hers and he stroked them. 'Coming here?'

'Yes. And no. You're in our lives now so we have to make something of that. But there's all this attraction getting in the way. I'm scared…angry, confused. And I want to kiss you again. None of it makes sense.'

He smiled wryly. 'No. It doesn't. If it helps, I want to kiss you again too.'

'It doesn't help at all.' Her body rippled with need at his words. She had to stay strong. 'But I'm not the same person I was three years ago. I've spent so long grieving for my family and building a new life for me and Harper. It's taken a lot out of me but I'm stronger for it. I know what I want, who I am.'

'I can see that. You've a lot to be proud of. You've had some terrible things happen in your life and yet you do amazing things, usually with a smile.'

'Apart from when I bit your head off earlier.' She shook her head. Why did he have to be so understanding? 'I hope that one day you'll trust me enough to tell me about what happened to you.'

'Mia…' He shook his head.

Frustration bubbled through her. 'Come on, Brin. I've been completely honest with you about my life. And I think there's things from your past that have impacted us too. That might still do, going forward. And I want to be prepared for that.'

His eyebrows knitted as he picked up his mug and drank. 'Like what?'

'Like, you don't have social media when everyone has *something*. You know a lot about parenting—more than someone like you should. It's not just your job, there's more. You're an uncle, maybe? But why not say something? None of it makes sense. And that first time we met you said you were running. I asked you why and you said, "you don't want to know". Why?'

Putting down his cup, he blew out a breath, opened his mouth, closed it and opened it again. 'Look, it's just demons, nothing dangerous or sinister. Some stuff happened in my past and I want to leave it there.'

'Why?' She knew she was pushing him further than he wanted to go but she wanted to break down this emotional barrier.

'Because what's important is now, Mia. I'm not running any more, that's all you need to know. I'm here. I'll be here for as long as you and Harper need me.'

She drained her cup and put it on the coffee table. 'It's really great for you to say that now, and to promise it too. I believe you mean it. But no one knows what's round the corner. No one can promise "for ever".' Her parents and her brother had thought they'd got many more years with her.

He leant forward, took both of her hands in his and looked deep into her eyes. 'I know you need certainty, Mia. I know you've had a lot of upheaval in your life and I'm not going to add to that, I promise. I want to help. I want to take some of the solo parenting burden from you. I want a relationship with Harper, but not at a cost to you. We can compromise. We can work things out together. Talk things through.'

She could deal with the practicalities. The problem was the threat to her emotional equilibrium. But he was committing to stay, so that was something. He'd also promised not to get in the way of her relationship with her daughter. Maybe she should start believing him.

Here, in the middle of the night, she almost could. Maybe Harper was the thing that had made him stop running—a tether to a new life in a new country. A future he could look forward to instead of looking backwards.

Her heart swelled. If they navigated the right way, they

could be good parents together, apart. They could share the load, discuss any issues. She wouldn't be on her own through this. 'Okay.'

And maybe later she'd find out what he'd been running from. He clearly wasn't going to elucidate…he clearly didn't fully trust her.

He dropped her hands and picked up his cup. 'See? I told you hot chocolate was the answer.'

A siren outside had her jumping and looking out of the window. A blur of flashing lights roared along the street below. 'I'm such an island girl, I'm not used to all this city noise.'

'Just the scratching of possums and the call of the *ruru* on Rāwhiti.' He laughed. 'Not sure I could get used to all those eerie animal night-sounds. I like the white noise of the city.'

'*Ruru?*' She sat back and regarded him. 'Owl?'

'Yes. I'm trying to learn a bit of *te reo Māori* so I can help Harper. They teach it in school, don't they?'

'They incorporate some of it into lessons—the basics, like counting—but the general population is far from fluent.'

'Listen…' He held up his hand and counted on his fingers. '*Tahi, rua, toru, whā, rimu, on—*'

'No.' She giggled. '*Rima* is five. *Rimu* is a type of tree.'

He shrugged. 'Ah, you know. It's difficult to learn a language at the ripe old age of thirty-four.'

'Seriously, well done. What else do you know?'

He patted his flat stomach. '*Puku.*'

'Yes, belly.' She laughed, her eyes drawn to muscle that arrowed down below the band of his boxers.

Oh, man. They were half-naked here. She swallowed and forced her gaze back to his face.

His expression had changed. His eyes were still alight with tease and fun but there was something far sexier there too.

'What else?' Her voice sounded breathy, raw and a little high-pitched. She cleared her throat. 'Any more?'

His head moved from side to side in a 'maybe' gesture. 'Okay, but don't laugh.'

'I wouldn't dream of it.'

He chuckled and shook his head. 'You just did.'

'Okay. I promise to *try* not to laugh.' She pressed her lips together and tried to stop smiling but couldn't. His gorgeous Irish accent, fumbling around the unfamiliar *te reo* vowel sounds, was cute as hell. 'Hit me with it.'

He pointed to his eyes. 'Um…*karu*.'

'Yes. Good.' She pointed to her nose. 'This?'

His eyes brightened. 'Yes. I know this one. It's…*ihu*.'

'Very good. And this?' She pointed to her mouth.

He slowly traced his fingertips across her lips. 'I have no idea what the word for lips is.'

She shivered at his touch, her body alight with a sudden intense need for his mouth to be exactly where his fingers were. She wasn't sure she would be able to form any words, but managed, *'Ngutu.'*

His eyes shone with glittering desire. 'You have a beautiful mouth, Mia Edwards.'

'Thank you.' The air around them felt heavy and swollen with need. She tried to breathe, but inhaled stuttering breaths. She touched his mouth with her fingertips. 'You too.'

'The *ting* is…' His voice was so quiet and reverent. 'I can't manage myself around you. You're so damned beautiful, so committed to your daughter and to your friends. You're compassionate and funny.' His thumb ran over her bottom lip. 'And sexy as hell. I can't think straight when I'm with you. All I want to do is…' His words trailed off and he shook his head, moving away his hand.

She couldn't bear *not* to be touched. 'What? What do you want to do?'

'All I want to do is kiss you, Mia. That night we shared has been going over and over in my head for the last three years—

taunting me, haunting me, exciting me. I've said it before—it was magical. Like a dream.'

Fire rolled through her, razing any rational thought. Every cell in her body craved his touch. Earlier she'd thought things were moving too quickly but now things were not moving quickly enough. She desperately wanted to hold him, to feel his strength around her. To sink into what they were both afraid of: that connection and intimacy. The attraction growing between them that was undeniable and off the scale.

Hell, if she didn't touch him, she didn't know what she'd do. 'It was real, Brin. Like this is very, very real.'

'But what the hell are we going to do about it?' He shook his head and laughed, as if it was all so hopeless, but she caught hold of his hand. 'We know it's reckless to give in to it. We can't.'

Reckless? Yes. She wanted to be exactly that. It had been so long since she'd let go of control on her emotions, her life and her heart. When her family had died she'd held on. When she'd discovered she was pregnant to a man she couldn't find again, she'd held on. She'd had to because she'd had no one to catch her if she'd let go. It had been years since she'd been touched, held, loved, caught.

Three years, to be exact. No man had ever instilled in her such need. No man had so much as captured her interest, never mind her heart. Not like Brin. He captured her thoughts, her heart and her soul. And she needed more from him. More scorching kisses, yes. More touching. Sitting here and not touching him, seeing him half-naked, being with him, made her feel dizzy with need.

If he was too good a man to initiate anything, then she would take control.

'Touch me.' She placed his palm on her chest. 'Here.'

'Mia.' His eyes widened as he groaned, a warning and a desperate prayer of reverence.

'Feel my heart. It's beating so fast because I want you so much. I want you to touch me.' Then she slid his hand down to her breast. 'Here.'

His eyes shuttered closed briefly, as if he was trying to stay in control but rapidly losing his grasp. He opened them again and ran his fingers over her nipple. There was no bra, just her thin tank top, and her nipples reacted immediately to his touch. '*God*, Brin. That's good.'

'Jeez, Mia. You're killing me.' He looked as if he wanted to devour her.

She held out her wrist to his face, the spot where she'd sprayed her perfume this morning, wondering who she was applying it for. Why she was putting on perfume, make-up, choosing her favourite clothes and packing skimpy nightwear.

It was all for him. 'Breathe me in.'

He did as she said and he smiled, pulling her across the sofa and nuzzling her neck. 'I love the way you smell— flowers and something that's just you. It's addictive.'

She curled into his touch, putting her hand where his warm breath grazed her skin. Desire wound through her like a fire. She pressed her cheek against his, breathing in his scent. 'You smell exactly as I remember, Brin. It's so damned hot. I can't resist.'

'It's the hot chocolate. Magic.' He chuckled as his hands skimmed down her sides, grazing the side of her breasts on the way to her hips, and he held her there in place.

'It's not that.' She smiled as she caught his gaze. 'It's everything about you, Brin, driving me wild.'

'I think I'd like it when you're wild.' He angled his head and for a moment she thought he might kiss her, but she wanted to keep her flimsy grip on control for one moment longer, so she moved back a few inches.

'See me.' She slipped off her top, revealing her naked breasts. She felt reckless, sexy, fun, desired...wanted.

He gasped and ran his fingertips over her beaded nipple. 'I have no words, Mia. You are even more beautiful than I remember.'

'I doubt that. I have stretch marks and I'm not as toned as I was.' The first time with him, she'd had nothing to lose. It had been a one-night thing and she'd thought she'd never see him again. Yet here he was, inextricably linked to her for ever. This time, her heart and her life were on the line. But not even that thought could douse the flames of desire inside her.

'You've done the most amazing thing, Mia.' His fingers trailed over her skin. His eyes gazed down at her, hot and intense. 'This body has grown and nursed a child. Our child. It's a work of bloody art.'

Her thoughts blurred as he stroked her breast. All she wanted, all she could think of, was to kiss him, taste him and feel him rock deep inside her. This man who had stalked her dreams for too long. He was here. He was real and he was hers. More, he was better than she remembered—kinder, funnier, sexier. He made her feel cared for and beautiful. Quite simply, he made her feel happy.

She shuddered, finally losing her grip on control. She crawled onto his lap and felt the hard rock of his erection underneath her core as she straddled him. 'Taste me.'

CHAPTER TWELVE

BRIN GROANED AS her lips touched his. All his attempts at denying their chemistry were faded memories. All sensible thoughts had vacated his brain. Because this could not, should not, be denied. He wrapped his arms around her waist and hauled her close.

He let her take the lead with sweet, soft kisses until he couldn't hold back any longer. He kissed her, hard and deep, cupping her breast, feeling the delicious swell of her in his palm, the tight nub under his fingertips. Then he slicked kisses down her throat to her breast. He sucked in her nipple and she bucked against him, writhing on his erection.

Her movements were rhythmical, incredible and so damned sexy, and he was fighting to hold on. He flipped her onto her back and slipped off her sleep shorts.

Then he kissed across her breast until he reached her nipple again. He sucked it in and felt the shiver of need ripple through her, the contraction of her belly. Her hands slid into his hair and she moaned as he kissed a trail lower, across the flat ridges of her rib cage to the soft sweep of her hip.

He paused as he looked more closely at the silvery lines below her belly button—the map of motherhood.

His throat suddenly raw, he traced the lines and wondered how she'd looked when ripe with his child.

'Brin!' She gasped, her hand on his cheek. 'I'm so sorry you weren't there. It was a miracle. She is our little miracle.'

'You are the miracle, Mia.' He kissed the silvery skin then dipped his head lower to the crest between her thighs. He parted her legs and stroked her centre. Slipped one finger then another into her silky softness.

She let go of his hair and lay back, moaning and whimpering with pleasure as he replaced his fingers with his mouth.

'Brin. Brin. Oh…' She rocked her hips against his mouth and he held her hips tight as she rode her pleasure. Her back arched as her body tensed and he tasted her sweet hotness. 'I need you inside me, Brin.'

'No way. Not yet.' He matched her frantic rhythm and felt the tightness swell around his fingers as she called his name.

'Now, Brin. Please. Now.'

The desperation in her voice matched the feeling in his skin, in his gut and lower, deeper. Urgency and need were stoked by her pleasure. He climbed back up the length of her, skin against skin.

Breast. Throat. Mouth. Lips. Hot. Wet.

'Up,' she commanded, encouraging him to lift his backside off the couch. She slid off his boxers and took him in her hand.

Her palm on his erection sent sparks of heat shimmering through him. He laughed, groaned and sighed at the same time. 'You're in one hell of a hurry.'

'It's been three years.' She laughed.

'It'll be over in three seconds if you don't stop.'

Condom…

'Condom.'

Wallet. Jeans. Floor. He reached, grabbed and tore then was sheathed, her mouth a constant on his neck, his cheek, his mouth.

He positioned himself between her legs and she clutched at his skin, urging him on. He kissed her again then, capturing her in a wet, open-mouthed, messy kiss. Then he gently nudged inside her. Her heat subsumed him and it took all his strength to hold back. He paused as she inhaled sharply. 'You okay, Mia?'

'Yes. Yes.'

'I can't believe this is happening.'

She held his face in her hands. 'I never forgot you, Brin. Not ever. I wanted you so much, through it all. I looked for you.'

'You found me.' He kissed her mouth, the bridge of her nose, her cheeks. 'I'm here, Mia. Here for you.'

'Those damned Fates meddling again.' Her eyes filled with tears but she blinked them away.

'Thank goodness.' He brushed her hair back, capturing her gaze, staring at those sultry brown eyes that had bewitched him from the start. At the mouth that had entranced him, mesmerised him. This fierce, soft, serious, funny, sexy woman had blown his mind and filled his chest with heat.

He pushed a little deeper inside her then pulled out.

'More,' she cried against his collarbone, bucking against him.

He caught her rhythm in long, deep strokes, felt white heat. With each stroke, pleasure balled inside him, tighter and tighter. She grabbed at his shoulders and he pulled her closer to get deeper, clawing, reaching, kissing until there was no air or space between them.

He felt her tighten around him, her head lolling back as she shuddered. 'Come with me, Brin.'

The way she said his name, like a solemn oath, was his undoing. He closed his eyes, rocked deeper and harder and chased her release over the edge until he was flying and falling.

Falling hard for the woman who had fallen into him three years ago.

After, once his heart had stopped ramming against his rib cage and he could breathe again, he tucked her into the crook of his arm and kissed the top of her head, breathing in the scent he'd craved for so long. He remembered how incredible it had felt last time, and this time had been five times more intense. He nuzzled her hair. 'That was amazing.'

'More than amazing.' Her laughter was light and a balm to his soul. She snuggled against him, branding him with her scent. Which was unnecessary: he was hers now anyway. And, truthfully, he'd been hers for the last three years. 'No tears this time. Well, almost, but I held it together.'

He squeezed her shoulder, remembering the way she'd sobbed that night in the hotel and how he'd cradled her. How this time was different—deeper, better.

He felt her cheek move against his chest and knew she was smiling. 'Is holding it together such a good thing?'

'I don't want to be that sobbing, emotional wreck I was back then.'

'Why not?' He edged back, creating space to look at her. 'Just be you, Mia.'

She sat up and looked at him, stroking her fingers down his cheek. 'I told you, I've changed. I'm older and wiser.'

'Or maybe you hide the pain of losing your family better. But I see it sometimes, in the way you stare out at the sea; the little frown at the storm clouds, as if you're telling them to back off. Sometimes it's an expression you have: I know you're thinking of them. I wish I could do something to make it better.'

Her eyes misted. 'It won't ever be better. I've just learnt to live with it. They're gone. They're never coming back.'

He took her hand and stroked little circles over her palm with his thumb. 'It takes time to come to that conclusion, right? You grieve, you hope, you get angry. You scream. And then eventually you realise that, no matter what you want, it's never going to happen.'

She stared at him for a few moments, as if trying to work out something, then asked, 'Who have you lost, Brin?'

Oh, damn.

There he was again, his mouth running away with itself, his brain hurrying to catch up too late. He scrambled for a palatable answer that wasn't lies, exactly, and might be enough to assuage her curiosity. 'Just…er…my dad.'

'Oh? All that emotion for losing someone you didn't like.' She frowned, her gaze intensifying. 'It doesn't ring true, Brin. Losing your mum, yes. But your dad? I think that's just a facade.'

Why hadn't he said his mum?

Her eyes narrowed. 'You also once said that a woman lied to you and that was why you didn't like me lying about my name. What happened, Brin? I need to know how to put all the jigsaw pieces together.'

Hurt pricked him. He'd thought he'd dealt with it, but he was reminded that nothing lasted for ever, even times like this with a beautiful woman and a warm heart. 'Some things are best not being known, Mia.'

'Bull.' She scrambled back up the bed and frowned, bunching the duvet round her naked body like a shield. 'You're deliberately being obtuse. How can we forge a relationship of any kind if you allude but don't explain? I'm not a mind reader, but if this affects us then I need to know.'

'It won't affect us.'

She pointed to the space between them. 'It already has.'

His gut tightened. Mia was right. She was pretty much always right. His obfuscation had only led to more questions. Avoidance wasn't working. If he didn't let go of the ache of his past, he might not wholly be able to move forward.

The weight of it all pressed on his chest, the past and the present—the little girl he'd lost and the one he'd just found. The betrayal of trust that had him running, and this new feeling with Mia that he wanted to sink into. But he'd been mired in his negativity for so long, he wasn't sure how to un-stick himself.

'Jeez, Mia. To be honest, I don't even know where to start. And if I do start, I don't know...' He ran his hand over his hair. Was bringing this negativity into their space wise?

Her tone was gentle. She covered his hand with hers. 'Don't know what?'

'If I'll be able to stop.'

She smiled softly and encouragingly. 'Oh, I know how that feels. It builds up inside, right? You want to throw things. Sometimes you don't think you can bear the pain any longer—you wish you felt numb. But feeling nothing is scary. I get it. I don't know what you've been through, but I get it.'

He breathed out. This amazing woman had been through so much, had lost so much, yet here she was, understanding him. Getting him. How could his pain ever match hers?

He owed her so much, owed himself so much, to give voice to what had been haunting him. And hopefully, by doing that, he'd let it go. 'I was married, Mia.'

Her eyes widened, and she looked briefly wrong-footed, but she nodded, digesting it all. 'Sure, you're thirty-four. We've all got baggage.'

'It wasn't the plan. The wedding, the baby—they were road bumps. We were just out of college and had secured jobs on a cruise ship. We were going to travel the world, but she fell pregnant, so we gave up those dreams and built a different life. We did the whole grown-up package: house, jobs, baby. We had a beautiful girl, Niamh. I watched her mother give birth to her. Celebrated her first steps, first words, first day at school. It was everything. We tried to make it work. I was happy.'

'And what happened?' Mia's eyes had filled with tears and her hand was at her mouth. 'Oh, Brin...she didn't...did she...?'

But he shook his head quickly. 'It's not what you think.

She wasn't hurt. She didn't die. She's fine. She's okay. She's healthy, she's good. I think.'

Mia breathed out. 'You *think*? You've got another daughter who you *think* is okay?'

He imagined what might be going through her head. 'I didn't abandon her. I would never do that. I loved her. *Love* her.'

'So…what happened? Why don't you know she's okay? Why isn't she here with you?'

He knew Mia couldn't contemplate being separated from her daughter even for one minute, never mind years. 'One day I came home early from work and found my wife in bed with my brother. As I confronted them, he proudly announced he was Niamh's father. That they'd been having an on-off kind of thing for years.'

'Oh, Brin. I'm so sorry. And she knew he was the father?'

'Yes. But she hadn't dared tell me. I guess she thought she'd pick the most reliable brother to bring up her child. The one who'd stick with her. When I caught them, she'd only just confessed the truth to him. A later DNA test proved it.'

Rage rippled through him even now. His brother—the one person he'd trusted more than anyone else in his life. They'd been inseparable growing up. United against a father who'd deserted them. United in their love for their mother. They'd shared the same blood, the same house, the same upbringing. But that was where the similarities ended. DNA could only connect them so far.

And his wife—the other person he'd loved, respected and trusted. How? Why? Why had they done that to him? It was so beyond his own standards and morals, he still couldn't fathom it.

But Mia's hand on his back soothed some of it as she said, 'I can't imagine how you felt, Brin. To have that kind of betrayal after giving up everything for them. After believing she was your girl. It must have hurt you so much.'

'I was stunned. I'd had no idea. I thought we were both happy.' There'd been no signs...or maybe there had been but he'd been delusional. Had allowed himself to sink into a dream. He wasn't going to let that happen again.

'Your brother, too. That's awful.'

'You should have seen him, Mia. He was hateful. Spiteful. Gunning for a fight. I don't know what I'd done for him to be like that.'

'Jealousy, maybe? You married "his" woman.'

'Grainne was my girlfriend. My wife. But maybe he hated that I was happy with her. That we had this family. *Family!*' He snorted. 'The only good thing was that I was the one who'd been at Niamh's birth, not him. I changed her nappies, I saw her grow every single day, not him. He missed out on all those milestones.'

'And now? They're still together?'

'No.' He didn't know whether he was glad about this or just sad at the whole sorry outcome. 'They broke up soon after the truth got out. Turns out neither of us O'Connor boys could trust her. But he gets to see Niamh, not me.'

'But why can't you see her? She's still your niece.'

'Yes. And I love her still. Do you think I'd give up that easily?' He knew his tone had been sharp. 'Sorry. I shouldn't have barked at you.'

But she gave him a soft smile. 'It's only natural to be upset about this. I know you, Brin. You would have fought for her.'

'I insisted I had access. I made her promise I could see Niamh at weekends, evenings. But they moved away to another town for a fresh start.' He shook his head. 'Because everyone we knew had found out and she couldn't cope with the backlash. But, once she'd gone, she made contact very difficult. Wouldn't answer my calls, turned up late for my afternoons with my girl. She told Niamh things about me that weren't true, which Niamh believed. She was…what?…nine or ten at this point. She was encouraged to call my brother, Padraig, "Daddy". Grainne said it was all too confusing for her to have me there too. I was…'

He breathed out his anger. 'The guy who'd brought her up for a few years. I tried, you know? I tried so hard to be the best kind of father. I was involved, interested, invested. It wasn't her fault her parents were messed up. She deserved to have me in her life. A steadiness. I'd been there all along. But then…'

'Then what?'

'Then Niamh announced she didn't want to see me. Parroted reasons from her mother. And I didn't have any options. I wasn't going to make her feel bad or cause trouble. I had no hold over any of them. She isn't my child, however much I want it to be so. I was just…paying.' Paying not only with money but with his trust too. 'Easily discarded as soon as the truth came out.'

'Oh, Brin.' Mia ran her hand down his back then sucked in a sharp breath. 'Now I understand why you needed the test, why you don't trust me to turn up. I would never do those things to you.'

'I know you wouldn't…' He paused because there were still traces of doubt at the back of his mind—not because of Mia, but because of Grainne.

Mia stilled, her eyes narrowing. 'But…?'

He raked his hand across his jaw. 'It's so much, you and me. It's like a flashpoint of need. But what happens when that flashpoint dims? Or stops altogether? I'm struggling with all this, Mia. What if something happened between us and that made you stop me seeing Harper? I've got no power here. You could do the same thing to me and then where would I be?'

Her eyes flashed bright steel. 'I am not your ex.'

'I know. You are far, far from that.' He reached out and stroked her cheek. 'Not in the same universe.'

She smiled. 'I would hope not. And see? Talking about it has made things clearer, helped me understand you a little more—why you were so adamant about the DNA test. Why you were angry about me giving you a false name. Even though I had good reasons, I can see why you'd be unwilling to believe anything I said. I wish you'd told me before.'

'How? When? We're just beginning here, Mia. This is the kind of thing you talk about when you trust someone. Not before.'

Her eyes widened, her smile reaching them and glittering there in the deep pools of brown. 'You trust me?'

Did he? His chest felt blown open. His pain eased. Hope shimmered, almost in reach, because he thought he actually might. 'Enough that I know you're not like Grainne. And I don't talk about it because I want to forget what happened, you know? Not forget Niamh—never—but I want to cut ties with my brother and with Grainne. I don't do the social media thing because I don't want to read about how they're doing, who they're with, what they had for breakfast. I don't care. I don't care about them at all.' He blew out a breath. 'And now you know everything about me.'

Except she didn't know about the panic rattling through his chest. The raw need for her. Even he didn't understand why it was so intense. Why the flashpoints of need hadn't dimmed.

Yet.

Because they inevitably would. Love didn't last. It was all tied up in pretence. His failed marriage and his brother's betrayal had taught him that.

But she might have suspected what he needed, because she edged closer and wrapped her arms round his neck. 'You're a good man, Brin O'Connor. You didn't deserve any of that. You lived through hell, had your precious daughter taken away.

And now here you are, facing it all again. Facing it with dignity and hope. I wouldn't do that to you. Harper is one hundred percent your daughter.'

If he was honest, he didn't dare to hope. He was living day to day here, minute to minute.

Feeling her skin against his had all thoughts of his past evaporating. She pressed her mouth to his and kissed him, long and slow, until his heart didn't ache for what had happened: it sprang to life with the now. He wanted this, he wanted her. Now.

He'd deal with what the future held later.

CHAPTER THIRTEEN

MIA MADE SURE she was early meeting Brin from the ferry—
no toilet stops to make him think they weren't going to be
there.

It was his third visit in four weeks, a routine of sorts. The
start of something, maybe. Each time he visited, they ended
up in bed. There was no way of controlling their desire, so
they'd agreed to go with it.

Each visit, he helped with fixing up the house—a coat of
paint, putting together flat-pack furniture, tiling the kitchen,
building a home for Mia and Harper to live in.

But not for Brin to live in. Because that had not been discussed. Neither had they made the step to suggest Harper call
him 'Daddy'. But it was coming; they both knew it. Harper
was more and more entranced by him every day and the feeling was clearly mutual.

Brin kept pushing for them to tell Harper he was her
father…whatever that would mean to a two-year-old. Truth
was, Mia wouldn't be able to bear it if Harper lost her father,
like Mia had lost hers. She couldn't bear to think of her daughter suffering such a loss, so she held off.

So, what *this* was, she didn't know. They hadn't put a label
on it.

It had been wonderful for him to confide in her at last. But,
regardless of what he said about his brother, he did care. Mia
could see that. He'd been hurt very badly and was trying to

be a good man and a good father to Harper, and she'd pushed him to talk, assuming he was hiding something that might damage Harper or her. The truth was, it was something that had damaged him. The hurt in his eyes told her he was still struggling at the loss of his first daughter.

Her heart jumped as he strolled off the ferry, his holdall slung over his shoulder, his eyes bright and smile wide.

God, she'd missed him.

He wrapped her into his arms and kissed her. And she didn't much care about people seeing her like this. Regardless of what he thought, he did have power in this. Power to make her breathless with a touch. Power to make her cry out his name. Power to make her dizzy with need. But in the matter of their daughter, yes, the law would doubtless be on her side. That was why he hadn't trusted they'd turn up and had almost left them standing on the dock. His trust in people had been trashed.

'Where's Harper?' He drew away but kept an arm round her waist as they walked along the harbour front.

'She's at a birthday party.' She shot him a smile. 'So, we get to play.'

He grinned, his eyes twinkling with promise. 'I like the sound of that.'

'With a new flat-pack set of drawers for Harper's room.'

'Oh, you know how to talk dirty. I can't wait to get my hands on that. And you.' He pulled her in for another kiss. 'One set of drawers, then I get to lose myself in you. Deal?'

'Deal.' If she could wait that long. 'I've got some lovely *Frozen* decals to stick on it. I want it to be a surprise when she comes home.'

'Sounds perfect.' He slid his hand into hers. 'Missed me?'

'Only your screwdriver.'

'More dirty talk.' He winked. 'Lead on.'

The buzz of a drill coming from inside her house had her

pausing, her hand on Brin's chest. 'Oh, yes, forgot to say, Nikau's finishing off wiring in the new lights in the lounge.'

His eyebrows knitted. 'I could have done that.'

'Nikau's the island's handyman. I willingly pay him. If you or I did that kind of thing, he'd be out of a job.' She leaned against him. 'Besides, I have other ideas for you.'

He nuzzled in her hair. 'Can't wait—'

A loud bang and weird fizzing noise cut him off.

'What the hell?' Mia ran towards the sound that had come from inside her house. Nikau was sprawled on the lounge floor with a cable still in his hand, shattered glass and ceiling plaster around him and an upended stepladder near his feet.

'Stop!' Brin was at her heels. 'He's been shocked. Don't touch him.'

'I've got it.' Heart pounding, she ran to the electrical switch box in the kitchen and flicked it off. 'Okay. The electricity's off now.'

Brin nodded and bent to examine her friend, feeling for a pulse and checking his breathing. 'His pulse is rapid and weak. He also could have hit his head or hurt his back when he fell. Nikau? Nikau, can you hear me?'

The slightest of head movements, a flicker of eyelids.

Mia breathed out. He was alive; that was something. 'I'll get the portable ECG and Owen. And call for an evacuation.'

Brin gave her a sharp nod of approval. 'And adenosine, if you've got it. Just in case.'

When she returned, she found Brin assessing a nasty electrical burn on Nikau's palm. She knelt down next to him. 'Here's some saline solution and an IV set. Owen's out on a call but Anahera's coming over. Chopper's on its way.'

Brin smiled and took the ECG from her. 'Thanks. You're good at this.'

'It's what I do.' These were her friends. More…they were her *whanau*, her family, and she'd move heaven and earth for them. She shrugged but felt pride shimmer through her. 'Right, Nikau, bear with me while I put up a drip with some fluids for you.'

'Have you got any pain in your back? Neck? Legs?' Brin did a thorough assessment and Mia was mightily relieved when she saw their patient move his arms and legs. Even so, she applied a neck brace and kept him still while Brin completed his examination.

Anahera came running through the door and threw herself at her son on the floor. 'Nikau. Oh God, Nikau.'

'Be careful of the broken glass,' Mia said, shifting sideways to let Anahera closer to her son.

Nikau blinked at the sound of his mother's wails. He raised a hand. 'I'm...okay...'

'We've called for an evac.' Brin looked from mother to son. 'He's had a nasty electric shock and some burning on his hand. We need to monitor his heart rate and make sure he didn't damage his neck or back when he fell from the stepladder.'

'Aren't I always telling you to be careful?' Anahera shook her head and stroked the back of Nikau's good hand. 'Thirty-five and still my baby.' She turned to Mia. 'You never have a decent sleep again, once you have kids. Even when they've left home. You always worry.'

'Too right.' Brin shot a sideways look at Mia and winked. His smile was tender, a secret shared.

Mia nodded. 'I don't think I've slept properly since Harper was born.'

Brin's smile slid and he looked...sad. He'd missed out on Harper. How hard must it have been for him to have no contact with Niamh too? How much must he have worried about her? He wouldn't be able to switch off that kind of parental love. No wonder he'd been running for the last few years, essentially trying to come to terms with losing a child. Never mind the break-up of his marriage and the bomb that his brother had detonated in his family.

She realised Anahera was looking at them both, confusion and questions in her expression. Mia had never discussed her private life with anyone here on the island. But she'd kissed Brin in broad daylight now so many times, she had no doubt the gossip machine was in full swing. She wasn't sure how she felt about that.

No one knew Brin was Harper's father, but was it only a matter of time before she let that slip into conversation too? Was she letting things get too cosy, being lured into a false sense of happy families? Was not putting a label on their relationship going to be a recipe for disaster? Did she and Brin have different slants on the way things were developing between them?

'Mumma! Mumma! I got a ice block!' Harper ran through the door with Carly and Mason in quick pursuit. They all stopped at the sight of the little huddle around Nikau on the floor.

Carly took in the scene and quickly moved the children behind her so they couldn't see the unfolding drama. 'Need a hand?'

'All okay, thanks.' Brin nodded. 'Helicopter's on its way.'

'Got you. Okay, kids, it looks like Mummy's busy. Let's go sit outside and eat the ice blocks.' Carly waved. 'In fact, we could have Harper stay the night?'

Brin and Mia both looked at each other.

They could have a child-free night, knowing that Harper would be safe at her auntie's house. They could talk freely about where things were going.

'Yes,' Mia said.

'No,' Brin said at the same time.

She flicked him a confused frown as something akin to

rejection skittered through her gut. Did he not want to spend the night with her?

'I thought you needed me to do some DIY?' He bugged his eyes at her. 'For Harper?'

Ah, that. He wanted to see Harper's surprise. 'Yes, of course.'

'Then we can have dinner together.' He grinned. 'The three of us.'

Mia checked herself because, after what he'd been through, he deserved to spend as much time with Harper as he could. She nodded at Carly. 'Okay. I'll come and pick her up in...?'

She looked at Brin for an answer. Since when had she deferred to someone else over decisions about Harper?

'Two hours?' Brin nodded at Mia.

'Okay. Shout if you need anything.' Carly gave them a thumbs-up sign. 'See you later.'

Anahera glanced at them both again and smiled knowingly. Then the sound of a helicopter rent the air and Mia focused back on their patient.

Thirty minutes later she was back in her house with Brin at her side, clearing up the glass and ceiling plaster. 'Thank goodness we arrived when we did. Thanks for helping out there.'

'Hey, it's my job.' Brin grinned. 'But, is it my imagination, or is there always a drama when I'm here?'

'Aw, no. Rāwhiti is a peaceful little idyll.'

'Except for cyclones and storms and electrical incidents and early labours...'

'That's what makes it special. Come, look outside.' She took his hand and drew him to the window. 'Look at that perfect blue sky, the little boats bobbing on the ocean. The bush across the bay. It's sublime.'

As she pointed, she glanced up at his face. Oh, he was smiling and nodding, but it was clear he wasn't as enamoured as she was. He didn't want to live here. This place wasn't imprinted in his DNA as it was hers. He didn't see the beauty, the community. Sure, he helped them; he was a good man. But he came here to see his daughter and to see Mia and she knew, without a shadow of a doubt, that he'd have gone anywhere they were. Rāwhiti was just another place to him, not a special one. He didn't have the history and the memories here.

So they needed to make some.

And here she'd been, lulling herself into thinking there might be a future as she peered across the water that had taken her family.

But Brin whirled round to face her and skimmed his hands round her waist, tugging her to him. 'It's pretty and all that, but I prefer this view. Very much.'

She placed her palm on his cheek and traced her thumb across his lips, wanting to erase all thought of her family's tragic end and fill her head with him. 'Well, I guess you're not onerous to look at either.'

His eyes danced with tease as he leaned closer and whispered, 'You are one hell of a woman, Mia Edwards. Come here.'

He slid his mouth over hers, kissing her long and slow. She wound her arms round his neck and sank into it all—to him, the kiss, the feel of him. And, as always, like a spark to a flame, one touch of his lips on hers made her body come alive with need.

What started as a tender kiss became frantic and desperate. Without lifting his mouth from hers, he slid down the straps of her dress. It pooled around her feet. She stepped out and tugged at his T-shirt, ripping it from his shorts' waistband and pulling it over his head, then making quick work of his shorts.

He laughed. 'What's the hurry? We've got plenty of time before we pick Harper up.'

'I need you, Brin. Inside me. I can't explain. I...'

'I know. I know.' He took both her hands and kissed them. 'You're like a drug. I can't get enough. All I could think of was getting here. The hours at work went so slowly. I love my job, but man, I needed to see you. I needed to do this. I need you.'

He slipped his hands behind her back and unclipped her bra. Then he stepped back to look at her. The intensity of his gaze heated every part of her. Her longing for him grew deeper and deeper every day through their messages and conversations, through the flowers he sent and the presents he brought over for Harper.

I need you.

She tried to be guarded around him, to hold back the truth of her feelings, but it was getting harder to deny them. And to deny all the complications that all this created.

But, oh, the way he caressed her, and the sweet roughness of his kisses, flared her need. She pulled him to her bedroom and removed the last of their underwear before they tumbled onto the bed.

Then he was sheathed and inside her. She held him tight, gripping his shoulders, wrapping her legs round his hips. Wanting to be over him, on him, next to him. Just him—Brin. Always Brin.

Every time she saw him was like the first time. It was filled with wonder, excitement and a building pressure of need in her skin, in her belly. She couldn't think straight until she'd kissed him or made love with him. Until the first rush of desire had been sated. Until the next built, rapidly, and burned through her.

This time it was slow and intense. He held her gaze as he entered her and with each stroke. He watched her as he kissed her, his eyes on hers. A meeting of need and more—so much more. A knowing, an understanding—deep. Soul-deep.

Then suddenly it was too slow and she bucked her hips, changing the angle so he could go deeper and harder. As he slid into her, she felt a growing light there. She chased it with her rhythm, over and over, higher and higher. 'Brin. I can't… Don't stop. Don't stop.'

'This is so good. We're so good together.' His blue eyes were swirling with affection, bright with light.

'Yes.' She urged him to rock faster as need spiralled. 'Yes.'

'You are so damned sexy.' He pushed harder into her, grinding his hips against hers until his body arched and he groaned her name. He was chasing the same light, chasing the release. She gripped his shoulders as it finally crashed through her.

He hauled her close, tight against him, as he pulsed inside her. 'Mia. Jeez. This…is everything.'

Everything.

Yes. Everything she ever wanted was right here.

She giggled as she loosened her grip on his shoulders. 'Happy now?'

'Very happy.' He pressed his forehead to hers as his breathing normalised. 'But I could be happier again in…say…ten minutes? Give me a chance to get my strength back.'

'So soon?' She laughed but had to admit a rerun would be very nice indeed. 'You are incorrigible.'

He shrugged and smiled. 'And insatiable when it comes to you.'

His fingertips ran little circles between her breasts, and he looked at her, smiling lazily. In that smile was a riot of emotions: tenderness; generosity; safety; vulnerability; strength.

In essence, it was Brin O'Connor stripped bare of any pretence, any guard, any mistrust. A naked honesty. This thing between them was as true and raw for him, as it was for her.

As he gazed at her, her heart felt as if it was filled with light. Her whole body cleaved to him. She felt excited and sated. Calm and yet vibrant. The minute she looked at him, this sense of something special filled her. It was the most intense, the most beautiful, feeling she'd ever had.

What was it about him? What was this feeling, that she couldn't bear to be apart from him? That she thought about him every moment of her waking life and many of her sleeping ones too? That her heart beat a special way when she saw him, that her soul felt lighter when she was with him? That he was her person. Her *one*. A final piece in her jigsaw puzzle.

Brin O'Connor.

Then it dawned on her, a slow realisation that stole through her unasked for, unwanted, unbidden: she'd fallen deeper than she'd ever thought possible. She cared for him. She wanted to make him happy, to ease his hurt. She wanted to wake up with him tomorrow and the next day and the next. She'd been fooling herself that she'd met him early at the ferry to ease his mind: it had been because she couldn't wait to see him. To kiss him. To spend their precious moments together. She ached for him.

She was falling in love with him.

Had fallen. Hard and deep.

And that only meant one thing: now…now she was at risk of losing him. Somehow, some time, somewhere. She'd believe he would always be here for her, with her. And one day he wouldn't come back.

And this time she didn't know how she'd survive.

Panic ripped through her. She eased away.

She couldn't love him.

They lived too far apart. It was too soon. It was folly.

It was danger.

CHAPTER FOURTEEN

BRIN WAS TRYING to make sense of the flat-pack instructions when Mia stuck her nose round the door. Her hair was mussed and she had sleep lines down one side of her face. In a nutshell: gorgeous. She yawned. 'Sorry, I must have dozed off.'

'You looked so peaceful, I didn't want to wake you.'

'I didn't realise I was so tired.' She came and sat on the floor next to him, close but with no kiss, no touch. She was probably reeling from her afternoon nap. She'd dressed again, not in her summer dress but in jeans and a long-sleeve top, as if she was cold despite the thirty-degrees day. 'You've been busy.'

He screwed in the last screw and moved back to admire his handiwork. 'I wanted to get this fixed up for when Harper gets home. I can't wait to see her face when she sees it.'

'She'll love it. She's impressed with everything you do. She's always talking about Brin this, Brin that.'

'Brin. I don't want that any more. When do we explain that I'm her daddy?' The words slipped out too quickly. He'd been thinking about bringing the subject up again but hadn't planned what he was going to say. Being here, surrounded by his daughter's things, had him wishing.

Mia's eyes briefly flickered closed and she looked as if she was trying to find the right words, to let him down gently. 'In time, Brin.'

'When?' It was always 'in time', 'it's too early'. He tried

to control his irritation as he applied the *Frozen* decals to the drawers.

She blew out a breath. 'Look, I don't know. I don't know how to say it: "Harper...Brin is your daddy". I mean, she understands that Owen is Mason's daddy, and that other kids have daddies, but will she be confused?'

'We could just say it. See how it resonates.' He wanted that. He also knew that he shouldn't push things. Mia was still getting used to having him in her life. Harper was still getting to know him. He wanted too much.

He wanted to lie with Mia until the sun rose. Until they were awakened by their daughter running into their bedroom. Until...

Until what, exactly? In Brin's experience 'for ever' was a distant dream that happened to other people. Or was cruelly snatched away by lies.

His brother had a lot to answer for. Because stealing his family hadn't been enough, no—he'd planted the seeds of mistrust into Brin's head and he'd let them grow.

But he had to keep showing up for his daughter. And he would. 'I'm here, Mia. I'm not going anywhere. The sooner we say it, the better. Then we can all get used to it.'

'It's a big step.' Mia sighed again and wrung her hands. There was something about her demeanour that wasn't quite right. Last week she would have sat on his knee, swiped a kiss on his head. Maybe she was still sleepy, but did he detect some emotional distance too? Was the smile not as ready? Was there some fragility in her voice?

Maybe she didn't believe in 'for ever' either. His heart crumpled. 'But it's the truth. Maybe we should have done it from the beginning.'

She looked at him for a long time and said nothing. A host of different emotions flickered across her features: confusion, worry and then something else. Something he didn't want to put a name to but he felt like a swift blow to his chest.

Eventually, she nodded. 'Okay. We can talk to her when I bring her back from Carly's. In fact, I should head over there now. We said two hours and it's been closer to three.'

'Okay.' Despite the fleeting wariness in her demeanour, his chest heated at the thought of the three of them being together again. 'I'll move the furniture around so it's ready when you get home.'

'Great plan.'

Home.

He looked round at the room decor chosen by Mia. It was their home, not his. Even though he'd helped rebuild it. Even though she'd talked her ideas through with him. Even though he'd helped her choose the paint colours and tiles. He didn't live here, he was always just a visitor sleeping in the spare room so Harper wouldn't get a shock at finding her mother and Brin in bed together. So he wouldn't disrupt their routine or their lives. And he went along with it all because he knew that, after everything she'd endured, Mia craved stability. She saw him as a threat to that.

As he watched her go, his heart contracted. Because the surprise of this whole thing was that, even after his brother had done the unspeakable, Brin did want it all. He wanted the happy-family thing. He wanted Harper to call him Daddy. Now, not later.

Mo stór.

The words fluttered around his chest and he wasn't quite sure if they were meant for Harper or Mia.

They were for both.

Talking to Mia was too easy. But spilling his guts to her had been a weakness. Making love with her was a beautiful, delicious weakness, a weakness that could be exploited. Alarm bells rang loud in his head, gripping his gut and twisting.

He shouldn't be here, doing this.

He should have put a stop to it for both their sakes. And for Harper's too. Because he was doing what he'd promised he'd never do again—he was falling too fast and he couldn't stop it even if he wanted to.

He was pushing the set of drawers back against the wall when his phone rang. Rattled by his realisation, he forced a smile into his voice. How was he going to navigate this? How could he do this and come out whole? 'Mia? Missing me already?'

'Oh, Brin.'

He could tell by her tone and the bubble of breathlessness that something was very wrong. His heart went into freefall. 'What's happened?'

In the background, mingled with the rush of air he could hear a small child crying—his child. Mia sighed. 'Look, don't panic.'

'I'm not panicking.'

He was panicking. His heart rate was skyrocketing, his chest caving. His daughter was crying and he wasn't there with her to stop her tears. It was always going to be like this if they lived so far apart. One of them would always be on the end of the phone in times of need, not there in the heart of it all.

'Tell me, Mia. What's happened?'

She gave a gulp and a stifled sob. 'Harper's had an accident.'

Mia cradled a still-sobbing Harper to her chest as Carly moored the boat at the harbour.

Brin was standing there, shivering in the dimming daylight, his face a map of worry and fear. He ran forward and took Harper from her. Mia watched him hold his daughter so tenderly, her heart felt bruised. This big man and her little miss—the love she felt for him was overwhelming, distracting and too much.

Too much.

She couldn't breathe at the thought of how much damage he could wreak with one callous word, one dark look.

He stared into Harper's blue O'Connor eyes. 'Hey, big girl. What did you do?'

'Ouchy.' Harper whimpered and heaved air into her lungs between shuddering sobs. 'Sore.'

'I think her arm is broken.' Mia tried to stay calm. It was bad enough she was rattled by her feelings for this man but now her daughter was hurting too. If only she could stop hurt, rewind time, right back to the day her family had left to go fishing. Or the day she'd met Brin. Or to a few hours ago, before she'd let Harper go with Carly so she could spend time in bed making love. But there was nothing she could do but live through it and provide comfort for her child. 'She's going to need an X-ray.'

Brin nodded as he rocked Harper in his arms. 'Tell me again, slowly, what happened?'

'She was riding Mason's little push-along tricycle and fell off at an awkward angle. It happens. Kids fall. It's part of growing up.'

'Should I call for a medical evacuation?' His jaw clenched and she felt a rail of judgement from his black look.

'For a broken arm? It's not that bad, Brin. They won't come for that. We have to get the ferry over to the city.'

'But she's—'

'Your daughter, and she's hurting, I know. They won't send a helicopter for this.'

'They sent one for an electrical injury.' He strode towards her house with his daughter in his arms and she had to run to keep up with him.

'We both know that could have had serious consequences. Nikau's heart needed monitoring. This is a broken arm. It could possibly even wait until morning.'

'No way. We go now.' His eyes shot sparks. 'I'll get my bag. Pack something for her and I'll take her to the hospital. Don't forget her blankie.'

Mia's heart buckled. Things were unravelling; she could see that. They weren't close enough yet and didn't have the longevity to weather a storm like this. She didn't want to have to explain to him that he didn't know what vaccinations Harper had had, or her medical history, and possibly didn't have her date of birth imprinted in his head. He probably didn't know their actual postal address. Besides, she was Harper's mother, and there was no way her daughter was going to hospital without her. 'I'm coming too. We'll get the last ferry over.'

As he threw things into a holdall, he didn't let up. 'This is ridiculous. If you lived on the mainland it'd take a fraction of the time to get her to hospital. She's in pain.'

'I know. And this is the best we can do.'

'It's so far away from anywhere.'

'That's why I love it.'

'So far away from me. All this weekend visiting—it's not enough.' He looked at her then, for a long time, and she felt the implications ripple through her. He needed more from them and he couldn't ask. 'And from the hospital,' he added.

But she couldn't give any more and put her heart on the line. 'This is the first time we've needed the hospital in her whole life.'

'It may not be the last.'

'No, but we can't wrap her in cotton wool, Brin. I've lived on the island my whole life. Many hundreds, if not thousands, still do, and we cope. We get through.'

'I don't want my daughter to cope. I want her to thrive.'

'She *is* thriving.' But she looked down at Harper, who was now lying on the sofa, at her shocked little face and her tear-stained cheeks, and Mia's heart broke. They'd always managed on the island. They were strong and resilient people. He didn't understand. He didn't want to.

The argument abated while they sat in the waiting room, surrounded by other people, and while Harper's X-ray confirmed a fracture. And even while the back slab was applied. They both focused on making their little girl smile, trying to distract her from the pain.

Trying to distract themselves from their own pain too.

'Mumma…' Harper sobbed after the back slab was finished, and put her good arm out to be picked up. Mia swept her up and held her close, stroking her hair.

But then came a restless wriggle, a grouchy face and, 'Bwin.'

She put out her arm again. Her chest was heaving and she made the little sniffling sounds of an exhausted child in pain. Mia's heart broke into tiny pieces. Nothing could calm her daughter. Nothing could soothe her, not even a game of hide-and-seek behind the blankie. Brin tried and tried, but failed to bring a glimmer of a smile.

That *always* worked.

'We need to get her home.' His tone was desperate. 'She needs some rest.'

Home.

Yes. Back to Rāwhiti. Mia didn't say it, she just nodded, because she knew he meant his place. Two parents. Two homes. Two lives.

And now two adults in stony silence on the drive back *home.*

It wasn't until dawn, when Harper was finally asleep in her room at Daddy's house, clutching her beloved blankie in her good hand, that he said the words that ricocheted through Mia's heart. 'I want you to move here. So we can be closer. It makes sense.'

'Not to me.' It had been a long and worrying night and exhaustion nipped at Mia's nerves. She beckoned him out of the room so Harper wouldn't wake to see the two grown-ups upset with each other. When they got to the lounge, she took a deep breath. 'I am not moving, Brin. Rāwhiti is my home. It is my everything.'

Only hours ago she'd thought *he* was. And he was… Oh, even now she ached to be held by him. For them to put this difficult conversation behind them and climb into bed together. But her heart was a shabby, soft, old thing that had been badly bruised. It leapt at any kind of affection, like a little excitable puppy. She wasn't young any more. She couldn't let her heart lead her down that path.

She loved him, but she could not let that be her downfall.

She had to let her head rule. Rāwhiti Island was her place, her life. It was where she'd grown up, where she'd lived with her family. That made sense, to her at least. He couldn't make her do it. She'd already sold her family home; she had to keep their memories alive, keep tethered to them by geography, keep them tied to the people who'd known them. And make sure that Harper got to know and love her heritage too. 'I can't leave. You knew that coming into this.'

He shook his head as he leaned back against the windowsill. 'I didn't know a lot coming into this, Mia. I came for a job and ended up with a family.'

True, he hadn't asked for this. But she knew how much he loved being with them. And how much she loved being part of this family of three. Oh, it was what she wanted. But how could she make it happen and then wait…*wait*…for it all to fall apart? How could she live through that torment, waiting for everything she loved to be lost? 'Is that what you want? A family?'

'I…' He swallowed and looked away. He'd had one before and it had broken him.

'Because, if that's what you really want, why don't you move to Rāwhiti?' The words slipped out of her mouth as a sudden flicker of hope slid under her rib cage. Maybe they could both override their fears. Maybe it could work. Love could find a way on her little island. Love could blossom there.

But his expression was utter sadness. 'You know that's impossible. My job isn't on Rāwhiti, it's in the city.'

'And you've already given up your life dreams for one family, right?' Why would he risk that again?

His jaw tightened and he turned away.

It was hopeless.

They'd avoided this conversation for too long. They'd hidden behind kisses and long lazy nights, behind getting to know each other in so many ways. Pretended they could do the impossible.

But she couldn't do it. And neither could he. 'I can't move here, Brin. This is not me. And I can't leave them.'

He turned back to look at her. 'They will get another nurse. They have Owen and Carly.'

I can't leave them.

He didn't understand. She was tied to the island inextricably. She couldn't just move away. 'They have me.'

'And I don't.' He turned away to look at the night.

City lights danced outside like glow worms and fireflies. She guessed that once upon a time she might have found it pleasing. Now she wanted to be back home.

He huffed out a breath. 'What would I do on Rāwhiti? I'm a paramedic. I'm based here. There is no paramedic service where you live. I can't just find a job there or make one up.'

'You could try. You know how much that place means to me.'

He walked across the room and ran his fingers along her arm, softly and tenderly. 'I told you before, you bring your family with you in your heart and in your memories. In your stories. We can't stay stuck in one place because of the people we loved there.'

She'd sold their memory and had got a nice new kitchen instead. She damned well would stay there to make sure they weren't forgotten. 'All I have left is a bench with their names on.'

'Bring that too. We'll find you a place with a garden. You know how much you and Harper mean to me.'

'I know you love your daughter.' But her? How did she fit into this for him?

He was suggesting they find a nice place for her and Harper to live on the mainland, not to live with him. Was he saying all this because he wanted Harper in his life with a convenient side serving of Mia? Did his picture of a family even include her? Did he even want a partner? Did he not trust her even now, after everything they'd done and said?

They'd both been alone and independent so long that when things started to get difficult they didn't know how to weather it together. They were too scared, too scarred, to be utterly vulnerable and make a leap.

And she couldn't say, 'I love you,' to him now. She couldn't tell him because that would smack of desperation or coercion. She had to step away before she made a fool of herself.

Her heart broke at the thought of losing him, but she had to do what was best for her family. Her little family of two, the way it had always been. She fisted away tears and dug deep for some courage.

'I'm here, Mia.' But he didn't double down on how much he cared. And he certainly didn't say he loved her.

'For Harper? Or for me?'

'For Harper, of course, and…' He visibly shook and stepped back. 'Mia, I had it all once. I gave everything up for it. Then I lost it.' His tone was raw and low, his breath shaky. 'I don't know… What if…?'

'You don't know if you can give everything up again—your job, your life—for someone who might decide they don't want you. Is that right, Brin? No matter what I say now, it won't change your fears for the future. So you won't give up what you've worked hard for. Not for me. Not for any idea of us.' She nodded. Tried to swallow away the pain in her throat. Tried to ignore the hurt ripping through her chest like a knife wound. This was exactly what she hadn't wanted, everything she'd been hoping to avoid. When he nodded, she bit her lip to stop it from trembling. 'Just so you know, I am not your ex.'

He pressed his lips together then breathed out. 'No.'

'But you still don't trust what we have. What we could grow between us on Rāwhiti.' At his silence, she sighed, almost moaned at the sadness of it all, but managed to hold that in. 'Then it's visits every other weekend only on the island, while Harper's so little. You'll have to find somewhere child-friendly to stay. When she's older, she can come stay here.'

She'd miss them both terribly while they bonded together without her. She would be excluded from their own little family. She was inextricably linked to him for ever. For the next few years, she'd be forced to see him every other weekend, and to message him on Harper's behalf. She'd get to share things with him, but not the private, intimate things, the difficult things or the lovely things. Just the mundane drop-off and pick-up details. The reminders of Harper's schedule. She'd have to watch him grow apart from her...perhaps fall in love with another woman. Maybe have another child.

No.

She couldn't bear it.

God. A scream rose in her throat but she forced it down. How had this gone so horribly wrong? Why did it have to hurt so much?

He shook his head. 'Mia, I'm so sorry.'

'Me too.' Because she loved him and this was the price—

her heart, her peace, her everything. She got the booby prize, got to sit on the side-lines of his life instead of being in the spotlight of it. She cleared her throat and made to sound as reasonable as possible, because if she broke now she didn't think she'd recover. 'We'll be gone as soon as she wakes up.'

He nodded, his eyes haunted with grief. 'I know.'

Then he turned and left the room.

And she leaned back against the door and finally let the tears fall.

Brin stormed out of the room, unable to control himself any longer. He'd tried to reason with her. He'd listened to her arguments. He'd answered her comebacks with logic. Moving here was the only sensible thing to do. Rāwhiti was magical, he couldn't deny, but it made sense for them to be here. She could get work at the hospital or any of the many GP practices. Harper would have the pick of schools. But Mia was so wedded to that island, she couldn't see past it.

He ignored the swathe of emotions that threatened to overwhelm him. He would not allow them to impinge on this important life decision. He needed to see his daughter regularly—end of. He'd risked too much in the past. Harper would not be like Niamh—collateral damage from a failed relationship. He would not walk that path again, would not allow his daughter to be used as ammunition—she deserved to have two parents in her life. And he would move heaven and earth for that to happen.

But then there was Mia. Beautiful, funny, gorgeous Mia. Stubborn, too. Independent. She'd had to be. Left alone to bring up a child, she'd learnt to fight. And he loved her for it. He loved her vibrancy, her compassion. He loved the way his soul felt brighter, being in her presence.

His heart rattled at that thought. *Loved?* Did he love her? *No.*

He was never going to allow that to happen. Care for, yes. Like, yes. Desire, yes. But more than that? His heart quivered at the thought of being so vulnerable.

The sound of a heavy-duty zip being pulled alerted him to her packing. He couldn't sit here in the bedroom and listen to her prepare to leave, so he grabbed his running gear and headed outside into the marmalade sunrise. Harper was still fast asleep. He had a while before they'd go.

Auckland had fifty-two volcanoes and it felt as if he pushed himself to the top of each one of them, trying to exorcise every feeling he had for Mia. To rid himself of the sweet, sweet memories and the fierce attraction.

His feet hit the tarmac over and over, a rhythm that soothed him a little. Maybe she'd rethink. Maybe they could sit down and chat over breakfast. Maybe…

When he rounded the corner towards his apartment, he saw Mia bending at the back door of a taxi, no doubt clipping Harper into a car seat. His heart lurched. He couldn't believe this was where they'd ended up. They were leaving and his whole world was folding in.

No.

'Wait!'

He raced forward as Mia straightened with such sadness in her eyes, it made his gut hurt.

'We were waiting for you.' Her voice was almost a whisper and her eyes glistened. 'To say goodbye.'

His gut hollowed out. He wanted to reach for her, to pull her against him, to kiss her and hold her. To tell her everything was going to be okay.

It's okay. It's okay. It's okay.

But it wasn't. He'd held back his emotions in the early hours but now they threatened to engulf him. He felt loss, dread, fear. A powerful love for his daughter. Something…*what?*… for Mia. So much, too much, that it clouded his reasoning.

'Bwin.'

He tore his gaze away from Mia to see his little angel, clutching her blankie to her cheek the way she did when she was self-soothing, tired or in pain. Her sleepy smile hit him square in the chest.

'Hey, baby girl.' He stroked her hair. 'You be good for Mumma, okay?'

'Yes.' His daughter blinked up at him and raised her broken arm. 'Ouchy.'

'Yes…' He tried for words, but his throat was blocked. In desperation, he turned back to Mia.

Her lips were pressed together but she nodded and swallowed. 'Bye, then.'

Don't go. It'll be okay.

But it wouldn't. Nothing would be okay again.

She climbed into the front of the car and closed the door, and it felt as if she'd closed off his lifeline.

The car started to pull away.

'Harper! Daddy loves you!' he shouted. She couldn't hear him so he blew a kiss, and she copied, her mouth moving, saying something only Mia could hear.

Mia turned then. His Mia. *Mo stór. My darling Mia.*

And her dark gaze latched on to his. He caught a glimpse of the swift swipe of her sleeve across her cheek. Then the car disappeared round the corner.

It was happening again. The two people he cared the most for in the whole damned world would be carving a life without him.

'No!' He raced after the car, wanting to…wanting to what?

Wanting them here, with him. Wanting to clutch them tight to his chest. To grow old with them, to nurture them.

Wanting Mia to be in his life. To *be* his life.

But, shredded on the inside, he watched them go. Because

he knew it couldn't happen. He'd learnt that over and over from his father, his brother, his ex.

Love didn't grow where Brin was. Only pain.

CHAPTER FIFTEEN

'So, I HAVE NEWS.' Carly beamed as she wandered into the staff lunch-room.

'You're pregnant?' Mia's eyes strayed from her sad-looking sandwich to Carly's flat belly and she felt a twinge of envy. Again. She could not be jealous of her best friend's happiness. Just because love was not on Mia's cards, it was lovely to have it in her friend's life.

But Carly's smile grew as she shook her head. 'No.'

'Then, what?'

'The new owner of the camp sent an email through asking about a few things and said she's going to turn the place into a wellness centre.'

'Oh? All yoga retreats and açai smoothies?' Perhaps Mia should have been more excited about this. But, truth was, she hadn't felt excited about anything for days, not since she'd left Brin's place almost a week ago. She was listless and empty— broken, in fact. Oh, sure, she was managing to put up a great front, so no one knew. But at night she gave in to the emotions and let her body sob out its loneliness.

She missed him. Missed what they'd had and what could have been.

Carly was still grinning. 'And meditation and mindfulness.'

'Sign me up,' Mia quipped. 'I could do with some quiet time.' Although, being alone with her thoughts was probably not such a great idea. Maybe she needed to be somewhere busy, vibrant, exciting, with a hum of white noise.

Like the city?

Like Brin's apartment?

No. It was all too late to think about that.

'Me too.' Carly sat down across the table from her. 'I would love a massage and some time out.'

'We should book a slot, then, as soon as it opens.' Mia could imagine the resort, with a spa and high-end apartments. It would bring much-needed dollars to the island but wasn't exactly how her parents had envisioned the camp turning out.

'But get this,' Carly added. 'She's also going to donate six weeks a year to Women's Refuge and host victims of abuse here to help them heal—for free. She wants to upgrade the playground, not tear it down. And she's keeping some of the bunk rooms so she can bring children, too, and turn the rest into higher-end accommodation to fund it all.'

'Oh?' Mia's chest felt suddenly a little clearer. 'So, not flash apartments, like we'd heard?'

'No. The real-estate guy had got the wrong end of the stick.'

Mia found herself smiling for the first time in days. 'I know it's none of my business what happens to it, but I'm thrilled it's not going to be a big resort. And helping charities too… that's great.'

Her friend nodded. 'I know you were feeling guilty—I have to admit, I was too. I didn't want you to think I was all about taking Rafferty's money.'

'I would never think that about you. You were my brother's wife. We all loved you.' A rogue tear slipped down Mia's cheek. She scrubbed it away. These days, tears were only a heartbeat away. She felt so sensitive, acutely reacting to every and any emotion.

Carly frowned and slid her hand over Mia's. 'Hey, I didn't realise you were so upset about selling the place.'

'I'm all kinds of confused, to be honest. I needed the money for a better life for Harper, and I can't do that without selling the camp. But I'm so glad it's going to help people too. Mum would have liked that. Dad too.' Mia's throat was scratchy and raw and she wasn't sure she was coping well, holding everything in the way she usually did. She took a deep breath. 'It's not just that. I…um…'

'What is it?'

Mia's brief happiness and relief took a nosedive. 'Brin.'

'I thought you were getting along. It seemed that way last time I saw you together.'

'Not any more.' Mia filled her in on the details of her last trip to the mainland. 'But he messages every day and tries to say goodnight to Harper every night when he can.'

Carly's eyes brightened. 'That's good, isn't it? He's a good dad. As much as he can be, from a distance.'

'I miss him.'

I love him.

It didn't appear that feeling would abate any time soon. Her treacherous bottom lip started to wobble. She pressed her lips together and willed herself not to cry.

'Oh, honey. Come here.' Carly pulled her into a hug, which made Mia feel even worse.

She tugged away. 'Stop being nice to me or I'm going to cry even harder.'

'Oh, Mia. I'm so sorry.'

'Me too.' Mia sniffed. 'I'm just going to have to be strong for me and Harper.'

Carly brushed soggy strands of hair from Mia's face. 'You are the strongest woman I've ever met. You'll get through this. You've got through worse.'

But this was a different kind of loss. A lifetime wouldn't erase the way she felt about Brin. 'I don't ever want to be in another relationship. It hurts too much.'

'After what happened to Rafferty, I used to think that too, but sometimes you've got to take the risk.' Carly handed her a tissue.

Mia blew her nose. 'I don't like taking risks.'

Carly gave her a curious but sympathetic look. 'You really wouldn't consider moving there to be with him?'

'How can you say that? Rafferty's here.' In fact, Rafferty's body had never been found. They didn't know where he was, or her mother. Her father's body had washed up on a neighbouring island. But there was something symbolic, almost sacred, about Rāwhiti, the place they'd made their home. 'You're not going to leave.'

'I was about to leave when we sold the camp, right? I came back for Owen and Mason, not just for Rāwhiti. But who knows what the future holds? Seriously, if we decided as a family that somewhere else was better for us, I'd go in a heartbeat. It would be an adventure. I met Rafferty travelling, after all. I never intended to live my whole life here.' Her friend's smile was soft and tender. 'Love is in your heart, Mia. It's not a place. You carry your family with you. If you lived on the mainland, you wouldn't forget this island. You'd visit. You'd keep the memories alive. Your family would not want you to be stuck here.'

Those last words had Mia blinking and sitting up. Was she stuck?

Was she using her past to glue her to the island when she should be teaching her daughter to move forward? To embrace new things and not to be afraid of change? A strange sensation slid into her chest. Was she *hiding* behind her lost family and community because she didn't want to take a risk with Brin?

Ouch.

Carly took a deep breath. 'Let me ask you a question, Mia. If Brin moved here would you want to be with him?'

'Of course. I think… Oh, I think I might have fallen in love with him.'

'Oh, trust me, we all know how much you care for him. We can see it. And how much he cares for you too. You're perfect for each other.' Carly squeezed her hand.

'But he wasn't willing to take that step either.' Mia sighed. Because he'd lived through a nightmare. Because she hadn't been willing to discuss their future unless it had been entirely on her terms and he'd respected that. 'I think we're both scared.'

Carly nodded. 'I was terrified of falling for Owen. But doing something scary is life-affirming. Perhaps it's time *you* took that risk, eh? You can't spend the rest of your life hiding here, trying not to care about people. You've got to live, Mia, in your family's memory. And to show Harper how to be a strong woman. You don't want her afraid to take risks, do you? You want her to be open and curious and willing to reach out, to stretch and grow.'

'I can grow here.' But Mia knew her friend was right. She needed to live her life to the full, not endure a half-life here, being scared and hiding away. She didn't want to be scared any more. She wanted to be the open-hearted woman she'd once been, before her family had been lost to the sea.

She needed to take risks, even if the biggest threat was to her heart. Because love was worth it. Brin was worth it. Their future as a family sure as hell was worth it.

She just had to work out how to convince him to believe it too.

'You're very quiet, Brin. You okay?' Lewis balled the paper bag that had held his sausage roll and threw it into the beach rubbish bin like a basketball player. Then he whooped. 'Slam dunk. Three points to me.'

It was the last hours of a gruelling nightshift, and they

were taking a very late break and grabbing some much-needed sunshine and sustenance. But every time Brin set foot on the beach he looked out towards the little islands on the hazy horizon and his heart felt crushed. Mia and Harper were out there. He was here.

'Grand,' Brin answered. Although nothing was grand these days. Sure, he had a daily update on Harper, via Mia's short messages. But he was missing out—not just on watching his daughter grow but on Mia time.

Ever since she'd left his senses had been on high alert, trying to find some fragment of her scent, or her presence in his house.

House. Yes, because it wasn't a home. It was a holding pen until he could find something that would work better for Harper and him. And, even though he had contact with Mia, nothing between them was the same. It was brittle, loaded and broken.

His gut tightened at the thought. At what they'd shared together and now lost.

Jeez, he missed her.

'Okay.' Lewis jumped up and shook his head, brushing sand off his trousers. 'Got to get the van back to base, then I'm out of here. I've got to be at St Joseph's before ten o'clock.'

'St Joseph's?'

'Primary school. My niece is getting an award and they're having a special assembly this morning. If I don't get there in time, my brother will kill me.' Lewis grinned as they walked towards the car park. 'Don't want to be Bad Uncle Lewis. Again.'

'Again?'

'Oh, you know how it is. I missed the Christmas play because I was working. I missed Christmas Day because I was working.'

'Sometimes shift work sucks. You and your brother close?'

Brin wondered how it felt to not hate your sibling with as much passion as Brin did. How it felt to see your niece on a regular basis. To have a family that loved each other.

'Twins. Tied at the hip.' Lewis shrugged. 'Any plans for your days off? Please tell me it's something more exciting than a special assembly.'

Brin couldn't think of anything better. Except a long, lazy night with Mia. 'Going to Rāwhiti.'

'To see Mia? Things getting hot there?' His boss's grin was suggestive and teasing.

But Brin's jaw set. Things were very definitely cold. 'It's autumn. Things are cooling a bit.'

Lewis laughed. 'I mean between you and Mia. You seem very close.'

Brin took a deep breath and looked his boss straight in the eye. 'I'm Harper's father. I try to see her when I can.' It was time to tell people. He wanted to scream to the world that he was that cute little kid's daddy.

Lewis's eyes grew wide. 'Whoa, wait, what? You and Mia?'

'Long story. And I'm not going to go there. But, yeah. Three years ago.'

Three years and he'd missed her every damned day. That was after one night. Now he'd had many amazing nights and many glorious days with her, he wasn't sure if his heart was ever going to recover.

He missed her smile, her laugh, her temper. He missed the chats they had after making love, missed holding her, sharing their lives, sharing Harper.

Jeez, he missed everything. He'd loved every minute of being with her.

That word again: love. It kept popping into his head, sliding under his rib cage. Love for Harper, yes, but a different kind of feeling for Mia. An ache that would never stop.

And there wasn't a damned thing he could do about it. Apart

from face her, smile and pretend he was okay. 'So I'm going to be requesting regular weekends off. Don't want to be Bad Daddy. Right?'

Daddy. He was going to tell Harper as soon as he thought the time was right. No waiting for Mia to be ready.

And yet, *damn.*

He wanted her to be ready.

Lewis's eyes were still wide with excitement at Brin's news as they climbed into the ambulance. 'Must be tricky with them being over on Rāwhiti and you in the city.'

'Yup.'

'So, you and Mia…?'

Brin held up his hand. 'I said don't go there.'

'I like Mia.' Lewis gunned the engine and steered into a gap in traffic. 'She's had a really tough time. But she's a tough cookie. Funny, too. Bet she'd bite your head off if you were late to assembly.'

'No doubt.'

She's mine. Hands off.

Possessiveness curled through him, ugly and raw. He couldn't think of Mia with anyone else. He wanted her. He missed her.

Jeez. Did he love her?

No, he didn't.

Yes, he damned well did. He knew it and had been hiding from it. Hadn't wanted to admit that he'd let himself fall so deep and so hard because the consequences would be devastating.

And they had been. Every minute since she'd left, he'd felt broken into a zillion pieces. He loved the woman and there was nothing he could do about it. She didn't want him, did she? She'd almost said so.

Stupid bloody eejit.

Wait…she'd *almost* said so. But she hadn't actually said it, had she? She'd said, 'Is that what you really want? A family? Why don't you move to Rāwhiti?'

His heart jigged.

Why didn't he?

Because he didn't have a job there. But, when Grainne had fallen pregnant and they'd cancelled their cruise jobs, he'd pivoted and retrained. So, he could do something else, right? The handyman was laid up at the moment. They always needed a first-aider. He could put his hand to something—pull a pint, learn how to sail…invent a job.

He had to do something to make things right. To shift this weight in his chest. More importantly, he needed to talk to Mia—really talk. Put aside what he'd been scared of and talk. He hadn't listened. He hadn't *heard* her. She'd never said she didn't want him, she didn't want to be forced to move. And why should she? She'd lived on that island her whole life. Why would she move her daughter's and her whole lives for him just because he'd been too damaged by betrayal to step into something that could be amazing?

He turned to his boss as they pulled into the station. 'Look, Lewis, I know I've just joined the service again, but I might need to leave. In fact, yes. I need to hand in my notice. Now.'

'What?' Lewis's mouth hung open.

'You're right, it's hard being away from them. I need to be on Rāwhiti. With my girls.' *My girls.*

Maybe…surely…they could make it work? The pieces of his splintered heart started to fit themselves back together as hope suffused his chest.

Lewis blinked. 'That's a huge call, Brin.'

'Yeah, I know. And it's about time I made it.'

Mia stood at the ferry terminal and watched the boat dock. Time was her heart would have danced at the thought of seeing Brin disembark. But he wasn't due for his parental visit until later in the week.

So, she was going to see him. A surprise. She hoped it would be a good one.

The last ferry from the mainland was always busy with people returning from city trips so she waited until the crowd had subsided before stepping forward to hand over her ticket to the deck hand.

'Mia?'

She froze at the sound of that voice—deep, warm and, even in such a short word, with a hint of an Irish accent.

She turned to see Brin striding towards her with a holdall slung over his shoulder.

'Brin?' Was she dreaming? What the hell? She ached to run towards him, but she anchored her feet firmly to the ground. Had he come to see her or Harper? Hope rose in her chest but she squashed it. This was how it was always going to be— her heart dancing at seeing him and then the swift realisation that he was not here for her. 'It's not your day until Friday.'

He nodded. 'My plans have changed.'

'Your roster?' Of course. A thick weight crushed her chest. 'You should have said.'

Close up, he looked nervous, tired. 'Mia, I needed to see you.'

'Me?' Her heart hammered hard against her chest wall.

The roar of an engine had him looking behind as the ferry started to glide away from the dock. 'You're missing the ferry. Where are you going?'

'To find you.'

His expression darkened to worry. 'Why? Has something happened? Why didn't you call?'

'I wanted to see you in person. I need to tell you, Brin. I'm sorry we left. I should have stayed and talked some more.'

He shook his head and walked towards the marina, where it

was quiet. 'We were all out of talking, I think. We were tired and stressed out.'

Did he understand what she was alluding to? 'No. I mean I should have stayed. With you. But...' Courage slipped away, but she grabbed it. 'I was scared of losing you, scared that if I allowed myself to fall for you it could all be snatched away. One day you might not come home.'

He was still frowning but it had changed into confusion and tenderness. He reached and cupped her cheek. 'Hey, nothing's going to happen to me. But, even if it did, then you'd still have my love. Alive or dead, you'd still have me, Mia. Totally, wholly.'

Mia swallowed. Was she hearing him correctly? 'You love me?'

He chuckled. 'Is it possible to love someone so fiercely, even if it's the first time you've met them? I mean, that was how you felt about Harper when you birthed her.'

'Yes, of course, but she's my baby.'

'*Our* baby. And it was exactly how I felt about you. Not love at first sight...but maybe.' He laughed. 'You fell into me, and I was all paramedic, assessing you quietly to make sure you were okay. But, really I was trying to catch my breath. You blew me away from that moment. And that night, talking, making love, my heart was yours—always and only yours. I've loved you fiercely since that day, Mia, and I love you even more each day. And the force of it all and what I could lose, how much risk there was... It scared me. I didn't want to lean into it, I wanted to run.'

'But I ran instead.' She couldn't quite believe this was happening. Tears pricked her eyes and this time they were happy tears and sad tears all mingled together. She should have stayed with him. But he was here now. He'd come for her.

He stroked her arm. 'I've been running from a broken family that doesn't love me, but why should I let that colour what

I could have? *This* family. I love Harper, obviously. But I *love* you, Mia.'

He loved her. She scrubbed away the tears. 'And I love you, Brin. I was coming to tell you. We'll come to the city and live there. We'll grow something new and good between us. My home isn't here with ghosts and memories. My home is with you.'

'Ah.' His eyes narrowed. 'I've handed in my notice. I'm coming to live here.'

She blinked up at him. 'You did what?'

He nodded definitively. 'I'm leaving my job. I'm going to come and live here, where you want to be.'

'And do what? You're a paramedic.'

He shrugged. 'I'll find something.'

'I don't want you to just find something. That's not what love is. I want you to be fulfilled in your job and your life. I want you to be happy.' She put her hand on his chest. 'So maybe we could do both? Work in the city and visit here at weekends. We've got my house here…it could be our holiday home. And we have your place in the city.'

'Our place in the city. For you, me and Harper. Our family.' He tilted up her chin. 'Any home with you sounds perfect.'

She laughed. 'You are perfect.'

'No, you are,' he teased, and wrapped her into his arms. 'Come here. I love you, Mia Edwards.'

'I love you, Brin. So much.' She looked up into his beautiful face and whispered, 'Kiss me.'

And he did.

EPILOGUE

Eight months later...

MIA STOOD IN her Rāwhiti Island bedroom and looked in the full-length mirror at a reflection she'd never believed she'd ever see.

Something old. She ran her fingertips over her mother's precious diamond earrings.

Your little girl's all grown up with a girl of her own. I wish you were here to share this. I miss you. I love you. And Dad and Raff. But I carry you with me in my heart. For ever.

Something new. She sniffed and smiled. No doubt Brin would be very happy with the fancy new lingerie under her gorgeous A-line wedding dress.

Something borrowed. Carly's diamond bracelet hung from her wrist. It had been Mia's parents' wedding gift to Carly all those years ago, so she wore it with pride, and thanks to her friend for her enduring support and love.

Something blue. She put her hand to her belly. She'd only done the test that morning. Two little blue lines explained the nausea…she'd thought it was nerves. But then, she wasn't nervous about marrying this wonderful, caring, handsome man. She slipped the little test into her bag to show him later.

'Mumma! Mumma! Come on.' Harper barrelled into the room, her flower headband at a jaunty angle. Her pretty white dress was slightly creased, but it didn't matter. Life with a toddler was messy and Mia embraced it all. 'Daddy's waiting.'

Daddy.

She couldn't hear it enough. Mia didn't think her heart had ever been so full. She slid her hand into her daughter's and they stepped outside into the sunshine to a chorus of whoops and cheers. It seemed the whole island was there, clapping and laughing.

Even though she lived in Auckland now and worked at a fabulous practice in the city, they spent as much time as possible here. Brin had kept his job as a paramedic and they'd made it work. She had two homes now and she loved them both.

A flotilla of boats followed hers over to the camp. Carly steered, of course. Mia wasn't sure she could handle a boat today. The new owner had jumped at the chance to host a wedding here and had gone a little overboard with the decorating. The jetty was festooned in white chiffon and flowers, a longer aisle than most, but just perfect.

Brin was waiting at the end, so smart in his suit. Her heart almost flew from her chest with happiness, as it did every day whenever she looked at her gorgeous man.

The ceremony took place in the grassy area in front of the beach. Then came a barbecue dinner, dancing and laughter with friends—Anahera, Nicole, Nikau and all the others. *Whanau*: family. Carly, Owen and Mason. Love. So much love.

Later, as they stepped into the honeymoon accommodation in a secluded part of the island, Brin took her in his arms. 'What a wonderful day. You, me and our daughter. A perfect family of three.'

'Ah. About that…' She put her hand on his chest. 'A family of…um…four.'

He frowned. 'What?'

'There's going to be a new addition. Happy wedding, husband.'

'For real? You're pregnant?' At her nod, his eyes grew

moist. 'Whoa. And you've just done the conga around the camp. Sit down. What do you need?'

'For a paramedic, you're mighty concerned about a perfectly normal condition.' She laughed. 'I need you. That's all.'

'How did I get this lucky?' He slid his hand over hers, cradling her barely-there bump. 'This time I get to watch you both grow. I love you, Mrs O'Connor.'

'I love you, Brin. More than anything.' She kissed him. 'Together, for ever.'

A family of…four.

* * * * *

RESISTING THE PREGNANT PAEDIATRICIAN

SUE MacKAY

MILLS & BOON

This book is for my good friend Vicki Rule.

There are days I'd go bonkers
if we couldn't have a wine together.

CHAPTER ONE

'WATCH OUT, YOU IDIOT!' Bella Rosso shouted at the car speeding past.

The driver cut in front of her.

She swore as she slammed her foot on the brake to avoid a collision. 'Some people shouldn't be allowed behind a steering wheel.'

The sun was on its slow descent towards the horizon and the road between Lake Orta and Stresa was busy with people heading home after work. Not a time for any driver to be pushing their way through the traffic. No time was right for that, Bella admitted, jerking forward when her car came to an abrupt stop.

The vehicle causing problems swerved back towards the centre of the road, then veered straight into a small cyclist on a child-sized bike. Make that cyclists plural.

Heart leaping to her throat, Bella eased her car off the road before leaping out to run over to the two small boys lying entangled in the bike frame and wheels. Shock stared up at her from their little faces. 'Hello, boys.' At least, she thought they were boys with their messy short haircuts and tee shirts with trucks on the front. 'I'm a doctor. I'm going to help you, all right?' She was already on her knees beside them, ascertaining the situation. 'Don't try to move until I say so. You might hurt yourselves even more.'

One began crying. 'The car hit us. We didn't do anything wrong.'

'I know. Let me check you over before we worry about that.' She looked around and saw other people racing towards them. 'Someone call the *polizia* and an ambulance.'

'The police are already here. They were on the other side of the roundabout watching the traffic when this happened,' a woman informed her.

'Hope that means they know what went down,' Bella said, half to herself. Because the driver of the car *had* been negligent, the driving shocking.

A man crouched down on the other side of the boys. A steal-her-breath-away kind of man. So good-looking, he couldn't be for real.

'I'm a doctor,' he said, bringing her back on track.

Just as well since there were *two* injured boys to concentrate on helping.

'Good. The more the better. I'm also a doctor.' Then she added for good measure, so he understood that she knew what she was about, 'A paediatrician.'

'Emergency specialist.' He was already carefully moving one boy's arm from between the steering bar and the asphalt path.

'The boys are in good hands, then.'

'You're local?' There was an intriguing accent emphasising his Italian words. Possibly British but she couldn't tell where from, which was odd considering she'd lived and worked in London for four years.

'Yes.' She felt over the head of the other boy.

'I'm currently working at the Stresa Hospital,' he told her.

Was this the temporary emergency specialist she'd heard was meant to start this week while she'd been working in

Milano? More than likely, it was, which meant that from what she'd heard about him the accent was from Scotland.

A woman suddenly shouted, 'Out of the way! I'm a nurse, I'll see to the children.'

The new doctor stood up, wariness all over his face. 'Easy does it.'

'They rode their bike in front of my car. It's their fault this happened.'

Something hard stabbed Bella's shoulder, sending her falling sideways. *Not exactly how I saw the accident unfolding*, she thought as she struggled to right herself.

'Hey, look out.' The wariness changed to annoyance as the doctor stepped between her and the ranting woman. 'Move away. Don't hurt anyone else,' he snapped.

'Not my fault the stupid boys rode in front of me.' The ranting woman tried stepping around him again.

'Lady, move back now.' He stepped with her to prevent the woman getting anywhere near Bella or the boys. She could see he was tense, as if he was expecting trouble. But he was probably used to that if he worked in emergency departments. When the fuming woman didn't move he turned his back on her and reached down to help Bella. 'Here, give me your hand.'

Looking up—a long way up—she nodded. 'Thanks.' One firm tug and she was on her feet, rubbing her shoulder where a small throb had set up.

'Let me through,' the woman shouted again, her arms flailing in all directions, coming up against the doctor's firm stance, whacking his arm.

Bella stepped back, but was too late to avoid knuckles striking her in the side. She gasped. 'Hey.' Her hand immediately reached for her abdomen. There was a baby in there.

'Stop that,' the Scotsman snapped, again stepping between Bella and the apparent madwoman. 'We're doctors and will look after the boys. Please move away. We don't need your help.' He looked around, and called out to the two policemen heading their way. 'Can you remove this woman? She's getting in the way of us seeing to the lads.' He wasn't hesitant in expressing his annoyance and was being protective of her and the boys. He'd definitely come face to face with difficult people before, she'd say.

His accent sent an unexpected thrill down Bella's spine. Totally inappropriate. As well as unasked for. Besides, right now it was the boys needing her attention, not her quiet, steady life. Kneeling down, she returned to looking after the kids, who were shaking and pale. 'It's all right, boys. You're going to be okay. What are your names?'

Her hands were moving up and down the left leg of one lad who, having been on the back of the bike, would've taken the brunt of the knock from the car, from what she'd seen. *Sì*, as she suspected, a fracture to the femur. Getting him free of the wheel wasn't going to be easy, or comfortable. 'Need painkillers fast,' she said aloud.

Neither of the boys had answered with their names. No doubt too shocked to understand what was going on.

'Fractured?' asked her counterpart as he concentrated on the second boy.

'*Sì.*' When in Italy speak Italian, even if she was fluent in English and this man's first language would be English. 'Have the police removed the woman?'

'Yes.' He nodded. 'There's a definite alcohol smell emanating from her.'

'Her driving was dangerous moments before she hit these two.'

'You saw what happened?'

'I did.' She'd talk to the police once the boys were hospital bound. 'I was behind her, and had to brake to avoid being hit.' She couldn't imagine the outcome had she taken the hit in her car instead of these two but they would probably still be happily biking along the side of the road.

The man opposite her was ever so gently moving the front wheel just enough to feel along the other kid's legs, quite the opposite to his manner with the deranged driver who'd caused the accident. 'Fracture in the lower leg.' He looked around as a siren cut through the chatter going on behind them. 'Not before time.'

Talk about impatient. 'That's a fast response,' Bella told him. It couldn't have been many minutes since the call went to 112.

'You're right. It's just that I always hold my breath in serious situations until an ambulance arrives,' he said quietly.

Something she could relate to. One time the ambulance had been too late for the man she was trying to stabilise after a cardiac arrest. Incidents like that never left her.

'Mamma,' finally screamed the boy she was looking after.

Running her hand over his right arm that appeared free of injury, Bella spoke softly. 'Mamma's not here but the policeman will bring her to see you at the hospital.' They needed some info to go on. The boys were wearing the local school's uniform, which was a start. Names would help a lot more. 'What's your name?'

'An-Andrea.' Tears streamed down the sides of his face. 'I want Mamma.'

Her heart was breaking for him. This had to be so frightening. Surrounded with people he didn't recognise, his mother not here to make him feel better, and then there was the pain and shock. If only she could lift him into her arms and hug away all the trauma. Instead she went with smoothing back the hair stuck to his forehead. 'What's your friend's name?'

'Mattia.'

The other boy was lying still, eyes closed, his breathing rapid and shallow.

'Can you hear me, Mattia?' the ED specialist asked. 'I'm Aaron, a doctor.'

The boy slowly opened his eyes, but said nothing.

Aaron. Come to think of it, she might have heard that name mentioned before. 'I'm glad they were wearing helmets,' she said. The consequences of being slammed into the pavement could've been far worse. Not that either of them would be cycling for a while to come. 'We need some serious painkillers here, otherwise extricating these two from the bike is going to be unbearable.' Not happening on her watch.

'Agreed.' Aaron looked around. 'Help's arrived.'

Within moments paramedics had taken over and were administering drugs to numb the pain before putting both boys on oxygen, then she and Aaron helped remove them from the mangled cycle to place them on stretchers.

Finally she was able to stand up straight, only to wince as a sharp pain stabbed her in the side. Her hand hovered over her abdomen. That woman had better not have hurt her baby. That would really get her wound up and on the warpath. Not that she'd be able to do a thing about it. But she wanted this baby so badly the mere idea of losing it made her blood boil. Jason might not be alive to meet his child, but she would do all in her power to make up for his absence. It had taken nearly three years for her to finally feel ready to have in vitro insemination and nothing, nobody, was going to get in the way of this pregnancy going full term.

'You all right?' Aaron stood in front of her, looking concerned.

'I'm fine, thank you.' But very angry.

Calm down, Bella. A smack in the side isn't likely to jeopardise your baby.

True. She did get a bit paranoid about her pregnancy at times. Doing it alone got her uptight whenever the slightest little thing went wrong. She chose not to download her worry on anyone, which got a bit lonely at times. While her family hovered over her pretty much non-stop, she didn't like to tell any of them her fears about something going wrong with the pregnancy. They'd only get even more determined to keep her wrapped up in cotton wool, and she was well and truly over that. Since Jason died she'd slowly got back on her feet and begun facing life again, and now she was not going back to that dark, sad place ever again.

'You sure?' The doctor was watching her very closely. Too closely for someone who didn't know her. There was nothing but concern in his face, but still. He didn't need to know about her pregnancy. Or her OTT worries.

But why was he so concerned?

She didn't need his concern on top of everyone else's in her life right now. 'Yes. What about you?'

'I'm fine.'

'Thank you for intervening with that woman. She was definitely on a mission.' Bella looked around for the police. She'd go and fill them in on the details of the accident she'd witnessed. Accident? Really? When the woman had been going too fast and was obviously under the influence? Technically the incident would be written up as an accident, but she'd seen the results of so-called accidents far too often during her medical training to think of them as anything other than bad decision-making with horrendous consequences for innocent people. 'I'll talk to the police about what happened.'

'I'm Aaron Marshall, and here for the next four months.' He held his hand out. 'I'm sure we'll see a bit of each other at the hospital. It's not exactly a huge place.' His smile had become warm and full of confidence, like a man used to getting his own way over just about anything and everything. Especially if he used that smile.

Well, it wasn't getting to her. She was immune to charming men. Jason had been the love of her life, and there wouldn't be another one of those hanging around for her. No one got two goes at such a deep love.

'I'm sure we will.' She shook his hand briefly, then stepped back, needing to put a hold on the sudden heat that flared between their hands. 'Bella Rosso. Nice to meet you.'

That suck-her-in smile remained. 'Not in the best of circumstances.'

'No.' She turned around to head for the policewoman talking to a man on the side of the road. There was no need to hang around being polite with Aaron. As he said, they'd bump into each other at work. That was enough. He might be intriguing with that spine-tingling accent and tall build—*why did tall men turn her on?*—but her future was mapped out and it did not include getting involved with the temporary ED doc.

Or any man, for that matter. She'd loved Jason with all her heart, and couldn't imagine loving another man as much. So far, the three dates she had gone on in the last year to shut her family down about getting out there again had been enjoyable but not filled with heat and passion.

Pleasant, not exciting. More about pretending to be having a full life so her family backed off.

Unfortunately those dates had only endorsed the fact the love she'd known with her late husband had been special and rare and wasn't going to be repeated. Now she had her wonderful career, and a baby to bring into the world and raise the best she could. Along with help and understanding from her three bossy brothers and parents who often hinted she shouldn't be doing this alone.

Tough. She was. Nothing was going to change that. Nothing and nobody. In the last weeks of Jason's life they'd talked for hours about her having their baby when he was gone. He'd been concerned that she might not cope alone while working at the career she'd always dreamed about, but he'd also made it very clear it would be amazing if she did go ahead. She'd pointed out that if she hadn't miscarried months earlier she'd already be facing parenting on her own. She couldn't make him any promises about going ahead with a pregnancy, even if deep down she knew she would have his baby. Their baby. It was a way to keep Jason with her. She didn't regret it at all.

It was too late for regrets, anyway.

Aaron pulled into Gino's *ristorante* car park and turned off the car. Linguine and a glass of Pinot Grigio was what he needed after a busy day in ED followed by that accident with the two kids knocked off their bike. He wasn't allowing any thoughts of Dr Bella Rosso into the mix. Not even how she'd turned her back on him and walked across to the officer to talk about what she'd seen go down when the car took out those boys.

Sure, she'd been doing the right thing, but she didn't

have to be so abrupt with him. He was only being open and friendly, which usually won most women over.

Did he want to win over this particular one? Why? Partly because she hadn't dropped to her knees at the sight of him as so many women usually did. Because of his famous family, his face and name went before him and made life tedious when it came to keeping clout-chasing women at bay. So far that hadn't happened here in Italy but he knew it was only a matter of time.

No denying a fling to while away the hours when he wasn't at work would be fun and would help him relax some, might even help him sleep a little at night. Plus it would add to his Italian experience. He sensed Bella wasn't going to be the one to make his nights pass in enjoyment and help him get his mojo back. She was a bit too serious for his taste.

You were at an accident scene. Of course she was serious.

There hadn't been any smiles forthcoming afterwards though.

She still had to talk to the police.

Seeing those two little guys slammed into by a car had probably wiped any thought of a smile off her lovely face. Plus the way that woman shoved her out of the way with no consideration for anyone else whatsoever. His initial reaction had been fear she might attack him or the paediatrician—a serious attack like the one that nearly took his life back in Edinburgh—but he'd quickly reclaimed his composure, and the need to protect had kicked in fast, as per normal. He'd been too late to prevent Dr Bella falling to the ground. He ground his teeth. What was that other woman on? He thought he'd smelt alcohol but could be wrong. She might just be OTT. Guess he'd never know, and didn't really need to. But the stunned look on Bella's face as she fell remained with him. He hadn't caught her in time.

'Give it a break,' Aaron muttered and shoved the car door open. He didn't need any hassles. He was here to get back up to speed after a galling incident back in Edinburgh. His left hand automatically rubbed the top of his thigh where the knife had sliced through the artery. Attacked by a drugged-up patient during an extremely disorderly night in the emergency department back home, he'd been lucky to survive. The blood loss had been serious to the point he wouldn't have made it if he hadn't been in the centre of the department with all the equipment and staff to deal with such an emergency. *And* if the security guard hadn't been right there taking down the man as he raised his knife to have another crack at the doctor who wasn't doing anything to fix his broken toe.

Aye. There were always egotists in emergency departments demanding they be seen to before anyone else, no matter where the triage nurse put them on the list of waiting patients. What a night that had been. One that wasn't going away any time soon. He'd barely slept since. Every time his eyes closed, a picture appeared in full colour of that knife arcing into him and showing the hatred in his attacker's eyes being replaced with glee when Aaron dropped to the floor in agony. No, sleep was highly overrated when it was full of images he'd give almost anything to forget.

A decent meal would go a long way to quietening the tension that rolled through him on a regular basis for no apparent reason other than he was exhausted and unable to put the attack behind him. A full night's sleep would be even better but not as easy to order up… *No*, make that impossible to order up!

After a quick stop at his house he'd headed to the restaurant he'd seen in town. As he walked in the sound of laughter reached him and he glanced around to see a large table by the far wall with what appeared to be a family having dinner.

His breath caught. Amongst the group sat Bella. And man, was she attractive when she was smiling freely. His gut clenched. He breathed deep and long, urging the tightness to back off. He'd known plenty of beautiful women yet this one seemed to flick a switch, tipping his carefully held-in emotions off balance.

'You'd like a table for one, *signor*?'

He'd far prefer to join Bella's group, but that wasn't happening. Something he should be grateful for. '*Sì.* Thank you.'

'Over here by the window. Not that you can see the lake now that it's dark.' The waitress laughed over her shoulder, her large eyes giving him the once-over. 'But it's a nice place to sit. Away from the noisy family too.'

The family looked right at home. The children were laughing and eating and getting the occasional growl from one of the adults. 'Is this their restaurant?'

'*Sì.* Gino and his wife own it, and the others are all relatives. They eat here most nights of the week.'

Bella appeared to be part of a large family by the looks of that table. A happy family with no restraints on their voices and laughter. Lucky woman. Not something he was used to. Taking the chair the waitress pulled out, he sat down. 'Could I have a glass of Pinot Grigio, please?'

'Certainly. Here's the menu. Tonight's special is the seafood spaghetti.'

Leaning back in his chair, he stared out of the window, aiming for peace and quiet, trying to ignore the unexpected longing bubbling up in him to be involved in such a display of closeness. Beyond the gardens surrounding the parking area, the road was quieter than it had been as he'd made his way to his accommodation after the accident. He'd rented a small house on the hillside overlooking Lake Maggiore for four months, and it was perfect. The views were amazing and the neighbours welcoming without being pushy.

Of course, they knew nothing about him, something he aimed for every time he went somewhere new. Being part of a famous family had drawbacks. He preferred to live quietly and get on with his own career without those of his parents and sister dragging him into media frenzies he disliked intensely. They took away his privacy and his individuality.

Despite the night view, he could see beyond the road to the bumpy lake surface glittering in the light of the full moon peeking over the Alps. The tiny island Isola Bella with its castle was dark except for a few lights on the lower floor. He couldn't have chosen a better place to take a break. The emergency department kept him busy in a more relaxed way than what he was used to. Which meant he wasn't continuously feeling uptight and frantic to keep the patients moving through the system, and not eyeing every one of them as a potential threat. Something else that was a hangover from the attack.

'Here you go, *signor.*' A glass of wine appeared in front of him.

After a quick perusal of the menu he ordered the linguine he'd been looking forward to and sipped the wine. Aye, not a bad way to end a day. Reflected in the window to his right was a view of the family on the other side of the wide room. Even sitting side on to him, Bella stood out. Appearing relaxed and happy, she was talking to the older woman next to her between mouthfuls of pasta. It was as if there were two Bella Rossos. He'd probably only get to know the serious version since they'd mostly see each other at the hospital and even then only when a child was in need of a paediatrician.

With a pang of disappointment he sipped his wine again. At least that was reliable, tasted the same as the first mouthful and wouldn't change by the end of the glass.

It was crazy he should be thinking he'd like to get Bella's attention when he spent most of his time avoiding being noticed. Growing up in his family came with its downside. Because his mother was an actress with multiple awards to her name and his father a top judge often causing a stir in court in London, everyone from the media to hangers-on thought they had a right to know what he was up to and who with any time they asked. As if it had anything to do with them. His sister soaked up the attention like a sponge as she made her way up the ladder as a camerawoman in the movie industry. Not him.

He'd always felt uncomfortable but it had got a whole lot worse when Amy came into his life. That was when he truly grappled with the consequences of his family's fame. In the end Amy left him because she loathed the constant pressure from the media.

Aaron sat back as the waitress placed a plate of linguine in front of him. *'Grazie.'*

Amy had taught him the biggest lesson of his life. Not to judge people until he knew the facts. He'd thought she'd be able to handle being with him because she was quite laidback and easy-going. He was clearly wrong, or she'd still be with him. Hence his dislike of the media had grown. All he wanted was to be able to get on with his work and personal life without interference, and to help others along the way, whether medically, financially or by lending an ear. One thing he was grateful for at the moment was that it appeared Dr Rosso hadn't recognised his face or name. Then again, here in Stresa there was less likelihood of that happening, which was why he'd applied for the job here.

So relax, why don't you? Make the most of where you are and what you've got. Stop worrying about what you can't change.

Not something he was good at, but he'd give it a go. For the millionth time. Otherwise coming here was a waste of time. He had to get over the attack so the nightmares stopped, so that he didn't get wound up whenever a patient raised their voice. Only then would life be so much easier to deal with.

The first mouthful of linguine slid across his tongue, exciting his taste buds. 'Delicious.'

'Isn't it?' agreed the waitress as she went past with three full plates balanced on her arm. The smile she gave him was open and suggested she was willing to share something else if he asked.

He smiled to himself. It would be nice to lose himself in a woman for an hour or two, but somehow he couldn't find the enthusiasm to do anything about it.

Sorry, but not tonight, if at all.

Tucking into his meal, he let the food, wine and general atmosphere take over dulling the permanent tension in his body for a while. Something easier to do tonight than he'd experienced in a long time. Nothing to do with Dr Rosso. Couldn't be. He hadn't glanced her way since ordering his meal, and he was trying hard to ignore the image in the window where Bella was now standing and gathering empty plates.

She turned and stopped, her gaze fixed on him. Of course she wouldn't know he could see her in the window. That could be called creepy. He focused on the view once more and forked up another mouthful of pasta. Breathed deep to find that relaxed feeling again. Sipped his wine. Ate some more. Working together was going to be tricky if this was how he reacted to Bella's image in the window.

'Can I get you another wine?' The waitress appeared on the opposite side of his small table. 'Or the dessert menu?'

He leaned back in his chair. 'I'll have a coffee, thank you.'

'Are you staying in Stresa long?' she asked as she took his plate. 'The tourist season is getting under way but already the number of diners at the restaurant is picking up.'

'Is accommodation a part of this business as well?' he asked, avoiding her question. Lights had been on in lots of rooms on the floor above the restaurant when he'd arrived. The car park was also full.

'Level two has eight hotel rooms. Then the top level is for Gino's family, along with a small apartment where his sister lives. She's having a baby and her brother likes to keep a protective eye on her.' This woman obviously had no inhibitions over talking about the people she worked for.

Best to keep well clear of her, even for a few hours. He knew where a loose tongue could lead and he didn't need that. No one did. 'Coffee?'

Her mouth flattened a little. *'Sì, signor.'*

'Grazie.'

Looking around the room, he noted he was the only one dining alone. Every table had people laughing and talking loudly. Holidaymakers or locals? Most likely a mix as the tourist season was getting up to speed with June being warm while not overly hot.

Coffee finished, Aaron stood up with the intention of paying his tab and heading out into the night. He'd take the car back to his accommodation then go for a stroll beside the lake. A glance across to the family table and he found Bella watching him. Changing direction, he headed her way. It would be rude to walk out without acknowledging her. 'Hello, Bella. I didn't expect to see you again so soon.'

'Aaron, welcome to the family restaurant. I hope you enjoyed your meal.'

A man sitting further along the table stiffened.

'The linguine was superb,' Aaron said. 'I'll be back to try some of the other dishes during my time in Stresa,' he added with a smile.

'You can relax, Gino,' Bella said. 'So, Aaron, have you heard how those boys are doing?'

'Mattia's had his leg put in a cast and is staying overnight in the hospital. While Andrea has been transferred to the main hospital in Milan where an orthopaedic surgeon will insert a rod in his femur tomorrow.' He'd called the ED to find out the outcome of the boys' X-rays before coming here. 'He'll be returned to us either tomorrow or the day after.'

'Bella's been telling us about the accident. You were there?' the man he presumed was Gino asked.

'Yes. I'm Aaron Marshall, working in the ED department over summer.' He held his hand out to the man.

'Gino Rosso, Bella's brother.' The man had stood up, back straight, a direct look at Aaron.

Your sister's safe with me, pal.

He wasn't interested in getting serious with any woman, not even a beautiful lady with eyes he could drown in. It would only lead to someone being hurt. But Bella was stunningly hot.

'Pleased to meet you. And yes, I reiterate, dinner was delicious.'

'*Grazie.* Do come again.'

Turning back to Bella, Aaron asked, 'How's your side where you took that blow from the woman's elbow?'

'What? Who hit you?' Gino snapped. 'Are you hurt? Bella, answer me.'

After glaring at Aaron, Bella faced off her brother. 'Calm down, Gino. It's nothing. The woman who drove into the boys on the cycle knocked into me when she rushed to check on them. I fell over, that's all.'

Not quite how it happened, but Aaron gave a mental shrug. She'd taken hard knocks in her side and shoulder, and he'd seen her rubbing where she'd been hit a couple of times at the accident scene. But if Bella didn't want her brother getting wound up by the fact that it had been a deliberate knock, then he'd go along with her. He had to work with this woman, and any hindrance could be a pain in the backside. 'It was a little chaotic for a few moments, but the woman was removed and we got on with helping the boys.'

Gino eyeballed him, then nodded. 'Thank you for being there for Bella.'

He'd have done the same thing for anyone. 'No problem.'

'I'd better get back to the kitchen. Those cooks are slack when I'm not there to watch over them.'

Bella shook her head at her brother. 'They're too scared of you to take a breath.' Her voice was full of affection. 'He only talks tough. He's a pussycat on the inside.'

Gino strode away without comment.

'Whichever, he's a darned good chef. People say pasta's pasta, how can you go wrong with cooking it? I disagree. Done well, nothing beats it.'

'You're from Scotland?'

'Yes. Our food couldn't be more different.'

'I lived in London for four years and hankered after Gino's cooking all the time.'

Glancing around to make sure none of the family was within hearing, he found he was being sized up by the older woman Bella had been sitting by.

Wasting your time, lady.

The other man still remaining resembled Gino, and Bella, he saw now he looked more closely. Another brother, most like. He turned back to Bella and said quietly, 'Are you sure you're all right? She did slam into you fairly hard.'

'I'm fine. Thank you for asking though. Now I'd better get the table cleared. I'll see you at the hospital tomorrow or later on in the week. Goodnight.' She added more dirty plates to those she already held and walked away.

'Goodnight, Bella.'

She didn't look back.

Fair enough. Though it was a new experience for him. It was usually he who drew the line under getting too friendly. He headed to the young man standing at the desk. 'I'd like to pay my bill, thank you.'

'It's been taken care of, sir. Gino said the meal was on him.'

'That can't be right. I only met him a few minutes ago.'

'You looked out for Bella today. That means a lot to this family. Goodnight, sir. Hopefully we'll see you again some time soon.'

Stunned, Aaron wandered outside. He couldn't remember ever being thanked in that way. People usually wanted something from him. Even though this family didn't know who he was, he doubted it would've made a difference if they did. He liked that a lot.

But a meal on the house? For helping Bella to her feet? Any decent man would have done the same.

Hold on. The waitress mentioned a sister living upstairs. A pregnant sister. Bella? That would explain the concern in her eyes as she rubbed her side. He hadn't noticed her being pregnant but then he hadn't been looking hard. If she was pregnant then she was out of bounds. There was already a man in her life.

Hard to explain the disappointment filling him as he walked out to his car though.

CHAPTER TWO

'BELLA, PHONE FOR YOU. It's ED.' Gita handed the phone over.

'Bella Rosso speaking.'

'Bella, it's Aaron. We've got a fourteen-year-old girl presenting with injuries after a fall. But I think there's something else going on that might've caused her to trip in the first place. Can you come along to see her?' He sounded professional, nothing like the sexy man she'd met three days ago.

Which was good since they'd be working together, and because she wasn't interested in him anyway, sexy or not.

Sure, Bella.

So why hadn't she been able to put him out of her mind ever since she'd first bumped into him at the accident, even when she had more important things to think about? 'On my way.'

'Thanks.' *Click.* He'd gone.

Not sticking around to talk about anything else, then. She should be thankful, given some of the locum doctors thought chatting about anything *but* their patient was fine. But she couldn't help but feel a little disgruntled. Hadn't he wanted to say hello? Or ask why she didn't want Gino knowing how that woman had flattened her so easily?

She'd seen the look on his face when she'd downplayed

the altercation. He'd clearly taken note of her reluctance to alarm Gino. Her brother fussed over her enough without adding to it with a minor thing that had no repercussions. 'I'm heading to ED,' she told Nurse Gita. 'Here's a new prescription for Joseph. I'm not happy with how the infection's taking so long to clear so he's to stay in for another night. We'll get some more bloods done too.'

Joseph had a high white cell count with abundant immature neutrophils, backing the diagnosis of infection in his abdomen where he'd had an appendectomy three days ago. She hadn't done the surgery, but had been left with the problem of clearing his infection. Now she was beginning to think there was more going on than just an infection.

She signed the lab form she'd printed off. 'There you go. Haematology and biochemistry samples.' Standing up, she rubbed the dull ache remaining in her side where that woman's elbow had got her. Better remember not to do that in front of Dr Aaron. He'd be quick to comment, and she already had enough people keeping a beady eye on her.

Anyone would think she was incapable of looking out for herself. So untrue. She'd managed perfectly well since Jason's illness and passing, thank you very much. Sort of, anyway. Lonely at times, and at first it'd been hard to make decisions about her future, but these days she was back on her feet and coping just fine. She'd also made a big decision and it was nestled inside her, keeping safe. Her hand slid to her growing abdomen, touched lightly. 'Hey, baby, how're you doing?'

'You all right?' Gita asked.

Damn it. She really needed to be circumspect on where and when she talked to her baby. 'I'm fine,' she said firmly. Then with a long sigh, 'Sorry, Gita. I didn't mean to snap. I had a bit of a sleepless night, that's all.' It was true. Dreams of Jason had got mixed up with images of a tall Scotsman looking out for her at the accident scene and then kept her awake for hours trying to forget them.

'I had lots of those during both my pregnancies. Worrying about everything under the sun.'

'Glad to know I'm normal, then.' She laughed tightly as she headed out of the door. Nothing normal about thinking of another man when she was carrying her late husband's child. *Or was it?* Who knew what was normal any more? Her world had been tipped upside down and sent spinning out of control when Jason was diagnosed with end-stage myeloma. She might be back on track, but there were days—and nights—when she really wondered if she was plain nuts to be having a baby on her own even when they'd discussed it in depth time and again in the final weeks of Jason's life. Talk was one thing, reality quite another.

It was strange not having Jason around to share the excitement and talk about baby's future with. He'd been happy for her to have their child, but it wasn't the same as him actually being here with her. She'd known what she was letting herself in for before undergoing the IVF—or so she'd thought. Some days it was a little scary thinking about what lay ahead, but mostly it was exciting.

'Morning, Bella.' Aaron crossed the emergency room when she walked in. Aaron's dark blue eyes were locked on her, sending an unexpected shiver down her spine. 'How's things?'

'All good, thanks.'

Apart from this sense of awakening that's developed since I laid eyes on you.

What was wrong with her? Even if she opened up to the possibility, there was no room for romance in her life with baby on the way.

'Glad to hear that.' He took a quick step back. Too close?

'Tell me more about your young patient.' She needed to focus on work, and ignore the odd sensations Aaron was causing. Odd in that she hadn't felt anything close to desire in years. Also totally out of place. Getting into a long-term relationship now she was carrying her and Jason's baby would be awkward. He'd never get the opportunity to meet his child, and to bring another man into the picture mightn't work. Anyway, she intended to raise it herself.

Don't say that to your brothers.

They were already getting their digs in about how to bring up him or her.

'Tish Gambolli presented with a fractured wrist and con-cussion after falling off a first-floor deck. There's a rash on her face and swelling in her arms. Her mother says the swelling and rash have been apparent for a couple of months but became worse over the last couple of days.' Aaron led the way to a computer and brought up the notes he'd entered.

'Is Tish a local?' If so there might be info from earlier medical incidents.

'The family's visiting from Genoa for a month, staying with relatives.'

Nothing to go by then. Leaning closer to read the brief notes pertaining to Tish, Bella tried to ignore the pervading scent of the outdoors emanating from the man beside her. Hard to do when he was so close. The smell brought back old memories of walking in the hills beyond the town with Jason the first time he came here to meet her family. How did this guy get that scent? It didn't come in an aerosol can. Had he been out walking in the early hours that morning? He might be someone who leapt out of bed when the sun peeked over the horizon and got outdoors to make the most of the day before it became too hot.

Talking about hot, there was a wave of heat blasting through her right now and it had nothing to do with her physical condition. Stepping sideways, she said, 'Take me to meet her.'

'Sure,' he drawled in that sexy accent.

'Sorry, I didn't mean to be so abrupt.' That was what happened when she needed to dampen down the sudden awareness of him.

'No problem. I told Tish's mother I was seeking your opinion. She's happy with that.'

'Good.'

'Along here.' Aaron led her past a row of unoccupied cubicles to the end of the room, where he swished back the curtain and indicated she should enter first. 'Tish, this is Dr Rosso,' he said over her shoulder, startling her. Damn, she was edgy around him.

'*Ciao*, Tish. Call me Bella.'

'My head hurts.' Her speech was slurred, no doubt due to the concussion Aaron mentioned.

'I'm sure Aaron has that under control.'

'I've administered mild analgesics,' Aaron told her. 'This is Gabby, Tish's mother.'

'Hello, Gabby. I hear Tish hasn't been feeling well lately, with rashes and some swelling happening.' The teen's face was red with a rash around her eyes. Aaron was on the ball with this one. He probably was with all his patients. He had that air of confidence about him that would lead patients to believe in him.

'That's correct.'

Why hadn't they been to a doctor about this? 'Tish, can I look at your arms?'

Tish nodded. 'All right.'

'Tell me if it hurts when I touch you.' The limbs were hot and spongy where Bella prodded carefully.

Tish didn't complain about any pain, which was a plus.

'I need you to sit up so I can look at your head.' Bella knew hair loss could be a side effect of lupus.

Tish shuffled up the bed, then swayed and fell sideways, her eyes staring sightlessly.

Aaron was immediately at her side, catching her before she slid over the edge of the bed. 'Easy does it.'

'What happened?' shrieked Tish's mother.

'She fainted,' Bella answered as she helped Aaron move the girl to the centre of the bed. What was going on? 'Concussion, then a faint.' Bella's finger was on Tish's pulse. 'Erratic.'

Tish's eyes opened. 'Mamma?'

'I'm here, sweetheart.'

'I feel sick.'

Aaron had a bowl out of the bedside cabinet and next to Tish before she'd finished talking. 'Use this if necessary.'

Bella gave her a few minutes then asked, 'I need to find out Tish's haemoglobin level. Do you get overly tired at times, Tish?'

'Sometimes,' she muttered reluctantly.

'Most days,' Gabby intervened. 'I thought that was due to her age and her body changing from a girl to a woman.'

Tish blushed and looked anywhere but at Aaron, who discreetly turned away to study the monitor by the bed.

Points for his empathy, Bella thought. Not a pushy male doctor who believed all female patients should accept his presence because he *was* a doctor.

There was quite a bit to like about him.

As in working comfortably alongside him when necessary, nothing else.

Right.

He was hard to ignore though.

'I'll arrange for some bloods to be taken and sent off to the lab.'

She had barely finished her sentence when a nurse appeared at the door. 'Aaron, the ambulance has arrived with two tourists who went over the side of the hill on cycles. One with serious injuries. Luka wants all hands on deck. He's already tied up with a cardio infarct.'

'Coming.'

'Need my help?' Bella asked, sensing the urgency in his voice.

'Sounds like it,' Aaron answered, already heading out of the cubicle. Then he spun back around. 'Tish, Gabby, we'll be back as soon as possible. In the meantime take it easy. One of the nurses will keep an eye on you. There's nothing to panic about.'

As Bella scrubbed up next to Aaron she couldn't help thinking how they were about to work together in an emergency for the second time in only a few days. It was rare for her to be helping in ED other than when it was a child specifically referred to her for specialist treatment. It was as though some outside force was saying, *You two are meant to be together.*

But they weren't.

Aaron made her toes tingle with just one look, but that was not a reason to get serious about him.

In medical situations he made everything look so easy. Was he like that outside the hospital walls? Or was this merely his professional manner and he was more demanding of people in his personal life?

He hadn't been the other night at the restaurant.

Instead he was quiet and appreciative of his dinner. He

didn't pester her about how she felt after being knocked over earlier once he understood Gino would get concerned. It didn't necessarily mean a lot. Aaron might've been on his best behaviour, though somehow she found that hard to believe. Everything she'd observed about him so far said he was a good guy who thought about others, the kind of man she went for. If she was going for one, which she wasn't.

She'd had the love of her life, and no one got a second crack at that. Not often anyway, and chances were she wouldn't. Taking another chance on love didn't feel right. She'd been so lucky with Jason. Now she was following up by having his baby. Her family had backed her all the way once Jason talked to them about it, as he did with his parents. They too accepted her decision to go through with motherhood, but she doubted they'd be so happy if she found a new man to live with, and thereby become the father of their son's child. After three years they were still clinging to Jason, almost as if he'd stepped out for a few hours and would be home any moment.

Entering the ED drew her attention back to the intense situation. A stretcher was being wheeled into the department, the young man lying on it attached to fluids and a breathing apparatus. A cervical collar held his head still. The paramedic handed Aaron a clipboard. 'Jonathon Stitchbury, twenty-four. He took full impact on the head when he went over the side of the hill on his bike, has no reaction in his feet to touch. He's been unconscious all the time we've been with him, and the people who found him say he was like that all the time. He also has deep lacerations to his lower back, shoulders and upper arms.'

'Thanks.' Aaron was reading the notes. 'Emano, tell Luka I need Bella with me on this one. He might need to call in someone else.'

The hospital was small and not set up to cater for a huge influx of patients or more than a couple requiring urgent attention and equipment, so in major emergency crises doctors from all the departments were available to help in ED.

'He's already onto it,' the nurse replied as he made ready with the spinal board for them to shift Jonathon across to the hospital bed.

Bella took her place at one corner. It had been a long time since she'd helped a patient with a serious spinal injury but she hadn't forgotten the tension amongst the medical staff as they raced to save the person from further problems all the while hoping against the odds that there'd be nothing too wrong.

'One, two, three,' Emano said, and he and the paramedic rolled Jonathon onto his side so Bella and Aaron could slide a board under him to lower his body down without inflicting more damage.

'Bella, you start at the feet while I check his abdomen and chest.' Aaron was already cutting the sports pants away to expose Jonathon's lower body.

'Onto it.' Definitely no response to the tapping and prodding on the man's feet. She lifted a hand and tapped the palm. The patient's fingers curled instinctively. Same result with the other hand. 'Feeling in both arms.'

'Internal injuries are likely given the impact he's obviously undergone.' Aaron's fingers were pressing gently around the abdomen, but there was an urgency about him that made her wonder if he'd already found an injury.

Placing the stethoscope on Jonathon's chest, she listened to the heartbeat. It was slow and erratic. Then…silence. 'Code one,' she snapped and clasped her hands together to begin compressions. 'One, two, three, four.' Continuing to push and release, she willed the young man to live.

Aaron stepped up, ready to breathe into the man's lungs when she reached thirty compressions. 'He's bleeding internally. Majorly, I'd say.'

Emano shoved the defibrillator into his hands.

Within seconds Aaron had the pads in place and was waiting impatiently for the machine to get up to speed. Moments later the alarm sounded and he said, 'Stand back, everyone.' After looking to make certain no one stood close enough to get an electrical zap, he pressed the button.

Jonathon's body jerked upward, fell back. The flat line on the screen began rising and falling.

Bella felt her heart begin pounding as she placed the stethoscope back in place on the man's chest. 'That was close.'

'I don't think we're out of trouble yet,' Aaron said. He looked around. 'Emano, get ready for a procedure. Bella, call the duty anaesthetist, though I can't wait if he's not in the hospital. I'm going in asap. I need to stop the blood loss before another cardiac arrest occurs.'

Bella raced to the phone on the wall and pressed the theatre number. It might be a small hospital but they had staff to cover most emergencies. She got a voice message and left one of her own just in case the anaesthetist got it in time. 'Jack, you're needed in ED. Now.' Slamming the phone down, she returned to Jonathon's side and took over listening to his heart and monitoring his obs so Aaron could prep for the incision he had to make. 'No one picked up.'

'Probably in Theatre,' Aaron acknowledged, his face grim. 'We have to do this.'

'Tell me what you want all the way,' Bella said, aware of every move he made and the tension growing in his shoulders. He was on high alert. Did he think his patient was going to bleed out before he repaired the injury? It was possible. Nearly an hour had passed since the man fell off the cliffside. 'You've got this, Aaron,' she said quietly.

'You don't know that yet.' He was inside the abdomen feeling for the bleeding site. 'Got it. Emano, suture kit. Bella, press here hard.' He took her hand and placed it where his had been. Sweat was breaking out on his forehead. Something was up with him. It was possible he'd lost a patient before in a similar crisis, and doctors never forget those experiences, questioning themselves over whether they could have done something more to save the person.

The heart monitor alarmed again.

Bella kept her hand in place until the last possible moment, stepped back while the shock was delivered, then returned to put pressure back on the bleeding site. 'At least his heart started again,' she said, more to herself than anyone else.

'One thing to be grateful for,' Aaron answered as he began suturing the torn blood vessel between Bella's fingers. *If this man doesn't survive I'm going to kick myself for ever and beyond*, he thought as he pulled the thread through and tied it off. His colleagues had done this for him the night he was attacked and they'd told him how hard it was with him being a mate and fellow doctor. He mightn't know Jonathon but the pressure to get this right even when he was on the back foot with it being so long since the injury happened was driving him hard.

Bella shifted her hand slightly to allow him to place the next suture. She had her eye on the job. Certainly knew what she was doing.

'Next needle,' he demanded.

Emano passed one over, took the other out of the way.

The needle went through, and he tied another knot. Nearly there. He held his hand out for another needle.

Bella leaned closer, said quietly, 'Breathe.'

He hadn't realised he wasn't. Inhale, exhale. Put another stitch in place. Inhale. Now Bella would have questions he had no intention of answering. Too bad. The bleeding was slowing as the hole became tiny. Almost there. He was winning. That was all that mattered. That and ordering O-negative blood for Jonathon. Damn, he should've done something about that already. As if there'd been time. 'Bella, can you call the lab for some blood?' He didn't need her pressure on the wound now.

'On it.'

He liked how she didn't muck around, just did whatever he asked. No ego in sight. This was his domain but over the years in emergency departments he had come across one or two specialists wanting to flex a muscle just to show they knew their job. 'Thanks.'

He doubted she heard him; she was only focused on what was important as she lifted the phone. They worked well together in emergencies. He'd laugh if it weren't ridiculous. They worked in different medical fields and for this to happen twice in a few days was weird. It was as if they were meant to get to know each other.

There, last suture done. He straightened up and stood back to look Jonathon over. His skin was white, his breathing laboured—but at least he was breathing with the aid of the oxygen pump. His heart rate was slow but stable. Aaron sighed with relief. He'd done it. They'd done it. Bella, Emano and him. This was one patient he wasn't going to spend weeks wondering if he could've done more for. There was still a lot to do, like getting blood into his patient, and preparing him for the journey to a hospital in Milan, but the odds were on Jonathon's side now.

'Here. For your face.' Bella was back, handing him a wipe. She must have noticed his moist brow. Then she went back to the monitors, studying them intently as though trying to give him some space.

Guess she'd seen another side to him. He *had* stressed, but nothing serious enough to get in the way of making certain his patient survived. He rubbed the sweat off his brow and face and tossed the wipe in the bin.

'You were a great help.' Very calm and logical. Beautiful came to mind. Beautiful in how she worked. Not once had she tensed or looked flustered. She'd got on with doing what needed to be done and did it competently, never questioning him. He gasped. When she'd told him to breathe *he* had calmed down and got a grip on his emotions. That attack in Edinburgh had a lot to answer for. He'd always wanted the best outcome for any patient, but since that horrific night he felt more in touch with what someone like Jonathon had just gone through. His actions weren't impeded, but his body reacted with tension—*and faulty breathing, apparently.*

Bella flicked him a brief smile. 'If you don't need me for anything else, I'll get back to Tish. I have some patient appointments to get back to at the clinic.'

The department would feel empty without her. 'We've got this now. Again, thanks for your assistance.'

'You're overdoing it.' She grinned.

And just like that, his stomach tightened and his head spun. Bella Rosso was something else. Something, no, *someone* he didn't need in his life right now. Somehow he didn't think that was going to change a thing. She was already nudging her way in without even trying. If she really turned her attention on him, he didn't stand a chance. He had to get real here. 'That's me. An over-doer.'

Two hours later Bella was back in the department, and his heart was beating faster than normal, telling him he needed to work at sorting his act out, because she was getting to him without any effort. The problem was he couldn't avoid her around the hospital. Nor did he really want to, if he was being honest with himself. 'Have you got some results back on Tish?' he asked.

Her nod was abrupt. 'I have.'

'Not good?'

'I'm certain about the lupus. Well spotted,' she added with a grim look.

'I was hoping I'd got it wrong, but the hair loss was a give away.'

'I know that feeling,' she said. 'I'll arrange for her to go to the children's ward for the night so we can get started on some treatment. I'd like her to get a good night's sleep too.'

Sleep. What was that? Suddenly Aaron yawned. It had been a big day and wasn't over yet. Dinner at Gino's *ristorante* was starting to look like a good idea. It was nearby and had a relaxed atmosphere, something he needed right now. All he'd have to do was turn up, sit down and enjoy the wonderful food.

Bella looked his way. 'Late night?'

'No, more of a restless night than any other night. Too much going on in my head.'

'I hate those nights.'

I hope your nights aren't as bad as mine, Aaron thought. Pictures of a knife-wielding man were not easy to get over, if at all. Sometimes he wondered if the nightmares would ever go away entirely, or if he had to accept this was his new normal. 'They're not much fun,' he said. 'Those results came back quickly.' The downside to being some distance from the city and the medical laboratories was how long it took to get tests done. Glancing down, he noticed her hand stroking her abdomen.

Did she realise she was rubbing her lower belly as she walked? He stilled. As in how pregnant women touched their stomach sometimes. So Bella *was* the sister living in the building where the restaurant was. So much for getting in a twist over her. She was already taken. Now he thought about it, her first reaction when that woman sent her sprawling on the ground was to touch her belly as she was doing now. He could be wrong, but his gut said not. Bella Rosso was pregnant and looking radiant. And unavailable for a quick fling, which was all he could give her right now. Not that he'd ever suggest it, but he had been thinking about it ever since they met. It was hard not to when she oozed sexiness.

There again, she always held herself back around him, making certain they were only on a professional footing. Even when he'd spoken to her at the restaurant she hadn't been overly friendly towards him. Now he knew she had a partner he could shut down the annoying pull that gripped him whenever she was near. Maybe not a husband though as there was no sign of a wedding ring, and she hadn't been with a man at dinner. Of course, the guy might be away for work or anything.

Stop trying to fill in all the gaps when you've got nothing to go on.

With a sigh he hated to admit was filled with regret, he got busy so he could stop thinking about one beautiful, confident doctor. Until the next time she came into the department, and he'd have to start over. She really was mucking with his head, and that was so unusual it was odd, and interesting. He liked Bella. Furthermore, he wanted to spend time with her and get to know her better. But the last thing she needed was him complicating matters for her.

'Want to come with me to tell Tish and Gabby?'

All right, she could surprise him. 'Since it's quiet in here now, yes.'

'Good answer.' She suddenly smiled.

His head spun a little. That smile should be bottled for bad days. 'Let's go,' he growled around the lump of longing forming in the back of his throat.

'Here they come,' Tish said in a worry-laden voice as they approached her bed. 'Good or bad news?' There was a brave smile on her pale face but her eyes were flitting everywhere.

As they entered the cubicle, Bella pulled up a chair and sat down looking at her notes. 'Tish, you do have lupus. The good news is that it's very mild and we need to focus on keeping it that way.'

'Can't you give me something to make it go away?'

Gabby reached for her daughter's hand and held it tight. 'Tell us more, Doctor. Is Tish going to be all right?'

'Yes, she is, but not quite as she knows things now. Tish, you'll probably have to take regular medications to keep your thyroid under control and that might interfere with your energy levels at times.' She was putting it mildly for now, aiming for a calm approach. The specialist Tish would see would dig deeper and let the family know more as he progressed. It wasn't her place to start going into what lay ahead.

'Do we have to go back to Genoa to see a specialist right now?' Tish asked in a quiet voice.

'I doubt it. I'm sending your notes through to a clinic today but, as we all know, getting an appointment with a specialist takes time. You can carry on enjoying your holiday with your cousins in the meantime. Just keep that cast out of the water while you're at it.' Bella stood up and gave Tish and Gabby a big smile. 'Have some fun, and try not to worry too much.'

'Easy for you to say.'

'Tish, that's not nice,' Gabby admonished her daughter.

Bella paused. 'Tish, I hear you. You have a lot to deal with and there will be days you'll struggle, but you're strong so I believe you'll do all right.'

Aaron blinked. Never had he heard a specialist be so honest with a young patient. 'Tish, Gabby, I told you Dr Rosso was good, didn't I?'

Tish was crying. 'Sorry, Bella.'

'It's fine. Trust me, you *will* cope.' She drew a breath. 'Tish, I want you to stay in hospital overnight so I can start you on some drugs to help lift your energy levels.'

'Do I have to?'

'Yes. I'll be in early tomorrow to check you over, then if everything's going well you can get on with enjoying your holiday, though at a slower pace. All right?'

'I suppose so.'

Gabby wiped a stray tear away. 'Thank you, Doctor. I'm so glad we met you.'

'If you've got any more questions, fire away. I'll give you my number because you're bound to think of something later on.'

When Bella left the cubicle Aaron could feel his heart pounding. She was special. Not only as a doctor. If she could be so understanding with her patient, then she'd be the same with everyone. Her baby was going to be one lucky individual having her for a mother.

Why did she have to be pregnant with another man's baby?

He would like nothing more than to get to know every part of her.

Thank goodness she was pregnant, then, because he wasn't ready to fall in love again. The last time had been a heartbreaker. Amy had been a nurse at the hospital in New Zealand where he was doing a post-grad year and he'd been smitten from the moment he met her in the emergency department. They'd moved in together within four months and everything was perfect. When he proposed and Amy said yes, he truly believed nothing could go wrong in his world. Except being on the other side of the globe, living a quiet life, he'd been letting his guard down over how the media would get into a frenzy when the news got out. Which was exactly what happened when his parents announced their son was getting married upon his return to Britain over the summer.

All hell broke loose. At first Amy coped with the drama and fame and being followed everywhere. She refused to be intimidated but at the same time preferred to remain in the background, making him relieved and so proud of her. She also supported him and became a part of his life in England. Then she grew quieter and less communicative. He tried to get her to tell him what was wrong, but she'd shrug away his questions. One night he came home from a harrowing day in the emergency department to find a letter on the table and one half of the wardrobe empty. Amy had gone. She couldn't handle the lifestyle that went with the Marshall clan and had gone back to New Zealand.

He followed her in an attempt to win her back but she

refused to give him a chance, saying she could not live with all that 'uncalled-for attention' for another day. Heartbroken, he flew home, swearing he'd never again hand over his heart so readily, if at all. Six months later he heard she'd married her childhood sweetheart. So much for loving him if she could do an about-face so fast. The lesson for him was that love came with a huge price tag he wasn't prepared to pay.

Which meant he'd better find somewhere else to have dinner tonight. The less time spent in Bella's space, the better. She was too attractive to ignore, too tempting, so putting distance between them whenever possible was the only way to go.

CHAPTER THREE

JUST AFTER SIX Aaron was ready to head out of the department. The late afternoon had turned busy with a car versus
truck ending with two seriously injured men being brought
in, and then a three-year-old with a dog bite arrived with her
mother freaking out. Add in the usual cases of suspected
broken bones and a woman with severe abdominal pains and
he hadn't been able to walk off duty at three when everyone was struggling to deal with the influx. It had been the
busiest day he'd had in this ED. Still a lot quieter than back
in Edinburgh. 'That's it. I'm heading away while I can.'

'Thanks for staying back to help us,' Tommaso said.

'No problem.'

'Where is she? Why can't I take her home?' a man
shouted from behind him.

Looking around, Aaron saw an older man charging
through the department, a look of pure rage darkening his
craggy face. Aaron's gut squeezed. There wasn't a knife
in the fist the man waved at a nurse, but still, he could
feel the anxious energy in his body building. 'Here we go
again.' His stomach tightened painfully as he started towards the guy.

Bella appeared at the other end of the row of cubicles.
'Hello. Can I help you?' she asked the man.

'Step away, Bella,' Aaron said calmly so as not to disturb

the guy any further, but he was going to intervene before anyone got hurt. Especially Bella. Stepping between her and the angry man, he stood straight and tall. 'Stop shouting and talk to me. I'm a doctor. Who do you want to see?'

'What's it to you? Think you can stop me, huh?'

I'll do my best.

'Slow down and talk to me,' he repeated. 'Unless you do, I won't know what your problem is.'

Knuckles slammed into his chest. 'My wife's been here for hours and no one's looking after her. She's sick, and no one cares.'

Fighting the urge to grab the man and hold him until security came, Aaron drew a breath and said with as much calm as he could muster, 'What's your wife's name?'

The man spun around and stormed over to a bed where a woman being monitored for heart murmurs lay looking embarrassed. Jabbing the air with his forefinger, he shouted, 'This is her. See? No one's with her. She needs to be looked after.'

The woman had come in alone an hour ago feeling unwell. Given her history of heart problems, she'd been attached to an array of monitors and a nurse had been with her most of the time. Except now.

'Come with me and I'll show you what we're doing to help your wife.'

The man whirled around and pushed his face right up to Aaron's. 'Why should I believe anything you say?'

'Because I have no reason to lie to you.' Thump, thump, went his heart. He doubted he was about to get attacked, but the day he was stabbed he hadn't seen the knife coming until it was too late.

'Mrs Romano is being well cared for. Her heart was erratic when she arrived but is returning to normal. We'll continue to monitor her for a while to come. She'll probably go to the ward overnight. Now, if you want to, you can sit with her.'

The man's shoulders sagged as the anger drained away. 'She's had heart attacks before. Nearly died twice.'

The poor man was terrified this might've been the time his wife didn't make it. Aaron relaxed as much as possible. But relaxing didn't come easy for him.

'I understand your worry.' Aaron suddenly realised how quiet the department had become. Looking around, he found everyone, patients, nurses and doctors, watching the unfolding scene. Bella's concern was all over her face. For him, if her focus was anything to go by. His chest expanded. The pounding under his ribs slowed.

He didn't attack, relax.

Bella was coming towards him, compassion in those beautiful green eyes. He put a hand up, embarrassed to see it shaking. 'Wait.' Turning to the patient's husband, he said, 'Can we have your reassurance you won't lose your temper again? Otherwise you will be removed from the department for the safety of other patients and their visitors, and all our staff.'

'I get so stressed every time Ro gets sick.' The man gulped. 'I'm sorry. I won't cause any more trouble.'

Tommaso, a fellow doctor, moved in and, reassuringly taking Mr Romano's arm, led him to a chair beside his wife. 'Sit here, and if you have any questions please wait until a nurse or doctor is available to talk to you.' He looked over his shoulder to Aaron. 'You're amazing. Now go home. See you tomorrow.'

Suddenly Aaron felt so tired he could barely lift his feet. Bella took his arm and gently tugged him away. 'Come on. We'll go outside and get our breath.'

Knowing she'd feel him shaking wasn't enough to make him pull his arm away from her hold. He needed her strength for a moment. It felt good to share his stress, even when she didn't know why he was acting like this. Her fingers were firm yet light and her shoulder brushed his upper arm as they walked out of the department. He couldn't help the lustful heat the subtle touch evoked within him.

Once away from everyone, she dropped her hand and put a gap between them, as though her gesture wasn't to be seen as anything too personal, clearly taking stock of how seriously he'd reacted. 'When did you last eat?' she asked.

That was unexpected. 'Some time this morning.'

'You're not looking after yourself, Aaron.'

'Now who's sounding like one of her brothers?' he quipped in an attempt to lighten her sombre mood.

'It's a family thing. You haven't heard my mother yet.' She smiled.

'Was she not there the other night?'

'She'd gone upstairs to check on one of the grandkids when you came over. Let's walk a bit to calm down after that altercation and then we'll head home for dinner.'

For someone who always seemed in a hurry to move on from talking to him, she'd just managed to surprise the pants off him. Not literally, thank goodness. 'That's not necessary.' But he'd like time unwinding with her, chilling out and putting the nightmare behind him. Though today's scenario had nothing on what happened last time, it reminded him how easily things could go from normal to terrifying in a blink.

'A meal with my noisy family can't hurt, even if it's not what you're used to,' she said. 'You were very composed dealing with that man. He was beside himself with worry.

I don't know how you managed not to get in his face and tell him to get out of the department.'

Nor did he. But then last time he'd been much the same. It was the same every time he was confronted by irate patients or someone with a patient thinking nothing was being done to help them. It must be part of him to remain cool and calm in adverse situations. Usually it worked—*until that last time in Edinburgh*. Though he'd been told he was very calm right up until the knife sliced into him.

'That would've exacerbated the situation.'

'You know that? From experience?' Of course she read him that easily. She was smart.

'Yes.'

Please don't ask any more.

'There's a shortcut to the lake along here. Come on.' She strode out, forcing him to increase his pace.

Not hard to do when he was enjoying being with her, despite what had happened minutes ago. It helped that she didn't follow up with intense questions he wasn't prepared to answer. 'We're not far from the restaurant, are we?' he noted when they reached the shore of Lake Maggiore.

'Just under a kilometre away.'

'Shall we walk there?'

'Of course. So you will join my family for dinner?' She sounded far more open to him than she had any time previously, making it hard not to accept her invitation. Even knowing he shouldn't be interested in anything about her outside work he couldn't say no. 'They won't mind?'

'Not at all. It's always a bit of a circus at mealtimes but it's how we like it. Happy families.' There was a lot of love in her voice.

Which made him a little jealous. 'When I was growing up my family was always too busy to sit down together at the end of the day and talk about what we'd been up to.' That was when he lived at home and wasn't at boarding school or living in student quarters at university.

'I can't imagine what that's like.' She paused. 'No, that's not true. Jason's parents were a little like that, always rushing in for dinner and rushing off to some meeting or work before they'd swallowed the last mouthful.'

'Jason?'

'My husband.' Bella went quiet on him. Needing space?

He waited for more as they walked along the narrow path towards town.

'He died three years ago.'

The air oozed out of his lungs at the pain in her voice. 'I'm sorry to hear that, Bella. Really sorry.' How did anyone cope with the death of their partner? 'It's not much, but I don't know what else to say.'

'It's enough,' she said through a tight smile. 'Better than saying something meaningless.'

So it wasn't her husband's baby she was carrying? She must've moved on despite that pain he'd heard. All number of questions were firing up in his head but he left her alone, knowing how much he hated people delving into his life. It was something he'd grown up dealing with. People thought they had every right to ask personal questions about his love life, his wealth, his career. About anything really. He wouldn't do that to her, but he did want to know more.

Ten minutes later they were walking up the road where Bella's family lived. Some of them, anyway.

'How many siblings have you got?'

'Three bossy brothers, three lovely sisters-in-law and five nieces and nephews.' Her hand did that touch-the-tummy thing.

'You're very lucky.' A wave of longing rolled through

him. It would be awesome to have his own family but he'd long believed it wouldn't happen. Not since Amy left and he'd decided he wasn't getting involved with anyone again. Having his heart broken was not something he ever wanted to face again. He'd really believed he and Amy were for ever. He'd given his all to their relationship. She'd cut him in half when she walked away. Yet here was Bella making him think about family and love. It didn't make sense.

'You're right, I am.'

He remembered something the waitress had said the other night. 'So you live above the restaurant? Along with your family?'

Her eyebrows rose in an exquisite manner, making him hum on the inside. 'Someone's been talking. Yes, I have the small one-bedroom apartment on the far side. At some point I'll get a place of my own, but for now the arrangement works well. I get to spend time with my family and Gino makes sure I eat way too much.'

Aaron laughed. 'Now, that doesn't surprise me.' What did though was that Bella was apparently on her own. No mention of a partner at all. Yet she was pregnant. Interesting. It wasn't any of his business but that didn't stop him wanting to know. He wasn't stupid though. Ask about that and he was sure he'd not only miss out on a wonderful meal but he'd be sent to emotional purgatory for the rest of his time in Stresa and working with Bella would become difficult beyond belief.

'Right, brace yourself,' Bella said, and they were inside the restaurant and she was heading to the same table she'd been at the other night where five children sat eating while four adults were talking with wine glasses at hand. 'Come on, Aaron. Time to meet the tribe for a grilling.'

That alone would've normally sent him running for the

door, but somehow he didn't think this was going to be too intrusive, and more like fun.

'Mamma, Papà, I'd like you to meet Aaron Marshall. He's a relieving doctor at the emergency centre and is in need of a decent dinner.'

'Welcome.' Bella's father clapped him on the shoulder. 'We like it when Bella brings someone home for a meal.'

That might be tricky. He was only a colleague. 'Thanks for having me.'

Her mother wrapped him in a hug. 'Hello, Aaron. Didn't you dine here earlier in the week?'

'I did, and the food was delicious.'

'I heard that.' Gino appeared from out the back.

'Just as well I didn't say it was awful.'

Gino laughed. 'You'd already be halfway across the deck if you had.'

He didn't doubt it. The man appeared fit and strong, despite a stomach that suggested he sampled his cooking rather a lot. 'I did plan on coming back during the weekend, but when Bella suggested I join you all tonight I couldn't resist.' It was true. He'd seen the love at the table last time he was here and felt envious. To give up an opportunity to join in would be crazy.

Bella intervened. 'We've been very busy at work, and have only just finished. I'm starving and think Aaron might be feeling the same.' She did the introductions of everyone around the table.

'I hope I remember all the names.' He chuckled. 'There's quite a crowd of you.'

Cara, or was it Anna, one of the sisters-in-law, laughed. 'I wanted them all to wear name tags when I first became part of the family. You'll soon know who's who.'

That sounded as though he'd be turning up regularly. 'I hope so.'

Bella pulled out two chairs and sat down on one. 'Here you go, Aaron. Get comfortable before the inquisition starts.'

Really? This family would start tormenting him with questions he hated answering? He hesitated. Bella looked at him and smiled. 'It's all right. I was teasing.'

Her smile went a long way to undoing the knots forming in his belly. It was genuine and, as far as he could see, not laced with an agenda. He sank further onto the seat before any more doubts crept in. 'So far I haven't known you to be so light-hearted.'

'There's a lot you don't know about me,' she retorted, then slowly smiled again. 'I know next to nothing about you either, but it doesn't matter. We can still relax and enjoy our meal.'

For someone to be so straightforward was new to him. It went to show how jaded he'd become over the years. Amy often said he was in a rut and needed to get out amongst it—whatever *it* was. 'Sounds good to me.' He wasn't mentioning how different this was from his usual experiences with strangers.

'Aaron, where are you from?' someone asked.

'Edinburgh,' he answered.

'Have you worked outside Scotland before?' Bella asked.

'London for a year and Auckland for another when I was getting up to speed.'

'I lived in London for years,' she told him.

'Is that where you qualified as a paediatrician?'

'Mostly, yes.' Ask no more, her expression warned.

He wanted to delve deeper but there was a stop sign blinking at him from her jade-coloured eyes. He got a lot of that with Bella, he realised. She was almost as reticent as him when it came to talking about herself. Which might mean something awful had happened to her at some point. Was that something to do with Jason? Again, he wasn't asking. Instead he stuck with the basics.

'We dragged her back here eighteen months ago,' Gino told him, obviously not concerned about Bella's need to change the subject.

'I can't imagine anyone dragging Bella anywhere she didn't want to go.'

'She did put up a fight,' Gino agreed. 'Tonight we're having lasagne. Hope that suits you?'

The subject was closed. Fair enough. 'Sounds wonderful, Gino.'

The man nodded once and headed back to his kitchen. Dinner confirmed, and Bella was relaxing.

Aaron's mind threw up a lot of questions. Why drag Bella back? She didn't appear to be a woman who depended on others to sort out her life. So something awful having happened that had the family rallying around to support her made sense. She'd said her husband died, and she might've struggled to the point she needed family to help her get back on her feet. It would be easier to watch out for her if she was here, not across the continent.

Bella's father leaned forward. 'So, Aaron, tell us about yourself. How many siblings have you got?'

Another change of subject. Talking about his family only wound him up but he'd give it a go as they'd been nothing but friendly and welcoming to him. 'One sister, Maggie. She's very busy and always telling me what to do. Not that I take any notice, but it's nice to get away at times.'

'What made you come to Stresa for the summer?' someone else asked. 'It's not usually a place where doctors come from other countries.'

'I can't see why not. It's beautiful, and not too big.'

Bella piped up. 'Aaron's only here for four months, then he's going back to Edinburgh.'

'He might not want to when his time's up. We live in one of the best places in Italy,' Bella's dad said.

Everyone laughed at that. 'Of course we do.'

He joined in the laughter and soon became immersed in fast banter that was hard to keep up with at times. Italians seemed to speed talk, or this family did anyway. At the same time they made him feel he'd been a part of them for a while.

'Let's take our coffee out on the deck,' Bella suggested when dinner was over and the children were being packed off to bed. 'Give you a break from this lot.'

'Good idea.' He picked up their cups and followed her out. Leaning against the railing, he peered down at the surrounding grounds. 'The gardens are amazing.'

'Papà spends a lot of time working in them. It's his passion now he's retired.'

'What did he used to do?'

'What do you think?'

'Chef?'

She nodded. 'He started out in a kitchen in a hotel in Roma with the dream of one day owning a small restaurant in the city. Then he met Mamma. She was a housemaid at the hotel and came from here. When they married she was already pregnant, so they moved to Stresa so Nonna could help with the baby while they worked all hours getting a local restaurant up and running.'

'Gino was that baby?'

A small smile tugged at the corners of her lovely mouth.

'He started learning to cook when he was about eight. Apparently it was a battle to get him to go to school because there was nothing else he wanted to be but the best chef in Italy.'

Aaron sipped the strong coffee and sighed with pleasure. Perfect. 'So why did you choose medicine?'

'I don't know a lot about cooking.' She laughed.

Hearing that laughter lifted his spirits further. It was new to him and made her so much more approachable. 'Guess you didn't have to take your turn with prepping vegetables for dinner.' He'd never had to do so much as cook a piece of toast if he hadn't wanted to. There'd always been a housemaid and a cook in his family home. Sometimes he'd wondered if he might've been a different person if he'd had to make his own bed and stack the dishwasher every night. Not that he'd behaved like a spoilt brat. He hoped not anyway.

'There were still plenty of chores to do.' Bella sank back into her seat, holding her mug in both hands close to her breasts. 'You seemed to enjoy yourself over dinner despite my lot never shutting up.'

'It was fun.' Nothing like dinner at the Marshall house, even these days. He felt ridiculously comfortable with Bella's family. There was a sense of having found something he'd always hoped was out there but believed unavailable to him. He needed to stop thinking this way because in less than four months he'd be packing his bags and leaving, heading back to Scotland and the empty house he owned there.

'So you're feeling more relaxed now?'

He wasn't surprised she'd known how upset he'd been after that man had lost his rag over his wife's condition. He presumed that was her reason for inviting him to dinner. Not just a friendly invitation to a colleague. 'A lot better. Thank you.'

'Good.'

He liked how once again she didn't press for information, and seemed to accept he'd talk if he wanted and left him alone when he didn't. Which made it so easy to say, 'Five months ago I was attacked in the emergency department where I worked in Edinburgh by a knife-wielding man on drugs. He believed he should be seen before anyone else although triage could find little wrong with him, apart from a broken toe.'

Bella shuddered. 'That's terrible. It's not uncommon for patients to think they should come first, but still.'

'Nor was the fact I was assaulted. But he stabbed me in the femoral artery. He seemed to know exactly where to strike. The fact I was in ED saved my life.'

Bella's hand covered his. 'No wonder you got uptight when that man lost his cool.'

'I feel bad now. There wasn't a weapon in sight.' There hadn't been last time either. Not initially. 'But it was an instant reaction to protect everyone in the vicinity.'

'I bet you'd have always done that.'

'True, I would have.' He stretched his legs out in front of him, enjoying Bella's hand on his. Such a simple touch, yet it filled him with wonder, and loosened some knots. 'The nightmares from that evening haven't gone away. They're why I don't sleep well.'

'Anything to do with why you came to Stresa to work?'

'Everything to do with it. I got burnout, and was always on edge at work. Still am, if I'm honest. The department head wanted me to take time off and go away for a long holiday. I prefer to keep busy, but not so much that I don't get to relax at work. I love what I do, but it became a chore.

So I took on board what he said and looked for somewhere to work for a few months. I found the ad for the temporary position here and delved into it more. Once I learned the ED was in a small hospital and wasn't going to be anywhere near as busy as what I was used to, I applied.'

'And here you are.'

He turned his hand over, the urge to touch her over-powering his every protest, and wound his fingers around Bella's. 'Here I am.' She made him comfortable with her straightforward manner and allowing him to decide how much to tell her. No wonder it had been too easy to talk about what had happened and how he felt when he hadn't been able to do that with anyone else. Not once.

Bella turned to study him. 'We don't often get aggressive people here. Today was a rarity. Tommaso told me in an aside when you were calming Signor Romano down that he's been known to lose his temper before. He doesn't always understand what's happening with his wife, whom he adores.' Her hand tightened around his. 'You were good with him. Firm but not nasty.'

The last of the tension gripping him from confronting the guy slipped away, replaced with relief and a new happiness. One he'd started to believe didn't exist for him. Lifting their joined hands to his lips, he kissed the back of Bella's. 'Thank you for listening and being so understanding.'

Pulling her hand away, with a hint of reluctance, she asked, 'Why wouldn't I?'

That was one question he definitely wasn't answering. He didn't want to spoil this tentative friendship by letting her know his background. If they got to spend more time to-gether outside work over the coming months, then yes, he'd have to come clean because he didn't want to be thought of as a liar, but right now it felt so good to be accepted for who he was without all the hoo-ha attached. Bella Rosso was special. What was more, she made him feel special. 'Sometimes it's good to be accepted without having to explain yourself.'

She leaned closer, her face only inches from his. 'Now, *that* I understand.'

Why? He wasn't asking. That'd be doing what he appreciated her not doing. 'I'm glad.' It would be too easy to lean close enough to kiss her tantalising mouth.

Bella's eyes were large and focused entirely on him. What was she seeing? Thinking? Was she thinking? Could she read his mind?

'Bella?' Lifting his hands, he took her shoulders gently and pulled her a little closer, gazing at her exquisite features. 'You're beautiful,' he murmured, then jerked his head back. He was way out of line.

She stood up. 'I'd better help clear the table.'

'Sorry,' he said.

'Why?'

Damned if he knew.

Hey, wake up. She's carrying another man's baby. That's why.

He tensed. 'I think it's time for me to head back to my place.' He'd leave his car at the hospital overnight.

She nodded in agreement. 'I'll see you at work tomorrow.'

The near-perfect end to a wonderful night. Except it didn't feel close to perfect now that she'd cooled towards him a little. There was an ache going on in his chest. He wanted more time alone with Bella. Further talk so he got to learn more about her, to find out more about her husband, and that baby she was obviously carrying. Which was all plain frightening when he didn't do talking about himself, and he couldn't ask her to talk about herself if he didn't reciprocate. 'Goodnight.'

I want more time with Bella?

But she must be involved with someone else. Where was the guy anyway?

Aaron's steps were hard on the pavement as he grappled with the truth. He liked Bella Rosso a lot and she wasn't available.

CHAPTER FOUR

'ANDREA WANTS TO go home,' Gita told Bella the moment she stepped into the children's ward on Thursday. Andrea had only returned from Milan yesterday. 'Says his mother makes better pancakes than what he got this morning.'

'I bet she does.' Bella laughed. The hospital kitchen wasn't known for its gourmet meals. 'It's not up to me. When's Alec due to do his round?' The orthopaedic specialist came up from Milan two days a week and was due here today.

'He called to say he's on the early train so should be here any time soon, I'd say.'

'That'll make one small boy happy if nothing else.'

'Morning, Bella, Gita.' Aaron strode into the area looking relaxed and happy.

'Morning. What did you have for breakfast? I could do with some if it makes you so cheerful.' Her head was heavy and there was a nagging ache in her lower back. Hopefully not caused by the pregnancy this early on, or she'd be in for a lot more as the months continued. At fourteen weeks people were beginning to notice her baby bump and ask questions about how far on she was and how long she'd be working. Aaron hadn't asked anything, though she'd often caught him looking at her as if to make sure she really was pregnant. No doubt he'd be confused as to who the father might be. She'd tell him next time they were together, alone. Funny how she wanted him to know the truth behind her pregnancy sooner than later. She more than liked him and didn't want any shadows hanging over their friendship or whatever it might become.

If it became anything more. There was a lot to consider before that happened. The decision to have Jason's baby had been made knowing she'd struggle with any other man stepping into the father role. This baby was her last physical tie to Jason and, while she knew she was moving on from his death, a part of her couldn't let him go completely.

Aaron interrupted her thoughts. 'Toast and jam. Very boring, but it filled the gap.' He looked across to the room where four boys sat in their beds talking as if there were no tomorrow. 'I've just come from the canteen. Thought I'd pop in to see Andrea for a minute on my way back to ED.'

He'd visited the lad on her ward twice since he'd returned from Milan. Sometimes she wondered if it was an excuse to stop and say hello to her too. She was probably way off track. Just because his mere presence threw her nerves into a frenzy didn't mean he'd noticed her any more than he did any other women. But he always went out of his way to stop and talk to her.

'You're good doing that for him.' Even in this small hospital the ED staff didn't usually drop by to see a patient who'd been through their department. 'Andrea thinks the sun shines out of your backside.' Even she was starting to think there might be a ray or two. He was rather gorgeous, and kind, not pushy. Something that always sat well with her. *And* had her looking twice at him. No, that was because he was so attractive with that slight body and sexy face.

'I always like knowing how my patients are getting on.

I'm even more invested in Mattia and Andrea since we helped them at the accident scene.'

'I get where you're coming from. I always feel better knowing my patients' outcome.' It was part of being a doctor. Even when a patient walked out of the ward for the final time she still wondered how they were getting on. 'Working in Stresa means I often bump into my patients around town, which I like.'

'Not all of them are from around here though.'

'At the paediatric clinic I get referrals from Lake Como and a few from Milan.' That was something she was particularly proud of, people wanting to bring their children all the way up here to see her. Her share in the Paediatric practice within the hospital aligned to one in Milano was growing as word spread she was good at what she did.

'I did wonder how you could be so busy with only the hospital patients until Tommaso mentioned a lad staying in town with his grandparents who presented with early-stage leukaemia that you recognised and got him into the right specialist fast. His parents keep bringing him up here to you despite his cancer specialist being in Milan.'

'Yes, they do. I think it's their way of showing their gratitude for me finding out what was wrong with the boy when he presented with very few symptoms. I was only doing what I'm trained for and have had nothing to do with his treatment. The outcome is fantastic and makes me feel good about my small part in helping him.' Anton was back at school, playing football, hitting the grades in all his subjects and talking about becoming a doctor when he grew up.

'The reason we do what we do—getting the best outcomes for people suffering.' His smile was wide and genuine.

'When you two have finished patting each other on the

back I have a prescription that needs finishing and signing, Bella.' Gita laughed. 'Her analgesics have run out,'
she added.

I was doing that?

Bella swallowed as she felt her face heat. 'Right, move
over and let me at the keyboard.'

The desk phone rang. Snatching it up, Bella said,
'Paediatrics, Bella Rosso speaking.'

'It's Tommaso. We've got a three-year-old girl presenting with vomiting and diarrhoea plus erratic heart rhythm.
I'm thinking severe allergy reaction, cause unknown. She's
on oxygen and her obs are not settling.'

'I'm on my way.'

'Bed three. Can you tell Aaron to get back too? It's gone
crazy in here.'

'Done.' Slamming the phone down, she hurriedly filled
in her code for the prescription Gita needed. 'I'm needed
downstairs.' Then she was on her way, talking over her
shoulder as she went. 'Aaron, you're required back in ED.'

A strong hand caught her wrist. 'Careful, you'll walk into
the wall if you keep that up,' said Aaron. 'What's the hurry?'

His touch was warm and she shrugged him away. She
wasn't even thinking about what that meant. She had a seriously ill child to worry about, not her reaction to a man's
hand. But it was great. He felt hot, sexy. No, he didn't. Yes,
he did.

'Bella?'

'A young child has presented with a severe allergic reaction.' A bee sting? Not likely or someone would've known.
A child usually screamed blue murder when they were
stung. A food the girl hadn't had before? Had she swallowed something that wasn't food? Or was it a reaction to
a stray cat or dog causing the problem?

Bella all but flew down the stairs to ED with Aaron right beside her every step of the way. Which was kind of nice and made her feel special even when that was probably the last thing on his mind.

'Bella, this is Maria.' Tommaso stepped aside for her to get close to the bed where a small child lay curled up tight. 'This is her *papà*, Davido.'

The man looked terrified as he held his daughter's tiny hand in his large one. 'Do something, please.'

Bella noted the sweat glistening on Maria's forehead and cheeks, and the trembling all over her small frame. 'Has Maria ever before had any bad reaction to something she's eaten? Even a small one, like throwing up or even just wanting to? Feeling cold after eating something?'

'No. Nothing.'

'Blood pressure is low,' Tommaso told her. 'I've administered a light sedative to keep her calm.'

The tiny girl tried to roll into her father, and began crying when the oxygen tube hindered her.

'Where was Maria when this started?' Bella asked as she noted the raised body temperature on the monitor. 'What had she been doing before you found her?'

'She went with her big sister to the woods. About two hours ago. They came back when Maria was sick the first time.'

Woods. The ground would be soft and covered in leaves and grass. An image filled Bella's head. Mushrooms. Bright red ones. Poisonous.

'Davido, did you see the first time Maria vomited?' she asked urgently. When he nodded, she demanded, 'What colour was it?'

'Pink, reddish, I think.'

'I need a stomach pump in here fast. I know Maria's

probably brought up most of her stomach contents but I need to be absolutely certain nothing's left.'

'Onto it.' Aaron was already moving, not waiting for a nurse to do as Bella had demanded.

She'd been so focused on the little girl she hadn't even realised he was still with her. 'Are there mushrooms growing in those woods?' she asked the father.

His face turned ashen as he nodded. 'Sometimes. A few. But Maria wouldn't eat them. They'd taste awful.'

'Bright red, very pretty to a little girl.' Bella took the pump Aaron held out.

'Want a hand inserting it?' he asked.

'Can you remove the oxygen and hold her?'

Within minutes Bella was removing the pump. There'd been very little content in the stomach. 'That's a plus. Maria's already got rid of most of what caused the problem. Those few small dark pink pieces in the fluid look like they're from a mushroom. I'll send it to the lab for analysis, but in the meantime we need to draw some blood to check her liver and kidneys.'

'Is she going to be all right?' Davido asked as tears slid down his cheeks.

'Maria's fast reaction to the mushroom is good. I'm going with that being the problem, all right?' She didn't wait for an answer. 'Her heart is beating unevenly, and her blood pressure is low so we will move her to the ward where a nurse will be with her all the time. She'll continue to be on oxygen until everything settles down, as well as intravenous fluids since she's already lost a lot of fluid and at this age children get dehydrated very quickly.'

'You haven't really answered my question.' Davido was smart, as well as terrified for his daughter.

Bella's heart was filled with compassion. This had to be

an absolute nightmare for any parent. 'I'll wait for the lab results for her liver and kidneys before I give you a definite answer, but I think Maria's going to be all right. Throwing up early on means the stomach didn't have time to absorb too much of the poison.'

'I need to talk to my wife. She'll be beside herself with worry. But she had to stay home with our other children.'

'Go outside where it's quieter and call her. I'll sit with Maria till you get back.'

Davido shook his head. 'I'm not going anywhere. I'm ringing from here.'

'I understand.' She wasn't leaving her patient either. Pulling up a chair, she sank onto it and watched Maria breathing, slowly and unevenly, her tiny face all but obscured by the oxygen mask. 'The poor kid,' she said to herself.

'Who is very lucky her paediatrician was on the ball,' Aaron said quietly as he picked up the pump.

Glancing at him, she saw only respect in those beautiful winter-blue eyes. Warmth stole through her. Which it shouldn't. She didn't need his approval, but it felt so good getting it. 'It's frightening how easy it is for something so horrifying to happen.' Her hand touched her stomach. The downside to being a parent would be the constant worry about all the things that could go wrong. Being a doctor, she was more aware than most parents of what those could be.

'And how fast.'

'*Sì,*' she sighed. They were only saying what she'd said and heard often over the years of her career, but with Aaron it felt as though they were on the same page about more than just patient talk. More personal, as though they were each letting the other in a little bit. Did she truly want that? When she believed she'd adjusted to living solo for ever? But then, letting Aaron in a little didn't equate to something deep and meaningful and long term. She leaned over Maria and studied her face. 'She's going to need lots of fluids.'

'We'll sort that before transferring her up to the ward.' He disappeared out of the cubicle, leaving Bella to catch her breath and put her out-of-sorts mind back in order.

Aaron managed to tilt her sideways ever so slightly without appearing to be aware of how he affected her. Which was a good thing, she reminded herself. The last thing she needed was a doctor she worked with thinking he was disturbing her like that. It could lead to all sorts of misunderstandings.

Though at the moment the only person not understanding the effect he had on her was herself. Why did her blood rush to her head whenever he came into the room? Why the sudden heat under her skin when he was beside her? Why the urge to reach out and hold him when he talked in that deep, sexy voice and his eyes sparkled with humour? A lot of questions she had no answers for, or answers she was prepared to take seriously. She had had her one love, and doubted she'd ever find another. Besides, in a few months he'd be gone and she wasn't moving away. London had been fun but it wasn't home.

Davido appeared on the other side of the bed. 'My wife says thank you for looking after Maria. She's so upset about the mushrooms and is going out right now to remove each and every last one she can find.'

'She'll have to check every morning until the season's over,' Bella said. 'Might be safer to talk to Maria and show her what made her sick in the first place. I can't imagine her ever wanting to eat a mushroom again, not even the good ones.' Which, considering how many people used mushrooms in their cooking, would cause a problem if she didn't learn to accept some fungi were safe.

Davido was gazing at his daughter, worry etching his face. 'We've been very lucky.'

Bella stood up. 'I'm just relieved we got to the cause quickly and there won't be any serious after-effects.'

A nurse appeared with a bottle of fluid and tubes to attach to Maria. 'Hey, little one, I'm going to give you a drink in the arm.'

Maria barely reacted to the nurse's words or the pressing sensation of the tube being attached to the needle already in place under her skin.

'She's exhausted,' Bella noted. 'I'll call the orderly to shift her to the ward where I can keep an eye on her.' Heading through the department, she couldn't help looking out for Aaron.

His deep voice coming from behind a curtain drawn around a bed was filled with concern. 'Signora Bianchi, you have fractured three ribs. You need to take medicine for the pain.'

The woman's reply suggested where Aaron could put the medication and it wasn't in her mouth.

Chuckling, Bella wondered how he'd deal with that response. She wasn't hanging around to find out. She was needed on the ward. But it was tempting to stay and listen to that voice that caused all sorts of unmentionable sensations to her body.

'Do you want to stay here all night?' Aaron asked calmly.

'No.'

Yes, thought Bella.

'Now, you see, here's the thing. The pain's going to cause you to lose sleep and be uncomfortable no matter what you're doing. A dose of pain-relief medication will help you move around and movement will help you feel better.'

Could the man sound convincing or what? Bella grinned

as she hurried away. She'd do well to remember that in the coming weeks when they got together again over a meal at her family's home and restaurant.

So she was going to invite him more often? Why not? It was good having his company and he wasn't full of cheek and bossy like her brothers. Throw in how sexy and intriguing he was, and she realised she'd missed that. Was this disloyalty to Jason? Or more like getting on with her life?

'Feel like going for a walk along the lakeside after work?' Aaron asked Bella late Friday afternoon as she signed off a six-year-old who'd presented in the ED with a severe sore throat and swollen lymph glands.

Bella had ordered bloods done to confirm her suspicion of glandular fever. 'You're not looking for another dinner with my lot, by any chance?'

The thought had never crossed his mind. He didn't do looking for freebies. 'Not at all. I was thinking of asking you to join me for a beer and pizza in town,' he snapped.

Bella put her hand up in the stop sign. 'Sorry. I didn't mean to say you were a freeloader. It's because you seemed to enjoy yourself the other night that I thought you might like to do it again.'

His angst dropped away. So used to others expecting him to shout them meals or drinks, he hadn't stopped to think she might be making a kind gesture. 'It's me who should be sorry. I'm not used to being invited into other people's families.' Not for a meal with nothing expected in return, at any rate. He'd become such a cynic. It was a barrier formed from too many let-downs. Bella didn't deserve it. 'I'd love to share a meal with your family again some time but to-night I'd like to relax with you without having to be on my best behaviour.' To be able to enjoy her sexiness and stunning looks without worrying what her family might think.

Her eyes crinkled at the edges as she laughed, sending his heart rate up a few notches. 'I'd love to go for a walk and work some kinks out of my back before we sit down to pizza and a drink. No beer for me, I'm afraid.'

Of course. The baby. 'Not a problem. I'm sure we can get some water.' He laughed. Doing more of that lately. Because of this woman? Or because he was working with a group of people who expected nothing more from him than his best medical abilities? Probably a mix of both, he decided.

'Give me ten minutes? I want to check up on a girl with bronchitis before I head out.'

'I'll change into some respectable clothes and wait for you in the car park. Don't hurry. We've got all night.'

When Bella blinked he realised how loaded that sounded. 'What I mean is—'

Her hand touched his shoulder. 'There's no rush. It's okay. I'm more than ready to get out of here. See you shortly.'

He missed her touch the moment she removed her hand. Plus the heady scent of roses she took with her as she strode to the elevator. She was doing his head in with that wicked laugh and those big eyes that didn't miss a thing. She was getting under his skin—that was what she was doing. Waking him up to possibilities he hadn't thought likely for so long. Hadn't wanted to consider at all. He liked keeping his heart safe. No, he didn't. It was hard work and brought no enjoyment, but it saved him from pain. Keeping it safe was the only way to go. Or he could leap off the edge and see how he landed. Maybe. Maybe not. A repeat of what Amy did was too awful to contemplate.

'Have a good weekend, Aaron,' Tommaso called as he

went past. 'Forget you're an emergency doctor and have some fun.'

'I'll do my best.' Starting with a walk along the lakeshore with a delightful woman who seemed to like taking time out in quiet ways too. A bonus that came with working in Stresa was the stunning scenery. Throw in how small and friendly the town was and there was a lot going for this place.

'Any plans for the weekend?' Bella asked as they sauntered down towards Lake Maggiore.

'I thought I might drive up to the Alps. Go for a bit of a hike. Nothing too serious, just like to get out in the fresh air for a bit. What about you?' That idea had occurred as he gazed north. 'Would you like to join me? Though I suppose it's not a novelty for you.'

'I haven't been over that way for years. I used to do quite a bit of hiking in the mountains before I left to go to university in Milan. After that I never seemed to make the time to get away and I've missed it.'

That wasn't answering his question. 'Still got your boots?'

'I doubt it, but I do have sturdy walking shoes.' She tipped her head to look up at him. 'I'd love to join you if you don't intend being over-exertive.' Then the twinkle in those eyes vanished and she looked away. 'As long as we're not spending too much time together. I have to warn you I'm not interested in getting too close. I'm running solo these days.'

He should be pleased to hear that.

His heart was safe.

Not if the sudden thud in his chest was an indicator.

'Fair enough.'

She was still staring straight ahead as they continued walking. 'The thing is, I'm pregnant.'

'I'd surmised that.'

Her head shot up. 'How?'

'You do a little touch-the-tummy thing at times that I've seen with other pregnant women through the course of my work. You were also worried after that woman elbowed you out of the way at the accident.' Plus her tummy was slightly larger than what he'd expect for someone so slim.

'Yes, I was.' Bella blinked, then gave him a lopsided smile. 'No hiding anything from you, is there?'

'I wasn't aware you tried to.'

'I haven't. Not really. We're not so close I feel I should be telling you everything about my life.' Her breasts rose on an intake of air. 'But I might as well finish what I've started since you will probably join my family for a meal again some time and they're already asking if you know about the baby.' A blush coloured her face. 'Not that it's any of their business.'

Unable to resist that delicate look and bemused expression, Aaron reached for her hand.

Whoa. Getting too close, man.

Jerking his hand away, he kept walking along the pathway as though nothing felt wrong. 'They care about you.'

'They do. Too much sometimes but better than not at all.' Again she drew a breath. 'The thing is, I'm having Jason's baby. We knew his life expectancy was short once the myeloma returned after a year in remission so before he died he had his sperm frozen. We talked a lot about me being a solo mother, and the choice to go ahead with it was entirely mine.' She paused, then, 'I fell pregnant in his last year but sadly it wasn't to be.'

Aaron was gobsmacked. That had never crossed his mind when he'd wondered who the father might be. 'Hence Gino's protective streak.'

'*Si.*'

'You're one very strong lady to be doing this.' She was also off-limits. Her late husband still meant so much to her she wouldn't be interested in getting close to another man.

'I don't always feel like it. Then I guess there'll always be days I'll feel incompetent even if I had a partner beside me.'

Did she want one? Seemed to him that her late husband had been her one and only. 'You waited a while. You did say Jason died three years ago?'

She nodded. 'I put my final year of qualifying on hold towards the end to nurse him so I wanted to finish that. I also kind of lost my way for a while. I think focusing so hard on study had me denying Jason had gone so I still had to grieve.'

When Bella opened up she certainly had no issues with telling him how she felt, and he felt special. Plus he was growing to care deeply for her.

'I reiterate—you are tough.'

'I hope so.'

'That's why your family's so important to you—for the days you're struggling.' If only his family had been the same. Instead they had never understood why he wasn't interested in being famous and wanting everyone to kow-tow to him, and that he disliked being used for his wealth and who his family were. But he wasn't being fair. There was one person who'd understood him all along. 'You'd have liked my grandfather. He was my rock when I was a kid, always there if I needed someone to talk to. He let me be who I wanted to be.'

'What about your parents? You said mealtimes in your house were the opposite to my family, but surely there were times they'd sit down with you if you needed their help?'

See? Bella had a way of making him open his mouth and talk about things he always kept close to his chest.

'Not often.' That was all he was saying. Please. He could not tell this wonderful woman how he could be followed by the media whenever one of his parents or his sister made the news over their work.

'So your grandfather was your go-to person. At least you had him.'

'Yes. He always had time for my gripes.'

Bella glanced at him. 'Better than having no one at all.'

It was too easy to smile. 'Quite right.' His parents would've been there to listen if he'd decided to aim for the top of the best emergency specialists list, he thought. Though that did sound as if he were bitter, which wasn't true. He loved them and knew they loved him. It was only that he had different goals from theirs and his sister's. He'd excelled in his speciality but didn't make an issue of it. Sometimes he had to wonder if he really belonged to his family or had been adopted at birth. Of course he hadn't been. One look at his grandfather and anyone could tell he belonged to the Marshall clan, but still. 'I take it Jason was English?'

'London born and bred. I once suggested we move to Milan as I missed home. Of course, that wouldn't have happened as he didn't speak the lingo and therefore would've had problems with work, but there was no way he'd have left London anyway.'

'Why's that?'

'His career was going from strength to strength and he became well known and sought after. I understood he'd always aimed for that and couldn't expect him to give it away to move here.'

Sounded like anyone interested in Bella would have to accept living in Italy or not bother. 'You're home for good, then?' Another reason he'd stay on the sideline. He was returning to his home after this spell in paradise. Though when he thought about it, did he have to go back to Scotland? Why not settle somewhere else, in an area no one was so engrossed in his family's life that he couldn't get on with whatever he wanted uninterrupted? So far Stresa had been quiet in that respect.

Early days, warned his ever-wary mind.

'I am. I'm a partner in a great practice, and my child will have lots of family to support him or her.' Bella withdrew her hand and looked ahead. 'Where were you thinking of having pizza?'

Subject closed. Fair enough. He'd learned more than he'd expected and knew not to push the boundaries. He named a pizzeria he'd been to a couple of times. 'That suit you?'

'Perfect.'

He smiled, feeling more at ease than he had in a long time. Bella wasn't hard to please, and straightforward in her requirements. No expectations of grandeur…just took things as they came. He could get used to this. Which was another warning to walk away fast.

Only he didn't know how to do that.

Not true, Aaron.

He was very good at walking away. The problem was, he suddenly saw, he didn't want to. He hadn't felt this sense of bonding with a woman since he met Amy, and with Bella there seemed to be a depth to what was forming between them. Possibly because they weren't rushing into intimacy. As if that were likely to happen. She'd already pointed out she wasn't looking for a relationship. Strange how that made him stop and really look at her; how it had him wanting to know more and more about what lay behind that beautiful face and those intelligent eyes, and her determination to do this alone.

Bella Rosso was proving to be difficult to walk away from, even when they were only going for pizza.

Bella nearly tripped over her own feet, thinking about how Aaron accepted what she'd said without too many personal questions. After all the feedback—mostly unwanted—she'd had from others since announcing her pregnancy, he was a breath of fresh air. Not that he wouldn't have a head full of questions—he was human—but so far he was keeping them to himself.

'*Grazie.*'

'For taking you out for a pizza?' he asked with a cheeky grin on that handsome face. 'No problem.'

She let it go, relieved to have told him about the baby and Jason even when there was no serious reason she should. It was because they got on so well and seemed to be becoming friends that she wanted no secrets to get in the way. At least none that affected their day-to-day friendship. He didn't need to know how much she'd agonised over taking the final step to getting pregnant because once Jason was gone it didn't seem as straightforward as she'd anticipated. All the discussions they'd had about how she'd manage seemed superfluous now the pregnancy was real.

'Jitters,' Cara had told her on one of her indecisive days. 'You'll handle it brilliantly and on the days you don't we're all here for you.'

Yes, she was lucky with her family. Unlike Aaron, by the sound of it. How could his parents not want to be there for him? But then, she didn't know the story behind what he'd said, not even a fraction of it. 'Where did you learn to speak Italian?'

No one had a problem understanding him. He'd never have got the position at the local hospital if he hadn't been fluent in the language, but he didn't even have much of an accent. 'Growing up I had an Italian nanny until I was sent to boarding school. She came from Sorrento. She was very homesick for the first year and I was often alone and unhappy so she'd talk to me in her language and I'd copy her.'

Boarding school? A moneyed background to go with the good looks and great career? He didn't show off or flaunt it, if that was so. 'But you're fluent, orally as well as on paper. Or should I say on the screen?' She laughed. 'I'd have thought you'd need more than that to become as accomplished as you are.'

'Turned out I have an affinity for languages and Sara soon had me doing my homework in English for her to study and Italian for me to learn another language.'

'Where is she now?'

'Married to my old teacher and living in Glasgow. Seemed she got over her homesickness after coming to watch me in the school play.'

'A happy ending. I like it.'

'You're all for romances and everyone getting their happy ever after?'

'Of course. A little bit of romance never goes astray.' She'd had more than a little with Jason. They'd been the happy couple everyone wanted a piece of from the day they met over a bad pie in the hospital canteen in London when she'd been there for a month's training on a paediatric cancer ward. They'd never looked back. A wave of sadness rolled over her. Damn but she missed him. But she also knew she had to look forward now, possibly even find another man to share her and her child's life. If she didn't she'd still be all right, and would not spend every day thinking about what might've been if he hadn't died.

'I see.'

'Do you though?' She glanced up and saw Aaron's cheeky smile back in place. It turned her toes and made her heart beat wilder. Was it possible he could be her second chance? Except she didn't believe she'd ever love as deeply again. Nudging him with an elbow, she laughed. 'Don't tell me you haven't been in love and felt romance in the air.'

The smile slipped. 'Yes, I have. Obviously it didn't last for ever.'

Nor did hers, but it wasn't because Jason chose to leave. She touched Aaron. 'I'm sorry to hear that. Life can be a bitch at times.'

'It sure can, but looks to me like you've found it can also be wonderful. When's baby due?'

Subject moved from him back to her. Fair enough, though it was unlike her to talk about herself so much. Another clue that she might be getting more involved with Aaron than was wise. He was only here for a few months while she was home permanently. Moving back to Britain wasn't an option. Italy was home for her. 'Early November.' Her hand touched her stomach.

How's it going in there?

'It's quite exciting really.'

When she wasn't worrying about how she'd manage baby and her career despite her family saying they'd be there for them.

'After I've left Stresa, then.'

'*Sì.*' Something she should remind herself of whenever she started to think how wonderful he was. 'Unless we wow you over so that you become a permanent member of the hospital staff.'

He shook his head. 'I'm still under contract in Edinburgh. This is a break, nothing more.'

'Point taken.'

This man knows what he's doing.

She should follow his example. Nothing changed because he was so sexy and exciting.

'I am enjoying working in a close-knit community. There's something special about the people around here. You all seem to stick up for each other no matter the cost to yourselves.'

Exactly why she loved home. 'Wouldn't you?' She'd read him entirely wrong if his answer was no.

'Absolutely, but not everyone I know is the same.' His mouth had tightened, warding off her next question. Was he talking about his own family? From his few comments about them it was more than likely.

Tempting as it was, she didn't ask. He might cancel dinner and she'd be gutted. His company was enjoyable, and something she hadn't had in a long time apart from her family, which wasn't the same. Not that she'd been looking very hard. The few dates she'd tried might've been about testing the waters but she hadn't been overly enthused. Yet somehow Aaron managed to wake her up to start looking around at her world.

Looking at him, more like, she told herself with a soft chuckle. 'Not everyone's perfect around here either.' But the ones closest to her were and she knew how lucky she was. Hopefully she gave back as much as she received.

Suddenly the tiredness she'd been fighting all day filled her and made her legs feel lifeless. 'Are we walking to the pizza place or going back to get our cars first?' The pizzeria was closest.

'Let's go eat first. We can always grab a cab afterwards if necessary.'

With a bit of luck, dinner would re-energise her so she was up to the return walk, at least as far as home. The car would be safe at the hospital overnight if need be. 'Works for me.'

'Glad to hear that. My stomach's starting to get impatient for food.'

Hopefully hers would feel the same soon. She did need to keep up her intake for baby. There were days when she struggled eating three meals. The midwife said she'd get past that soon. Right now energy was a requirement so she had to eat. Force-feed herself if necessary. 'Nothing worse than a hungry man.'

CHAPTER FIVE

'SORRY, BUT I'M not going walking with you today. I've had a sleepless night and don't feel one hundred per cent this morning,' Bella told Aaron over the phone the next morning.

'You were shattered last night. Why didn't you sleep well?' Was this normal for Bella or was there something wrong? It was the beginning of the weekend and she didn't have to go to work.

'I've had a few nights like that since I became pregnant.' She hesitated, as though tossing up whether to say any more. 'To be expected, I suppose.'

He wasn't buying it. 'Have you talked to someone about this?'

'Aaron, I'm fine.'

'And I'm a concerned colleague. And friend,' he added because colleague didn't explain his feelings about her. 'How's your blood pressure?'

'Normal.'

'When did you last check it?'

'Aaron, stop it. Go enjoy your walk in the hills. I've got chores to do.' *Click.* Gone.

'Well, Bella Rosso, I've got more important things to do than go walking. I'm coming to visit you and make sure nothing serious is wrong.' He tossed his phone on the table and picked up the bowl of breakfast cereal he'd been eating when she called. The problem being he wasn't Bella's doctor and had no grounds for checking her out. She could very easily kick him off the property without talking to him. Gino would be right behind her if he upset the chef's sister.

But he wasn't about to ignore the need to make sure Bella was all right. He had to know, to help her if necessary. Just as her family would if they knew.

He'd had a cab drop Bella back at her apartment after they'd finished pizza last night. She'd looked tired beyond belief and hadn't argued when he'd told her he was calling up a ride for her. Something that should've told him she wouldn't be walking today, but he'd been too happy in her company to think about this morning. A simple meal in a noisy pizzeria filled with locals celebrating the end of the working week, and he'd relaxed so much he'd felt a different man, almost as though he'd found a town he felt totally at home in.

But he had noticed Bella's exhaustion. Hard not to when dark shadows stained her cheeks beneath those usually gleaming eyes. It hadn't been only the doctor in him keeping an eye on her. He wanted to make sure nothing was wrong. He cared about her. Probably looking for signs of a deepening friendship that weren't there. Deepening friendship or something more? No, couldn't be anything more. Mustn't be.

He was returning to Edinburgh at the end of this contract. *You don't have to.*

Yes, he did. He owed it to his colleagues after all they'd done to help him through the aftermath of nearly losing his life. He also had his dream career there.

Plus he was still having the nightmares and until they were gone he had to concentrate on sorting himself out. It wouldn't be fair to dump his problems on Bella. Nor did he want her knowing how screwed up he'd become since that attack, though after his reaction to Signor Romano she probably had some idea of that.

But the biggest issue standing between them getting close was that she was having her late husband's baby. She was comfortable with what she was doing and didn't need another man in her life sharing her child. Or did she? Behind her brave face she might be in a right old state about raising a child on her own, yet it wouldn't be easy to let another man who wasn't baby's dad into her life.

Yet the most important reason for not getting close and falling for Bella was that she did not need all the publicity that went with being a member of his family. He wasn't implying she'd become his wife. Not yet anyway. If ever. But she didn't have to for the media to start chasing her down and asking questions that were none of their business. If they did fall for each other, what was to say she wouldn't wake up one morning and walk away when it all got too much? Because it would. It always did. Amy had done it when she'd been his support system, and said how much she believed in him—and loved him.

So he had to stay away from Bella. After he made sure she was all right.

Snatching up the keys to his car, he headed over to see Bella.

Gino opened the side door to the stairs Aaron presumed led to the upstairs apartments. 'Hey, Aaron, you here for Bella?'

'Thought I'd drop by.' Lame, but Bella would be furious if he mentioned her being so tired. Gino might already know but he suspected not. She tried to keep worrisome things from her family.

'You've just missed her. She's gone to pick up her car and then to see a friend out Orta way.'

Great. Had she figured he'd come round? 'No worries. I'll catch up with her some time over the weekend.'

'You could call in after lunch,' Gino said. 'She'll be back by then.'

Because I'm meant to be walking the hills all day.

As she well knew. He should go do it. The idea had been very appealing yesterday, even this morning until he'd learned he'd be doing it alone, and now it was the last thing he wanted to do. 'I might just do that,' he told Gino before heading back to his car. In the meantime he'd stock up on groceries and other bits and pieces he required.

'Aaron,' Gino called. 'Bella looked a bit pale this morning. Can you check her out without letting her know what you're doing?'

His heart swelled at the thought this protective brother trusted him to look out for his sister. 'Already onto it.'

Gino stared at him, but only nodded before he finally turned away.

This family was drawing him in, like it or not. Truth was he did like it. Just didn't know how to go with this because someone would end up getting hurt. The last person he wanted that to happen to was Bella. She did not deserve it. Nor did he but he knew the risks. She didn't. Except now he could not walk away from Gino's challenge. Because the man was setting him up to see how he fared. 'See you later,' he called as he opened his car door. He got no reply, which wasn't a surprise.

'What happened to your walk?' Bella asked when she opened her door to him mid-afternoon.

'Changed my mind about going and did a few other less

exciting but necessary chores around town.' Those dark shadows were still darkening her face. 'Coffee?' He held up a cardboard tray with two paper mugs.

Suspicion blinked out at him from tired eyes. 'What's this about?'

He wasn't going to get past the door until he told her, and he wasn't going to lie. 'You're exhausted, too much even for a busy week in your current condition. I want to make sure there's nothing untoward going on, Bella.'

She gave him the same stare Gino had earlier in the day. She didn't like anyone interfering with her life.

He was going to be sent on his way.

Then she slowly stepped back. 'Come in.'

Surprised, and relieved, he followed her into a bright, sunny apartment with cream furniture piled with cushions in every colour of the rainbow. 'I like it.' The warmth and homeliness made him smile.

'I'm not a monochrome kind of girl.' She slowly returned his smile. 'That coffee smells good. Just what I need to perk me up.'

It was an opening to press her for more info on how she was feeling, but Aaron also saw caution in her countenance. 'Me too.'

She sat on the couch while he took a chair further away. Popping the top on his coffee, he sipped tentatively. 'What have you been doing this morning?'

'I went to see a friend I've known since school days. Didn't stay long as her kids were needing various things done and she really didn't seem to have time to sit for even five minutes.'

'Does that worry you for the future? Having to cope with a busy child on your own?'

Her laugh was brittle. 'I'll leave worrying about that while I get through the baby phase first.'

Aaron winced. She wasn't in a good place right now. Placing his coffee on the side table, he turned to face her, and took her hand into his. 'Talk to me, Bella. You're tired, and sounding flat.' Lonely was another word that came to mind but he kept it back. 'I've got broad shoulders.'

'I've noticed,' she quipped, but her face didn't lighten.

'Then use them.' *Any way you like.* Silence fell.

Bella appeared to be contemplating how far to trust him. 'It was a big decision to make about having our baby,' she said.

He relaxed. 'Any regrets?'

Her hair flicked back and forth on her shoulders. 'None at all. It was hard getting the positive result and not having Jason there to celebrate though.'

'I can imagine.' It was going to be even harder giving birth without him at her side. 'One step at a time.' Becoming a parent wasn't something he dwelled on. Opening up to finding the right woman to share that experience with came first. Bella? Right now he needed to focus on her and her physical concerns. 'Have you been more tired than usual lately?'

'Only over these past couple of days. My back's aching and I get the odd sharp pain in my stomach.'

'Have you talked to your midwife?'

'She says to rest and let her know if nothing improves.' The eyes Bella turned on him were filled with concern. 'She knows what she's doing but that doesn't stop me worrying myself sick.'

'Any blood spotting?'

'No.'

'Show me where the pains occur.'

Her hand tapped her lower stomach on the left side. 'Which doesn't make a lot of sense.'

No, it didn't, but sometimes pain didn't always hit where it came from. 'Can I check your BP?'

She nodded. 'My medical bag's in the bottom of my wardrobe.'

'I'll get it?'

'Do you mind?'

'Not a bit.' She was accepting his help. That was what mattered. He got the bag and removed the monitor.

She held her arm out. 'So far I've never had high blood pressure, but pregnancy can interfere with that.'

'You're a worried mother-to-be and a doctor to boot. They say doctors and nurses make the worst patients.' A minute later a relieved sigh slid across his lips. 'Normal. Which, given how worried you are, is a bit of a surprise. Have you had back problems prior to getting pregnant?'

Another nod. 'I once had a severe sprain in the lower region after a skiing accident that sent me tumbling down the slope while entangled with another skier. That was about eight years ago.'

'Spinal injuries are notorious for recurring. Though I'd have expected it to cause trouble further along with your pregnancy when you're carrying weight at the front, not now so much.'

'The pain's to the front, remember? And it's not constant. Just the occasional stab.'

'I think you're having minor tweaks that come with your body adjusting to the pregnancy, but, for peace of mind, let's get you thoroughly checked over, internally and externally. Ask your midwife to meet us at the hospital. Or we can see one of the doctors in the emergency department. Your call.'

He was all right with the external work, but would not

do anything else. They were friends. Some things were best left for the professionals, which in this case he didn't feel he was. So much for keeping space between them. He was being wound in closer and closer like a salmon on the line, and resisting was impossible. Especially when Bella needed him.

'Thank you for understanding. I'm being a worry-wart at the moment, but I miscarried four years ago so a check-up might shut up my nagging fears, though you've already shut down most of them,' she said with a little smile. A more relaxed smile than he'd seen so far today.

'Come on. I'm driving.'

'I wouldn't have expected anything else.' Now her mouth curved upward and some of the tension in her face disappeared. Then she blushed. 'Now you won't think I'm the strong woman you first thought.'

Taking her shoulders in his hands, Aaron gazed down at this woman who already had him wondering if he might change his life for something better. 'Bella Rosso, wash your mouth out. Don't ever think like that. Even the strongest have moments when they're uncertain. You want this baby. You're ready to give up so much for it. I'm sure your feelings are perfectly normal. If they aren't then you're setting a new trend.' He held back from brushing a light kiss on her forehead and growled, 'You've got this.'

Now let's get the hell out of here and get you checked over before I make a complete fool of myself by hauling you into my arms and kissing you until neither of us can stand through the need filling our bodies.

Make that until *he* couldn't, because he didn't have a clue how Bella might feel. She'd probably slap his face if he tried to kiss her.

She was still gazing at him, but now the tip of her tongue was moving across her bottom lip. 'Aaron?'

'Yes,' he managed around the sudden desire in his throat.

'You're special.' Then those full lips were on his mouth and her tongue was tasting him.

He was special? Because he supported her? Believed in her? Heat swamped him, had him deepening his kiss. 'You're the special one,' he whispered as his arms wound around that stunning body and brought her close to him, so close her breasts pressed into his chest and her thighs were hard against his legs, and that small baby bump was pushing into his gut.

Baby.

Bella's and her late husband's. Not his. Nothing to do with him. Flipping his head up, he lowered his arms and stepped back. 'Bella—'

'Yes, sorry, I guess this is all wrong. You're being kind and I got carried away.' She walked out of the apartment, leaving him behind.

'Bella, wait.' He went after her.

'It's all right, Aaron. I understand,' she threw over her shoulder.

'No, you don't. Hell, I don't.'

That made her stop and turn around, a bemused look on her face. 'Not used to being kissed out of the blue?'

'More like not used to not knowing what to do.' Bella was getting to him in unprecedented ways.

'Now what?'

He drew a long breath. He'd love to haul her back into his arms and continue that mind-blowing kiss, followed by another and another. 'We'll get you checked over and then we'll see where we go from there.' He hesitated.

Go on, say it. Tell her you want her.

No, they weren't ready. He wasn't anywhere near ready. Might never be.

'We'll see where we go from there,' Aaron had said. Back to her apartment for another kiss? Despite the exhaustion dragging at her, that was where she'd like to go, but Bella knew it wasn't happening. She should be grateful Aaron had come to his senses and pulled on the brakes, but she wasn't. Not a bit. It was the first kiss she'd had in years that she hadn't wanted to walk away from. The men she'd dated hadn't stirred her blood or made her excited.

Aaron did that without even trying. Now she'd kissed him she wanted more. But it wasn't happening. She was going to have a baby and start a different life that probably wouldn't enthral him at all.

'Let's get this over with.' It might be best to go alone but she needed his support. He was a doctor so would keep her grounded if there was a problem. He wouldn't wrap her up in cotton wool and tell her what she couldn't do. For a few blissful moments with him she'd forgotten her concerns about the baby and her exhaustion, which showed how much he disturbed her equilibrium. 'Let's go.'

'Do you lock your apartment?'

Her shoulders sagged. How had she forgotten that? She didn't leave the door wide open for just anyone to wander in. The kids had no barriers at times. 'Not always but I've left my handbag behind.'

'I'll wait here.'

Staying safe from her? Fair enough. If she could kiss him without warning, then who knew what else she was capable of? Except she'd just had a quick, short lesson on how to behave around Aaron. They might be getting involved, but he wasn't keen on knowing her too well.

Snatching up her bag and phone, she closed the door and headed for the lift, Aaron beside her. Protective to the core, that was him. Plus genuine, caring and the sexiest man she'd been lucky enough to meet since she'd found herself single again. Lucky or unlucky? Because now it was going to be hard to remain casual around him at all times. Even when she wasn't actively looking for a man to have fun with. She was carrying Jason's child, which was a huge barrier to letting someone into her life.

Aaron opened the door for her when they reached his car. How many men did that these days? Sinking into the seat, she buckled herself in, and drew a breath as he got behind the steering wheel. 'Why did you really change your mind about going hiking? You were quite excited yesterday.'

The engine roared to life.

'It didn't appeal as much after you cancelled.' Blunt but honest.

'I couldn't have walked to the end of our drive this morning,' she told him. 'I barely made it round the supermarket, and when I got to my friend's house I was almost glad she didn't have the time to sit down over a coffee with me.' As long as the tiredness was normal for this stage of her pregnancy then she'd relax, but not until she was certain.

'I'm not having a poke at you, Bella. I'd have been more upset if you'd joined me because you felt you had to. I'll do the walk another day, with or without you.'

So they were still friends. Which sounded childish, but these days she couldn't always be certain she understood men. One she'd dated had got uptight because she didn't want an affair with him, and accused her of using him because he was rich. He'd shocked her because he'd seemed a quiet man who only wanted to share a meal or go to a show with a friend. Another told her she was too boring after saying how excited he was at going to the theatre with her.

'I'd like that. I promise to eat lots of energy bars the night before.'

'Don't you dare. We'll go if and when you're up to it, not because you've had a sugar overload.'

'Yes, boss.'

'Better believe it.' He was laughing.

Which took the edge off her fear that she might've lost a friend when she kissed him. Aaron had only come into her life very recently but already she couldn't imagine not having him there in some capacity.

'Who's on duty this weekend?' The emergency department sometimes struggled to provide enough doctors over the busy summer period now in full swing.

'Tess took today and Tommaso is on tomorrow.' He glanced her way briefly. 'You okay with Tess?'

'As in a female doctor to check me out? Absolutely. We get along fine workwise. Someone has to deflect the male medics' cheeky comments at times and I support her whenever I hear them.' It was all in good fun as the staff got on well, but she was glad Tess would be there. Everyone had warned her she'd lose all her inhibitions now she was pregnant, but to do so with a male colleague seemed harder to handle. She knew she was being precious but she was allowed some pride.

'When did you last have your haemoglobin tested?' was Tess's first question.

'I can't remember.' Bella thought back as far as possible and shook her head. 'There's been no reason to.' She never got sick.

'Then guess what? Today's as good a day as any to take a blood sample. Plus we need to know your iron levels. They're the first to take a hit when you're pregnant.'

'I'm not quite four months on.' Iron deficiency tended to happen more in the third trimester. Anyway, her diet was healthy, no reason for low iron levels. Her doctor brain kicked in. Diet wasn't the only cause. Internal bleeding was another. 'Take the sample.'

'Have you had an ultrasound yet?'

'No. I keep meaning to make the appointment but it never seems to work out with my work schedule.'

'It's your lucky day. The radiology technician on duty is qualified to do them so we'll get one done this afternoon.' Tess was smiling as she felt around Bella's abdomen. 'This feels fine, but better to be safe. Right, knees up, I'll do an internal before phoning Radiology.'

'All good so far,' Bella told Aaron when she was dressed again. 'Tess has arranged for me to have an ultrasound so if you need to get away I'll phone one of the sisters-in-law to pick me up afterwards.'

'I'm not going anywhere until you're ready to go home.'

She hadn't realised how tense she was until he said that. 'Thanks.'

'Want company while they slide the camera through the goo on your stomach?'

Her eyes widened as she looked at him. 'You'll come with me?'

'If it makes you happy to have someone with you, then yes.'

From all accounts it wasn't an uncomfortable procedure but what if something was wrong? 'I'd like that,' she said quietly, suddenly frightened of what might be happening.

It didn't feel strange accepting his offer. His support would help a lot.

Aaron took her elbow. 'Let's do this so you can relax and feel better.'

He seemed to have no hesitation about being seen with her in the hospital. It wasn't bothering her either. They were adults, free to do as they pleased. Not friends with benefits but friends in a good, caring way. She managed a small laugh. It had been so long since she'd felt the touch of a man. Until Aaron she hadn't wanted to, and now she didn't want him to pull away. That kiss had hyped her up. Something exciting was happening. 'More likely I'll fall asleep when the pressure's off.'

'Talk about exciting.' Aaron grinned, unaware he'd repeated the same word that explained her sudden happiness. Exciting did it every time.

'I know. Watching paint dry would be more fun.' She turned into Radiology, then hesitated. 'What if…?'

'We'll sort it, whatever it is.'

She shivered. The excitement was gone. There were some conditions that couldn't be sorted. Yet when she looked to Aaron she saw his strength and belief in her and instantly calmed. He'd told her she was strong, and it was true. She'd come this far following Jason's death and now wasn't the time to stumble. 'You're right. I will.'

'Think I said *we* will.'

She had no answer. She liked he'd said that even though it was too soon to be including him in everything tied to her pregnancy. Or her life. She was running solo. Which didn't explain why she felt good having him at her side right now.

Together they watched the screen as the technician scanned her uterus. Bella's heart rate had increased from the first moment the wand touched her stomach, and she reached for Aaron's hand.

'Nothing out of order,' said the young woman. 'But a radiologist will read the results on Monday to be absolutely certain.'

'I'm not miscarrying?'

'No. Baby looks very comfortable in there.'

She couldn't ask for more than that. This woman would've done hundreds of ultrasounds and know what she was looking at. 'I feel better already.' Surprisingly, she did.

'Do you want to know the sex of your baby?'

Bella hesitated. In the beginning she'd thought she'd wait until the baby was born, but lately she'd started thinking she'd like to have a name ready the moment she laid eyes on him or her. 'Yes, I think I do.'

'Want me to leave you alone?' Aaron asked.

'Not at all. If you're happy to stay, then I'm happy to have you here.'

Wow, they were getting in deep.

It's the baby's sex, not a binding agreement to spend the rest of our lives together.

'Thank you.'

She was doing him a favour? Or was he feeling close to her and wanting to be involved in everything? Too soon, yet she couldn't tell him to go. Her hand tightened around his. She wanted him here more than just about anything. She'd think about that later. 'Right, let's find out.'

More goo and pressing from the wand and soon Bella was staring at the image on the screen, a tear trekking down her cheek. 'A girl?' Not a boy from what she could see in the grey picture.

'A girl.' The tech nodded as she pressed print. 'Here's the first photo of your daughter.'

Bella stared at the image, barely able to take it all in. 'That's my baby,' she whispered.

Aaron rubbed her back in slow, soft circles. 'Yes, Bella, that's your daughter.'

The technician stood up. 'I'll leave you for a moment to take it all in.'

More tears escaped. 'I'm having a daughter. Sophia Justine.' The names spilled out with no input from her brain, though Sophia was her grandmother's name and Justine was Jason's mother's.

'You'd already thought of names?' Aaron asked.

'No, those just happened.' Sort of. They had been playing around in her mind on and off. She paused, breathed deep. 'But I like them. Really like them.'

'Sophia Justine, eh? Well, little girl, you grow big and strong for your *mamma*.' Aaron looked away, but not before Bella saw a tear appear at the corner of his eye.

'You ever thought of having kids?'

'Who doesn't?' He was talking to the wall. Not a defining answer, but he'd said yes in his own way.

'It's natural to want to be a parent. That's the easy bit. Finding the right other half to do it with is harder, and then there are all the other considerations. To work or not, to want one or more, where to send them to school. The list goes on and on.'

Be quiet, Bella. You're overdoing it.

Now Aaron looked at her. 'I didn't realise you spent so much time thinking about it. But then I shouldn't be surprised. You like to be prepared, if nothing else.'

'I also like some surprises every now and then,' she said a little too acerbically.

'I wasn't criticising. I'm in awe of how you manage your work, and plan for your child's future so that it will go well.'

'Isn't it what all expectant parents do? You can't have a baby without some forethought.'

'True. I'd be much the same if the opportunity arose.'

The sadness in his voice had her wanting to reach for his hands but she sensed he wouldn't thank her. He seemed to be in a bubble of his own. 'You never know what's around the next corner, Aaron.' That applied to good and bad events, but she wasn't saying so. 'If you're open to accepting whatever comes along, that is.'

'So if a woman with six kids and a horse is around the corner waiting for me I'm to leap in and invite them to my home, never to let them out of sight again?' he asked, smiling.

'Absolutely. Your place would probably be more spacious than their caravan.'

'You always know how to cheer me up, don't you?'

She wasn't aware of that. 'Glad to be of some help.' A yawn ripped out of her. 'Can you give me a lift home? I feel even more shattered now I know nothing's seriously wrong.' It was as though she'd let go the last worry holding her together and wanted nothing more than to curl up and sleep.

'Your place or mine? I've got a comfortable sofa and I can whip up a light meal while you take it easy, if you'd like.'

She didn't have to think about it. 'If I go home I'll have to tell the family they're getting a granddaughter and a niece and then there'll be no end of talk and everyone dropping in to let me know how they feel, which will only be good, but I'm not ready for them just yet.'

'My place, then.' He tugged her to her feet, put an arm around her waist. 'Let's go.'

It was too easy to snuggle in close to that firm, warm body and let Aaron take charge for a little while. Too easy and right now she didn't care.

* * *

Aaron wrapped a light blanket around Bella as she slept on the sofa. She'd barely touched the tuna salad he'd made, and even her cup of tea had gone cold without a sip being taken.

'You're beautiful,' he whispered. A strand of dark hair lay on her cheek, tempting him to lift it away, but he refrained. If she woke because of his action he'd be in deep trouble, even if they'd edged closer over the afternoon. If only he could hold her in his arms while she snoozed the evening away.

She'd let him stay for the scan. Seeing that baby image was beyond description. His heart had swelled and he'd felt a tug of love for Bella's child. It had been an incredible moment that he wasn't likely to ever forget.

He couldn't remember when a woman had sneaked under his radar so effortlessly. Apart from Amy and he wasn't going there. He'd always been alert to being used by anyone he encountered, and especially the women who appeared nonchalant around him only to be trying to win him over. Amy hadn't done that. Nor did Bella. She treated him as she did everyone—by accepting him for who he was and not trying to change anything.

Except she doesn't know who you are.

Therein lay the problem. One day—and that was getting nearer every hour they spent together—he was going to have to fess up, and hope like mad she still accepted him for who he truly was. Not only an emergency specialist and a keen hiker who enjoyed a bowl of good pasta and sitting on his deck having a wine, and who, yes, one day did want a family of his own, but the rest as well. Son of wealthy parents famous for their careers and social life, and brother of an aspiring camerawoman fast making a name for herself who also loved being in the spotlight and sharing everything about her life with anyone who'd listen. He really was the odd one out in his family.

Aaron walked out onto the deck and leaned against the railing to stare at Lake Maggiore as the sun went down. Stunning came to mind. He could go a long way before finding anything else quite so breathtaking. He was probably biased because of the woman lying on his sofa. She added to the mystic beauty of this area. He'd never again think of Stresa without thinking about Bella. In his mind they went hand in hand. He was smitten with them both.

His gaze dropped to the semi-ruin covered with ivy on the opposite side of the road. There'd be history behind those walls. Like the local hospital with its stone walls evoking a sense of awe in him. It underlined how comfortable he'd become so quickly in Stresa. The people were friendly and never in such a hurry they didn't stop to say hello, making him think he belonged in a way he'd never known.

He was nowhere near ready to return home, even if he could get out of the four-month contract, which he wasn't prepared to try because that'd mean letting the hospital down, as well as all the staff who'd welcomed him with open arms and whom he got on with very well.

Nor had the nightmares abated. He hadn't been here long, but he'd hoped there'd be some sign they would go by now. A good reason not to go to sleep while Bella was here. The last thing he needed was her hearing him crying out in the middle of the night. She might know about the stabbing, but she had no idea just how badly it had screwed with him.

Mind you, with Bella within range the chances of him sleeping were zero anyway.

The air shifted around him and Bella was there, standing beside him, looking in the same direction as he was. 'Magic, isn't it?'

'Yes.' The lochs at home were equally stunning, but it was the warmth and relaxed atmosphere here that got to him. Bella added to his enjoyment.

'I should be getting home.' Not a lot of enthusiasm going on in her voice.

'Sure you want to?' he asked.

She turned to lean back against the railing and locked those sensual eyes on him. 'Not really.'

Drawing a quiet, slow breath, he lifted the strand of hair away from her cheek to tuck it behind her ear. 'We have some unfinished business that I'd like to see through to the end,' he said quietly, watching her closely.

'We do.'

They continued to look at each other, the silence and expectancy drawing out between them. They reached for each other in the same instant, hands gripping each other, mouths meeting, opening; tongues touching and entwining. She tasted wonderful. She felt sublime in his arms, against his tight body. She smelt of roses and sun and life. A different life. A promise that hadn't been made but might come true if he opened up to it.

He knew he was risking everything he'd spent a lifetime trying to save, but for once he had no control over his emotions. Or he didn't want to control them. They'd started running rampant when he'd seen that image of her baby daughter and the tears pouring down her face as love warred with fear of getting it all wrong in her eyes. 'Bella?'

'Sì?'

'Stay the night with me.'

'Sì.'

There was nothing more to say. Any other words would spoil the magic surrounding them, isolating them from everything and everyone else. Lifting her into his arms, he strode inside and along to his bedroom, where he placed her gently on the bed.

'I'm not made of glass.' She laughed and bounced up to hold his head while she planted a long, intoxicating kiss on his mouth.

When he finally came up for air, he was rock hard and pulsing with need for her. 'Steady. We don't have to rush.'

'Can't see me being able to go any slower. I want you, Aaron. Now.'

'Not happening.' As much as he was struggling to keep control of his own desire, he was not diving in without first pleasuring Bella. 'First time I've known you to be impatient.' He grinned as he began unbuttoning her blouse and exposing the sexiest breasts he'd ever seen. His hard-on got harder and his pulse felt as if it were about to explode.

Added to by the hot sensation of Bella's hands on his waist, unzipping his shorts and pushing them lower. Sliding inside his pants and finding his need, wrapping around him, squeezing, caressing, turning his head to a molten mess. But not quite enough to hand over to her. 'Bella, wait.' When she didn't stop, he begged, 'Please.'

'Touch me.'

His hands lifted those hot breasts, his fingers tweaking the hard nipples.

'Lower.'

He deliberately took his time feeling her breasts and leaning in to kiss each one thoroughly before kissing a light trail between them and down to her belly. His tongue tasted her left and right, up and lower. His hands felt the tension tightening in her body as she cried out to be taken.

Sliding further down the bed, he found her sex, licked it until she was pushing upward and crying out louder. When he slid his finger inside, her whole body shuddered.

Bella shoved her fingers through his hair, caught his head and pulled him away. 'No, no more licking or I'll come. I want you in me for that.'

He was more than ready. So was Bella. Her hot, wet sex took him in, tightened around him as she rocked her hips upward. And he dived deeper into the heat, only to pull back and press in again and again, until he was out of his mind with need and Bella was crying out and shuddering all around him. Then he let go, and joined her in wonder.

Later they lay spooned together, with Aaron's arm over Bella's waist, his hand splayed over her baby bump. It felt wonderful. The most natural thing in the world, and it wasn't his baby. His hand tensed.

Bella covered it with hers. 'Relax. It's all right. We haven't done anything wrong.'

No, but the baby was beginning to intrude on his happiness. Not because he didn't want it there, but it indicated lots of issues lying between them. Important problems he wasn't prepared to ignore. Nor was he ready to take them on and tell the world to go to hell because Bella would get hurt if he did, and she was the last person he wanted to upset. She was too important to treat as a one-night stand. Or to have a brief fling with. Too late. They'd already started something. He rolled onto his back and put his hands behind his head, stared up at the semi-dark ceiling. 'You're right, we haven't. But I hope we haven't spoilt a great friendship.'

'Lovers can be friends too.' Then she gasped. 'What am I saying? That I expect more after this?'

His pride stepped up. 'Don't you want more?'

She rolled over so she could eyeball him. 'Aaron, we both know we've got our own futures sorted and they don't include us being together.'

'That wasn't my question.' Though he did want to know where she was going with this. 'But carry on.'

She surprised him. 'Making love with you was amazing. How's that for an answer? It's true, in case you think I'm trying to soothe your ego. I feel like I've been to the stars and back.'

His finger traced her lips. 'You know how to make me feel special.'

'As for your other question, I can't imagine I can let you walk away without making love to me again, but I am saying that I am not looking for anything permanent. I'm sure you understand why.'

'The baby? You don't think you can share your life once you're a parent?' A wave of sadness rolled over him. For Bella and himself. Solo parents found partners all the time. Why not Bella?

'It's a lot to ask another man to take on Jason's child when I've deliberately got pregnant.' She looked sad. 'It's different from having been left with a child to raise alone.'

'Is it though? I guess some men might think you'll never get over losing Jason and they'd be competing for your love, but I'd say they'd be short on self-confidence.' If he fell in love with Bella and she reciprocated the feeling then he'd run with it, and never stop to look back. Because true love accepted *everything*. Except history had proved him wrong with Amy.

'You think?' She was smiling now, the sadness slowly taking a back seat.

If he'd made her happier, then he was glad to have helped. 'You know me well enough to understand if I say something I mean it. Or think it,' he added with a smile of his own. 'Now roll over and back in so I can cuddle you to sleep. You still look tired.'

'I wonder why.' Her smile stretched wide. 'But yes, I could do with some more Z's.'

Her firm butt pressed into his groin, making him horny as, but he resisted because Bella did need to catch up on sleep if she was going to function at all well in the morning. His arm slipped around her waist, her warm skin like silk against his palm. She relaxed against his chest as her breathing deepened and slowed.

Lying there, holding Bella, Aaron tried not to think too much about the future because really they didn't have one. As she'd pointed out, they had their own plans mapped out, which didn't include each other. Though that was getting harder by the day to accept. Nothing was fixed in concrete. He'd have to be an egotist not to be prepared to change anything to fit in with a woman he loved if that came about, and Bella was getting closer to his heart with every breath she took.

This was so cosy. Comfortable, mentally as well as physically. Something that had been missing for a long time, especially since the attack. His eyelids lifted and he stared over her shoulder at the far wall.

Under his arm Bella's chest rose and fell in soft movements. She was out to it. So trusting.

His eyes closed. He pushed them open. Breathed deep, long and hard. *Stay awake. Enjoy the warmth, the sharing, the trust.* Shouting in his sleep would be a nightmare for them both. His breathing slowed along with his heart rate. So cosy.

The next thing Aaron knew he was opening his eyes and looking into Bella's steady gaze. 'Hello. Did I fall asleep?'

'You were out for the count when I woke about an hour ago.'

'You're kidding me.' He couldn't have been. He never slept more than a few minutes at a time.

'Why would I?' Then understanding dawned on her face. 'That attack haunts you at night.'

'Every night since it happened—until now. Unbelievable.' Even more unbelievable was how he was talking about it when he never mentioned it to anyone, not even his closest friends.

'You were comfortable with me.'

'True.' Could she stay every night from now on? Chance would be a fine thing. 'Or so completely relaxed after making love that nothing could intrude.' Not even a man with a knife.

'I know that feeling very well.' Her smile was infectious.

He laughed. 'Come here. Want some more comfort?'

'Can't think of a better way to start the day.' Her lips were heat on his mouth.

CHAPTER SIX

'JOHNNY'S AN ASTHMATIC,' Aaron told Bella. 'He presented with a serious headache on the right side. A migraine by my reckoning.'

Poor lad. 'Has he had them before?' Bella asked the distressed woman sitting by the bed.

'Never. He gets mild headaches during an asthma attack but nothing like this.'

'Johnny, what have you been doing today?'

'Swimming and riding my bike.'

'Did you fall off your bike? Bang your head on anything?'

'No, but there was a lot of glare on the water when I was swimming.'

'That could do it at a pinch.' Some people were more vulnerable than others. 'Do you do a lot of swimming?' she asked as a way of getting Johnny to relax. The tension wasn't helping his breathing and therefore his asthma attack was getting worse.

When he started gasping for air Aaron handed him the oxygen mask. 'Put that on, and don't take it off this time.'

His mother took over. 'He swims as a way of expanding his lungs and keeping his breathing as normal as possible. But today he came home early because of his headache. Said it was really bad so I brought him here. Dr Aaron thought you should see him. Do you agree about the migraine? Johnny doesn't need any more problems.'

Bella nodded. 'I'm sure he doesn't, but Aaron's right. Johnny's suffering from a migraine, and since his asthma is flaring up I'd like to keep him in for a night to monitor his blood pressure and vitals to be sure it is a migraine and nothing else.'

Johnny stared at her. He was gasping for the oxygen and sweat had broken out on his forehead.

'I don't think there is another problem but I like to be certain. Anyway you need that oxygen at the moment. That's not a light asthma attack.' Bella looked to Aaron. 'Have you given him anything for the pain?'

He nodded and named the drug he'd prescribed. 'Johnny took it about twenty minutes ago so it should be kicking in by now.' Turning to their patient, he asked, 'Is the pain any better?'

Johnny held up his thumb and finger with a small gap between them.

'Good.'

'I know you're thirteen but I'm taking you to the children's ward. The general ward is full at the moment.' Bella gave a little laugh. 'You can be the boss of all the kids.'

He did an eye-roll, and tugged the mask to the side. 'Thanks a lot, Doc.'

'You're welcome.'

'He's spent enough nights in children's wards they feel like home to him,' Johnny's mother said.

'He has a lot of severe asthma attacks,' Aaron added.

She'd seen that in the notes. 'You're not locals or I'd have met you before.'

'Milan,' Aaron answered for Johnny. 'He's here for a school trip. His mother's a teacher's aide.'

Then he ended up in here. Her heart tugged for him. But to be fair, he wasn't behaving as if he'd been handed a raw deal. He was used to it and getting on with what needed to be done with the occasional grump. 'Are you having more or less attacks than you did as a child?'

This time his mother answered. 'No change really. Until today and the headache.'

'You haven't taken a tumble in the last day or two, have you?'

Johnny's eyes widened. He tugged the mask away. 'I fell off the bed yesterday.' Gasp. 'Me and another guy were horsing around.' Gasp. Deep inhale on the oxygen. 'I did knock my head but not hard and no headache.'

'But it might have started something.' Bella straightened up. 'Let's get you upstairs and I'll talk to your doctor back home.'

'Might be too late in the day for that,' Aaron pointed out. 'It's after six.'

No wonder her stomach was rumbling. Food was needed and the sooner the better. Her appetite had returned with a vengeance over the past couple of days. 'I'll give it a go anyway.'

'You were working late,' Aaron said as she headed to the desk and a phone.

'I've got a ten-year-old with leukaemia who returned from treatment in Milan about an hour ago. I like to make sure everything's going all right before I leave. I'll be keeping an eye on Johnny too.'

She glanced at Aaron and felt her heart swell. It was nearly a week since she'd spent the night in his bed. Far too long. They'd both been busy all week, her with extra appointments with patients from further afield, and Aaron on night shifts, so no catching up between his sheets. But she was also being cautious. Despite how much she wanted him, she was aware that whatever they'd started wasn't going anywhere long term. That made her wonder if she should call it quits before she was too involved, or if she should grab what was on offer and make the most of the time Aaron was in Stresa.

The thing was, he also seemed a little reluctant to rush into a full-on relationship. She didn't know why, but she couldn't argue with him because basically they were on the same page about not getting in too deep. She didn't know if he even wanted to see her again outside work. She thought he might, but wasn't certain. The man could do aloof very well. Add in the fact she wasn't used to getting into new relationships and it was a bit of a quagmire.

'I'll be around here if you happen to get called in later.' His grin was wicked and did little to cool the need simmering in her veins.

Did that mean he might want some more time with her? She refused to overthink the answer. She'd already done six days on her own since they'd made love. She was starved for his company. 'Want me to bring in some spaghetti, by any chance?'

His eyes widened and his tongue did a lap of his lips. 'Yes, please, thank you, Doctor.'

She'd get Gino to put together two meals and join Aaron in the department tearoom. 'See you later.' Sounded like a promise, one she was glad to make. To hell with the future. Tonight she'd enjoy sharing a meal with Aaron amongst his calls to the ED.

'Delicious as usual. Gino's cooking would be as good a reason as any to apply for a permanent position here, if I didn't have a job back home.' Aaron pushed the plate aside and leaned back. Not quite as good as the one where he got to spend more time with Bella. If she was willing.

'I'll let him know.' She grinned. The grin disappeared as she became thoughtful.

'Maybe not?' Gino mightn't approve of him getting too close to his sister. He wouldn't want her being hurt again, though he did seem keen for her to find a partner so she wasn't raising her child alone.

Bella gave an exaggerated shrug. 'He likes the compliments as much as anybody.'

That was not what was putting the caution in her expression. 'Try again, Bella.' He was in the mood to push her a bit. They'd been relaxed around each other ever since making love. There hadn't been any talk of what came next, but neither had that caused tension whenever they'd caught up. If there was a problem between them, surely it would've been apparent? He knew he had to keep his distance when it came to his heart, but a little relaxation and fun didn't mean he was going all out to win her over.

Her sigh hung between them. 'Gino wants nothing more than for me to find a husband. He won't accept I'm not interested in another relationship. Not yet.' She was staring at her hands clenched together on the tabletop.

Okay, so he already knew this, but for some reason it hurt to hear it. Especially since they'd connected so well when they'd made love. Of course she was right, but that didn't make it any easier to accept. Pride? Probably. It was new for him to be turned away. Women flocked to him and it was usually him turning *them* away. Not that Bella was saying they'd have nothing to do with each other now, but still. He did have red blood in his veins and a big heart that needed filling. He shouldn't be thinking that. That was not up for grabs. Not until he was certain the woman he came to love could handle his lifestyle and background. He wasn't sure how Bella would cope with any of that. If she did keep it all in perspective, she'd probably still be worn down by all the hype eventually. He'd seen it before. Talk about jaded.

'Aaron? Have I gone too far?'

'No, I like your honesty. It leaves no doubts. More than that, I understand what you're saying.' Mostly, anyway, and not necessarily liking it, even if she was being honest, because it raised questions about his own reasons for staying single. Was he a coward? Should he take a chance? There was a lot to win, and a lot to lose. 'How about you tell him I thoroughly enjoyed dinner and that we are getting along fine without any expectations of a future together?'

Bella winced.

He'd touched a nerve. Who knew what that meant? She must have doubts about what she wanted looking ahead. Who didn't in situations like theirs? He wasn't asking for another round of honesty just yet. It was painful for both of them. Leaning forward, he covered those tight fists balled in her lap.

'Bella, it's all right. You and I know where we stand with each other.' Did they though? 'That's all that matters. As you've pointed out, we have our futures planned and they don't include each other beyond whatever happens over the next few months.' He hated saying that, but he was supporting her, and repeating what he'd agreed to. 'It has nothing to do with your brother.' Gino knew Aaron would never deliberately hurt his sister. That was what mattered here.

A nurse appeared in the doorway. 'Aaron, you're needed. An elderly man's had cardiac arrest and the ambulance is only minutes away.'

'Coming.' He stood up and reached for the dirty plates.

'I'll look after those,' Bella told him. 'Then I'll check on my patients before heading home.' She looked a bit woebegone.

'Bella, don't overthink everything.'

'Actually, I was going to say let's go for a walk tomorrow afternoon once you've caught up on some sleep, but I shouldn't be walking too much and you like to get out amongst it.'

Knock me down. Now I'm really confused.

So, he'd go with what he'd honestly like to do. 'Here's another idea. I could take the chairlift from this side to the top of the hill and hike down into Orta and meet you there for a late lunch.' He did like to stride out hard and fast. Over the past few weeks he'd come to realise how much the hiking was rejuvenating him physically and, more importantly, mentally. Though some of the mental improvement he put down to time spent with Bella.

Her hair fell across her cheek when she nodded. 'Agreed. I can go for a small stroll by the lake and pretend I'm being physically active.' She wasn't happy about staying off her feet as much as possible, but he knew how determined she was to keep this baby so she was taking it seriously.

'Decision made. I'll set my alarm for eleven in the morning. I'm not rostered on tomorrow night.'

'I'll drive you back to your apartment afterwards.'

He didn't bother arguing. It didn't matter who was behind the wheel. Only who he was with, and Bella was his pick.

So much for keeping his distance. He'd get back on track next week.

Which meant he had no hang-ups about making love to Bella when they got back to his apartment. Nor could he stop smiling when she curled into him and said she'd like to stay the night with him. More hugs, cuddles, kisses and love making eventuated, making him happier than he could ever remember being.

Hard to put up the barriers after that and the following days were filled with more of the same.

The next week Bella blew his socks off once more. 'It's my parents' wedding anniversary in a couple of weeks and we're having a family day out on Isola Bella. Would you like to join us?' she asked when they crossed paths in the hospital. 'The restaurant owners are friends of Gino's and they're organising everything, even the catering.'

Aaron laughed. 'Bet that's got Gino in a lather. He does like to be in control of the food.'

'Believe me, Micco is in charge. They go way back and Gino knows when to behave.'

'This should be interesting. As for your invitation, I'd love to come. Are you sure your parents won't mind?'

'It was Papà's idea, though I had already been going to ask you.' Bella's mouth twitched. 'My family seem to have taken a shine to you.'

'I'd better be on my best behaviour, then.'

'Why spoil things?' Bella grinned.

His stomach knotted with desire. She could turn him on with nothing more than a glance, so a cheeky grin was like adding fire to dynamite. 'That's the last thing I want to do.' He felt the note of caution in his words, and hoped Bella hadn't.

Isola Bella was a popular tourist attraction, which raised caution. Back home, whenever he went to a function, the first thing he thought about was how to avoid the media. Here, where he could still walk around town freely, he hadn't had to do that yet. The last thing he wanted was anyone with a microphone or camera turning up to ask him about the people he was keeping company with. So far he'd escaped attention in Stresa, but old habits didn't die overnight. Long may that last. He knew no matter how hard he tried to stay in the background, it was impossible if the media wanted to know what he was up to.

'You've gone quiet on me.'

He shook his head abruptly. 'Didn't mean to. Tell me where I meet you all and I'll make sure I'm there on time.' Without any nosey followers.

'Come around to my apartment and we'll go from there. We'll probably have a carload of excited kids to cope with.' She laughed. 'Hope you're up for that.'

'Totally inexperienced but happy to give it my all.'

'No nieces or nephews?'

'My sister isn't in a relationship; too focused on her career. I doubt whether she'll ever settle down enough to have a family.' Kind of sad, but then he wasn't sure if the opportunity would arise for him either for different reasons. Having kids of his own with the right woman would be wonderful. His eyes flicked to Bella.

She would be the right woman. She'd be a fantastic wife. And she was going to be a wonderful mother.

Yeah, and you're so not ready for that.

But he was thinking about it more often these days. Not so long ago thinking like that about a woman would never have occurred to him. Bella had him warming to the idea of taking another chance on love.

Bella nudged him in the side. 'You're doing it again.' A stern look came his way. 'If you'd prefer not to come, just say so.'

'You couldn't be further from the truth. I can't wait to spend time with you, and your family since they're so accepting of me.'

'Why wouldn't they be?'

If only she knew. No, he didn't want her finding out about his lifestyle back home. Not yet. There was no avoiding the day when he had to tell her, but he wanted to make the most of the time he had with her uninterrupted by nosey parkers thinking he owed the world something. He faked a shrug. 'Who knows? You're their daughter and sister. They might be picky about who you see.'

'You're failing to convince me that you're being completely honest here, Aaron.'

Fair enough. 'I'm not used to being accepted without lots of questions about my future and what I want.' It was true, in a roundabout way.

'Why would that be?'

No getting off lightly. 'This is bigger than a two-minute discussion in the hospital hallway. Can we defer it till another time?'

Bella leaned back against the wall, her hand on her baby bump. 'Are you avoiding something?'

Absolutely. Who wouldn't if it meant curtailing what was turning out to be the best experience he'd had in years? 'I have been, but you're right, the time has come to talk to you.' Two nurses walked past, laughing over something one had said. 'Not here though.'

A phone rang. Not his.

Bella looked disgruntled when she realised it was hers. 'Saved by the phone, eh?' Pressing the phone to her ear, she answered, 'Dr Bella Rosso.'

It would be too easy to walk away while he could, but he wasn't a coward. He might loathe the hype that surrounded his family but he wasn't about to turn his back on Bella when she'd been so understanding about his nightmares over the attack.

'I've got to go. That was a pathologist from Milan. Haematology's back on a two-year-old boy. Acute myeloid leukaemia.' Her shoulders sank in on themselves as her face darkened. 'I hate these moments. Now I'm going to be a *mamma* it's even worse, if that's possible.'

Aaron placed a hand on her shoulder. 'Breathe, Bella. In, out. That's it. You've got this.'

For a long minute they stood like that, then she straightened, drew a deep breath and gave him a crooked smile. 'You make me feel I can do anything. I'll see you later?'

'Yes.' Whether to discuss his family or her afternoon that was about to unfold he had no idea. Possibly both, but he'd be there for Bella. No way he wouldn't be. 'You can count on it.'

'Thought I might be able to.'

Or should I have said, I was afraid to trust him not to let me down? Bella pondered as she headed for the children's ward and the nightmare waiting there. She preferred thinking about Aaron's hesitancy and what it might mean to their growing friendship than facing what she now had to tell Nigel's parents. Yet he'd been quick to touch her with that tenderness he seemed to keep bottled inside. He understood how tough this was for her.

'Put your big girl's pants on,' she admonished herself. This wasn't the first time she'd had to deliver heartbreaking news to parents, nor would it be the last. It still didn't make things any easier. Her hand did a circle of her baby bump. Doing something like this was even more real. Being a parent made a person vulnerable.

'The file's on screen for you,' Gita told her as she swept into the office, trying to look more confident than she felt.

'There's a bed reserved at Milan Hospital for Nigel. We need to arrange a transfer asap.'

'I'll get onto it right away.'

Dropping onto the hard chair, Bella swiped the screen and tapped 'open', then proceeded to read all the data the pathologist had summarised over the phone. It didn't make pleasant reading, even when she'd been warned about what to expect. Finally she stood up and, holding her head high, went to talk to her patient's parents.

'I'm shattered,' Bella told Aaron later that night as they sat on his veranda and watched the sun sink behind the Alps. 'Explaining the leukaemia to Nigel's parents was hard work. They're struggling to believe it, as has every parent I've ever told something similar to. I can't begin to imagine what it must be like.' Both her hands were on her stomach, protecting Sophia from all the horrors out in the real world.

'Here, get this into you.' Aaron placed a mug of green tea on the small table by her chair. 'My landlady swears it's the best thing for stress.'

'Better than wine?' Which she wasn't having while she was pregnant.

'Probably not, but we're behaving.' He sank onto a chair beside her and reached over to rub between her shoulders.

How did he know there was a tight knot there that ached whichever way she held herself? 'That's good,' she murmured, sipping the tea. 'The tea's not too bad either.'

'Want to talk?'

'Nigel's on his way to hospital in Milan as we speak. His mum's with him and dad's following in the car. The grandparents are looking after their other son, who's five.' Another sip of tea. 'The pathologist is going to take a bone-marrow sample first thing tomorrow morning. Then he'll start treatment as soon as he's read the smears.' She shivered. 'That's it, really. Acute leukaemia can have a good outcome in young children but the treatment's harsh.' She would not cry. She wouldn't.

'Here, take a handful.' Aaron passed her a box of tissues.

Maybe a few tears were allowed. 'I'm the kid's doctor. I'm not supposed to cry.'

'You're also human. It would be odd if you didn't get tearful. Hell, I feel a bit that way and I've had nothing to do with your patient or his parents.'

She reached for his hand, because he made her feel better without any falsehood. A genuine guy through and through. 'The downside to being a doctor, isn't it? It's even harder in this case because I know the family. Jenny grew up in the same street as me, though she's a couple of years younger, and we were best buddies.'

'She hoped you'd perform miracles when you mentioned why you'd ordered haematology tests?'

'You're onto it. Though I didn't mention leukaemia, I did say Nigel looked very anaemic, which went with his lethargy. Then there are all the bruises covering his body. Jenny's no slug. She cottoned on to the fact I was thinking something more than a minor illness.'

'Why didn't you hand Nigel over to someone else?'

'Who? It's a small town. Everyone knows everyone. One of the other specialists at the practice isn't a local but he's away on leave this week. Besides, it's probably nicer for Jenny and Geo that they know me.'

'Fair enough.'

Baby kicked. Bella gasped, and placed her hand on the spot. 'Wow. Are you going to be a footballer, my girl?'

'Baby's letting you know she's awake?'

'Do you want to feel her kick?' She held her breath. Was

that going too far? Probably. This baby had nothing to do with Aaron, and, while he was very supportive of her, it didn't mean he wanted to get too close.

'Can I?' he asked. 'I'd love to.'

'Give me your hand.' She placed his palm on her abdomen, refusing to think about what might be going on in his mind. 'Just wait. There. Feel that?'

The look of wonder in his eyes told her yes.

'Wow. That's amazing. I've never known that before. Well, not quite true. When I was training there was a six-month-pregnant woman in our class who let everyone touch the spot where her baby was moving, but that was impersonal. This...' He paused and looked at Bella. 'This feels different. I've held your body. Made love to you, and now to feel your baby move is wonderful.'

Blow her over. When the man put his soul into it, he could say the most heart-rending things. 'That's how I felt the first time Sophia moved, and I have every time since. It's like she's telling me she's in there and I'd better not ignore her. I never understood how intense being pregnant could be, and I should have. I've heard plenty of women say the same thing, but I guess when it came to me I believed being a doctor would take some of the gloss away.'

'It hasn't, has it? I'm stunned and I'm not the one carrying the baby.'

Nor was he the father. That was what he was really saying. Which kind of saddened her. He'd be a great dad. Talk about getting ahead of herself. They were friends who'd become lovers. Best not to hurry and find out what lay ahead, and instead make the most of what they had together. One day at a time, she reminded herself.

She was still in the dark about how far she wanted this to go. Aaron ticked a lot of boxes, but when she'd decided to become pregnant with Jason's child she'd planned on going it alone. To bring Aaron into the picture needed a lot of consideration from all aspects. He had to be one hundred per cent on board, and they were nowhere near that with a lot to share about their pasts and what they wanted further ahead. It was quite possible they'd never be that close. She went with light-hearted because to get too deep wasn't a good idea at the moment.

'Men get the easy job when it comes to babies.' She laughed.

'I reckon. But then there are all the years that follow, and dads are very involved then.'

'You would be. I know that for sure.'

'Thank you for the vote of confidence.' He looked pleased.

Didn't he get many compliments? When everyone at the hospital thought he was a superb doctor? When her family believed he was a genuine man who wanted nothing more than to be a part of everything going on? When he had her back even before he got to know her? 'I could go on but then your head might get too big to hold up.'

He leaned back in his chair and sipped his beer. 'You know something? I haven't been so relaxed with a woman in for ever.'

'Why not?'

'You don't want so much from me that I forget why I liked you in the first place.'

There was more to that than first seemed likely, but right now she wasn't about to dig deep. The tension brought on by Nigel's diagnosis was slipping away and she was feeling comfortable again. All due to this man. No need to spoil the moment. Turning to him, she leaned close and kissed him. Lightly, softly. Her heart squeezed. He was just who she needed right now. Pressing harder, she kissed deeper, slipping her tongue into his mouth and savouring his heat.

'Bella,' he groaned under her mouth.

She pulled back enough to say, 'What I want right now is for us to make love.'

He took her face in his hands and locked his eyes on her. 'I'd like that very much.'

What could be better?

Later, as they lay in Aaron's bed, holding hands, Bella stared at the ceiling and said quietly, 'Tell me some more about your family.' More? She knew nothing.

His hand stiffened. Then he withdrew it. 'What would you like to know?'

So he was putting it back on her. Avoiding something? 'You've said my lot are close and all encompassing, unlike yours. Why are they so different?'

Silence. The frown on his brow suggested he was thinking about where to go with this.

She waited patiently. Forcing Aaron to talk might cause distress, but at the same time she wanted to get to know him better. Needed to if they were to stay together for longer than a fling.

He rolled onto his side, his head on his hand. Looking at her, he sighed. 'My parents have always been deeply involved in their careers. To the point the careers came before me and my sister.'

How could any parent do that? 'That must've been hard.'

'It was. My sister's much the same now, though at least she understands it wouldn't be wise to have children and then treat them the same way we were.'

'What does she do?'

'She works in the film industry as a camera operator. A very good one, at that.'

'Being very good must run in the family as her brother's an exceptional emergency doctor, by all accounts.'

His smile was tight. 'Thanks.' He huffed out a breath. 'My father is a high court judge and my mother is a well-known actress. They make the headlines often, including my sister. While I'm happy for them all, the hype that goes with that is mind-boggling at times and drives me crazy. There's no such thing as privacy for any of us.'

'Even you?'

'Even me.' He was watching her intently. 'My family's wealthy, which only adds to the media circus. They seem to think they have the right to ask personal questions and get abusive when I don't give them the answers they want. When I was young I thought it was normal and fine, but out in the real world I began to understand what it was like for other people living quieter, less fortunate lives. Strange as it sounds, I wanted that.'

'You'd like the family life I grew up in?'

'Absolutely. I'm used to being followed and hassled by media, but there're times when they interfere in my private life too much. It affects relationships and friendships in ways I don't like.'

'I can imagine.'

'I doubt it. Though I also believe you wouldn't like the attention either.'

'I'd hate it. I had a couple of encounters with the media when Jason hit the headlines over a life-changing medical technique he developed.' The reporters had wanted to know all about her, which was so irrelevant. No one had the right to shove a camera in anyone's face so they could get a story to titillate the readers and probably be forgotten by breakfast time the next day. 'Was the attack on you in ED made into a big deal because of who you are?'

'Yes.' He rolled onto his back. 'The thing is, that attack would've made headline news no matter who the victim was. It was horrendous. But because Aaron Marshall was nearly killed the stories went on for ever, making it hard to go into work and carry on as though nothing had happened. It seemed as though every patient wanted me to be their doctor so they could say they'd been treated by someone famous.'

Bella felt her heart expand for this man who had been hurt physically and mentally by a crazed person. Also by his family, if she was reading him right. Moving closer, she wrapped her arms around him and held him tight. 'You're awesome.'

He stiffened. 'You think?'

'I do. I can't begin to imagine what you've been through. But you're here, carrying on as though nothing happened while looking out for others. It's your nature to be a caring doctor and nothing's changed in that respect because of what happened.'

The tension eased out of him. He placed his hand on her back, his fingers making light circles on her skin. 'You're different from any woman I've been close to before, Bella. Thank you.'

For what? Being herself? That could be the case. Fame brought its own problems. She kissed his chest, then tongued his nipple, and felt him hardening against her. What better way to move on from his telling her about his life, albeit nothing too deep, and be able to let go the tension completely?

Reaching between them, she took him in her hand and began to make him harder.

CHAPTER SEVEN

'HAPPY ANNIVERSARY, Angela and Marco. Forty years and still counting.' Aaron handed Bella's mother the gift he'd bought them.

'*Grazie.*' Angela leaned in and brushed a kiss on his cheek. 'You didn't have to buy us anything. Enjoying the celebrations with our family is enough.'

'Maybe, but I wanted to get you something special.' He'd spent his day off during the week in Milan, taking in some of the sights, and when he'd walked past a shop with hand-crafted wooden artwork in the window he'd stepped inside. Blown away by the beauty of some of the pieces, he'd known the bowl he kept returning to touch would be the right present for this lovely couple. They had a couple of pieces on the counter in the restaurant that he'd twice seen Angela caress as she walked by.

This family was coming to mean something special to him. Not only because of Bella, but because of how they accepted him into their midst without question. That was such a new experience he couldn't resist even though he knew it might bring trouble to their door if he got too involved. It was almost guaranteed the day would come when the media would learn where he was and who he was dating. Reporters seemed to be born with extra-sensory noses for trouble.

'It's beautiful. *Grazie*, Aaron,' Angela said.

Bella came to stand beside him. 'It's just the sort of thing Mamma loves.'

Glad he'd got it right, he gave her a smile. He'd been doing that a lot since he'd told her about his family. 'Thank goodness I followed my gut instinct.'

Bella hadn't overreacted or asked more questions about the wealth or fame that made life difficult for the Marshall clan. Basically she'd accepted what he'd told her and continued on as though it didn't matter. She might be a good actress but he didn't think that was the case. They'd shared his bed twice since and she'd been as enthusiastic as ever without appearing to be trying to inveigle her way into his heart. Yes, he was being cynical, but that came with the territory. Though if he wanted a real life that included a woman and children it was time to move on from that.

'Come and meet some more family.'

When he winced she laughed.

'I'm Italian. There're a lot of aunts and uncles and therefore cousins.'

'You're saying you all have large families?'

She grinned. 'I intend having at least six kids.'

The crazy thing was he could see her surrounded by that many, all laughing and demanding attention—which they'd get, along with lots of love. 'One at a time, eh?'

'Realistically, probably only this one.' Her hand did his favourite circle thing on her stomach.

Then he really heard what she'd said. 'You don't intend having more?'

'None that are in the plan at the moment, but—' Her shrug was eloquent. 'Who knows what lies ahead? I'm not racing to unravel the future. One step—one baby—at a time.'

'Fair enough.' Hopefully she also meant she was open

to a different man in her life for the next one. If he was her
pick, that was. Because no matter how hard he was trying
to deny he cared a lot for her, he was well along the path to
being in love with her.

'Come on. Let's stop being serious. This is supposed to
be a happy day.' Taking his hand, she led him across to a
group of people leaning over the balustrade facing out over
the lake. 'Hey, everyone, I'd like you to meet Aaron. He's
relieving in Stresa's emergency department. He's also a
special friend of mine.'

Special, eh? He'd take that for now. 'Hi. I'll try to remember all your names.'

'These are my brothers. Elio has an IT business based
here, and Marco works in Roma.'

He shook hands with the men and received kisses on his
cheeks from the women, along with a few studied looks
from the brothers. Did he make the grade? He hoped so.

'Aaron, there you are. I need some help.' Gino appeared
from the building.

'Whatever with?'

'Salmon. You're a Scotsman, you must know the best
way to cook one.'

'I thought you had the day off from the kitchen.'

'*Sì*, and you'd walk away from someone needing your
medical help because you were at a party?' Gino laughed.
'Come with me.'

'Cooking's not my forte.'

'What's the best meal of salmon you've ever had? That's
what I want to know.'

'Have you got some honey?'

'*Sì.*'

'Garlic and lemon?'

'You're in Italy, man. What do you think?'

Hadn't he said cooking wasn't his thing? 'Right, let's go.'

Inside the kitchen, Gino handed Aaron a beer. 'Tell me, is Bella over whatever made her so tired last month?'

Ah ha. Away from his sister, Gino wanted info. 'She isn't so exhausted, and is trying to take it easy. Or at least be less physical than usual.' Other than in his bed, where she was very energetic.

'That's what she told me, almost word for word.'

'Then believe her.' Aaron wasn't about to go into detail about Bella's pregnancy worries. It wasn't his place, and wouldn't earn him any points if she found out.

'I do. Because she told me that there's been some spotting and she's being extra careful now. She also said it is quite normal, but she's taking it as a warning not to overdo anything.'

Relief filled Aaron that Gino knew. 'That's also true.'

Gino thumped him on the back. 'I like you. You're discreet. I think you care about my sister.'

How discreet did the man want him to be? 'I do.'

That's all I'm saying.

'About the salmon?'

'Under control. But I do like the honey, garlic and lemon idea too. Come on, there's another salmon in the chiller. Let's see what we can do to that one. You go and keep my sister happy.'

'Yes, sir.' He grinned, his heart as light as air.

From the patio Bella watched Aaron kneel down to tie a shoelace for one of the boys, and smiled to herself. He was quite at ease with everyone.

From the little he'd told her about growing up, being so comfortable around her family wouldn't come easily. Hard to imagine not having his parents there to talk and play when he needed them. To be sent to boarding school at the age of ten seemed cruel. Why have children if you weren't going to be a part of their growing up and see them change daily? It was unfathomable, and not the kind of parent she'd be. Sure, she still intended working, but not every hour of every day. She wanted to be there for and with her daughter.

'You're smitten.' Cara stood beside her, a glass of wine in hand.

'Not sure that's a good thing.' Bella felt a pang of love for Aaron. 'I'm carrying Jason's baby. It'd be a big ask for Aaron to accept that. I'm not sure I'm ready either. We're not so involved to be discussing a future together,' she added hurriedly.

Her sister-in-law might've guessed she was keen on Aaron, but she didn't need to know how much. Next thing the whole family would be at her to grab him while she could. They really longed for her to find another man and settle down again, but they also had to understand she had to be ready. As much as she was falling for Aaron, taking that last step and admitting her love would be huge. There'd be no turning back if she did, so she had to be certain it was the right move—especially for her daughter.

'Don't go making problems if there aren't any,' Cara warned.

'Good point.'

'Did you and Jason discuss you marrying again?'

They'd brushed over the topic but as it had made her uncomfortable they'd moved on fast. 'Not really.' Though Jason had said she was not to remain single for ever, that she deserved a second chance. She just wasn't sure if and when she might be ready for such a commitment, but if the way her heart went into overdrive when Aaron was around was anything to go by she was inching nearer.

'He's a good-looking dude.' Cara laughed.

'I'm not denying that.'

'Bella, take your time. We're all here for you and will support you no matter what goes down.'

'I know, and I'm very grateful. Family is everything, isn't it?' Something she'd like to give Aaron. She took a good look at that lithe body strolling towards her. Those firm thighs and that strong chest turned her on in a blink, and had her wanting to kiss him until she was senseless with passion. Yes, he was becoming more than a friend with benefits, way more.

The nights she spent in his apartment were the best she'd known in a while. He made her feel cared about in a way that was personal, deep and meaningful. A lot like how Jason had loved her. Dared she admit that? Hard not to when it was the truth. But she wasn't comparing. Not really. As far as personalities went, the two men who had inched into her heart were poles apart.

Jason was louder, more out there, and had fully expected her to follow his lead in a lot of their lifestyle decisions. Of course, she'd stood up to him on numerous occasions, and he'd once admitted he'd have been disappointed if she hadn't, that her strength was one thing he loved about her. His career had been just as important to him as Aaron's was, but he'd also made sure everyone knew how good he was.

Quite the opposite to Aaron, who was exceptional and put his patients before his ego. Jason had loved her so much that she'd always felt special. She suspected Aaron would be the same if he were to fall for her. He always had her back, even around her family where it wasn't really needed but appreciated just the same.

'Catch, Zia Bella.'

A ball flew past her head. She resisted spinning around

to snatch at it. Baby had only just settled down from a long kicking match of her own and no way did Bella want to shake her out of her quiet time. 'Catch it yourself.' She laughed at her nephew.

'Do they ever run out of energy?' Aaron asked as he joined her.

'Not very often.' She glanced up at him. 'You're looking very relaxed. Sleep well last night?'

'Only woke once and that wasn't because of a nightmare. I seem to finally be moving on from those a little.'

'I'm glad.' It must be hell having a rerun of that hideous attack every night.

He brushed a kiss on her cheek. 'You have a lot to do with it. All the walking I'm doing is good for me too. I start out feeling average and by the time I'm done I feel on top of the world.'

'The exercise will help you sleep better too.' He didn't go for strolls—unless with her—but seemed to hike hard and fast up in the hills or around the lake.

'Stresa has a lot going for it.' He grinned.

'There's a position coming up later in the year.' It'd be wonderful if he moved here permanently.

Hold on, Bella. That would mean opening up and becoming serious about your feelings for him.

Maybe that was the nudge she needed to move forward, to start a new life with another loving man. A big step. She never used to be afraid of taking those. That had been before she'd known how fast and hard the rug could be pulled out from under her and leave her in a heap on the ground, which was not an excuse to hide from life. She just hadn't thought she might get to be so lucky twice. Not that she knew if that was the case with Aaron yet. Too soon, too confronting maybe.

Looking at him, she added, 'Think about it. But don't wait for ever. Someone else might beat you to it.'

He nodded. 'Management mentioned it last week. I'll consider it, but there's still my job back home. I also think I'd miss the intensity of the larger EDs long term.'

Swallowing the disappointment that brought on, she said, 'Your call.' No wonder she was trying hard not to rush into anything too serious with him.

'If I decide to move here, I need to be certain it's the right thing to do. It would mean letting down the people at Edinburgh Hospital who've supported me so much, and...' He paused, looking at her intently. 'I don't want to take advantage of us, and you, and how well we're getting on. I would prefer to see where we're going first.'

Her heart stuttered. He was getting serious about her and them. He was also being cautious and considerate. She could go with that. 'You're amazing.' Leaning in, she kissed him.

His mouth opened under hers and he kissed her back before withdrawing. 'We need to be a little circumspect.'

'True.' She sighed. For once she wanted to let go and forget how her family would be coming up with any number of ideas about where this was headed.

Aaron laughed. 'One day at a time, remember?'

Had they really agreed to that? 'I hate it when you're right.'

'Sometimes I do too,' he agreed with a wicked glint in his eyes. 'Let's go and join the adults and keep our feet firmly on the ground.'

'What are you doing tonight?' she asked as they strolled around the side of the building to the lawn sweeping down to the lake edge.

'Hopefully taking a certain paediatrician home and having my way with her sexy body. Oh, and her mind,' he added cheekily.

Taking his hand in hers, she smiled. 'I'll be there.'

'I think we've got an audience.'

Looking around at everyone sitting under the awning stretched over the lawn, she felt a wave of happiness roll through her. Her family were watching them with nothing but acceptance on their faces. 'I could say let's give them a show, but better not.'

'No, thanks.'

Yes, please.

Aaron longed to sweep Bella up into his arms and rush away to somewhere quiet and private so he could kiss her blind. With her family watching on that wasn't happening. Instead he'd go with enjoying the day and this wonderful family who seemed to accept him for who he was and nothing more or less.

That alone was wonderful, and so new. Of course, they knew nothing about him outside Stresa. Not one of them could've looked him up on the Internet or he'd know. There'd be some look or question that'd have alerted him. Especially from Gino. He knew the signs all too well not to recognise when a person was digging into his background. Today he was a part of the gathering to celebrate Angela and Marco's wedding anniversary, and he felt good. So good it had him wondering if he *could* move here permanently. To be with Bella and her baby, to have a real family life and a future with this wonderful woman. Forty years of their own?

'Stop thinking too much.' Bella nudged him. 'Just go with the day and what it has to offer.'

It scared him how well she read him. 'Yes, ma'am. What can I get you to drink?'

'Sparkling water with a squeeze of lemon.'

It was late by the time they made it back to the apartment. The celebrations had gone on long after the enormous meal with endless toasts to the happy couple. 'That was a fantastic day,' Aaron told Bella as they settled on his deck with mugs of tea in hand. 'I'm glad you invited me.'

'Any time,' she replied. 'It can be a bit overwhelming if you're not used to so many people crowding around and acting like they've always known you. I know Jason found it daunting the first time he came to my family events. It's the Italian way, I suppose.'

'I like it.' More than liked it.

'Which reminds me, I'm heading across to London in a week to see Jason's parents.' Her shoulders rose and fell. 'It's something I'm going to do every couple of months so they don't feel I'm leaving them out of the pregnancy. They are my baby's grandparents and deserve to be kept in the picture. Literally, as I will take a copy of that scan for them to see.'

'You're not close?'

'Not the same as my family, but Jason's family have always been a bit more remote. They've supported me having this baby though, so I will support them in whatever they're doing.' There wasn't a lot of enthusiasm in her voice. 'I think they worry I'll fade out of their lives, taking Sophia away from them, but I'd never do that.'

'Will you stay with them?' His sister kept emailing to ask when he was going to go visit her. Something about catching up before she headed to the States at the end of July, where she would be working on a film for the rest of the year.

He could go over to London the same weekend as Bella

and spend some time with her when she wasn't tied up with Jason's family, but that made him uncomfortable. He wasn't ready for the repercussions if the media saw them together. Eventually they'd have to face it if they were going to continue in this relationship but right now the idea of exposing Bella to all the hype and finding she wanted out didn't sit well. Of course, sooner rather than later was the best option and then he'd know where he stood, but the thought of losing Bella made him tight in the belly. No way. The idea chilled his skin. She was wonderful.

'I'll stay a night with them and then head home, unless you wanted to meet up for a night somewhere afterwards.' Again she'd read his mind too easily.

Sweat broke out between his shoulder blades. She seemed to be in agreement when it came to spending time together. But for him a night in London was another step forward and he wasn't sure he should be taking it. Was this make-or-break time?

'I'd prefer to stay here and share the night with you when you return. When I came to Stresa I decided I wasn't going back to Britain until my four months were up.' It was true. 'I wanted a complete change and to immerse myself in Italy as I tried to get past what kept me awake at night.'

'Fair enough. It could've been fun getting away together, that's all. We seem to be getting along so well sometimes I forget we've agreed there is no future together.' Heat spread across her face.

'Does that bother you?'

'A little.' She swallowed hard. 'I don't usually speak my mind so freely. Well…' Her blush deepened. 'I haven't exactly come out with startling news but it's more than I've said about my feelings for a long time.'

'To think when I first saw you at that car-versus-cycle accident I thought you were aloof.'

'I didn't want you thinking I might fancy you.'

'Did you? Then?'

'Not a lot. I was trying very hard not to anyway.' Suddenly she laughed. 'This is a crazy conversation.' She drained her mug and stood up. 'Take me to bed, will you?' Then she winced and her hand instantly covered her baby bump.

'Bella? What's wrong?'

She huffed out a breath. 'A sharp twinge. That's all.' Her eyes were wide as she stared down to where baby Sophia lay.

'Easy does it. Sit down.' Holding her elbow, he pressed her gently back onto the chair she'd just vacated. 'How sharp was the twinge?'

'Four out of ten.'

'This isn't a time to downplay the level of pain.'

Her worried eyes locked on him. 'If anything I'm exaggerating. I do not want anything going wrong with this pregnancy.'

'Fair enough. Anything more going on? Pain anywhere else?' He was in emergency-doctor mode, only it was difficult when the patient was Bella. Instinct told him to wrap her up in cotton wool and protect her and baby.

'No.' She was holding her breath, definitely waiting for something more to happen. Another stab of pain in her abdomen, or in her back? Or even a contraction?

'Bella, look at me.' He held her hands firmly and waited for her to raise her head. The worry in her eyes nearly undid him. She was terrified something was about to go horribly wrong, and if it did what were the chances he could prevent it? 'Hold onto me. Lean into me. Breathe evenly and regularly. It's been a busy day and you're tired. This could be a reaction to that. Twinges during pregnancy are not uncommon.' They'd dealt with this only weeks ago.

'I know. On one side of my brain anyway, but the other side's doing panic circles. I can't lose Sophia now. She's real, especially now I've seen her and named her. Why did I do that? It was tempting fate.'

Her lips were chilly when he kissed them lightly. 'You did what the majority of would-be parents do. You fell deeper in love with your baby and naming her brought her closer. It does not mean she's in trouble.'

She hadn't had another twinge unless she was hiding it from him, and he doubted that. Her expression was all about worry and fear but nothing sudden or sharp had deepened it. 'You're doing fine.'

'You think?'

He couldn't answer yes and later be proven wrong. 'I think you should go to bed and get some rest. I'll take your BP for peace of mind but, as that hasn't been an issue so far, I can't see that being the cause for a twinge of pain. But first how about you check for spotting?'

Fear appeared in her face.

'You know it's the right thing to do and most likely will ease your mind a little if there's nothing there. I'll also check your abdomen once you're in bed, if that's all right?'

'You're so patient with me.'

'Why wouldn't I be? Apart from it being my normal doctor approach, I care too much about you, and therefore your baby, to be anything else. I've got your back, Bella.'

'Don't I know it? Fine, I'll be the sensible patient and lie down so you can make certain everything's in place.'

He put on his stern voice. 'After you've looked for bleeding.'

Her smile was tight but it was real. 'Of course.'

No spotting, and everything seemed to be in the right place in Bella's abdomen. No more twinges either. He breathed in relief. Shrugging out of his clothes, Aaron climbed into bed and wrapped his arm over her waist. 'Go to sleep. I'll be here all night.'

Twisting over onto her side, she kissed him. 'You make sure you get some sleep too.'

'Only once you've shown me how.' He kissed her back, a kiss filled with care and love. He wanted this pregnancy to work out for Bella almost as much as she did.

'I'll do my best.'

'Then baby has nothing to worry about.'

When she rolled onto her other side he spooned behind her and held her throughout the night, sleep not coming his way once.

'I look like I've climbed the Alps overnight. The swelling under my eyes is terrible.' Bella regarded the image staring back at her from Aaron's bathroom mirror. 'My patients are going to run when they see me.'

'Sure you don't want to take the day off?' he asked as he picked up his shaver.

'No, I'm good to go. Tired and looking awful, but otherwise all good. I won't go rushing around like a demented cat, but sitting around home doing absolutely nothing would drive me insane and have me imagining all sorts of things going wrong with Sophia.'

'I get that. Have you got a full workload today?'

She nodded. 'From what I saw on Friday it's going to be busy but I'll manage.' She wasn't turning into a wimp no matter how important this pregnancy was to her. Being weak wouldn't help the baby, nor her own mind.

'No surprise there.'

She watched as he shaved, the passion that had taken a back seat last night suddenly rushing to the fore. Aaron was unbelievably hot. That firm jawline turned her on, as did his naked body. If only they had time to get down and sexy before heading out to work, but Aaron was due in the emergency department in forty minutes and she needed to get home for some fresh clothes and breakfast before heading to the paediatric centre. Forgoing breakfast was possible despite feeling starving hungry, but yesterday's clothes definitely needed changing. It might be time to carry a small bag in the car with spare gear in it.

'Are you going to work full-time right through to the end of your pregnancy?' Aaron asked.

'No. Luna's going to take on some of my hours in the third trimester.' Her partners, Luna and Alberto, were going to share the ED calls and her patients who came back for repeat visits. She'd talk to Luna later today and explain how tired she was getting and about the twinges to pre-warn her that she might have to step up earlier than planned.

'I'm glad you've got that in place. I had an awful thought you might work right through to the last moment.' He wasn't joking if the severe look on his face was an indicator.

'I am not taking any risks, which means cutting back my hours as I see fit.' Did he think she'd be irresponsible? If so then he didn't know her at all, and she was certain he had come to understand how important this baby was to her.

He held his hand up in a stop sign. 'I didn't mean to sound so harsh but I know how worried you are about seeing this through to the end safely. I was only adding my two euros' worth. I don't want anything going wrong either.'

Swallowing her ire, she nodded. She was more sensitive to criticism these days. 'Take no notice of me. I get a bit wound up at times. Right, I'll see you later.' She stretched up and brushed a kiss on his newly shaven chin. 'Hopefully not in ED.' Though she did like working with him, she didn't need young patients being admitted just so as she could see him.

'I agree.' He didn't return her kiss, and his smile appeared a little remote.

'Problem?'

He shook his head. 'No, but I'd better get a move on. The time is ticking by and I'm due on duty soon.'

You could still give me a smile.

She shrugged. 'I won't hold you up any longer.' Only minutes before he'd been acting as though he had all the time in the world. 'Bye.' She'd even wanted to return to his bed. Thank goodness she hadn't mentioned that. What if he'd turned her down flat? It would've hurt.

'See you.'

What was that about? Bella wondered as she climbed into her car. One minute all was good, then they start talking about when she was giving up work and his mood changed entirely. Whenever she chose to take leave was her business, not Aaron's, but lately she'd shared any information about her pregnancy plans with him. Too much? Was he getting cold feet? They were having a bit of a fling, nothing more. Definitely nothing serious enough to be making plans for a joint future. As much as she was falling for Aaron, she was not ready to step up and tell him so, nor was she ready to move in with him. Her baby had priority over every other decision she made in the coming months, and that meant not getting too involved with Aaron.

Her heart ached for what might've been if they'd met under normal circumstances. A fling possibly leading to a full-on relationship and then moving in together. That wasn't happening when she was pregnant with Jason's baby.

Though to be fair, Aaron had never once hinted that he wouldn't care for a baby that wasn't his. She hadn't actually asked how he'd feel about that. It would sound as though she wanted to get involved full-time and they'd agreed that wasn't happening. Once Sophia arrived, she'd be too busy with her and work to continue the fling, let alone anything deeper and more fulfilling.

At home she headed for the shower and a long soak to ease the tension in her shoulders.

Men. Love them but they could tear you apart at times.

Bella sighed. No denying Aaron had got to her when she wasn't looking. She hadn't needed a man in her life, and still didn't. Except it wasn't so easy to believe that now she'd come to know this one, and let him into her heart when she wasn't thinking about it.

After drying herself, she wrapped the towel around her breasts and headed into the bedroom to find something to wear that was comfortable and yet didn't make her look dull and unattractive. If she did bump into Aaron at work she wanted him to take a second look.

A tune rang out on her phone.

Aaron.

'Hello.'

'Bella, I'm sorry for being obtuse. I get worried for you and it got out of hand this morning.'

The tension relaxed out of her body. 'Apology accepted.'

'Thank goodness. See you later?'

'Of course.' Then it dawned on her what might've put him in a funk this morning. 'Did you have a nightmare last night?' He hadn't had one during any of the few nights she'd stayed over but last night could've been the first.

'I did. I intended staying awake all night so I could keep an eye on you, but some time after two I must've dozed off.'

She hadn't been aware at all. 'You should've woken me. I could've hugged you until the gremlins went away.'

'You need your sleep at the moment.'

'Aaron,' she growled. 'We are there for each other. This is not a one-way relationship.'

Silence.

They hadn't called it a relationship before—because it was a fling, nothing more. Calling it a relationship meant getting deep and serious and, as she'd already had that discussion with herself this morning, she had nothing to say along those lines. 'What I meant—'

'I know where you're coming from, Bella. We're in this together and therefore we watch out for each other. My only issue is I'm not used to anyone doing that for me.'

Aaron handed his patient a prescription for analgesics. 'There you go. Take these until you run out. Don't stop when the pain decreases or you'll start using your arm and that wrist isn't ready to do any work.'

'*Grazie, Medico.* I will do as you say.'

The man's wife shook her head at him. 'Like you do me, huh?'

'*Sì.*'

Aaron smiled. These two hadn't stopped giving each other cheek since the man had presented querying a fractured wrist. Fortunately it was severely sprained, not broken, though a sprain could be as painful. 'Take care, and I hope I don't see you back here.'

'So do we,' the wife told him with a wide smile. 'Thank you for your help.' She took her husband's good arm and led him out of the department.

Aaron watched them go, wondering what it was like to be in such a loving relationship for so long. They'd know each other almost too well, but that had to be special. If only he got the opportunity to be a part of something similar.

Bella. It was annoying how her name kept banging around his head, along with an image of her beautiful face wearing a wide smile and cheerful eyes. Plus the one where she was fearful of something going wrong with her baby that made him want to reach out and hold her for ever and keep her safe.

She was in his heart now. No point denying it any longer even when he was trying his damnedest to remain careful. Hence his sudden abruptness with her that morning. Hearing her say she was going to work, and would continue doing so right till nearly the end of her pregnancy, had brought his protective instincts into play. Again he'd wanted to wrap her up and keep her safe.

He had no right to do so, or even to say anything about it, but it was hard not to when he cared about how this pregnancy went for her. She wanted her baby so much it was hurting her. To be nudged aside and basically told to mind his own business about what she chose to do in the coming months had hurt. It'd also been a timely reminder he didn't have any say in her decisions. The baby wasn't his. Though he'd love to be a surrogate dad for Sophia. As much as he'd love to pair up with Bella for the rest of their lives.

If only he could. But underneath these buoyant loving emotions he still feared being rejected once she came to fully understand her life would never be as private as it was now. She didn't put herself out there to be noticed, but there'd be no stopping the media once they learned she was in his life. He no longer even considered she might be interested in his family's fame and fortune. She wasn't rich, didn't have lots of high-end clothes and shoes, or live in a mansion, but didn't appear to want any of that either.

What she did have—and he didn't—was such a loving family that she was ensconced in happiness. In his book that came before all else. Jealous? Kind of. The real problem here was he was in too deep, couldn't pull out without hurting, and yet was afraid to risk taking a chance. Amy had hurt him so deeply, he knew when Bella realised she didn't want to put up with his lifestyle he'd be beyond hurt. Even if they stayed here, the media would follow them. It always did, no matter how hard he tried to get away.

'Aaron, a twenty-four-year-old man's being brought in by ambulance after a cycle accident on the hill. A metal object has penetrated his chest. His heart is erratic.'

'Bring him to the resus bed,' he told the junior doctor. All the equipment they'd need for X-rays, cardiac arrest, haemorrhaging and any other unforeseen event was on hand there. 'How far away is the ambulance?'

'Four minutes.'

'Right.' He went to scrub up. This sounded serious and the readier he was, the better.

CHAPTER EIGHT

BELLA STOOD UP and rubbed the small of her back. 'Luna, I'd better go over to the hospital and do a round before heading home.' Aaron might be somewhere in the building too. She had no real excuse to drop by the ED other than ask him to join the family for dinner. The thing was, she'd done that on Wednesday and he'd declined, said he had other things on. Like what? She hadn't asked, but felt peeved. He'd been as friendly as usual when she'd had to go into his department for a patient, but there'd been no phone conversations out of hours. So much for thinking everything was fine after his apology about being abrupt on Monday. Seemed he was still annoyed with her. She could try again, apologising and inviting him to dinner, but she wasn't going to. She didn't do kowtowing.

Nothing had changed when it came to how she felt about him. Her heart hadn't done a U-turn, but whether it was good for her was something else to consider. Loving Aaron had come about so easily and naturally it was a little scary. When she fell for Jason it had been quick, and totally perfect, but there hadn't been a baby involved. A baby whose father was still a part of Bella's life and who she was, who she'd become.

Kick.

She laughed. Little Sophia had an innate sense of timing.

'Yes, little one, I'm thinking about your father.' What she was struggling with was how she'd love for her daughter to have a living father, a man who'd cherish her as much as Jason would've.

Kick.

Bella touched her stomach. 'What are you trying to tell me?'

Nothing.

'Great. So I have to make all the decisions?' Fair enough. Just not right now. Instead she'd go to the ED after she'd done a ward round and see if Aaron was still there. If so, she would invite him to join the family for dinner. It didn't mean she was planning a wedding or getting him to commit to anything. It was all about relaxing and being comfortable in each other's space. It didn't mean she expected to go back to his apartment afterwards to share his bed. She might want to, but only if he was in agreement, otherwise she'd feel awkward—and unwanted.

'I'm on duty till six so won't be able to make it till a bit later but if everyone's okay with that, I'd love to come,' Aaron told her when she found him filling in a patient's details in the ED and invited him to join her for dinner.

'No one clocks us in, so you'll be fine,' she said through a relieved smile.

A paramedic was pushing a patient into the department on a trolley. Aaron stood up. 'I'd better go.' But he didn't move away immediately. 'How have you been this week?'

Lonely. 'Good. No more twinges, just lots of kicks. I still think Sophia might be a footballer in waiting.'

His smile looked tired. Not sleeping well again?

'All those cousins will make sure of that.'

'I'd better go. See you later.'

'You will.'

She still felt he was uncomfortable joining her but she wasn't going to push for reasons why. Could be he was stepping back to assess his feelings, as she'd done earlier. Better before baby arrived than afterwards when things could get complicated.

Baby Sophia. Everything came back to her and doing the right thing by her. To find her a father or to raise her alone with Jason in the background in the form of photos and words Bella could remember. She'd far prefer Sophia had a living, breathing *papà* who would read her bedtime stories and cuddle her, heat her milk and wipe away the tears, laugh at her antics and cry when she was sad. Jason would always be in the background. Always. But Sophia should have a *papà* at her side too.

Aaron was more than capable of being that man. He didn't turn away from responsibility or protecting those he cared about. His family weren't there for him in the way he'd like, but she doubted he'd ever walk away. As far as she could see that was Aaron, through and through. An ideal father figure.

An ideal partner for her? She wanted him to be, but wasn't certain. It was early days to even be wondering, but when she'd met Jason her attraction to him had happened in an instant. No doubts whatsoever. So to be having similar feelings for Aaron scared her into wanting to take time to get to know more about him in case she was trusting her instincts too much just because they'd worked well the first time.

'Thought you were heading home.' The man confusing her usually clear thinking appeared before her. 'You are all right, Bella?'

'Yes, I'm fine. I was just thinking about… About— a patient.'

Pathetic. No patient would want anything to do with her if that was all she could come up with when Aaron queried her state of health. But she was hardly going to admit her mind had been on him. Not when he'd been wary around her lately.

'Save it for Monday. Go home and take a break before dinner.'

He could be quite bossy without any real effort, she realised as she tramped along the corridor to the back exit. Used to getting his own way? If he was, he didn't overdo it. Or hadn't with her. Something to watch out for? Or she could ignore it and go with the flow, learn more about him without looking for pointers that might lead her in the wrong direction, which sounded far easier than the first option.

Shoving Aaron out of her head on the short drive home, she thought about her wardrobe and what to wear tonight. Not a lot of choice unless she was okay with looking like a beached whale. It seemed only days ago she could slip into any of the dresses or trousers hanging in her wardrobe and feel comfortable in a fashionable, and a little bit sexy, way. Not any more.

Bring on the shopping expedition she planned doing while visiting Jason's parents at the weekend. Nothing better to make her feel good about herself than some new outfits that highlighted her good features and dulled the not so good. Baby certainly had altered her shape dramatically in a hurry. While she was excited about that, she still wanted to look good—hot—so Aaron couldn't ignore her.

Pathetic. If he wasn't interested, why bother? She didn't want to drag a man into her arms, preferred he come flying at her because he couldn't resist her. Their fling had to mean he did find her attractive. Didn't it? 'So, what to wear tonight? For an everyday meal with the family who'd not notice anyway? OTT, Bella girl.' Yeah, well, sometimes that was her. Especially with Aaron in the picture.

She chose sky-blue three-quarter trousers and a chintzy white blouse that dipped to her growing cleavage and showed off her tanned skin to perfection. Staring at her image in the mirror, twisting this way and that, she had to admit her breasts were filling out quite nicely. Give them another month or two and they'd probably be ginormous and she'd be hating them, but for now she could be happy with how they filled out the front of the blouse to perfection. There were some pluses to growing a belly so fast it looked like a balloon that someone had forgotten to stop pumping full of oxygen.

Aaron crossed the restaurant to the seat next to Bella, his eyes entirely focused on the beautiful sight before him. She got more attractive by the day, and she'd started out close to perfect in the first place. How was he going to walk away at the end of his contract? It was all very well saying he was protecting his heart, but he was already too late for that. So he'd stick to the fact that he would do anything to keep Bella safe from the media hype. So why had he agreed to come here tonight? Because he just couldn't turn her down. Couldn't not be with her.

'Evening, Bella.' Leaning in, he placed a light kiss on her cheek. Light. Not sexy or deep. Damn it.

Deep green eyes met his gaze. 'Hi. You got away on time, then?'

'Despite what you said, I couldn't risk Gino refusing to feed me because I was late.'

From the far end of the table, Gino laughed. 'So I scare you more than a patient? Perfect.' He might be joking, but Aaron was aware that the moment he did something to hurt

Bella, Gino would be on his case in an instant. Which only backed up his own thoughts about staying away from getting too close. Hard, if not impossible, to give up a fling that was making him happy in so many ways he once hadn't believed possible though.

'Ignore him,' Bella whispered close to him.

Breathing in roses, he leaned back in his chair and laughed. 'That's like suggesting I wear a jersey to dinner. Impossible.' The outside temperature had been posted at twenty-eight last time he'd looked, an hour ago. Inside the restaurant the air-conditioning was doing its bit to keep it down but there was no avoiding the fact it was a hot day. The heat had slapped him in the face when he'd walked out of ED at the end of his shift and he was still reeling. Edinburgh didn't quite match Stresa when it came to summer temperatures.

'I'm hoping for slightly cooler in London. Though the shops are usually cool enough to enjoy. I think the owners know having good air-conditioning keeps customers happy and in the shop, and therefore buying their goods.'

'What time are you flying out?'

'I catch the nine o'clock flight.' Which meant an early train to Milan.

'Want me to drive you to the airport?' he offered.

'Thanks, but I've got it sorted. What have you planned for the weekend?' she asked.

'I haven't been to Como so figured tomorrow is as good a day as any. I'll take my walking shoes and find a track to hike.' The more walking he did, the more he wanted to do. It was turning out to be so good for his stress levels. He thought about the attack often as he strode along and for some inexplicable reason the fear didn't raise its head. Now that only happened in the dark of night, and not when Bella was with him, except they hadn't got together in his bed this week.

If only he'd leapt out of bed and headed away at the crack of dawn on Saturday morning, Aaron reflected through a moment of despair when he opened his door on hearing the chime ring to find his sister standing on the doorstep with a suitcase.

'Surprise,' cried Maggie as she wrapped him in a hug.

'You could say that,' he muttered as he hugged her back.

'I got tired of waiting for you to come home to see me before I head away so I decided to drop in and hassle you.' Maggie laughed. 'You'd better not say you're working this weekend because I already checked.'

'You did?' Someone had told his sister he wasn't rostered on?

'A nurse who was more than happy to talk about you said you had the whole weekend off so no excuses for not spending time with me.'

'Sounds good.' He meant it. They mightn't be the closest family about, but he loved his sister and spending time with her was great. He automatically glanced down the path to the road. No cameras, no nosey reporters to spoil the moment. Yet. Thank goodness Bella was out of town for the weekend. 'Come in and get a load off.'

'Not bad,' his sister said as she looked around the house. 'Stunning view, though awfully quiet.'

'That's one of the reasons I like living here.'

'How long have you got left on your contract?'

'A couple of months.' Maybe a lot more if he got around to making up his mind about his future and Bella. 'After that, who knows?'

'You're not thinking of walking away from your position in Edinburgh?'

Sometimes Maggie read him too easily. Like Bella. 'Nothing's definite. Stresa's wonderful and there must be other towns around Italy where I could work.'

'Me thinks there's someone here keeping you entertained.' Maggie picked up an obviously female sweater. 'A woman who might be pressing some buttons, huh?'

From a sweater to a relationship? Only Maggie would come up with that. True as it was, he wasn't talking about Bella. Maggie would never stop asking more questions he had no firm answers for, so he downplayed the question. 'No harm in a little activity outside work.'

'No harm in finding the right one, either.'

'I was about to make breakfast when you turned up. Have you eaten?'

'Coffee and a stale bun on the train doesn't count.'

'Then I'll whip up something while you put the coffee on.'

'Let's go out. I want to see the town and get the feel of the place you think so highly of.'

Aaron shivered. Go out, and have Maggie recognised? In Stresa? Not likely, unless an overzealous reporter had followed her here, which happened often enough to make him edgy. 'You sure you're on your own?'

'I overnighted in Milan and if anyone was going to make themselves known that's when I'd have noticed.' She wouldn't have been looking very hard.

'There's a patisserie a few kilometres away towards the town centre. We'll go there.'

'Whatever.' Maggie shrugged. 'You know the area.'

Yes, and which restaurant to avoid while you're in town.
Maggie was not going near Gino's.

* * *

'I've named her already,' Bella told Jason's parents as they gazed at the scan image she'd given them.

She'd spent the afternoon wandering through the local market with Jason's mother, and checking out a few shops, trying to get comfortable with her. Normally it wasn't so hard, but the thought of how close she was getting to Aaron kept her wondering how these two would accept him if he became a serious part of her life.

'What have you chosen?' Justine Wright asked.

'Sophia Justine.'

Justine gasped. 'You've used my name for her middle one?' A small smile followed the question. 'Thank you, Bella.'

'It's a no-brainer. Sophia was my grandmother's name.' Jason's parents had been disappointed she'd never taken their surname when they married but for her it had been a show of independence. Not every woman took her husband's name these days and Rosso was on all her medical certificates, something she was proud of. She was a Rosso through and through. It seemed she'd made Justine happy about this though.

'It brings Jason a bit closer,' Colin admitted as he continued to stare at the framed image.

'He is Sophia's father, and I will make sure she knows about him. You being in her life will strengthen whatever I tell her. I'm never going to keep her from seeing you.' Bella had lost count of the number of times she'd told them, but it seemed they couldn't quite accept it.

'What happens if you meet another man, remarry?' Justine asked.

Bella felt her face warm. 'Nothing changes in that Jason

is still Sophia's father. Naturally if I do find another partner he will be a big part of her life, or I wouldn't want him.'

Colin was watching her closely. 'Have you met someone?'

Here we go.

Best to be upfront though she knew it was going to hurt these two. The truth was it would hurt them ten years from now. Jason had been their only child and they were struggling to move on. 'I've been dating a doctor who's working in Stresa temporarily. So far it's nothing serious.' Pants on fire? 'I'm very hesitant about getting close to someone after Jason. We had a wonderful marriage, and, honestly, my main focus is my pregnancy and the baby.'

'You have to be open to another relationship, Bella,' Colin said, surprising the air out of her lungs. Never would she have expected him to say that. He'd always been so closed when it came to her moving on from Jason's death. 'All we ask is that you be careful, take your time.'

Sounded to Bella as if Colin and Justine had discussed this. 'Thank you. I'll always be open with you both. You're part of my life, and that's not going to change no matter what lies ahead.'

Justine surprised her further by standing up and crossing over to give her a rare hug, which told her how much they cared for her. 'Thanks,' she whispered. 'None of this is easy but you've just made it a little more so.'

'Right.' Justine stepped away and brushed her hands down the front of her trousers. 'You said you intend to go shopping tomorrow before flying out. How about we go into the city together and have some fun? I'd love to buy some clothes for Sophia and you can make sure you like my choices.'

Another surprise. Not a person to enjoy shopping with

others because it always took twice as long, nonetheless she couldn't say no. That'd undo all the ground she'd made up today.

'Sounds perfect. I need to find some outfits that will see me through the coming months.' She gave a little grin. 'I can't wait to see what's available for my baby girl either.' Then she rubbed the small of her back. 'I'm going to bed now if you don't mind. I seem to get tired all too easily these days.' It was barely nine o'clock but all she wanted to do was lie down somewhere quiet. Thinking about Aaron and how he'd fit in and how Jason's parents might react had drained her. The fact they'd said she had to be open about another relationship was good but added to the pressure somehow. She'd have to get it right or they'd never forgive her. It was also strange how little she was thinking about Jason when she was here. Seemed she was looking forward more and less at the past.

'See you in the morning, Bella.'

As she lay between the crisp white sheets, Aaron slid into her head yet again. What was he doing? Dinner with Tommaso maybe. They got on well and had taken to visiting the inn together one night a week. She suspected Tommaso was partly getting onside with Aaron to help entice him to stay on at the end of his contract as it wasn't easy finding specialists for the small hospital. Chances were Aaron wouldn't stay. He had pointed out he still had a job to return to in Scotland, and he probably preferred the more intense departments of larger hospitals. She hoped he might change his mind—if that meant he wanted more with her, that was.

Loving Aaron had come about so easily and naturally it was a bit scary. It was different from when she fell for Jason. That had been quick too, and totally perfect. But there hadn't been a baby involved. A baby whose father was still a large part of who she was, who she'd become.

Kick.

Warmth filled her. 'Yes, little one, I'm thinking about you and your *papà*.' But she'd love her daughter to have a living father, a man who'd cherish her as much as Jason would've if he'd been here. Aaron was caring and compassionate, and loving. Yes, she could see him in the role of Sophia's *papà*. Jason might even have agreed.

Kick.

Bella touched her stomach. 'What are you trying to tell me?'

Kick.

'You're persistent, aren't you?' Picking up the novel she'd brought with her, she tried to divert her mind by reading, except the words blurred as her head filled with Aaron. She needed to learn more about him and his reticence was starting to rub her up the wrong way. She'd been open about her love for Jason and her future and her family and anything he wanted to know. Come to think of it, he didn't ask a lot of questions about her. That might be because he didn't want to reciprocate.

His mother was an actress, his sister a camera operator making a name for herself, his father a high court judge.

Sighing with frustration, she reached for her tablet. It wasn't the way to find out about Aaron's family but neither could she wait for him to decide when it was time to talk about them.

As she didn't know anyone's first name she keyed in Aaron Marshall and held her breath while waiting for the screen to deliver.

Aaron Marshall wasn't an uncommon name, but only one on the screen was an emergency specialist practising in Edinburgh. Slightly out of date, but the photo of Aaron dressed in hospital scrubs looking anything but pleased to be in the limelight snagged her attention. He was so gorgeous. Sexy as, and so good-looking her mouth watered. The headline read: *Judge Marshall's son attacked by knife-wielding man in ED*.

Numerous entries followed, all with Aaron's name in the headline. Aaron in a tux, dressed in hiking trousers and shirt with a pack on his back, wearing a suit heading into a theatre where his mother was performing. In each and every one of the photos he looked confident and unassailable. Every photo made her heart squeeze a little harder.

She adored him.

She stared at the screen. Putting up with the media at every turn must be hell. Delving further, Bella found Maggie Marshall, the camera operator who'd won awards for her work with a movie camera, Diane Marshall the actress in a current British television saga, and the judge, John Marshall, who'd sentenced a local parliamentarian to six years for embezzlement that the man still swore he hadn't had anything to do with.

Shutting down the website, Bella slid the tablet onto the bedside table and snuggled down under the covers. There was a lot more to Aaron than she'd supposed despite what he'd told her about his family getting quite a lot of attention. He'd held back on the details. Not that she could blame him. It showed he wasn't into all the hurrah. He'd said as much, but she hadn't realised how well known his family was. No wonder Stresa was a calm place for him. Could that play a part in his decision to move to Italy?

Thump, thump, went her heart. Was she reading too much into this because she'd love him to move to her home town permanently?

Looked as if the time had arrived for them to have a serious discussion about their relationship. No more messing around. Either they were together or they weren't.

Spending time with Jason's parents had made her realise she was ready to move forward and have a complete future.

She was ready to accept him into her life, and into Sophia's life.

Yes, she definitely was. This had nothing to do with his family and who they were, but the fact he didn't flaunt it, and, she suspected, rued it a lot of the time, made her love him even more. She was ready.

CHAPTER NINE

THE PLATFORM WAS crowded as Bella stepped off the train at Stresa, hauling her now over-full case behind her. 'Wonder what's going on?' she said to the woman she'd been sitting beside on the trip from Milano, a friend from school days.

'I'd say everyone's waiting for the southbound train,' Terese said as she looked around. 'I'm glad we weren't affected as I'm on duty in two hours.'

Bella stifled a yawn, grateful not to be working until tomorrow. 'You weren't leaving any room for error, then.'

Terese laughed. 'Hugo said he'd cover for me if I was late.'

'You got a good one there.'

'I know.' The love in her voice spoke volumes, and had Bella remembering when it had been like that for her and Jason.

It also got her wondering if she could have it again with Aaron. Whenever she thought of him that wonderful warm, soft feeling of wonder filled her head and heart and had her daydreaming of wonderful things. Shaking her head to clear away those thoughts, she pushed through the crowd. 'Let's get out of here.'

'Maggie, there's nothing you can do about this but be patient.'

The voice that filled her dreams last night had her turning around to scan the sea of heads. 'Aaron? Is that you?'

'Bella? Hey there. I wasn't expecting to bump into you, but then I didn't think my sister's train would be running so late. It was held up by a truck hitting a car on a crossing further north but now it's only minutes away.'

His sister was here? He hadn't mentioned anything about her visiting over the weekend. Bella shrugged. He didn't have to let her know everything that was going on in his life, but she couldn't help feeling left out of something. They were better than that, surely? 'Catch up later. I'm getting out of here.'

'Hey, wait.' His hand was on her arm. 'You'd better meet Maggie.' He was making an effort, if a little late.

'Sure, but can we move away from the crowd? I'm getting a lot of elbows in my side and stomach.'

Annoyance crossed his face. For her being knocked about or because she wanted to be somewhere quieter, she didn't know, but she wasn't standing here any longer. 'I'm going downstairs to the entrance.'

'Maggie, follow me. I want you to meet someone.' Aaron still held her arm and now he was reaching for her case with his other hand. 'Give me that.'

She wasn't incapable, but it was nice having a man taking care of her. 'Sure. Watch out. It's heavy.' She'd done a fair amount of shopping for herself and Sophia. Then there were the toys and tiny dresses and outfits Justine had bought adding to the weight. Thank goodness for expandable cases with wheels.

At the bottom of the stairs Aaron led her to a corner away from the frustrated crowd milling about.

She'd have preferred to go outside but realised that his sister would want to get on the train as soon as it arrived so even coming down the stairway was a bonus. When she looked at Aaron, her chest tightened. She'd missed him more than she'd have believed. 'Your plans for the weekend changed?'

'Maggie turned up unannounced yesterday morning.'

'Since Aaron was being tardy about coming to London to catch up before I head across to the USA I decided to gatecrash his weekend.' A stunning woman of a similar age to Bella stood before her. 'I'm Maggie, Aaron's annoying sister. You must be Bella.'

'That's me.' So Aaron had mentioned her. Or had Maggie heard him call out to her on the platform? 'I hear you're moving to America?'

'In four weeks, and with the weeks flying past and getting busier by the day, I grabbed the opportunity to come across to catch up with Aaron while it was still possible. There's so much to do with the current programme I'm working on while getting up to speed with the film I'm going to be involved with in LA.' The woman could talk, for sure.

A light flashed behind them.

Aaron's mouth tightened.

Maggie didn't blink.

Bella glanced around, wondering what was going on, and saw a man holding a large camera above the people standing in groups as they waited for the next train. The camera was pointed in their direction. She already had her back to him so she turned her head back to face Maggie and Aaron. 'It's great you could make it over here. Did Aaron show you the sights or were you both too busy talking to go anywhere?'

'The sights and the eateries. We took the cable car up the hill and the views are stupendous. No wonder he likes Stresa so much. It might be hard to get him to return to Edinburgh.'

That's what I'm hoping, Bella admitted to herself.

'Too quiet for me,' Maggie carried on. 'I love big, busy, noisy cities.'

'We didn't go to Gino's,' Aaron said sharply. 'Though Maggie wanted to. I wasn't having her followers tagging along and upsetting things in the restaurant. Gino would've kicked my backside.'

Gino would've made the most of it and suggested the reporters take a table and order a meal like none they'd had before. He'd also have made sure no one left their table to harass any other diners, including her family. 'I expect the restaurant was busy.' The tourist season was in full swing so Gino's was buzzing every night, though her brother would've made sure Aaron got a table.

'I understand you're a paediatrician,' Maggie was saying, her eyes giving Bella the once-over at the same time. 'A pregnant one, at that.'

So? 'Yes, I am both of those.' The words came out a little sharper than she'd intended but she didn't like the way Maggie was eyeing her up.

'Take no notice of me. I often speak before thinking. I didn't mean to insult you. Nor upset you. Having a baby must be exciting.'

'It is.'

The loudspeaker interrupted all talk. 'Passengers travelling to Milan are to go to platform two as your train will arrive in two minutes.'

Maggie threw her arms around her brother. 'See you in LA, Aaron. Bring Bella with you. I want to get to know her better.'

'We'll see,' Aaron growled before returning the hug. 'Take care and make a success of the movie.'

'Why wouldn't I?' Maggie grinned, then turned to Bella.

'I mean it. Come and visit when Aaron does. Bring baby with you.'

This woman was full on, but underneath all the talk Bella suspected she might be a bit lonely. 'As Aaron said, let's wait and see. All the best with your movie.'

'Thanks.' Maggie was already turning to rush up the stairs. 'Guess I'll have to fight my way to a seat.'

'Come on. Let's get out of here while everyone's focused on reaching the platform.' Again Aaron had her arm in one hand and case in the other. 'With a bit of luck the reporters following Maggie will be on the train with her.'

'Why wouldn't they?' she asked when they reached the outside.

'Because they are unpredictable, and if they sense a story elsewhere they'll hang around like a dog sniffing a bone.'

'So you're a bone?' She laughed.

His face was grim as he shook his head. 'You don't understand. Until now the media didn't know where I was working, and probably didn't care too much as I haven't done anything worthy of reporting lately. Unfortunately now they've seen me with you there are bound to be questions about our relationship.'

'What relationship?' The question was out before she knew she was going to ask it.

'Not the one we know we have, but whatever they choose to make up for a good headline. I shouldn't have called out to you when I saw you in the crowd. It was instinctive. I'd missed you and there you were looking happy and beautiful and I just couldn't wait to be with you.'

'Aaron, it's all good. No one's going to take the slightest bit of notice of me. Why would they? I'm a local doctor, nothing more.'

Flash. Another camera appeared in front of them.

'Bugger off,' Aaron said under his breath.

But she'd heard and felt the tension increasing in his grip on her arm.

Flash.

'This is exactly what I was warning you about.'

'Aaron, tell us about your partner. Who is she? When's the baby due? How do you feel about becoming a father?'

Bella's head whipped up and she stared at the man standing directly in front of them. 'Excuse me. You're in my way.'

'What's your name, lady? Are you from around here?'

'If you don't mind getting out of my way. I am not talking to you.'

'How long have you known Aaron Marshall?'

Bella ignored him and walked straight at him so he had to step aside or look stupid when she bumped into him.

'You're carrying his baby.'

Bile soured her mouth. What right did this man have to pluck ideas out of the air and put them on her? She continued walking, head high, mouth tight.

Aaron's hand was steady around hers as he said, 'Fergusson, you couldn't be further from the truth if you tried so how about leaving us alone? We'd appreciate it.' Then he added quiet enough for only her to hear, 'Like that's going to happen. I am sorry, Bella.'

She refused to look anywhere but in the direction she was headed. This wasn't an entirely new experience. 'Not your fault,' she said just as quietly.

'Lady, when's your baby due?'

Bella stopped, drew a breath and locked her eyes on the despicable man. 'That's none of your business, as are none of the answers to the other questions you asked. I will not be talking to you about anything.' She started walking again, head high, heart thumping and her hand tight in Aaron's.

'You're no wimp,' Aaron muttered. 'But I have to warn you, it won't work. Not unless there's a bomb blast in the next few minutes. My car's over there.'

Relief at being able to shortly shut the door on the reporter filled her. 'That's better than walking down the hill to home.' It was barely a kilometre to the apartment but that was a long way if she was going to be plagued by nosey reporters who had nothing better to do with their time. It was none of their business who her baby's father was, or that she was pregnant, or that she and Aaron were close. Pressing her lips tight, she headed to Aaron's car and tugged the door open the moment he flicked the locking device.

'So much for getting home and having time to unpack and get ready for the coming week after a lovely weekend in London.'

'You enjoyed your time with Jason's parents?' Aaron was pulling out of the car park before he'd even closed his door.

'Did I say that out loud? Yes, it was good.' Only she'd been brought back to reality in a hurry. A new reality. She was beginning to seethe at the rude behaviour of that reporter. Her life had nothing to do with him and would be as dull as dishwater to anyone reading whatever story he could come up with. 'Who does he think he is?'

'Someone who believes he has the right to ask personal questions and then share the answers with readers.' Aaron had got who she was talking about. 'Not all reporters are like him, only the worst, but Maggie and my family seem to attract those ones along with the respectful ones.'

'It wasn't Maggie he was harassing.'

'He had been. Which makes it even more stupid of me for coming over to you.'

'You can't live your life dodging what you want because of people like him.' Whenever Jason had made the headlines she'd tended to keep out of the picture, but she hadn't stopped doing the things she'd wanted to.

'Believe me, I've made it an art form.'

'So they win.' Of course, she hadn't been exposed to anything like what she was starting to realise Aaron had. She might've reacted differently when with Jason if the intensity and regularity of reporters and their questions had been more aggressive and frequent.

'Not always.' Aaron pulled up outside the restaurant, which thankfully hadn't opened yet. 'I won't come in.'

So much for catch-up time. If she weren't so angry at the reporter she'd have laughed at herself. Catch up after a couple of days apart? But she'd missed Aaron, even when she was busy shopping or having dinner with her in-laws. Her anger increased. 'So he wins,' she repeated scathingly.

'I can't—no, I won't cause more problems for you, or any for Gino and his restaurant for that matter.'

'Gino can handle things.'

'You have no idea how persistent that man can be, or what he'll do to get inside info on you and your family.'

'How do you know that? You don't know the half of what my family have done over the years.' Now her anger was focused on Aaron. All she wanted was to be with him and here he was, doing his utmost to get away from her.

'Bella, believe me when I say I've seen the worst of him, and others like him. There's no dealing with them. Now that Fergusson has seen me holding hands with a pregnant woman he's not going to go away quietly. I'm trying to protect you.' He didn't reach for her hands as he usually did when he was being serious. There wasn't a hint of longing in his face; more like a look of withdrawal.

She stared at him, her anger boiling over. 'Are you sure it's just me you're protecting?'

His mouth opened, closed again. Then he shoved his door open and removed her case from the back seat and wheeled it to the building's entrance.

She followed, her anger dissipating in an instant as she waited for him to turn around and haul her into his arms and kiss away this nightmare. To tell her he was wrong, they were a couple and would get through whatever happened as a team.

'I'm sorry it's come to this, Bella.' He strode past her, back to his car. Then he drove away. Not a word. No answer to her question. Nothing. *Niente*. A very cold shoulder from the man who'd been so caring. If he couldn't talk then there was no hope for them. Talking was important.

Her heart cracked as his car disappeared around the corner. There was a lot he didn't know about her. It included the fact she loved him. Because she hadn't told him. She wasn't any better at talking. She didn't want to risk her heart a second time. Losing her first love had been hard, and she couldn't face that again.

Except she already had.

CHAPTER TEN

AARON CHECKED HIS rear-view mirror as he turned into his drive. Still no one following, but then there hadn't been time for Fergusson to get a car before he'd driven Bella away from the station. He liked to be prepared, not blind-sided with a camera in his face. Fingers crossed the man had boarded the train to stay near to Maggie and note what she was up to.

Maybe, but unlikely if the guy already knew Maggie was returning to London. He wanted to get mad at his sister for visiting, but he couldn't. They were close in their own way, and he'd been happy to see her. But to have Bella accosted like that and asked about the baby and the father made his blood boil. He should never have got so close to her, should never have fallen for her.

But I have.

There lay the problem. He had to walk away, leave Bella to get on with her life and have her baby and raise her in the best way possible—without photographers and infuri-ating reporters hanging around every corner. Leaving her meant hurting himself, but he was doing it because he loved her. Yeah, sure.

'Are you sure it's just me you're protecting?' Bella's ques-tion echoed in his head. He'd known she was no slug when it came to understanding him, but he hadn't expected that. Because truthfully? He was looking out for himself. He didn't want to end up heartbroken again. Only problem was—it was already too late. He was hurting big time.

What happened next? He'd love to see her and have a deep and meaningful talk. The only problem with that was at the end they'd still go their separate ways, especially once Bella understood how harrowing all the publicity could be.

To hell with this. He needed air and space and time to think without anyone interrupting. Not that there was anyone in his apartment, but he could picture Bella sitting on his deck or on the couch or lying in his bed curled into him, or making love.

Grabbing his hiking boots, Aaron headed out of the door. Away from searing memories, away from confronting the fact he'd well and truly messed up, and on with his future. Without Bella Rosso in it.

His phone pinged.

Bella.

Ignoring her wasn't the answer. He had to tell her in no uncertain terms they were no longer an item. Their fling was over. 'Hello.'

'Can you come over to my apartment, please? We can't turn our backs on what we have. Not without talking about it first anyway.' She wasn't pleading, or sounding as if he'd pulled the floor out from underneath her. More as though she was being strong and coping better than he was, which suggested she wasn't as involved as he was.

She had said they couldn't ignore what they had between them. He had to. For her sake as well as his. 'There's nothing more to say, Bella. I'm sorry it ended this way, but I don't want to continue with our fling any longer. There was always an end date approaching. It's arrived sooner than expected but nevertheless it's here.'

'You don't want a full-on relationship, then? One where we help each other through the awful times and love the good ones?'

'No, I don't.'

I can't. Someone has to look out for my heart and that comes down to me.

'I never did, and I don't think I ever indicated otherwise.'

That was met with silence. Who knew silence could be so loud? It was as though the air were thick with hurt and anger and disappointment.

And guilt. Oh, yes. Guilt filled him, twisted his gut, clouded his head and brought tears to his eyes. Guilt for hurting her. For upsetting her. For letting her down—though that was a two-way issue because this was all about protecting her—*and* himself.

'I can't argue with that.' Bella cut through his turbulent thoughts. 'But I thought you were getting more into us than what you're showing now. Guess I read you wrong.' She paused.

He waited, the breath stuck in the back of his throat.

'Or not.' *Click.* She was gone.

Leaving Aaron confused. No, not confused, but rattled, because once again Bella was showing him how well she had come to understand him. If only he could go around to her apartment and take her in his arms and hold on for ever. But he'd done that with Amy when she'd said she couldn't cope and she'd pushed him aside, said she didn't love him enough to live with his family's noise. This time it was him not coping and so pushing Bella away.

Noise. That was Amy's word for all the turbulence. He actually got it. It was noise. Loud and intrusive at its best. While Bella seemed to want to pursue what they'd started he understood the slow eating-away at a person's resilience the noise did and therefore how the day would still come when she'd pack her bags for good.

Yes, he loved her and was hurting, but to become a true couple in the eyes of her family, and then watch her walk away, would be excruciating. Maybe he was a coward. He did want love and family. More than anything else. Almost.

How was he going to manage avoiding her when they had to work together at times? So much for considering applying for the permanent position in the department. He'd always known the day would come when he'd have to accept he couldn't stay and fit in with Bella and her daughter. Of course he'd known and had done from the first time he'd sat down at the Rosso family dinner table beside Bella and relaxed in a way he hadn't ever truly done before.

Then go see her, have that talk she wanted, explain yourself.

He kept striding along the pathway, heading out of town, away from the tourists and locals and Bella.

'This is Katie White,' Aaron told Bella when she stepped into the cubicle a nurse had indicated. 'She's got a temperature of thirty-nine and complains of sharp aches in both ears.'

'Hello, Katie. I'm Bella Rosso, a doctor, and I'm going to see what's going on with you.' Bella turned to the woman sitting by the bed. 'You're Katie's mother?'

'Yes. Katie's never had anything like this before.'

'Dr Marshall says you have an infection in both ears, Katie. We need to find out what's causing them.'

Dr Marshall was still in the cubicle. Never had she called Aaron 'Dr' when with a patient, but they'd become somewhat remote with each other in the hospital over the last five days. It had to stop. They were being ridiculous, child-ish even.

'Katie doesn't seem to have any other infected areas and her ears have been painful for more than two days,' Aaron said.

Bella continued. 'We'll take swabs and send them to the lab, but they take a couple of days for the results to come back. In the meantime we'll put you on antibiotics. First I want to take a look at your ears and listen to your breath-ing and heart.'

After examining Katie and organising laboratory tests, Bella headed back to the ward to check on little Francesco, who was recovering from a severe bout of asthma. She hated walking away from Aaron but confronting him at work wasn't professional. Besides, he seemed determined to keep the barriers up, only talking about patients whenever she was called to the ED. It was as though they'd never slept together, or gone for a walk, or laughed and talked. When she had tried to mention anything that didn't involve work he'd clammed up, or been particularly polite and walked away. No wonder she wasn't sleeping or even eating proper meals. She was hurting, badly.

After looking in on Francesco, she spent time on the computer updating files and checking other patient results from the lab and Radiology, before deciding it was time to go home to her quiet, empty apartment.

Out at her car she hesitated, tempted to go and find Aaron and ask him to call in on his way home so they could at least talk, but, looking around the car park, she couldn't see his car so he must've already finished for the day.

She'd see if he was at home. He wasn't. Calling his phone got her nowhere either, other than to leave a mes-sage. 'Aaron, give me a call when you're free.'

He must've had a very busy night because he didn't ring.

When Bella was called into the emergency department two days later he was nowhere to be seen. 'Aaron not on shift?' she asked Tommaso.

'He swapped with me so I can go to my son's tennis game tonight. I was surprised really as he doesn't like night shifts.'

He was avoiding her. He won. She'd stop trying to make contact. She got the message. Aaron did not want anything more to do with her.

Then late Friday afternoon he called her to see a two-year-old girl. 'Greta has epilepsy but I would like you to check her before we allow her to go home with her mother.'

Nothing unusual in that. 'On my way.'

When she walked into the department Aaron stood up from his desk and crossed to join her, unlike other days this week. 'Thanks for this. I'm sure Greta's fine but her *mamma* is overwrought with worry so I thought you might be able to calm her down.' There was even a small smile on that divine mouth.

For her? A quick look around told her no one else was near. 'Let's get this sorted.' Did a softening in his stance mean he was starting to see things differently? She wasn't pushing for more. He'd probably close down on her again.

Twenty minutes later she stood up from the computer and picked up her bag. Work was over for the week, and she was so tired. Her whole body ached with weariness. Not so much because work had been busy but because sleep had been as elusive as snow in summer. She missed Aaron. Seeing him in here on the occasions she'd been called to the department didn't make up for sharing a meal or a hug or making love. Especially since he seemed determined to stay uninvolved. Too late. She couldn't be much more involved if she tried. 'Goodnight, Aaron.'

'Have a good weekend, Bella.'

That was likely the last thing she'd have, wondering where he was and what he was doing. Though he was definitely warming a little. 'Would you like to join me for dinner tonight?' she asked thoughtlessly.

'I don't think so. Thanks anyway.'

She couldn't help the next things to come out of her mouth. 'I can't believe how you've cut me off so completely. What's wrong with sharing a meal with me?' It was almost as if she didn't exist and they hadn't had a fling and talked about their futures.

'Fergusson's back in town. He tried to talk to me this morning.' Aaron leaned against the doorframe. 'Since he put that photo of you and I online along with the article about Maggie you are fair game for any reporter to do a number on you. Especially if I'm anywhere near you.'

The article hadn't pleased her but she'd shrugged it away. Nothing she could do to make it disappear. The postulating about her baby's father made her teeth grind, as did the guessing going on about the relationship Aaron was having with her, but she'd ride it out. Her life was boring by most people's standards and eventually she'd be yesterday's news. 'I've been here before and survived. I'll manage this time.' So much for thinking he was softening. She headed down the corridor.

'What do you mean? This isn't new to you?' Aaron was keeping pace with her, which in itself was new for this week.

'I told you Jason occasionally hit the headlines with something he'd done in his medical field which saved a patient who'd had no chance. When that happened I'd be pursued for a bit of scandal about the medical specialist's life.' It had been vile the way those scumbag reporters had thought they could do that, but she'd stayed cool and eventually they'd got fed up with her and gone to find someone far more intriguing.

'I didn't think it through.'

'Maybe I should've explained more but it had nothing to do with our relationship and therefore I didn't bother.' Why would she when she'd worked hard to avoid talking about that time in their lives where she and Jason didn't always see eye to eye about what was going on? He'd loved the limelight. She'd hated it. Still did, but that didn't mean she was going to run and hide if confronted again. She had a life to live and she wasn't stopping. Her chin dropped. With or without Aaron.

He was still with her. Interesting. 'Fair enough. I didn't come forward about my family in the beginning, and certainly never mentioned how intense the media got when it came to my mother and sister.' That was more than he'd said to her all week unless talking about patients.

Bella kept walking, not wanting to give him cause to head away in another direction. 'For you, it's important, I know. You want me to understand and be prepared.' So why hadn't he explained earlier?

'I do.' Aaron sighed. 'I admit to enjoying the weeks I had when no one knew who I was and anything about my background. I didn't want it to stop. I believed you'd never abuse it, but there've been some tough lessons in my past when it comes to trusting women and how they react to the fuss that goes on at times, and I can't forget them.'

Now she had to look at him. Her heart felt heavy for what he might've missed out on in the past. No matter they weren't seeing eye to eye or that he'd snubbed her all week, her heart skipped as she drank in that sexy face.

'Aaron, I can't say I understand everything but you have to be loyal to yourself first and foremost. Protecting your heart is a part of that, but please don't think we're all the same. I am not interested in the nonsense that obviously goes on in the background of your life, but that doesn't mean I want to walk away from you. Not without knowing we can't make a go of what we started anyway.'

'Ah, Bella. If only it was that simple.'

'Why can't it be?'

'I don't think I'm ready.'

Of course she overcomplicated things when it came to her love for Aaron. She was always looking for what could go wrong and not what was so good about being with him, yet now she was ready to take the last step to be by his side for ever.

'Will you ever be?'

The entrance door slid open. 'Bella, Aaron, look this way. We want a photo of the both of you together.' Fergusson was back.

'Not now.' Bella drew a breath, held her head high, and continued on out to the car park and her car. By now the reporters knew where she worked and lived, what she drove, probably what she ate so she wasn't bothering with trying to hide in plain sight. If only everything else were that straightforward.

Aaron watched the love of his life walk out of the building as if there were nothing unusual going on. Dignified came to mind. Bella had an air about her that said, 'Don't mess with me.' Not that Fergusson and his ilk took a lot of notice, but neither did they get right into her space as they were prone to do with others.

'Leave her be, Fergusson. Miss Rosso has nothing to say that'll make you top reporter for the week.' Aaron followed Bella to her car and opened the door for her to get in. 'Take care,' he said quietly.

'No other way to go,' she said as she touched the ignition button.

Aaron looked at her hard. Tears were slipping from the corners of her eyes. 'Bella?'

'See you around.' She grabbed the door and pulled it shut with a bang.

She was losing it. Big time. Bella didn't do tears. Not that he'd seen anyway. Was this because of the paparazzi? Was his fear she'd become unable to cope with all the nonsense coming true already? When he'd seen how well she managed? How dignified she was? Or had he got to her by turning down the opportunity to talk over a meal?

His gut instinct was to follow her back to her apartment and have it out with her. To get it across to that stubborn mind that he knew what he was doing by staying away, that nothing would ever change, and that eventually she'd get fed up and leave him.

He would not be telling her he'd barely slept all week for thinking about her, and missing her in his arms. There'd be no mention of wanting to propose to her and have a real family life with the woman he adored so much. No, he'd stay away. Today he'd struggled with maintaining his aloof façade. Hell, it had been impossible not to smile at her a couple of times. But that was where it had to end.

He pulled his car key from his pocket. Then shoved it back. He wanted to follow Bella home so badly he knew if he got behind the wheel that was exactly what would happen. Which in turn would fuel Fergusson's inquisitiveness. Even Gino might have trouble getting rid of the reporter then. Though Aaron couldn't help the smile that lifted his mouth. Probably not. Gino was a force to be reckoned with and when it came to looking out for his sister there'd be no holding him back.

He needed to be like that himself when it came to Bella and look out for her, stop worrying about his heart so much. He'd been protecting her by keeping his distance, but maybe he'd only made it worse because now Fergusson wanted to unravel the puzzle that to him was Aaron Marshall and Bella Rosso. Aaron stared at his feet. Had he blown the one real chance of happiness he'd had in years? He should fight for Bella, not against her. He needed to fight for both of them, for their future. Damn it.

First he had a phone call to make.

When that was done he got into his car and headed to the Rosso apartments. It was time to sort this out, to lay everything out so Bella totally understood why they couldn't be together.

Or he could go home and sit on the deck and watch the sun go down on another grotty day.

Or he could lay his heart on the line, show Bella how much he loved her, and ask for her forgiveness and another chance to make her happy. To make *them* happy.

There really wasn't an option.

Bella sat at the family table alongside her *mamma* and stirred her spaghetti round and round with a fork. Her appetite had vanished along with Aaron. Even Sophia was quieter than usual.

Mamma nudged her with an elbow. 'You've got a visitor. We'd better make a space for him.'

'Come in, Aaron.' Gino was already bringing a chair over. 'You sit with Bella.'

Gino hadn't asked her much about what was going on, but that didn't mean he wasn't aware they were having problems. He was setting Aaron up so he couldn't walk away. Gino liked Aaron a lot. That didn't mean he'd let him away with anything though. 'It's seafood spaghetti tonight.'

'Is this all right with you, Bella?' Aaron asked.

'Didn't I invite you to dinner?' Her heart was hammering. The fork slipped out of her fingers with a clatter. He'd come. What had changed his mind? Swallowing a big mouthful of sparkling water, she held onto all the questions buzzing in her head. No point in scaring him off before he'd sat down.

He sank onto the chair and looked directly at her. 'I'm sorry.'

For what? 'We'll talk later. Enjoy dinner first, and relax amongst the family. They've missed you.' It had only been two weeks, but they were the longest weeks she'd known in a while.

Aaron blinked and looked around. 'Hello, everyone.'

And just like that all the chatter started up again with everyone talking over each other. Aaron slowly relaxed and joined in the noise as though there'd never been a glitch in their relationship.

Gino placed a large bowl in front of him with a clap on his back. 'Get that into you,' he ordered.

Bella forked up a mouthful from the mess she'd made in her bowl and munched away happily. Whatever Aaron had come to talk about didn't matter right now. He was here, and that was what was important. It was a start.

Later, when they sat on her deck with coffee at hand,

she wondered if she'd expected too much. Aaron had gone quiet on her again. 'Don't do this,' she said.

'I don't know where to start,' he admitted. 'I don't want to make a bigger mess than I already have.'

'Try the beginning. It usually works.'

'When I was qualifying in emergency medicine I did a term in New Zealand where I met Amy. We fell in love and got engaged. It was wonderful. Then we went to London and the fun began. Mum was getting continuous attention from the media over a movie that hit the screen big time, and Dad was hitting the headlines daily about a murder case he'd ruled on. In other words, it was the usual world for my family. At first Amy coped, but slowly she began withdrawing. The worst was her pulling back from our relationship. Then one day she upped and left, went home to Auckland. I flew down to see her and tried to rectify our engagement but she shunned me, said she never wanted a part in my family again. Within six months Amy was married to her childhood sweetheart and having a baby.'

Bella reached for his hand, and held tight. She couldn't imagine how that had felt. No doubt beyond painful. 'No wonder you're afraid to love again.'

'You always read me too easily.'

'The thing is, Aaron, it's not hard to know where you're coming from. I loved Jason so much I've always believed I'd never be that lucky again. Some people don't know the kind of love I've had, and to think I'd find it again was beyond comprehension. That's why I was reticent.'

'Your honesty doesn't leave room for manoeuvre.'

'You want me to sugar coat it?'

He shook his head and smiled. 'Not likely. I haven't finished what I want to tell you.' He sipped his coffee. 'The way you've handled the media over the last few days makes me hope you wouldn't walk away when the horrendous days occur. But I've seen this before. I know how Amy was ground down so quickly. I am afraid of that happening again.'

'Are you saying you'd like a relationship with me?' Her hands were shaking and she pulled away from his grip.

'What I'm getting around to telling you, Bella Rosso, is that I am so in love with you it hurts not to be with you all the time. I want to risk everything for you. I can't not take the chance because to walk away from you would undermine everything I believe in.'

'Which is?' she whispered.

'Love.'

Love. There it was. One word said it all. 'I love you so much, Aaron. I want to share my life with you. To share my daughter and my family. Everything I have.'

'Love, Bella.' He was standing, reaching down for her, lifting her up into his arms, holding her fiercely as well as gently, and then he was kissing her as though he'd never stop.

Sinking into him, she let go the last worries that they might be making a big mistake and took a chance on for ever. Love for ever. Aaron in her life for ever.

Then he was pulling back, but she trusted him. He wasn't about to say he'd made a mistake.

'Bella, I'll also be there for Sophia all the way, will try to be the best dad I can.'

'I never had any doubts.' He was kind and caring, and what more could she ask for when it came to her daughter? 'You'll make a great *papà*. The best.'

'Will you marry me?'

'Yes. Try and stop me.' She stretched up to kiss him some more. No such thing as too much of those lips.

Loud clapping interrupted them from down on the restaurant veranda, followed by shouts and laughter.

'Get down here so we can celebrate with a bottle of the best champagne in the house.' Gino of course.

Bella grinned. She hadn't felt this good in such a long time. 'Welcome to the family.'

'Guess your father isn't so good at keeping promises.' Aaron laughed as he took her hand.

'What do you mean?'

'I went and saw your father before I came into the restaurant. Asked him if he minded if I proposed to his daughter. Looks like he's told everybody.'

Papà would be stoked. 'You're more Italian than many men I know.' Then she couldn't resist asking, 'What would you have done if he'd said no?'

Aaron laughed. 'Talked him into saying yes.'

'Come on, you two. The champagne's getting warm.' Gino again.

As if. 'I'm going to have a very small glass of that. I am not going to miss celebrating my engagement to the sexiest, loving man in my life.'

Kick, kick.

Bella drew a breath, and took Aaron's hand to hold it over her belly. 'Sophia approves. That's the hardest kick in a week.'

'Hi, Sophia. Looks like we're going to be a family. What do you think?'

Kick.

'No more questions, please. That was too hard.' Bella grinned.

'One more thing,' Aaron said.

'What?'

'I'm taking over Giuseppe's role in the ED three days a

week. I'm going to find a part-time job in Milano as well to keep up to date with any changes that happen in emergency medicine.'

'This couldn't get any better.' Bella laughed as she dragged her fiancé out of the apartment and downstairs to join the family.

EPILOGUE

Restaurant Closed for Family Celebration

'DON'T KEEP QUIET about the wedding, will you, Gino?'
Bella muttered happily as she looked at the large sign her
brothers had hung on the gate that morning.

So much for keeping her wedding a small affair that only
family and friends knew about. But then again, with the
Marshall clan involved it was never going to be a secret.
The media were already hanging around outside the property, kept there by manners, and when those were ignored
by the pushier reporters the security company Aaron had
hired quietly dealt with them.

Despite all that she couldn't be happier. She'd found love
for a second time, and Aaron had settled into life in Stresa
as if he was always meant to be here. His nightmares had
all but vanished, and he'd obtained the perfect two-day-a-
week job in Milano's largest hospital. Now they were getting married and soon Sophia would arrive.

'You ready, Bella?' Her father stood in the apartment's
doorway, dressed to the nines in a three-piece suit, and
looking so proud.

'Yes, Papà, I'm ready.' She'd been ready since the moment Aaron proposed. Slipping her arm through Papà's,

she looked over her shoulder to her sisters-in-law. 'Come on, let's get me married.'

A gentle kick reminded her there was more excitement to come in a couple of weeks. She'd wanted to wait until Sophia was born before having the wedding, but Maggie was on a short break from LA at the moment and so they'd brought the date forward so she'd be able to attend. Rubbing her tummy, Bella whispered, 'You're still coming to the wedding, darling. Just not quite how we'd planned it.'

'You look beautiful,' Aaron said, his eyes full of love, as she walked up the makeshift aisle between endless vases of roses.

He still stole her breath away. Just like that very first time she'd laid eyes on him. When she reached him, she stretched up and kissed him.

'Hold on,' Papà growled. 'I haven't given you away yet.'

Everyone laughed, and she told the marriage celebrant good-naturedly to get on with the job.

He obliged, and within minutes Bella's *papà* was sitting down beside Mamma and wiping his eyes as his daughter became Aaron's wife.

'I love you,' Bella whispered to her new husband.

'Same back at you.' Aaron swung her up into his arms and kissed her hard.

'That's enough, you two. Let's go celebrate.' Gino had all his chefs working in the kitchen and they came out to toast the couple before heading back to finish preparing the four-course meal.

Three hours later, Bella leaned back in her chair, holding her breath as a sharp pain shot through her abdomen. 'No way. You can't turn up today, Sophia.'

'You all right?' Aaron asked.

'I think so.' Was this the beginning of her labour or just a harder than usual nudge from her daughter to let her know she wasn't going to be forgotten during the celebrations?

Ten minutes later Bella had her answer. 'We're not going on our honeymoon,' she gasped.

'What?' Aaron's eyes widened when he noticed her clutching her stomach. 'You're kidding, right?'

'You think so?'

'No, I don't.' He stood up, sat down, looking confused. 'What now?'

She laughed. 'Carry on as we were, at least until the contractions are closer.'

Twelve hours later, Bella gave a final push and Sophia arrived in the world.

The midwife wrapped her daughter in a small blanket and placed her on Bella's breast. 'There you go. She's lovely.'

Bella swallowed the tears clogging her throat and kissed Sophia's brow. 'Hello, sweetheart. You are gorgeous.'

Her husband sat on the edge of the bed beside her, his eyes full of tears and love. 'She certainly is.'

'Sophia, meet Papà.' Bella placed their daughter in Aaron's arms, her heart expanding with every breath she took. She had got lucky again. 'I love you both,' she whispered.

* * * * *

COMING SOON!

We really hope you enjoyed reading this book.
If you're looking for more romance
be sure to head to the shops when
new books are available on

Thursday 21st December

To see which titles are coming soon, please visit

millsandboon.co.uk/nextmonth

MILLS & BOON

MILLS & BOON®

Coming next month

SURGEON PRINCE'S FAKE FIANCÉE
Karin Baine

'In that case, we'll announce the engagement as soon as possible. I know you want time to let your family know what's happening, but I think the truth is going to come out sooner or later.'

He watched Soraya's face contort into a puzzled frown as none of that would have made any sense to her whatsoever.

'What on earth—?'

The second she made it obvious she had no idea what he was talking about the game was over. He would never recover if he was exposed as a liar in the press even if it had been done with the best of intentions. There was only one way he could think of temporarily stopping her from breaking their cover, and, though it might earn him a slap, he had to take the chance. It would be easier to explain things to her later than to the entire country.

Raed grabbed her face in his hands and kissed her hard. He expected the resistance, her attempt to push him away. What he hadn't been prepared for was the way she began to lean into him, her body pressed against his, her mouth softening and accepting his kiss. All notions of the press and what had or hadn't been captured seemed to float out of his brain, replaced only with thoughts about Soraya and how good it felt to have his lips on hers.

She tasted exactly how he'd imagined, sweet and spicy, and infinitely moreish. He couldn't get enough. Soraya's hands, which had been a barrier between their bodies at first, were now wrapped around his neck, her soft breasts cushioned against his chest in the embrace. Every part of him wanted more of her and if they'd been anywhere but in the middle of a car park he might have been tempted to act on that need. It had been a long time since he'd felt this fire in his veins, this passion capable of obliterating all common sense.

He knew this had gone beyond a distraction for any nearby journalists but he didn't want to stop kissing her, touching her, tasting her. Once this stopped and reality came rushing in, he knew he'd never get to do this again.

Continue reading
SURGEON PRINCE'S FAKE FIANCÉE
Karin Baine

Available next month
www.millsandboon.co.uk

LET'S TALK

Romance

For exclusive extracts, competitions
and special offers, find us online:

f MillsandBoon

𝕏 @MillsandBoon

◉ @MillsandBoonUK

♪ @MillsandBoonUK

Get in touch on 01413 063 232